IND

Mark Tufo

CreateSpace Edition
Copyright 2009 Mark Tufo
Discover other titles by Mark Tufo
Visit us at marktufo.com
and http://zombiefallout.blogspot.com/ home of
future webisodes
and find me on FACEBOOK

Editing by:
Monique Happy
Editorial Services
mohappy@att.net

Cover Art:
Dean Harkness

Dedicated to my wife, who is my muse, my inspiration and my partner in life. (Just like a woman to be able to multi-task, I'm lucky if I can make toast and tie my shoes at the same time, although why I'd need to do those two things at once, who knows?)

To the brave men and women who protect and serve, I salute you all.

Foreword: Hello Dear Reader so some of you may stumble upon this series after reading the Zombie Fallout stories, and you'll get to the beginning and be like 'WTF is Michael Talbot doing in this book? Oh he's just trying to capitalize on that name.' I can assure you that is not the case, this story was started some 25 years before Zombie Fallout ever saw the light of day. I can see your next question, 'So then why stick with that name in the Zombie Fallout books?' valid question it is. I guess part of it is that I never thought so many folks would love the ZF series and I was more writing it for myself so that I didn't drive my wife nuts while I was once again laid off from corporate America. There was a point where I could have changed it either in this series or the other but by that point I came across the idea that these are the misadventures of Michael Talbot's alternate realities. I feel sorry for the bastard he sure has a penchant for getting in to trouble. I don't think I'll write another series with Michael as the lead protagonist maybe it's time he got to go out to pasture. So with that in mind I do hope you enjoy this book.

Introduction

Hello, my name is Michael Talbot, Mike for short. I'm 25 years old and a Colonel in the U.E.M.C., (United Earth Marine Corps) and war has been raging on our planet for almost seven years now. I'm writing these memoirs now because I don't know if or when I will ever be able to again. The woman I love with all my heart is sleeping, she sleeps a lot these days, and I want to leave something to the child she carries within her. Tomorrow begins our final assault for good or bad, and if I should fall I want my unborn son or daughter to know all the grief, suffering and hope that I have carried these seven long years. So this is my story - I'm not William Shakespeare, I'm not George Orwell, hell I'm not even Stephen King. (Don't get me wrong, I love Stephen King, I've read all of his stories.) But back to the point, I'm just a person with a story, but please don't be let down, it's one hell of story. By now you know the ending of thus far... I'm alive. But how I got here might be a tale worth sitting down to and reading. The parts I didn't physically witness I was able to fill in along the way. And if I'm lucky and I last long enough, I may be able to tell you how this whole mess ends up. Well, if you're ready dear reader, my child, I'm going to get this show on the road.

CHAPTER 1 – Journal Entry 1

The year was 1984, September 1984 to be more specific, I had just started college and my new life; I was finally out from under the rule of my tyrannical mother, your grandmother. I had begun to date who I thought was the perfect woman, all was well with the world. Eighteen and in love, there can be no better feeling. But maybe I should stop there, I'm going to go back a little further in this story. Four years and some change to be exact.

June 1980. I did the majority of my growing up in the suburbs of Boston in a tiny little town named Walpole, with a non-existent father and an over-bearing mother. Oh, the stories I could tell you about her, but I have no desire to write a Psychology 101 book. We had lived in Boston proper for the first thirteen years of my life, and then my mother decided that the house I had grown up in was too big. The dice had been rolled, my parents had made the most fateful decision regarding this story. We moved out of Boston and its 'bad' schools and into the past. At least that's what it felt like to me. Here we were in downtown Boston where everything and everybody was going a mile a minute, to Walpole, Massachusetts, a town right out of a Norman Rockwell painting. They even had soda fountain shoppes. I was going friggen nuts. The boys around here liked to do things like go fishing or hiking at some place called 'Indian Hill.' Gee, did they go to 'picture shows' on Saturday nights too? Golly gee willickers, Mom, the ice cream man's coming, can I have a nickel? Did you wash behind your ears? I thought I was in 'Leave it to Beaver' only this was more Twilight Zone-ish because I wasn't watching it, I was now part of it. That first summer was the toughest in my young life.

None of the kids I semi-hung around with wanted to do anything that I thought was pretty cool. Like throwing rocks at the passing trains or stealing liquor out of mommy and daddy's liquor cabinet, or pilfering Playboys from the local variety store. They wanted to fish and paint fences and suck cow teets. It was hell. The upcoming school year did little to improve my mood. Great, I thought to myself, now I get to be exposed to the whole damn crazy village as opposed to just a few of the village idiots. My mother couldn't figure out why I wasn't out with the other boys enjoying the fresh air. And do what, Ma, plant flowers? So the summer pretty much came and went without too much fanfare. I had a couple of people you might call friends, but I wasn't sure if I'd even get wet if they were drowning, if you catch my meaning. September came and I trudged myself to school, my mom had offered a ride but I was having a hard enough time adjusting without my mother dropping me off in her beat up station wagon. I had slumbered through the first five periods of my first day of junior high, only perking up enough to check out a couple of the finer things, I mean girls.

Eating lunch alone was a blast (that would be sarcasm). My semi-buds had the next lunch bell. Oh man, this school year was going to be as painful as the summer. And then came Algebra. I didn't think much of it, what teen does. I sat as far from the front as I could, which luckily with all these Johnny's and Becky's wasn't a tough seat to get. Last row, far left. The teacher had turned to write her name on the wall. I was just getting ready to write her name down, when 'splat' a huge spitball landed right next to her face. She had spit juice all over her face and the front of her blouse. Whoever had been working on that beauty must have started two periods ago, that sucker looked to be two whole sheets of paper. Of course she immediately looked at me as did the rest of the class.

"Mr. Talbot, I need you to go to the principal's office," one exasperated teacher named Mrs. Weinstedder said.

"I didn't do anything!" I pleaded. I sure didn't need my mom picking me up on the first day of school.

"Come, come, Mr. Talbot, we all know you're the new boy here and I've never had this problem before." She now had her arms crossed and her left foot was tapping on the ground.

"Mrs. Weinstedder, I didn't do it!"

Her foot was going faster, any faster I figured and she was going to take off. "Young man, you march down to the principal's office right now or I'll drag you there by the ear."

That got a snicker out of the class.

"Mrs. Weinstedder, check my notebook, I don't even have any pages ripped out of it."

She started to head towards me, at a svelte 250 pounds I had no doubt she would make good on her threat. I grabbed all of my stuff and headed toward the door. The other students were almost choking they were so intent on holding in their laughter. I was so pissed I must have turned four shades of red.

"That's right, class, we don't need his type in here now do we," I heard her say scornfully.

"Why don't you shut up you fat cow!" I spewed. That was the line that got me three days suspension. But it was worth it. And I walked out of the class and down the hall towards the principal's office. I had been taking my sweet time, I was in no rush to go meet Mr. Ratspindler. You knew just from the name what kind of person he was, he'd have my mother up here before I got the seat cushion warm and then the real fun would begin. I had gotten about two-thirds of the way down the hallway when some kid I had never seen before came half running with his books and bookbag out of the class I had just been ejected from. You could hear the class roaring in laughter as he made a mad dash out of the class.

"I know your mother, Mr. Ginson, don't think that I won't be talking to her after this little incident!"

"For your information Mrs. Weinstedder, she is *not* my mother, and that other kid was right, you are a fat cow." The class was now bursting in laughter, a few of the teachers even opened their doors to see what all the commotion was about.

"Hey kid, hold up."

"You talking to me?" as I pointed to myself.

"No, the *other* kid that just got kicked out of Algebra."

"Well, I'm Michael, not 'kid,' and my friends... at least the ones from back home... call me Mike."

"Well 'Mike,' my name's Paul Ginson. My friends call me Ginner."

"Nice to meet you," as we shook hands. "What are you here for?"

"Well, when she turned back towards the board I nailed her with the second barrel of my spit cannon."

"Oh, so *you're* the one that got me kicked out of class."

"Hey, I'm not the one that called her a fat cow first."

"Yeah, that's true."

"Hey, I know a short cut to Ratsniffer's office."

"What could be shorter? He's right at the end of this hall."

"Do you really feel like going down there? Mrs. Fat Cow, nice call by the way, doesn't know how to work the intercom. She won't even be able to tell him about the whole thing until after class, by that time we could be long gone."

"But we'll get in trouble."

"Too late for that."

I thought about it. "What do you have in mind?" And that was how I met my best friend.

CHAPTER 2 – Journal Entry 2

We spent the day up on the local supermarket's roof, of all places. If you pulled the dumpster over just a little bit you could climb on that and up a drainpipe and onto the roof. It was an easy climb for a spry 14 year old. I didn't think my mom would be coming to get me up here any time soon. The thing that struck me the most when I got up there was how huge it was. It looked like a giant shingle parking lot. There were all sorts of vents and air conditioners and fans all over the place. I stood there kind of slack jawed taking in the scenery.

"Come on!" Paul yelled. "If you stay too close to the edge and a passing car comes by they'll be able to see you."

I started to move toward the center, but I was getting the willies in my stomach. What if the roof gives, what if someone in the store hears us? What if….

"Come on man." Paul saw my hesitation. "Don't worry, the roof won't cave." He then proceeded to jump up and down on it. I motioned him to stop and put a finger to my mouth. He yelled at the top of his lungs, "Don't worry they can't hear us either!" Then in a more user-friendly voice, "Come on man, I want to show you something." He headed toward dead center of the roof where a huge air conditioner was. He then opened up a little trap door that seemed to be there for maintenance, and pulled out five beers. "It keeps them cold," he said casually as he tossed me one.

"Thanks man," as I stared in wonder. I popped the top and he wasn't kidding, I nearly froze my throat and I got a brain freeze to boot.

"Slow down, dude, you act like you've never had a beer before."

Well technically no, it wasn't my first, more like my

fourth but I wasn't going to tell him that. "Man, I've been hanging around this whole summer with Billy Summers and John Smithstone."

"Oh man, I'm sorry," he said in mocking tones. "Those two turds would probably shampoo with the beer before they'd drink it." We both laughed.

"Tell me about it," I said.

"So what's your story, Mr. Talbot?" he said in his best Mrs. Weinstedder impersonation, which wasn't all that bad. I told him about the deal with my controlling mother and my dad who headed out to parts unknown every Friday night and magically reappeared every Monday morning. And even the times when he was physically present, he was nowhere near the vicinity mentally.

"Ah, that ain't nothing," Paul said as he tossed me another beer. "My dad and my real mom got together in one drunken moment and produced yours truly. They tried to make a go of it, but when my dad decided to go to AA and then tried to get my mom to enroll she wigged out and left him. He then married some born again Christian lady named Barb."

"Like barbed wire," I said, now starting to catch a little buzz.

"And that she is, a big fucking barb in my ass." The visual was too much. I laughed and sprayed beer all over the place. Paul joined in the festivities.

"Anyway," he started after we had calmed down a bit. "She has no clue at all. Dude, I'm not kidding but she actually pulls out a child-raising book whenever she has a problem that she doesn't know the answer to. She makes me and my sister have family discussion hour after dinner every friggen night. I don't know what to say to my girlfriend for an hour, what the hell am I going to tell this lady?"

"So what do you do?" I couldn't believe it. His family sounded as dysfunctional as mine; apparently all was not well in Smallpole.

"Well mostly I just nod and go yeah, uh-huh, exactly.

Luckily my sister loves to yack so she takes up the majority of the hour."

"What does your dad do during all of this fun time?"

"He sits on the couch, watches sports and drinks bourbon and coke."

"I thought you said he went to AA."

"He did, but he didn't like the part about complete abstinence regarding booze. He doesn't get smashed like he used to, but I can tell he's definitely getting buzzed."

"Your mom, I mean, Barb doesn't care?"

"Oh hell no, she's to busy with her nose in some parenting book trying to find new ways to cope with teenagers."

"Dude I thought I had it rough."

"Don't sweat it I'm pretty much used to her now, besides I read the books she's looking at so I know how she's going to approach almost every scenario."

"Brilliant."

"Yeah, not bad huh?"

"Where'd you get the beer? We're running low."

"Well, we can't get it in this town, the friggen mayor would know about it before dinner. If we go to the town over, Norwood, they have an area called the Flats. Sort of the seedier side of Mayberry. There's a bum there. If I give him the money and one of the beers he'll buy for me."

"Awesome, I have five bucks. You got anything, maybe we could get a twelve-pack?"

"Yeah I've got four, that should be plenty."

We split the last beer and climbed down a little groggier than when we had climbed up. "So how do we get there from here?" I asked, more than a little pleasantly buzzed.

"You can't get there from here." Paul did his best impression of a Northern Maine resident. "We're going to have to be very careful, we have to get out to Main Street and hitch."

"Hitch? Really?" I had visions of my mother pulling

over to give us a ride on our shortened school day.

Paul, seeing the trepidation on my face, piped up. "Dude don't worry we won't have to be visible for long. I've done this a dozen times and I never had to wait more than ten minutes."

"Ten minutes is a long time to have your dick blowing in the breeze," I said out loud.

"Come on man, we'll be fine," as he wrapped an arm around me.

"Well I don't know, maybe we should just go and see Ratsniffer."

Paul stopped dead in his tracks and eyed me suspiciously thinking that perhaps he had let me in on too many things. Then he realized I was joking, once he saw the grin on my face. "You ass, you had me there for a moment." And then he chased me to the street.

Eight minutes later, according to Paul's Timex; we were in the back seat of some old VW van. The driver was a serious hold over from the sixties: Long hair and beads abounding. Luckily for Paul and I, this was a short drive, because 'Windstar' as he liked to call himself rambled on incessantly about how 'The Man' was trying to keep the people down. I don't think 'Windstar' picked us up for any altruistic reason. I think it was so he could have a captive audience for his rhetoric. The bum had been right where Paul had said he would be and we made our business transaction. But this time it cost us two beers. By the time we were able to hitch a ride back to the supermarket, school had long been over and luckily my buzz had long ago worn off. At least the ride back had been a bit more normal. It was just a businessman finishing up his day. The ride might have actually been enjoyable if it weren't for the jazz blaring through the speakers. Maybe he thought he was giving us some culture. Zeppelin it wasn't. The only thing I wanted now was maybe a hamburger and a nap. I figured it was going to be about twenty to twenty-five minutes of listening to the ranting and raving at home before I got either of those things though. We climbed back up the roof and put the beer away in our makeshift cooler.

"Well buddy," I said. "Are you ready to face the music?"

"Oh yeah, I'm all set," Paul said smugly. "I'm pretty sure I'm going to get the 'I'm very disappointed' speech tonight."

"Well, that's better than the cussing and cursing that I'm about to get."

"Good luck, bud." And I knew he meant it. "Bring a good book tomorrow."

"Huh? Oh for detention?"

"You forget about that part?" Paul grinned.

"Are we going to get suspended?"

"Hell no, they know that'd be too much fun for us, we are going to get in-school suspension."

"You mean we just sit outside of the principal's office all day?"

He shrugged. "Yep. Like I said, bring a good book."

"Thanks, man."

And then he shook my hand, not in the way old men do, but the way you sometimes see in the movies when someone is falling off of a building and the person still on the roof grabs him up around the elbow. That one motion seemed to cement our friendship, and I think he realized it too. And then we parted ways to each receive our vastly different forms of punishment. Vastly different from what either of us expected. Apparently Barb had a conflict with Paul's dad and was unable to resolve it, so when Paul's new little infraction came up she had not had proper time to look it up in one of her books. She blew her top at him; she reamed him up and down the wall. Not that he paid her all that much attention but he was mildly surprised at this form that her attack came in. She was usually much more subtle. Oh well, he thought, he'd have to file this one under rare. I, however, was completely unprepared for the way my mother decided to deal with the situation. I can just tune her completely out when she starts in on me. It's actually relatively easy; I think that I learned the technique from my father. At least he taught me something. The louder she screamed the deafer I got. It was a perfect defense, she would get louder and louder screaming and cussing and I would pretty much go about my business as if she wasn't there, it drove her nuts. Finally she would shut up and I could go in peace. But I no sooner walked through the door, and she hit me with the surprise attack, 'I'm very disappointed in you.' It caught me so off guard that I actually was taken aback. That was all she said as she turned and walked away. I think I stood there for at least five minutes, I didn't know whether I should go and apologize to her or go cry in my bedroom, that's how unprepared I was. I didn't do either of those things but the idea that she had unsettled me so much was, well, unsettling.

CHAPTER 3 - Journal Entry 3

Paul and I spent the remainder of the school week in detention. It amazed me how incredibly boring this means of punishment was. We sat outside of the principal's office all day. At lunchtime we ate a supervised lunch meaning one of the teachers literally sat with us. Yeah, that was a barrel of laughs. We were allowed two bathroom breaks a day, obviously they were at different times, heaven forbid that we actually got to talk to each other for three minutes during the day. School generally seems like it takes forever but you've never experienced anything quite like this. I think that this type of detention actually defies the laws of quantum physics, only in reverse. Instead of time travel, this was a time stoppage. The rest of the world was speeding by at light speed and our time line had just plain old stopped. I can look back on this and see the pure brilliance of it, but at the time I was ready to split out of my skin. The thinking behind it had to have been that a parent can only yell at a kid for so long before they either have to do household chores or go to work. Once that's over the kid can pretty much do whatever they feel like. But with in-school suspension, you are trapped. Trapped in a world where time does not move, and they made sure that you were in line of sight of every student that had to pass by that way. Suffice it to say we were laughed at and pointed at. I was beginning to feel like a caged monkey. The principal should have handed out rotten fruit to the student body and then it would have been just like being in the stockades back in the colonial times. The principal had officially made it to Paul's and my short list. And sooner or later we would exact our revenge.

Well, contrary to popular belief, the week did finally end. My mom still hadn't talked to me and my dad had taken

off for parts unknown, so to my way of thinking I had paid
my debt to society. Paul's pseudo-mother had softened her
stance. Her newest book said that teenagers, and I quote,
'Teenagers must explore their path unhindered and
unadulterated.' Paul thought that he should write a thank you
letter to the author. He was pretty much free and clear to go
'find his own way,' as Barb put it. Parents will never get it.
They must lose it somewhere along the way. They keep
telling us that they were teens once, but you'd never know it
by looking at them. I wanted to live my life like The Who
song, 'Hope I die before I get old.' But I wonder if I would
still hold true to that since now I am getting older? Who
knows? We still had a ten pack on the roof of the local stop
and shop and Friday night loomed large ahead. Paul and I
both chowed down our respective dinners as if they were the
last meal we would ever eat. Well, when it's already 6 p.m.
and you only have until 11 p.m., you have to pack in as much
fun in that time period as teenagerly possible. I beat Paul to
the roof and had been tempted to pop open a beer while I
waited but while I was trying to figure out this moral
dilemma I heard someone scaling the wall. Paul's head came
up over the lip of the building and I rushed over there to
extend a helping hand. With a grunt and a heave we were
both on the roof, previous problem solved.

"Hey bud, how was dinner?" I asked laughingly.

"How would I know, I'm not sure what I even had I
ate it so fast. How was yours?"

"I wouldn't know, the dog ate the majority of mine,
but he did look a little green around the snout when I left."

"Is your mom still not talking to you?"

"Yeah, it's kind of creepy, but since my sister moved
out she's been up my ass constantly. This is kind of a nice
break."

"Well enough of that crap, did you break the beers
out yet?"

"Naw man, I was waiting for you," I said with a slight
grin.

"Bullshit, you didn't have enough time or you'd be sipping one by now."

"Yeah, probably." We popped open a couple of them. They were unbelievably cold on this relatively balmy autumn night. We talked all night, from how big Betsy Whitestead's tits were getting to how much of a cow Mrs. Weinstedder was to how screwed up our family lives were. It was a good night, at the time I had no idea what the word meant but if I had been able to vocalize my feelings the correct word would have been cathartic. I had been unable to release so much of this baggage that I had been carrying around. My brothers were almost a generation older than me and had long since moved out. My sister had left only months before and as I was affectionately known around the house as 'the mistake,' that did wonders for my self-esteem. We had moved away from everything and everybody I cared for. I had begun to build a wall around myself. If Paul had not come along when he did, that wall may have grown to unassailable proportions.

The fall semester flew by. We played football with a bunch of other kids that more closely matched our type of personas. It was amazing what you could discover if you pulled away the fake veneer that covered a lot of these guys. Most of them had just not been shown that path before so they didn't know how. But we made sure to corrupt as many as possible. I guess that's not truly fair, we just wanted to have a good time and whoever wanted to come along was welcome. Which was vastly different from the status quo. The popular sect at school resented us, but we honestly weren't trying to lead a counter-culture revolution. In the popular crowd you were either a 'has' or a 'has-not,' whereas with us it was pretty much if you can catch up, join in for the ride. Don't get me wrong, we still had lines drawn in the sand of who belonged where, but we had definitely blurred the edges.

CHAPTER 4 – Journal Entry 4

The first half of the year had come and gone.
Christmas break finally arrived. Christmas really didn't do
much for me, but the thought of not having to do anything
academic for two weeks was of great relief. It was during this
break that I had my first girlfriend. It wasn't much of a
romance, the whole thing fit inside the break. Patty Ryan
called me the day after Christmas to see how I was doing. At
the time I didn't think too much about it. After I told Paul he
called me a bonehead.

"Why am I a bonehead?" I asked incredulously.

"Patty Ryan calls you out of the blue to say hi. What
are you doing? Smoking pot?"

"No, why?" I asked still dumb-founded.

"Dude, she called you hoping that you'd ask her out."

"Are you kidding me?"

"Not at all bud, did you get her number?" I nodded.
"Yeah, well, you should call her back before she realizes her
mistake."

"Thanks buddy, and by the way… Kiss my ass."

"You're welcome."

So I did as I was instructed and I invited her out to
dinner the next day. For all you people who are new to this
whole game, if you ever invite a girl out or are invited out
yourself, never go to an Italian restaurant. It's way too
messy. I had spaghetti sauce all over the front of my shirt.
It's kind of hard to put on the moves, not that I had any, on a
girl when you have food stains on you. Otherwise the date
went fairly well. She didn't invite me in for cocktails and she
didn't even give me a peck on the cheek. But I did get one
thing, a reprieve; she invited me over the next day. I was on
cloud nine, I had made it through my first date without

making myself look like too much of an ass and she had invited me over for round two.

"Dude, you're in," Paul said as he high fived me. I had stopped over at his house on the way home from hers. "Smooth move with the sauce though."

"Come on, man, I feel stupid enough about that already."

"Do you really think that I wouldn't use that as ammunition?"

"Well, I *had* hoped."

"Dream on, sauce boy."

"Dude, I've got to get home before my curfew is up. I'll talk to you tomorrow."

"Yeah, let me know what base you get to."

And that was all I could think of that night and into the next day. Base, was I really going to get to a base and if so how many? This was intriguing. I hadn't even thought about that. I knew I wanted to kiss her but I really hadn't thought it out beyond that. I didn't sleep much that night and even when I did all I could dream about was Patty Ryan's breasts and would I get to touch them over or under. I went over to her house around one that afternoon and when I got there she told me that both of her parents were at work. I heard the fireworks going off in my head; I hoped that she hadn't noticed. And then she invited me down into her basement to play ping-pong. And all I could think was, yup, I'm going to play ping-pong with your breasts alright. But she honestly meant ping-pong. I was truly perplexed. Her parents weren't home and we were down in her basement and she actually wanted to play ping-pong. Where had I gone wrong? And then I made the fatal mistake. She had informed me that she had been taking lessons and not to be surprised if she 'whooped my butt' as she called it. So I let the competitive side of me take over, and I crushed her five straight games before she told me that her parents were going to be home soon and that I should leave. I'm not sure to this day if she would have let me touch her boobs or not. But by beating her at her own game I had effectively eliminated any such chance. And that was the beginning and the end of my first relationship with a girl. Won't get much mileage out of that one, but I realized that sometimes you have to lose in order to win. You just have to be careful with the balance. If you lose too much the girl will think you are a loser. So it is a fine line, but if you want to touch the boobies you need to learn how to walk it. Paul laughed his ass off after I told him the whole story.

"So you think she's not going to call me anymore?"

"Dude, it's over. I wouldn't sweat it though. She's just the beginning in a whole string of relationships you're going to mess up."

"Thanks for the vote of confidence, break out the Nintendo, will ya."

So my day ended with me kicking Paul's ass on his new Nintendo game system that he got for Christmas. I got socks. Don't get me wrong, they were nice socks, but you couldn't shoot down alien ships with them.

CHAPTER 5 – Journal Entry 5

I dreaded the thought of returning to school. Mr. Ratsniffer, everyone's favorite principal, had been following us around since our little spit ball incident and our subsequent walking out of punishment. Being on the principal's shit list did not make school any easier. I once caught the guy actually following me around in one of the few times (luckily) that I wasn't causing mischief. He was literally waiting outside the bathroom door probably wringing his hands hoping I would light up, oh and joy to the gods if it was some type of illegal substance. He pretty much had his ear right up to the door so that when I opened it up I startled him. What a dick.

"Man, Ratsniffer's so far up my ass he knows what I ate before I fart," I groaned.

"How does he do that?" Paul bemoaned back.

"Do what?" Now my curiosity was a little peaked.

"Dude, every time I turn around the little bastard could read the soles of my sneakers. How is he in two places at the same time?"

"Maybe he's only half of a set of freakish twins." We both laughed a little.

"Talbot, we can't go the rest of the year with him following us around, we need to throw him off of us and onto someone else."

"Any ideas? Or are you just talking out your ass again?" To which Paul punched me square in the shoulder. "Alright, alright, I'm listening."

"Meet me at our favorite drinking location after dinner, and wear dark clothes."

"Wear dark clothes?" But Paul had left the vicinity to make sure he didn't miss his next class. The day dragged by as I pondered all the possible things Paul could be talking about, and did I really want to add fuel to a simmering fire. Ratsniffer might actually back off in a month or two or three...'Fuck it, I'm in.' I thought to myself. I picked through the majority of dinner. My nerves were starting to get the best of me, but since my Dad only read the paper and my mom spent the majority of the time glaring at my dad, my lack of appetite went completely unnoticed.

"Mom, I'm going to Paul's to study!" I shouted as I headed out the door. She barely glanced in my direction; she probably figured if she glared at my dad's paper long enough it would catch fire.

"Be back by curfew!" she shouted. With all the effort they put in to my rearing I often wondered why in these times they actually went through with the pregnancy. There was no spark whatsoever between my parents and I was fairly certain my dad had far greener pastures to sow on the weekends, but enough dilly dallying, Paul and I had some unknown business (at least to me) to finish with Ratsniffer. I made it down to the Stop and Shop in record time. Paul was already waiting by the dumpster.

"Hey bud," I half yelled into the wind. "You heading up?"

"Naw, too cold, anyway we have too much work to do to be messing around up top."

"What's with the book bag? You going to the library?" I quipped. I wasn't sure if he even knew which way the library was.

"Actually, yeah."

"What?!"

Paul laughed when he saw my face. "Don't worry, I'll explain on the way." He proceeded to tell me in detail his plan, and how every good crime needed a solid alibi.

"So we're going to do some face time in the town library, but won't people see us leave as soon as we enter? What's the use in that?"

"There's the beauty my friend, we can sneak down

into the basement, get out of the library, do our business and be back inside without anybody being the wiser."

"Dude, you're a genius," I exclaimed as I slapped him on the back.

Too bad the genius was short lived. We entered the sparsely populated library, making sure that our presence was noticed by being a bit loud upon entry. The head librarian was quick to shush us and look us up and down in that disapproving way adults do. Paul even made sure to go up to her and ask her for assistance in helping us locate a book for a report we had to do. When she realized that maybe these young hooligans were actually here to study, her demeanor softened a bit. We both made sure she got a good look at us and talked to us for a bit before we retired off to the far reaches of the south corner, and surprise, surprise, right next to the basement door.

The basement was far more disorienting then I would have expected. It seemed to be the repository for lost books… globally. Random stacks of books rose from the floor like literary stalagmites. We took great care to avoid these; one spill could alert the librarian something was amiss, or at the very least shoot holes into our alibi. The window, which I figured would be painted shut, flew open with the slightest push. The fates were definitely shining down upon us, at least that was the theory at the time. We took extreme caution to make sure that our operation went completely undetected; it would do us no good to be caught running around Ratsniffer's neighborhood moments before some ghastly deed was done. We even took to diving in hedges before passing cars.

"You sure you know where Ratsniffer lives?" But before Paul even responded I saw it, a brand new white Cadillac. How he affords that thing I had no idea.

"Dude, put these on," Paul said as he handed me a pair of surgical gloves.

"Good call. You really thought this out."

"Shhh…" Paul said as he pulled me to the ground.

"Dammit!" Ratsniffer was in his living room watching TV in full view of his new Caddy and us. "Now what? Do we abort?"

"No fricken way," Paul said. "We just stick to the rear of the car, he can't see us from there."

"Yeah, but passing cars can."

`"Then we'll have to be fast. Here, put this on," Paul said as he handed me a ski mask.

"Dude, you have way too much time on your hands," as I handed the mask back to him.

"Would you rather do in-school suspension until we graduate?"

"Good point," I said as I put the hat on.

"I'm gonna run over to his rear bumper. I'll motion you when to come."

My heart was thumping. Before this everything was just talk and bravado, now we were going to actually do something. I thought about backing out, but just then Paul motioned. Well, I couldn't leave him hanging, so over I went. My heart was racing so fast I almost didn't hear him.

"Dude, slide!" Paul semi-shouted.

"Wha..?" And then I saw Paul doing the universal slide symbol for baseball, it didn't take a rocket scientist to figure that out. I slid so hard I landed half under the huge car. My heart was hammering, my leg was cramping underneath me but I didn't dare move. From my vantage point I could see that Ratsniffer had gotten out of his Lazy Boy and was peering out the window. He really did have a sixth sense for trouble. Luckily for me Ratsniffer was suffering from a malady I really wouldn't understand till much later in life, night blindness. If he put his hand out the window he most likely wouldn't be able to see it after the flooding of light in his living room. But I'd swear to this day that he was looking right at me. Finally, after what seemed like hours but was more likely the end of the commercial break, he left the window and returned to his seat.

"Paul."

"Yeah."

"I think I crapped myself." We both laughed hysterically as he dragged me out from under the car.

"Alright, let's get this started," Paul stated as he pulled the can of spray paint out of his pocket. "You keep a look out and I'll do my artistry." I began to peer over the bumper at Ratsniffer who was most likely engrossed in a 'when wild animals screw' documentary when I heard Paul mutter "Aw shit." Without taking my eyes off Ratsniffer I asked him what was wrong.

"The nozzle on the paint is frozen, do you have a lighter?"

"Come on man, what kind of special op would this be if I didn't have a lighter?"

"Then get over here and dethaw this thing."

I lit the lighter carefully to shield the bulk of light from Ratsniffer's direction while Paul kept the pressure on the nozzle just to make sure that it wouldn't refreeze on this blustery winter night. And then it happened, our rude shove into hardcore crime. The nozzle unleashed its load into the waiting arms of the Bic, paint spray can instantly turned into flame thrower and as luck would have it, it was aimed squarely at the car's tail pipe. Yes, the same make and model that was later recalled for excessive fuel spillage through said tail pipe. Paul and I barely had time to notice the blue flame as it snaked its way straight to the fuel injectors. The rest, as they say, was history. We had barely traveled fifteen feet when the first explosion ripped the hood clean off. It would have been an awesome sight if we weren't in such a rush to leave the scene. The second explosion was much more pronounced and we would later learn smashed windows two houses down from Ratsniffer's. We had barely made it to the library before we heard the familiar blare of the town fire siren. By now sweat was pouring off of us.

"Ginner, we can't go up into the library looking like we just ran a marathon."

"Dude, we're gonna have to take that chance, we

can't mess around now. We definitely have to make it look like we were here all night. Wipe the sweat off and let's go."

We had barely managed to grab our seat when the cacophony of police and fire sirens wailed by.

"Oh my, I wonder what happened," Miss Crinkage, the head librarian said as she came shuffling to a window near us to see what all the fuss was about. "Oh dear, it appears to be a fire," she said as she squinted. I let out a heavy sigh of relief. Paul looked at me with questioning eyes and mouthed 'what?' I made two circles with my fingers and held them up to my head and mouthed back, 'no glasses.'

"Oh," he sighed back. We hoped her limited eyesight would not be able to detect our glistening foreheads or rosy cheeks. We did little more than stare at our respective books, but we dared not leave until well after the fire was dispelled and the police had done all of their questioning, We wanted to make sure that our time line was as solid as possible, because we were definitely on a short list of suspects that Ratsniffer would point out. And a short list it was. We most definitely headed straight to the top of his list, primarily because we were ultimately the suspects closest to the proximity of the crime. Ratsniffer already had us convicted but of course the complete lack of evidence and the rock solid statement by the head librarian pretty much kept our heads off of the chopping block. After that incident Ratsniffer backed off of us and actually took a job to be head Dean at a private school in Connecticut. We weren't going to miss him.

The rest of the school year hauled ass, especially with us not having to look over our shoulders all the time. And to be honest we had been pretty freaked out about the whole incident, we were only aiming for a little graffiti, not grand larceny and arson. So for at least a few months Paul and I became model students. Our collective parents were duly impressed.

CHAPTER 6 – Journal Entry 6

Summer hit with all the oppressive heat and humidity that only the New England region can deliver, but generally as kids you don't notice it too much. Playing baseball took up the majority of our time, that and a thing we liked to call night games. At night we would play this game called jail. There were two teams and the object was for one team to hunt down the other team and put them in 'jail.' But the real reason for the playing of this game was Lacy Mullins. Paul and I both wanted her; she was literally the girl next door. And any chance we could have to chase her was well worth the effort. Lacy wasn't overly pretty, she just had something about her. She was sort of sultry, I mean as sultry as a fourteen year old can get, anyway. She mainly dug Paul but when they had an occasional spat I was more than happy to lend a shoulder to cry on. I didn't truly realize it then but this girl put a lot of stress on my and Paul's relationship, and had we not had such a strong bond the fate of our planet might actually have turned out vastly different, all for a girl, wouldn't be the first time I suppose.

The summer all in all was the last truly innocent or better yet naïve summers of my life. To me I still seemed to be a kid, I still loved to play baseball and expand my baseball card collection. Besides a little macking with Lacy, the opposite sex was still a complete mystery. My parents were still omnipotent, the thought of driving seemed eons away. And so, we cruised controlled our way into the 10th grade, high school. And like a punch drunk fighter who has cold water splashed on their face, my eyes were beginning to open up wide. Much of that awakening can be attributed to a girl named Tracy Potter. She was a transfer student from Pennsylvania. The first time I saw her I knew she was trouble, but as a young teenager, not much machinations of the brain are present. Most of my thinking was being driven by the excessive hormones my body was producing. I'm not sure what she saw in me, maybe it was that we were so completely different; she was a flower child burn out. You know the type, suede jacket with the fringes, sundress, hell she even had flowers in her hair. And a sly smile that melted my heart. I was hooked and we hadn't even kissed yet. The rumor mill had her pegged as a slut that would do it with anybody any time, I think that only heightened my desire for her. Her bright auburn hair matched her eyes down to a tee. And the way she moved her ass, hell even *I* knew I was in way over my head, but where the penis leads the body will follow, and somewhere in all that mess is the brain completely covered over in moss and virtually useless. She taught me more in the three whirlwind months we went out, than obviously the two girls before and most of the women I would later meet. She was my first love and she broke my heart in such a way that I never thought I would trust a woman again, and truly for the most part, I don't. Christmas pretty much sucked, especially with me sulking through winter break. My mother actually expressed some concern over me, but that quickly faded as she realized that she still despised my father; the hate consumed most of her existence. Just hearing her talk on the phone to her friends or sisters about how much she hated him was a constant reminder. But God has a plan for all of us, so I'm told. He taketh away and he giveth.

CHAPTER 7 – Journal Entry 7

A freak cold snap… We went back to school in January in one of the worst cold snaps recorded, it was the kind that when you opened the door and took your first breath the snot in your nose would quite literally freeze. It wasn't a pretty sight. I had begged my mother for a ride, but she had refused. She hadn't woken up with me since the third grade, and she saw no reason to start now. So there I was at the bus stop dancing around like the other ten idiots trying to keep from freezing solid. I was in entirely too much misery to take too much notice of my fellow sufferers, they weren't any people that I hung out with anyway. I recognized all but one. I tried but I couldn't recall ever seeing him in school. Oh well, must not have made that big of an impression, and to be honest I didn't care much beyond the thought of the once again late but heated school bus making a hasty arrival. The bus was packed which at this point was a great relief; more bodies meant more body heat. I don't think I stopped shivering until we finally got to the school, and then I had to get off the damn thing. I was going to have to make sure that I begged my mother for a ride tomorrow, station wagon or not. This was ridiculous. I trudged my way up to the third floor where my home room was, I just wanted to get rid of my books and my jacket and gloves and all of the other gear that rounds out a day in frigid New England. I sat down at my chair, which by the way was now one removed from the back row. It used to be the back row, but an extra row had been added in the off time due to a teacher's illness. The school administration had not been able to replace her before the start up, so in their infinite wisdom they had simply dispersed students throughout the rest of the classes. I turned to see the person who had enviably taken my favorite seat from me. It was the kid from the bus stop. He couldn't be from around here, I knew everyone in my class, whether I liked them or not, and he was neither. I just didn't know him. I guess the Yankees hat should have given him away. Nobody with half a brain wore a Yankees hat in the heart of Red Sox country even in the winter.

"Hey, my name is Dennis," as he leaned over his desk and extended his hand. I had almost been ready to turn back around without taking the proffered hand but that gesture would have had cataclysmic effects further on down the road, and I also would have missed out on the person that would share co-best friend honors. Not that I knew it then. And he still had that friggen Yankees hat on. But we shook hands and went on from there. I told him my parents were going away this weekend (not together I might add), and I was having a party and that he was more than welcome to attend. He thanked me and told me that he was new to the area and would look forward to meeting some new people. I told him that if he had any inclination of getting somebody to actual talk civilly to him and girls to even look at him, he might not want to wear that hat. He laughed and assured me that it wouldn't matter what hat he wore, girls loved him no matter what and everybody else could go screw themselves. We both knew it was male bravado, but we laughed anyway.

The week stayed in the below zero range; my mother never budged on the whole ride thing. Dennis and I never talked much at the bus stop more than your average pleasantries, it was just too miserable. Homeroom really wasn't the place to develop relationships either, everybody was too busy wiping the snow from their shoes and attempting to rid the chill from their bones. Early January in New England can be among the most severe weather in the nation and this one was no different. The school week sludged on by, and I was actually too busy concentrating on heat that I didn't piss off one teacher. It had to be a record. Friday came at last. I reminded the appropriate people about the party so that they would disseminate the information.

Dennis assured me that he would be there. To be honest, at the time I didn't care one way or the other. My dad left right after dinner Friday night to parts unknown, I knew without a shadow of a doubt that I wouldn't have to worry about him till late Sunday night. My mother could be the trickier of the two, she played cards every Friday night, and she was about fifty/fifty when it came to spending the night over at her friend's house a few towns over. If she did not stay the night, I could expect her home like clockwork at 1:45 a.m. That might put a damper on the events to unfold but it sure wouldn't stop them. My mother got a late start getting out of the house, that was the most nerve racking part. I had told people to start showing up at 7:30 p.m. and she was just walking out the door at twenty past. Dodged that bullet, now I had the gut twisting time of being in an empty house. This is the time when you wonder if people like you or not. There are no guarantees when you have a party even in near frigid temperatures, if people don't like you they won't come. So you sit there in anticipation of the first guests' arrival. Inevitably they are your closest friends, which can be a blessing or not. If they are the first and only to arrive you can be labeled a loser by the ones that are closest to you. So I waited. 7:30 p.m. came and went, not a big deal, nobody shows up on time right? 7:45 p.m. came and the bell rang. I opened the door. It was Dennis. 'Oh great,' I thought to myself, 'now the new kid is gonna think I'm a loser.'

"Hey, Dennis how you doing?"

"Not bad, sorry I'm late," as he walked into the house. "Where is everybody?"

"Well, you know how it is, you tell everyone 7:30 and nobody shows till 8." At least I hoped that was the case.

"Yeah," he said but I'm not sure if he said that more to allay my fears or in agreement. Oh well, I guess only time would tell.

"Want a beer?" I asked.

"Sure, what flavor you got?"

"Mostly Moosehead, but there's some Budweiser in

there."

"I'll take a Moosie."

I no sooner turned to get the beers and the doorbell rang once again. It was Paul and another one of our friends, Kevin Thomas, but what was of much more interest to me was the line of people coming down my street. My first official party looked to be getting well under way.

"Dude," Paul said as he pulled me aside. "Who's the guy in the Yankees hat?"

"That's that new guy Dennis I told you about."

"He better hope nobody wants to kick his ass when they get drunk."

"Yeah, that definitely takes some balls to wear that thing around here."

"Balls or stupidity, sometimes the two things can be so closely intertwined as to be indistinguishable from each other."

"Dude, big words," as I high fived him.

"Did you like that?" he said with a big grin. "I've been working on extending my vocabulary."

"Save it for the girls, Einstein. Want a beer?"

"I never thought you'd ask," as he put an arm around my shoulder and we headed into the kitchen. "Dude, how did you get all this beer?"

"I told my sister I was having a party and she bought it for me."

"When?"

"While she was home for her winter break from college."

"You've been sitting on this stockpile for a week and you never told me? I'm hurt," he said mockingly.

"Dude, you know if I told you, you would have wanted to raid it from the get go, and we'd be high and dry for the evening."

"You're probably right my friend."

"Probably?" as I raised my eyebrow at him.

"Just get me a beer so I can scope out some honeys."

The party was cranking, the girls were gorgeous, and the beer was flowing. The cops hadn't busted it up and I was sucking face with some little honey. Damn, I hoped she wouldn't ask me what her name was, cause I didn't have a clue. Midnight was rapidly approaching and my mother would call like clockwork to let me know if she was spending the night at her friend's. Luckily I had just enough presence of mind, though not much, to lower the music and let everybody know what was going to happen. I wish I had a video camera because what was two minutes ago a loud beer guzzling, girl chasing event now turned into a quiet waiting game. Everyone was literally staring at the phone, hoping that it would ring so that the fiesta could continue. Twelve o'clock came and everyone, even Chris Smith who was puking in the bathroom, held their breaths. Okay twelve o'clock and ten seconds, alright twelve o'clock and twenty seconds. How much longer could we hold our breaths? At twelve o'clock and forty-two seconds the phone finally rang, and everyone let their breath out. I put my hands up to hush the already church-like crowd.

"Hello?" I said, trying my best to sound tired and not drunk.

"Hi honey," my mom said through the phone line. "We're going to be playing late tonight, I'll be home in the morning."

"Okay Mom."

"Is everything alright?"

Oh no, did I slur? "Yeah everything's fine Mom, I'm just really tired." And I did my best exaggerated yawn; I even moved my arms much to the delight of the anticipatory crowd.

"Alright honey." Thank God nobody else could hear this. "Sleep good."

"Thanks Mom. Bye."

"Bye."

I hung up quickly because I knew Paul's hand was on the stereo volume control. He had the music cranked back up before I had the phone in the cradle; luckily I had pushed down the tab first. The crowd did a collective "hurray" and resumed their previous business. Whether it was drinking, smoking, sucking face, or as in poor Chris' case, just plain old puking.

Dennis came up to me. "Hey Mike, great party."

"How could you tell, your face was planted in that girl's." We laughed.

"Yeah, pretty good huh? I had to come up for air and beer. Thanks for inviting me."

"Hey, one thing Dennis."

"Yeah, what's that?" as he turned to face me.

"My friends call me Talbot."

He looked for a second at me before the light of recognition lit up; beer can significantly affect this by the way.

"My friends call me Wags, short for Waggoner."

"Good to meet you, Wags," as I extended my hand.

He took it. "And you too Talbot."

"Dude, I wouldn't leave that girl for too long, I think she'd suck face with whoever walked by next."

"Kiss my ass," as he laughed and headed for the fridge.

The party rolled till around the 2:00 a.m. hour, I can't be sure because it was very difficult to focus on things that small. But that was roughly about the time the beer dried up and curfews became an issue. Dennis and Paul stayed the night. Much to their chagrin, their dates did not.

The next morning was the realization of what fifty drunken teenagers can do to a house. The place was trashed. And I had somewhere in the neighborhood of two hours to get it looking like home again. With this crippling hangover I didn't see the point in even trying. I heard noise in the kitchen, loud bottles rustling around. Oh man, was somebody still looking for beer to drink? They were some hardcore mothers, I thought to myself. I pulled myself up from the grasp of gravity, damn she was unrelenting. I strode my green-gilled self to the kitchen to see what was going on. I was pleasantly surprised to find Dennis in the midst of throwing out the first of many trash bags.

"Thanks man, I appreciate that."

"That's what friends are for."

And then it was my turn to reflect on his words; yeah I guess that's what they were for. Friends were there for you when you couldn't do it alone. What an awesome concept, hardly new, but new to me.

"Where's Paul?" I asked groggily.

"That Ginner guy?" Dennis responded in kind.

"Yeah." I figured he had split hours ago.

"I think he's in the bathroom cleaning up some mess."

"Ooohh, better him than me."

"Dude, smelling old beer is hard enough, smelling vomit would put me over the edge."

"Just talking about it is killing me."

"Hey Talbot, do you have the key to your parents' liquor cabinet?" Paul asked as he came out of the bathroom holding a trash bag as far as humanly possible away from his face. He even had huge rubber gloves on. I was tempted to ask him where he had found those but that seemed like entirely too much effort.

"Yeah, I've got the key, but why do you want in there?"

"I learned a little trick of the trade from my dad."

I opened up the cabinet and Paul started mixing away.

"Dude, I have no idea what you're doing but I don't want any part of it. I don't like vodka and I hate tomato juice."

"Dude, trust me on this one."

Dennis wasn't even looking over at the bar, so intent on hoping that one of those wasn't for him.

"Alright guys, come on over."

'Me too?' Dennis' eyes seemed to say.

Paul held up his concoction proudly. "This is called a

Bloody Mary, or in other words, 'hair of the dog.'"

"Are you sure about this?" My stomach was quaking at the notion of putting more alcohol into it.

"Trust me man, try it. We've got maybe an hour or so till your mom gets home, and at the pace we're going at, we'll never make it."

He was right and I was feeling entirely too shitty to have my mother rag on me for the rest of the weekend. So I opened up the hatch; the drink was refreshingly good. Dennis seemed to enjoy his too. We spent the next few minutes intent on finishing our wonder elixirs. And damn if Paul wasn't right, I felt like a new man. Everybody seemed to have an extra bounce in their step. We finished cleaning the house at least a full thirty minutes before my mom's due back time. But I had no desire to stick around just in case she found something.

"Paulie, what do you have going on today?"

"Well, there is homework." Dennis and I both looked at him before we pushed him off of his chair. "What's the temperature outside?"

"It's warmer than it has been," Dennis said.

"Hold on, I'll check." I went to the kitchen window to see the strategically located thermometer outside. "Damn it's thirty two."

"It's a heat wave!" Paul yelled a decibel or two higher than I really wanted to hear. "Let's go to the S&S."

CHAPTER 8 – Journal Entry 8

"The S&S?" Dennis asked.

"You'll see, it's kind of our home away from home," I piped in. "Cause I sure don't want to be at this home when my old lady shows up." We bundled up in layers, the only appropriate way to dress in New England, and headed out. It would be the first of many in our exploration of new realms. The roof of the Stop and Shop was another ten degrees warmer than the surrounding air, which made the day seem even warmer after the cold snap we had just endured. We had even taken a few layers off by this time. To be young again, those were the days when you could drink all night and get up the next morning and start all over. Nowadays, if I were to drink on a Friday night I might start to feel human by late Monday, early Tuesday. How bad does it get if I make it to my forties? We had been on the roof for an hour or so, when Dennis asked what 'that' was.

"What's what?" I asked, now seriously starting to catch a buzz. It doesn't take much if you already started off with alcohol in your blood stream.

"That," as he pointed off into the distance. It was a field maybe a mile away, straight back from the rear of the store. The majority of Paul's time and mine was usually spent in the middle talking or towards the front of the store where we could see down the shirts off some of the hotter women. Even some not so hot, we were teenagers, what did we care. But you had to hide behind the Kihei sign, (The local Chinese restaurant) to make sure no one spotted you. Once Paul had drooled, I'm sure it was by accident but she *was* pretty. We almost got busted that time, but when her boyfriend looked up he must have thought it was condensation from the a/c, he didn't look too bright anyway.

"I'm not sure what that place is, I've kinda never noticed it before," Paul answered, a little embarrassed for not even knowing a place in his own hometown.

"You guys ever been up there?" Dennis asked.

"No dude, to be honest it's never even caught my eye before," I added.

"I think we should go check it out," Dennis said with a gleam in his eye. Paul and I weren't too thrilled.

"But what about our folks?" I whined (just a little). The thought of hiking in eight inches of snow didn't entice me too much. And there would be no hot heat exhaust vents to lean against if it got too cold. What could I say, I was a city boy; not much hiking goes on in downtown Boston.

"Come on Talbot," Dennis goaded. "I can pretty much guarantee my parents aren't going to be up there, do you seriously think your mom is going to be up there slogging around looking for you?"

"He does have a point bud," Paul chimed in, with a smile I might add.

"Yeah, you're right, I guess." But I still didn't feel good about it. We climbed down off the roof and the temperature immediately plummeted, back on went the layers. "How are we going to get over there?" I asked, hoping that this one little fact might thwart the whole attempt. "There's a river between us and the embankment."

From the back of the Stop and Shop was a small alleyway that the cargo trucks used to transport the food and beverages, and past the alley there were wetlands and woods for a quarter or so of a mile. Then we would have to go down a fairly steep embankment to the river, which wasn't the Mississippi, but at sixty to seventy feet across was still formidable. And to fall in at these temperatures could be near fatal without proper attention. I was liking this idea less and less. But the more faults I found, the more reasons Paul and Dennis found to make this journey.

"There's got to be a bridge or some way across," Paul said.

"Yeah, how else would our parents make it over to bust us?" Dennis emphasized *parents* just to let it sink in a little bit more.

"Are you messing with me?" I asked as I ran at him.

"Of course I am," as he danced away from my halfhearted jabs at his arm.

"Ass," I answered, but I felt better anyway. "I think they'd come in from the other side anyway."

"Really, you don't think there is an entrance this way?" Dennis asked incredulously.

"I don't know man, we've never been up there," I answered.

"Come on!" Paul threw in. "We're never going to find a way in if we sit here and debate about it. I don't think we should go straight back, we'll end up in the swamp and I'm definitely not in the mood to be wet."

"Then I guess we should decide which way we should go along the river to find a crossing," I said, finally giving my two cents' worth. Better to be part of the team than to sit on the bench watching.

"Which way goes where?" Dennis asked.

"Well if we head that way," Paul said, pointing south, "we'll end up in the center of town, and that could be scarier than running into the principal on a skip day."

"Yeah, I'd rather fall into the river than run into any of our parents," I said.

"Alright, so south is out," Dennis noted. "So north it is. Where's that head?"

"Into the woods," Paul said as we all turned to the north. The woods were dark and quiet and somehow foreboding, but with three of us together what could possibly happen? That was the best argument I could come up with to allay my fears. The bluster seemed to wane a little in Dennis and Paul both, but nobody was going to back out now. So into the woods we went and we never even saw Little Red Riding Hood or the Big Bad Wolf.

We had walked roughly a mile with the river always

on our right hand side, but not once did we see a way to cross, not a bridge, not even a fallen tree like in the movies. We had been tempted to turn around when Paul noticed up ahead a train trestle that crossed over. We were thrilled, we were like nine year olds on Christmas day. Or possibly fifteen year old drunks, either way the euphoria was the same. We started running towards the trestle overhead, but much to my impending chagrin being the fastest of the trio I was out in front. My foot plunged into icy coldness; it felt like little leprechauns were stabbing me through my boots. I had crashed through the ice of an offshoot stream. I wasn't in danger of drowning but I now had the uncomfortable feeling of having an icy wet foot. At the time the thought of frostbite never entered my mind. Dennis and Paul, having seen my slip-up, easily traversed the six foot wide stream and then had enough energy left over to turn and laugh at me as I pulled my foot out of the darkness.

"Son of a bitch!" I yelled.

"Yes you are," Paul laughed, and smacked Dennis on the shoulder.

"That's jacked up," Dennis said, but it didn't stop him from laughing. I wiped off most of the mud and leaves that were stuck to my boot and made the jump.

"I'd kick your ass with my wet foot if I didn't think you'd go crying home."

And we all shared in the laughter. We scrambled up the embankment as best we could. It was slick with snow and ice and the fact that it was a 30-degree pitch didn't help either. We reached the top and viewed our next endeavor. The trestle crossed over the river at an angle, making the bridge easily a hundred and fifty to two hundred foot span of metal and wood with a fifty foot drop into icy water. But that wasn't the scary part. The scary part lay in the fact that once in the middle of said trestle there was nowhere to go. With a bend in the tracks roughly a quarter of a mile up that would obscure our vision of any oncoming trains, that didn't leave much room for error.

"Oh *hell* no!" Dennis moaned. "There's no way I'm going over that thing! There has to be another way."

"Dude, you saw yourself there is no other way. We've been walking down this river for a while now and there is nothing else. You're not gonna puss out now are you?" Good old Paul, he could always be trusted to pull out the peer pressure card.

"No, I wasn't going to puss out, I was just hoping there was another way across," Dennis said staunchly.

"Well, we either go this way or find another way, but I'm not standing here too much longer. My foot is starting to freeze," I said. The trestle didn't look like that much fun to me either, but Wags was on the short end of this argument.

"Wait, I think there *is* another way across," Paul said as relief flooded Dennis' face. "If we stay on the tracks going the other way, we should come to Plimpton Street and then there's a car bridge that goes over this."

"Yeah, let's try that," Dennis said just a little bit too eagerly.

"We'll have to be careful," I added. "That exposes us to passersby and this town is small enough that our parents could find out. Make sure the beers are hidden."

"Alright, let's give it a shot," Paul said and then he started whistling. I was about to yell at him. What the hell was all the racket about, we were trying to be stealthy. It only took me a moment to realize it wasn't Paul, it was a passenger train coming from the center of town. It whipped around the bend and was heading straight towards us. We jumped off the tracks and melted into the woods a few yards away and waited for it to pass. The sight of the huge metal machine roaring by scared me deep within. To see something that big moving that fast chilled me even more than my boot. Nobody said anything but had Dennis not hemmed and hawed about crossing we would have been dead smack in the center of that thing when the train came. It would have been a near suicidal plunge fifty feet into icy cold water or a race to the finish on slippery wood and metal. Both thoughts made my stomach turn. The next few moments we traveled in silence as we all thanked whatever higher force had been responsible for that lifesaving delay. After another quarter mile or so we came to the intersection where the tracks went over Plimpton Street, so down the embankment we went. We waited by the edge of the woods to make sure the coast was clear, then sprinted across the bridge and back into the woods. Whether or not anybody saw us or even cared didn't matter, we were on a mission. The woods were entirely too thick with brush to try to get in from here, so we hugged the tree line near the road where it wasn't too dense. We jumped deeper in whenever someone passed by. We had almost given up all hopes of finding any inroads into Indian Hill as we later found out it was called, when we quite literally stepped onto a small path. It was absolutely invisible from the road. We went onto the road and checked. A huge oak tree had been strategically placed at the head of this small footpath. I had to think to myself that there were probably only a handful of people that knew about this, and of that handful none had been up here lately. The snow was pristine. The path was no more than two feet across but straight through the brush it went. We reasoned that it had to have been used, but from the condition of the snow we knew it hadn't happened in the last few days. Wet, scratched, tired and buzzed, we headed up the hill. The snow seemed to get deeper the further in we went, it seemed mystical but more likely it was just that we were getting more tired and therefore couldn't get our feet as high as we previously could. A few hundred yards later we came out from the woods and discovered one of the most awesome sights I had thus far encountered. Indian Hill spread out before us in a meadow to the left and right, with another rise directly in front of us, albeit it was another three or four hundred yards or so across the field. It was gorgeous with the snow and ice hanging from the trees. But what immediately caught our attention was a huge solitary oak tree in the center of the field. It was enormous, gnarled and twisted; ice clung to it like a lover on a spring day. We were transfixed.

"The hobbit tree!" Dennis yelled.

"What?" I said as I was shocked out of my reverie.

"It looks like a tree that would be in the Lord of the Rings trilogy!" he yelled again.

"You're right," Paul said as he turned from the tree to look at Dennis. And from then on that tree was and always would be known as the hobbit tree, even after its untimely demise almost ten years to the day. But that part will be saved for a later entry. Today, well today is dedicated to a place that would truly become our home away from home. We would spend a great deal of time growing up in those woods and hills, exploring every nook and cranny. And inevitably when we all went our separate ways in life we would on occasion make a special journey back to these magical and mystical woods that would one day become the place where our fate as a planet would ultimately be decided. This initial visit did not last as long as we would have hoped. My foot was frozen, the sun was beginning its early ending for the day and the temperature was plummeting nearly as fast as the setting sun. Apparently the warm front had worn out its welcome, old man Winter was back and he was pissed off that someone had stepped in while he took a break. The wind picked up, the wind chill factor had to be somewhere in the neighborhood of minus ten, and we were roughly dressed in layers equivalent to the mid twenties. None of us looked forward to the long walk home but our steps were lightened with the knowledge of this new and wondrous land that we were going to explore when the weather allowed. Like the lunar mission, we didn't stay very long but the impression was indelible. And unlike the lunar mission, we would be back and soon.

"Where have you been?" my mother asked as she stared straight at me, and unless I was being paranoid she was looking closely at my eyes. Looking for some evidence of what I am sure she was suspecting. But it's amazing what you can hide behind a bottle of Visine and a pack of

Dentyne.

"I was just hanging out with Paul and Dennis, Mom. No big deal," I added.

"Don't you get flippant with me young man, if your father were here he'd have your hide for talking to me that way."

"First off, Mom, I didn't talk to you 'that way,' and as far as worrying about what Dad would do if he were here, not necessarily something I'm too concerned about." That shut her up faster than a roll of duct tape. To see my mom wordless was truly a rare occasion. Her mouth was moving but no sound was coming out. I'm sure she had a string of curses on her tongue, but as of yet had not unleashed them. That was fine with me, the longer I stood face to face with her, the more likely I might burp and she'd catch wind of my choice of afternoon beverages. I had turned and was going to seek refuge in the confines of my room when her brain engaged with her mouth.

"Why is the house so clean?" she asked with an edge. I knew she was sniffing, but what did she smell? I had prepared myself for a lot of possible defenses; this was not on the list. Luckily I still had some wits about me.

"Geez Mom," I said in my best-exasperated tone. "I try to help out a little around here and you question my motives." That should unsettle her a little bit.

"It's not that I'm questioning your motives, it's that you *never* clean up around here and now all of a sudden... I just don't know what to think."

Light bulbs lit up in my head; I'm a genius! I turned back around to face her. She braced herself as in preparation for battle. I knew that was what she wanted. I headed straight for her. She had not been ready for that; she began to shy away. I grabbed her and gave her a bear hug. I made sure to keep my head next to hers but my face opposite, so she wouldn't smell through me. I told her I just wanted to surprise her and clean up because I loved her. That made her quieter than my original quip; I disengaged myself from her and went into my room. I didn't look back for fear of giving up the ruse, but I'm pretty sure she stood there for a full five minutes with the slack jaw and all. She had been so ready for a verbal scrape she had not prepared for my super secret stealth attack. I completely disarmed her, but now I wasn't sure if this meant that I had to now keep helping out around the house. If that was the case, who truly did win this battle?

CHAPTER 9 – Journal Entry 9

Fast forward some. Sixteen and heading into junior year, all seemed right with the world, at least up until the point Paul and Dennis died. Okay, okay, I'll ease up on the drama. ALMOST died. Paul was the first of our bunch to get his license and a car. Sure, I had a license but the only good it did me was for locked doors, if you catch my meaning. My parents barely wanted me in their car when we went somewhere, they sure as hell weren't going to let me drive it. Dennis seemed less than interested in getting his license, he was pretty much in the same boat as me, no money and parents that were not going to hand him keys to the Mercedes, or in this case an Oldsmobile. So there we were pretty much leaving our lives on the line to a guy who would snort salt off a table on a fifty-cent bet.

We had gone to probably the last show for the season at the local drive-in. It was a Cheech and Chong movie festival which in its own right would have been funny enough, but we upped the ante a little. Every time Cheech & Chong lit up, so did we, and until you actually do this you wouldn't believe how many times they do it. I'm pretty sure we mowed through at least a half-ounce of some primo California goldies, and I know we single handedly sent the drive-in restaurant owner's son through college. My gut ached from the cokes and fries and Raisinets and hot dogs and cheap imitation hamburgers on stale buns. There was cardboard pizza, which by the way when you are stoned is phenomenal. None of us was awake for the end of the third movie, it was an usher knocking on the window that finally got us rolling, no pun intended. Paul was lit up like a Christmas tree although so were Dennis and me, with one huge difference - we weren't driving. Well, inexperience and drugs rarely lead to good things and unfortunately this was no exception.

"Dude, you okay to drive?" I mumbled as I tried to sit up straight. My gut ached and my eyes burned, but I didn't want to leave Paul hanging. I figured as long as I talked he would be good to go.

"Yeah, I'm fine," he said as he mimicked my movements by rubbing his eyes. "Holy shit Talbot, I'm cooked."

"You and me both. Dennis still hasn't woken up."

"Do you think we should shave his eyebrows?" Paul said with a near sinister sneer.

"Bud, if I could muster enough strength, probably, but right now I just want to curl up in my bed and dream of Cathy McCabe's breasts."

"I hear you man." And with that Paul started the engine to his 1970 Buick Century. It roared to life in a way that only a 350 four barrel can. Paul peeled out, narrowly missing the speaker pole in front of us. He didn't even notice. I sure as hell did though, and my feeling of unease began to grow. I had contemplated putting my seat belt on but that would have labeled me as a wuss and I had no desire to lower my status. So we just kept talking, smoking and joking as they say, that was of course until Stairway to Heaven came on, and then the music became decibels louder making it nearly impossible to talk but that was just fine. Music can be one of the best stimulants on the planet if you immerse yourself in it and let it take you for a ride. Unfortunately Paul decided to ride that wave a little further than he should have of, he literally became engulfed in the song. My memory became a little fragmentary, time seemed to come sliced into mini segments each of which I was able to analyze in full depth as it occurred but could barely remember upon retrieval. As if off in the distance I heard what I thought were tires screeching but it made no sense cognitively until the car was violently thrust to the left, pinning me against the passenger door. I turned in surprise to look at Paul whose expression was one of complete terror. I wasn't sure why until I looked up and through the windshield to notice the rapidly approaching tree. We were in trouble now, he knew it, and I knew it. And for better or worse Dennis still had no clue. The car slammed into the tree with all the fury a two-ton machine can muster, I vaguely remember Paul becoming pinned between the driver's seat and the steering wheel as I flew by. Yes flew, my momentum was hurdling me out through the already smashed windshield on a collision course with said tree. I thought for a moment that I must be back in my in-school suspension, for time had seemingly stopped. I played out that moment frame by frame, my mind was racing at such an extraordinary pace, and I was instantaneously able to relive most of my high points and subsequent low points as I hastily exited the vehicle. Halfway through the window, and I was five years old playing with our family dog futilely wrestling an Easter egg out of his mouth. Feet clearing the windshield, I was seven, my sister was dressing me up for our cousin's wedding, and I was crying like a, well a seven year old I guess. Halfway across the hood, a starry night with Tracy and my first foray into manhood. Three quarters past the hood, THE break-up. And countless other images raced, the closer my ultimate fate became, the quicker my mind went into overdrive. And then contact, not the brain crushing mind-ending life stopping contact I had been expecting, but more of a glancing blow. I was amazed at the detail in the bark of the tree as I cruised on by; I even saw an ant hefting up what looked to be a cricket leg. My mind struggled to understand what was happening and then terror again rose up as I tried to remember what else was on this stretch of road. Was I going to be spared the tree only to go crashing into a even less yielding stone wall? At this point I even wanted my mother, I *must* be going to die. And then my upward arc ended, gravity took over and my descent began. Would I land on skin ripping pavement? Head first? My mind might have been racing but the speed at which I was traveling completely prevented me from doing anything about my predicament, and I'm not sure if anything I did then would have made a difference anyway. So I traveled through the air and through the years of my life. Castles made of sand eventually melt into the sea and so did my trip through memory lane. I landed with an audible thud and resounding crack, then I bounced at least another five feet in the air. It was the second landing that proved the most painful, with my now fractured arm pinned under me I cried in pain and anguish, but on this lonely stretch of road there was no one to hear me, not even my friends. Paul and Dennis, what happened to them? Panic nearly engulfed me. Vomit was quite literally on the tip of my tongue. I was somehow able to force down the shock that threatened to completely shut down my nervous system. I had to help my friends. And then I saw it, a tiny spark under the car; the fuel line caught and I knew what would happen from here. Did they get ejected too? No, I knew Paul was still in the car, the steering wheel made sure of that. What about Dennis, did he ever wake up from his slumber? Maybe he was better off.

"Help," I heard weakly, to be honest I wasn't sure if I had muttered it or I had heard it.

"Help," I heard again. I was sure this time that I hadn't said it but honestly I wasn't 100% sure.

"Dude. I'm coming," I rasped out just in case it had been Paul. I knew he didn't hear me because *I* barely heard it and he was at least forty feet away. Flames began to lick up the doors of the car; even from this distance I saw the horror in Paul's eyes as he turned his head and looked toward me. I stood up slowly, fearful that I had broken my leg, back or neck for that matter, and I would have to sit here helpless as my friend or friends cooked alive, and then I puked, but I did it as I was moving. I couldn't waste time worrying about the muscle cramps, but my arm, that was another crippling matter. I knew beyond a shadow of a doubt that there was no way I was going to be able to use it when I got to the car. My forearm was bent, was the only thought that ran through my head at the time. I would later learn that this type of break was called a compound fracture worsened by the effect of the bone poking through my skin. Would I be able to do what needed to be done with one arm? Fear raced through me and adrenaline surged. I lurched forward dizzingly slow; my mind was still in hyper drive making my movements seem even more exceedingly slow. My friend(s) was/were going to slow roast while I shuffled over. But in reality little more than twenty seconds passed from the moment I stood up until I reached the car. I could feel the heat of the flames a full ten feet before I got to the door. Paul was frantically trying to pry the steering wheel off of his chest, as it had effectively pinned him in like a vise. And to add to my horror I could see Dennis' leg sticking up from the back seat. I had no idea if the force of the crash had killed him instantly or merely stunned him, but either way it didn't appear to me that he would be making an exit on his own volition anytime soon. I stared at Paul in panic, searching in my mind for some way to help; with one good arm I didn't like the odds. And then without thinking I opened up the passenger door, which was in surprisingly good shape considering the front end of Paul's car was now shaped like an inverted 'v' to make way for the new oak exterior. One good arm might not do the trick but with two good legs I should be all right, I figured.

"Paulie, you all right?"

"Yah, except for the broken ribs and potential barbecuing I'm doing dandy," he wheezed.

"Paul, I'm going to get Dennis out first." Paul understood the equation. Dennis wasn't pinned against anything, so if the car blew at least somebody would survive.

"Dude, just hurry, Barb's gonna be pissed if I ruin this new shirt she bought me." He grunted a little with what could have passed for laughter.

"Dude, save your strength, I'm gonna need your help when I get to that steering wheel," as I showed him my broken wing.

"I didn't know you were double jointed?" Paul said. I wasn't sure if it was an attempt at humor or if he had slammed his head too hard on the steering wheel. I was trying my best to stave off shock but Paul was rapidly succumbing, maybe that wouldn't be such a bad state to be in considering we could be fire fuel real soon. Sirens were wailing in the distance but I knew they were too far off to be of any assistance to us now. It was going to be up to me, but I wasn't feeling up to the challenge. I reached down thanking all the gods I could think of when I felt a belt around Dennis' waist; I jerked with all my strength wincing as my broken arm was pushed against my body and the seat. Dennis huffed as I tugged on his belt. Thank you God, I thought to myself, he's alive, but the blood flowing from his head completely convinced me that he was going to be of no assistance once I released him from our fiery prison. Halfway up the seat and I almost dropped him back down as my protruding bone had now broken skin on my rib cage. The pain was excruciating, my vision began to blur, my peripheral vision shrank to pinpoints. If I blacked out we were all toast, pun intended. So I braced my legs up against the seat and pulled for all I was worth, Dennis rolled over the top of the head rest and square onto my broken arm. I screamed like a girl, a deep throated loud girl, and for a moment I did pass out.

"MIKE! Wake up! MIKE! Help!!" I could hear it in the distance, it sounded vaguely familiar but for the life of me I couldn't figure out why my alarm clock would be saying my name. Man it's hot in here, my parents were too friggen cheap to even get air conditioning. Fans in the summer time don't do squat except move hot air around.

"TALBOT! Get up!" There it was again. And the heat and the smell, what is that smell? Even after a night of heavy beer drinking my farts never smelled like that. It smells like burnt plastic and rubber and what's that other smell, oh yeah, hair. Burnt hair? Burnt hair. Burnt hair! I jolted awake, pain flooding my every sense. Confusion was the norm. Dennis was in my lap, Paul was on fire. Huh?! I swept through the cobwebs as quickly as I could, shoving Dennis off of me and turned to look at Paul, his eyes pleading with me to not leave him there.

"Paul, I just want to get him clear." So I bent down once again, grabbing Dennis' belt and dragging him about twenty feet from the car. I took off his jacket before I ran back. I hopped back into the car and threw Dennis' jacket over the flame that had started on Paul's left sleeve. I braced my back against Paul's seat and once again thanked anyone that was listening that Paul's car had a bench seat. With the heels of my feet I pushed for all I was worth on the top part of the steering wheel. At first nothing happened, I began to wonder what burning alive would be like, because I knew in my heart of hearts there was no way I was leaving him here alone.

"Paul, I'm going need your help."

"Mike, I don't have much left."

"Bud, whatever you got, because we either both get out of here or we're both going to be on the school lunch menu tomorrow."

"Fuck that," he croaked.

"When I say three." But there was no time for a count down. "Three!"

Paul gripped the bottom part of the wheel and pushed up while I continued my assault from the top. At first nothing happened, and then above the sizzling of the polyvinyl there was an audible creak, something was giving and hopefully it wasn't Paul's ribs. The steering column moved a fraction of an inch at a time at a painstakingly slow pace. To make matters worse, as it moved so did Paul's semi-collapsed chest, giving the illusion that the damn thing wasn't going to yield its prize. Like some macabre woman holding onto her dead baby, the Buick did not want to die alone. With a renewed second effort Paul and I pushed with one final exhaustive burst of strength and there it was, daylight, well not quite, more like fire light, but I could see light between Paul and the steering column.

"Dude, this isn't going to feel good."

Paul barely had time to mutter "What?" as I grabbed the material on his shoulder and unceremoniously hauled him out of the car. His butt slammed off the ground sending sparks of pain to his neural center, now it was Paul's turn to scream like a girl. 'Well, at least now he couldn't use that against me,' I thought as I dragged him further away from the wreckage.

The police and the fire rescue squad arrived as Paul's car popped and shattered through its death throes; there was no Hollywood theatrical blasts, just more of a slow melt down. Besides a few broken bones and some burnt up pot we were no less for the wear. Dennis awoke three hours later at Norwood Memorial Hospital with one hell of a headache, the result of a fairly serious concussion. He missed the entire event, not being able to recall one single detail for the police. They thought he was covering for Paul, but he had been passed out and then knocked out. Waking up in the hospital had been a complete surprise for him, and after he had the tale retold to him, he said he was glad he wasn't around for it. Paul was a little worse off than my broken arm. The doctors assured me I would only have to wear the constricting itching device for a mere six months. Damn casts. Paul had broken two of his ribs, scraped his lung and bruised his liver. Nothing deadly but extremely painful and with the smoke inhalation he had suffered, the coughing fits were making his life a living hell. Even Barb at her best, or worst, couldn't touch this pain he was feeling. I ended up receiving an award for my bravery, but I didn't see it that way. Would I have done it for strangers, I don't know. I did it for the love of my friends and the cowardice of knowing that had they died it would have been because I didn't try to do anything. I guess the outcome was the same but I was approaching it from a different angle. The more I look at this story as I write it the more believable the tale of the butterfly in Japan setting off a hurricane in Florida becomes. Little events seem to ripple out and cause greater change as they go. I will never forget that night, except mainly for the details.

Dennis exited the hospital the very next day, the

lucky bastard; we made him swear to us that he'd sneak us up some Chinese food from the Kihei. I stayed in Jell-O hell for another six days, but Paul took the prize at a whopping two weeks. It was during these healing times that we stumbled upon probably one of the greatest board games ever created, Risk, the game of global domination. Some might have thought we were crazy to stay in on a Friday night to play a board game, but Paul couldn't fart without crying, my arm was locked from the shoulder down and Dennis occasionally suffered from some mind numbing headaches. We could usually rope a couple of our other friends in to join the fray. We spent many a recuperative night learning the ins and out of strategy and tactics and I guess diplomacy. Hell, nobody wants to go out first. I loved these times, they were the most unhindered aspect of our young lives. We were in the company of great friends and we were alive. You always hear the clichés about people who say they have a renewed sense of what was truly important in life when you come face to face with death, and for the most part they were right. The bond between myself, Paul and Dennis had become rock solid. What I lost that night, though, was the feeling of invincibility, which all teenagers seem to have innately built within them. Maybe that was a good thing, the jury is still out.

CHAPTER 10 – Journal Entry 10

Senior year came and blurred on by. The Friday night Risk games turned into the Thursday night occasional Risk games so as not to interfere with senior partying times. My love life had taken a twist that not even Paul or Dennis saw coming. For the most part I had flitted from girl to girl without so much as looking over my shoulder. I guess at the time, although the term wasn't being used yet, I was something of a player. Don't get me wrong, I wasn't any Rico Suave, I just usually let the girls do the work for me. It was so freaken easy. She would just blab away about how this or that friend thought I was sooo cute. And I'd be like 'Oh Reeally,' what was her name again? And then I'd just give the friend a call. Women are funny like that, they won't think twice about stepping over their 'friend' to get to a guy. Guys though for the most part have an unwritten rule about seeing a friend's ex unless it is clearly stated by the ex that he has no problem with that arrangement. Of course there are exceptions to that rule. But even so, guys will beat the tar out of each other, pick each other up, buy each other a beer and be done with the whole situation. The girls, well, they'll pretty much be enemies for life, never going to fisticuffs but at the drop of a pin they will tongue lash each other at every given opportunity. And this is where my so-called player days came to a screeching halt. Her name was Mandy, and she just plain out floored me. The last thing I was looking for my senior year was a steady. But I just couldn't help myself. She was gorgeous, she could cook, and she had the brains of a turnip, pretty much the three qualities any guy is looking for in a relationship. And she genuinely loved me, and I think that at that time I might have actually had some of those same feelings for her. The problem was that Mandy was and most likely still is a small town girl, she had no desire to go to college or even the next town over. She probably figured with my advanced degree in partyology I wasn't going anywhere either. So when I received my acceptances from four different universities I couldn't find the intestinal fortitude to tell her. I basically just wanted to get up one late August day and be gone. Do you think she'd miss me? I began to let everything slide once I realized that I didn't have to impress any more acceptance boards. I coasted through the remainder of the year usually in a drug or alcohol induced daze. Two of the acceptances were from the Eastern Seaboard and never saw the light of day. I burned those into ash so my mother or Mandy would never see them. My options, as far as I was concerned, were CU in Boulder or UCLA, but I was never a warm weather fan or an earthquake fan for that matter. A lot of crazy things happen in this world. Planes crash, people die, but the Earth, well that's never supposed to move. So CU it was.

Suffice it to say, the University of Colorado in Boulder was almost too close a distance to my mother. It came as quite a shock to her how I could possibly have been accepted to a Western State college when all the applications she gave me were for Boston based universities. With tears (of joy) in my eyes, I packed and I left. And I did tell Mandy but not until the first of August. If I had realized what her response was going to be I would have told her months sooner. Mandy tried her damnedest to get pregnant, but I wasn't having any of that. She told me she was on the pill and that we didn't need condoms anymore. If I hadn't seen through that one I guess I would have been the stupider of the two. So for that month we did it like rabbits. I guess she figured that with a one percent chance of getting pregnant using condoms, that eventually she would hit pay dirt just by sheer numbers. It was a great month but I think I aged two years in that span. As the end of the month got closer Mandy became more frantic. I was afraid that she might just do it with somebody that looked like me just to get pregnant and keep me here. Would I have stayed? No, not a chance. I felt like I loved her, but what were we going to do? Live at her folks? Was I an ass? Probably, but I was 17, what did I care. She called me on the day I was leaving to tell me how much she hated me. I knew she was lying but it still struck me deep in the chest. It was a long time before I got over that conversation.

I had to take a Greyhound bus out to Colorado because my mother was too pissed to spring for the airplane flight. It didn't really bother me, three days on a bus was still better than the three days extra I would have had to spend with her. That final summer with her was a nightmare. She harangued me from the moment I got accepted till the day I left. "How could you do this to me?" "Why would you want to leave me all alone?" "Your father's never here, why should you be!" Three days on a bus far outweighed the alternative. I guess the only thing that really began to bother me during that trip was the constant smell of urine. I don't know do bus riders just pee wherever they are? They truly are a different class of passenger. Too cheap, poor, stupid or possibly a combination of all three to take alternate means of transportation. But that also has very little to do with the tale I'm telling. I got off the bus in Boulder, Colorado. Is it me or does the air in Colorado just smell better? Even the urine-bleach odor of the bus depot smelled a little sweeter.

I stepped out from the front of the depot and actually hailed a cab, I thought that only happened in movies, and directed the driver to the University of Colorado, Boulder. Apparently he was very familiar with college students, he hurumphed and grunted and I think actually passed a little gas before proceeding to take me on the exclusive city wide tour of Boulder, so forty-five minutes later and fifty-two dollars poorer I stepped out of the cab and right in to the arms of Beth. No, literally, I stumbled on the damn curb and fell into the assistant R.A.'s arms. Maybe the oxygen is a little thinner, but I don't know if that could even begin to explain the swoon I felt when she touched me. Her fingers were electric, I don't know if she felt it too or she was just reacting to the goofy look on my face, but she held on to me just a little longer than she had to before she propped me back up on my semi-stable legs. She was 5'2" of pure female perfection, her auburn hair trailed down her back just to the point of caressing one of the finest sculpted buttocks (okay asses) I had ever seen. Her almost oval face was dominated by a radiant smile and eyes as blue as the sea, but not your average sea, more like the sea off the coast of Hawaii. I felt from that one look she directed at me that she could and had read my soul. (But I actually found out later that she had felt bad for me, thinking that I was part of the Special Ed class. Oh well, not every fantasy can be perfect.)

"Whoa, you alright?" she said with a gleaming smile

"Uh, yeah, I don't think I twisted anything," I murmured sheepishly.

"Are you part of the...?"

"Yeah, I'm in the freshman class of 1988."

"Oh," she said, "Do you know which dorm you're in?"

"Yeah, uh Baker's Hall, room 312."

"Oh, that's great, I'm the assistant R.A. for that floor"

"That's awesome!" I said a little too energetically, hope and desire surging through me.

"Alright, you should probably get your stuff and get to your room so that you can get acquainted with your new roommate. Oh, and there's a floor meeting at seven o'clock tonight in the third floor lounge."

"Thanks, I'll be there!" Man, could I be more lame. The girl of my dreams is standing before me and I sound like a kid at Toys R Us, even my mom knew it was better to remain silent and be thought dumb than to open your mouth and remove all doubt. I proceeded up to the third floor, I was able to circumvent the elevators because everything I was bringing to college was either in the backpack I was wearing or the duffle bag I was carrying. Mother felt that I had no need to bring my stereo or any other personal belongings to school. "You need to just concentrate on your grades so that you can graduate and get back here as soon as possible." As if I was going anywhere near the East Coast when I graduated. I guess I better get down to the registrar's office and see which degree would take the longest amount of time to acquire. Maybe I could just stay and go for my doctorate. Deep in thought, I had my second near collision of the day, good thing I wasn't driving.

"Whoa dude, what's your rush?" a voice drifted into my daydream

"Sorry bud I wasn't, just deep in thought," I replied, obviously without even considering my words.

"Are you stoned?" the voice came back.

"No I'm not stoned," I said indignantly as I finally looked up at the voice ahead of me.

"Do you want to be?" he said.

"Paulie, how you doin' my friend? How long have you been up here?"

"At least long enough to deseed half an ounce and roll a fattie."

"Awesome, bud."

"Yeah it is awesome - bud," and we both laughed at that. And then we both stopped to admire the fine looking brunette striding on by. Man she was hot and we both knew she wouldn't give us types the time of day unless we asked it from the posh interior of a Porsche. But it didn't stop us from admiring the view.

So that's how I ran into my best friend at CU. Paulie and I had planned this from the get go. We had applied for CU in secret hoping to get as far away from our parents as humanly possible and still stay in the country. I was truly glad Paul had decided to take his acceptance here. My self-esteem and confidence were shaky at the best of times. But Paul always seemed to be one of those people that you just felt good to be around. He brought out the best in the people around him. When we both decided that we were going to college we figured what the hell, let's apply to the same school, maybe we'll get lucky. Whereas my mother couldn't believe I was leaving her, Paul's parents couldn't wait for him to leave. He had just taken his final bags out of the room and his dad started stripping the wallpaper. Something about a hot tub or an office. Paul didn't know and he didn't care. For him also, two thousand miles might not be far enough away. He was a couple of inches taller than me, and definitely the type of guy that ladies approve of, dirty blond hair with piercing blue eyes. He was always quick with a smile and a joint. His laid back manner seemed to attract the ladies like a magnet. He was the kind of guy I had always strived to become, but I guess I just had too much of my mother's uptightness in me.

"It's good to see you my friend, step in to our palace." He motioned with the wave of a hand. And unless I was already stoned I could swear he had somehow already produced the joint we were about to partake from.

"This is our room?" I asked

"What do you think man?"

"It looks like you've been here a lot longer than a couple of days."

"Dude, my parents were so stoked I was leaving they would have put my ass on a Concorde if it had been an option. I'm telling you I've only been here for a couple of days."

I stepped into my new abode and into an alternate universe. He had the place decked out. There was a black light on, three different black light posters, one each of Jimi Hendrix, Led Zeppelin and Cream. There was a strobe light going off in the far corner, and painted in glow-in-the-dark paint were stars on the ceiling. I sort of had the feeling I sometimes got when I was building models and I left the glue open a little too long. The room was laid out in the shape of two squares that offset each other, giving the room the appearance of a Z shape. Of course being the last into the room I got the half that opened up to the doorway. Paul half-heartedly asked if it was okay if he got the half that faced the windows. It looked like he had been prepping his side for the last twenty-four hours with the posters and the lights and the glow in the dark nightline. I acquiesced, with the only condition being that he help me get my side to look like his. His smile spread from ear to ear. Well, I thought to myself, if being stoned could make you that happy, bring it on.

We smoked, laughed and ate; he had a box of Devil Dogs, which we devoured in record time, in four minutes if my watch was working correctly. I learned a new card game called 45's but I wasn't sure if I'd even remember it when we came down.

"Dude, its ten past seven, we gotta go the floor meeting," Paul said, half smiling.

"Oh man, I have no desire to be out in public right now," I said, slurring or at least it felt that way when it came out of my mouth.

"You'll be fine, but you might want to wear some sunglasses."

"Whattaya mean sunglasses, it's seven o'clock and we're inside.

"I know that," he laughed "but your eyes are glowing."

I looked in the mirror and could hardly believe the image that reflected back at me. I really did now look like a kid from Special Ed; the Devil Dog crumbs on my chin only amplified the effect. My eyes glowed like embers in a fire, and my lids drooped so low it looked like I was asleep on my feet.

"Use this, you'll be fine," Paul said as he threw a small bottle at me, which proceeded to bounce off of my arm and onto the floor. "Gets the red out."

"Thanks man, I definitely appreciate this, I wish I had something that would take the buzz out, I really don't want to act like an idiot in front of the assistant R.A."

"You mean Beth?"

"Yeah," I said with a sheepish grin.

"She's out of your league, she was a counselor at the

camp I used to go to during the summer. She's a great person but she's got more ambition and drive in her than anybody I've ever met. I tried to go out with her for two years, and she was having none of it."

"Oh, so you figure if you couldn't get her nobody could, huh?" I said nonchalantly, but in reality I was thinking to myself, if he couldn't get her there was no way on God's green earth that I would be able to. "How come you never told me about her?"

"There's nothing to tell. She was a girl, alright a hot girl, that I never went out with. Not the kind of thing I like to spread around," he said mockingly, "Naw, it's just that she was always looking ahead. If I remember correctly, in high school she was going out with some football player in college, a big dude. She showed me his picture."

My hopes had been dashed. They felt as if they had been literally smashed against the rocks. Paul, seeing the change in my expression, spoke hastily. "Don't sweat it, for every girl you can't get, there are two you can." It was small solace but it would have to do for now. So off to the third floor lounge we went.

"So glad you could make it," Beth said sarcastically as she glanced up at us. To me it appeared as a knowing glance at Paul and a disapproving one at me. Or maybe it was just the marijuana-induced paranoia. The only thing I remembered about the next hour was that I didn't drool, which is a good thing, and how mesmerized I was with the way that Beth would flip her hair away from her face from time to time. I hoped it wasn't too apparent that I was staring, but Paul noticed and would nudge me from time to time as if to awaken me from my stupor. So began my college career.

The first few weeks of college flew by at a surprisingly fast pace. I even made it to some of my classes when Paul and I hadn't partied too much the night before. But I had perfect attendance at my English lit class. Yeah, you guessed it. It wasn't the subject matter that did it, Beth had the class also, although we never talked in class. She was too busy taking copious notes (which I gladly used for study material before classes). We always talked after class, she had an hour and half break before her next mod, and I gladly pretended that I did also. Calculus, as far as I was concerned, could wait. At first we would be courteous to each other, say our pleasantries and then head in opposite directions, but after the first week or two we would begin to talk a little more, then eventually we would walk together and then on occasion we would get lunch together. After another week of beating around the bush, I finally asked her out on a date. The let down was almost more than I could bear.

"Beth, I feel like we've really been getting to know each other and I was wondering if you might want to go out to a movie or something," I half stammered. Damn, it's not supposed to be this hard.

"Mike, I like you, I like you a lot, more than I actually should."

'Here it comes, nothing good can come from this,' I thought to myself. The BUT should be coming at any moment now.

"But..."

Bingo, I was right

She continued, "I'm in a serious relationship with someone."

"I know," I said "With that football player from Penn State, I just figured we could try like the song, and love the one you're with." Oh no, I didn't really just say that, why can't life be like the movies so that we could cut out a bad scene and have a redo. But she actually did laugh at that. Unfortunately, lunch after that conversation had an awkward quietude to it. I actually excused myself a little early so that I could attend the last half of my Calculus class. I must have been upset. So for the first time in two weeks I actually attended all of my classes, more so that I could think through this new development with a clear mind. If I went back to the dorm I would more than likely end up in some drug induced stupor. I attended every class, but only in the physical sense,

I could not help but wonder if I had done the wrong thing. 'Was it to soon to ask her out?' 'Did I mess up a budding friendship?' I mulled over those problems all day long until eventually I ran out of classes and had to return to my dorm, no more the wiser for my musings. Paul had heard about a huge party off-campus that night and asked if I wanted to go. I declined, I told him I was actually going to try and study.

"Dude, it's Friday night, nobody studies on Friday night! Mike, this isn't about Beth is it? Come on bud, she's going out with a friggen running back from Penn State. The guy's a stud. Let it and her go. There's going to be so much tail at this party tonight, you're not going to know which way to turn," he said almost pleadingly.

"Hey man, I appreciate the offer, I do, and it does have a little to do with Beth, but I'm so far behind I just won't feel right NOT studying tonight. You know if I flunk out I'm gonna have to go back to Boston, and I really don't want to compound my woes with that."

"Well my friend, if you feel like coming out later, I'll be there all night, unless I get lucky, well okay maybe I won't be there that long," he said with a wicked teeth-flashing grin.

"Dude, you are the dog you make yourself out to be."

"Not a dog, my friend, more like a wolf." He semi-howled.

"Get outta here before I change my mind." Because I knew just being around Paul would greatly increase my odds of being with a girl tonight. He couldn't have them all, there would have to be one or two that fell to the wayside, even a castoff is better than being alone.

"Later Mike, I'll be thinking of you, for at least the first ten minutes," he laughed.

"Late," I replied without much enthusiasm.

I studied for what seemed like days, in all reality it was more like three hours, but that was probably two and a half more hours than I had studied for the entire semester thus far. I guess I must have dozed a little because I awoke to a light knocking on my door. I almost believed it was a dream, but no, there it was again. Who the hell would be knocking on my door at eleven o'clock on a Friday night? Maybe it was pizza. That would be good. I opened the door to a waking dream.

"Hi," she said.

I gaped for a minute. Beth had come to my room in a long skirt with a blue top that almost perfectly matched her eyes.

"Uh hi, you want to come in, have a beer or a soda?"

"No thanks, I was wondering if you'd come for a walk with me."

"Uh sure." Now I'm like most men, I can't figure out women to save my life, but now she had me completely befuddled. She already pretty much told me no way, did she just want to reiterate the point? Because I was really not in any mood to have my ego bruised any more than it already was.

So walk we did, around the entire campus. Conversation was at a minimum, mostly small talk. What the hell was going on!? Then it happened, she grabbed my hand, not in a friendly come here way but a way in which only lovers do, with their fingers entwined. I know it sounds foolish but just the touch of her hand made me hard. I hoped beyond hope that she didn't notice me constantly reaching down and adjusting the front of my pants. If she did notice, she never did say anything. After a few blocks of hand holding she led me to an adjacent playground, thankfully abandoned by any seesawing kids at this time of night.

"Come here," she said with a gleam in her eye. And it was then and there in that playground that Beth and I finally and blissfully became lovers.

I wish I could say that this was the end of our problems and that we became a happy couple, but that interaction only made things worse, at least for the time being. Beth became so guilt ridden over our love making session that she began to completely ignore me. And not being Mister Self-Confident anyway I was under the impression that my clumsiness at lovemaking was what drove her off. I had only Mandy to compare this too, and I had never felt the sensations with Mandy that I was feeling with Beth. Did she feel them too? I didn't know if I was a porn star or a man with ten thumbs. The great freeze thawed out at fractions of a degree. Occasionally I'd get a "hi" on campus or a smile at floor meetings, but nothing more than that. I was distraught; I began to ignore my classes, even more than usual, which at the time was a very difficult thing to achieve. I couldn't figure how making love could ruin us, I was under the impression it strengthened relationships; I guess you can refer back to me not understanding women. Beth finally approached me three weeks to the day of our last rendezvous.

"Mike, we need to talk."

"Alright," I stammered.

"Why haven't you been talking to me?" she blurted out.

Now I was completely confused. "You've been giving me the cold shoulder for three weeks and you want to know why *I* haven't talked to you?"

"I'll admit I'm feeling a little guilty about the whole thing but after what we shared I thought that you'd try a little harder instead of just falling off the face of the planet."

"Huh?" I couldn't even begin to grasp where this conversation was going. "I thought that you didn't want anything to do with me."

"Whatever gave you that impression?"

"You did. You've been extremely cold and distant."

She completely blew off my argument and headed off in her own little tangent. "I've talked to Mark." I looked at her with an unknowing stare. "The halfback at Penn."

"Oh," I answered.

"I told him that I wanted to break up." My heart was doing backflips. "I'm not ready right now to be in a steady relationship, but if you'll have me, I'd like to start again with you. But slower." Now my heart was doing front flips. I must not have been all thumbs if she was breaking up with the Penn state stud for me. And then like a needle she burst my bubble. "I told him that long distance relationships are too tough and that I just couldn't afford the time away from my studies to keep visiting him."

"So you never actually told him about us?"

"I didn't think that there was much to tell actually." My stomach started its somersaults routine all over again.

'Slow' quickly turned to smoldering and then like a couch with a hidden cigarette it burst into a bright flame. We missed whole days; we'd emerge from our shade drawn candlelit room only out of necessity. Food, water, bathroom breaks, that was about it. I learned more in the next two months then I would learn for the rest of my life. I ate, slept, and drank her in. If she left the room I couldn't wait for her return. Our relationship was that intense. Paul began to become a little perturbed that the time he and I were spending together had been reduced to virtually nil. And even on those rare occasions when we did hang out, it was usually with Beth along. Our friendship was strained a lot throughout freshman year, but I didn't even notice it then. I was so in love I couldn't even see straight.

CHAPTER 11 – Journal Entry 11

I was able to gain a little perspective during winter break. Paul and Beth both went back to Massachusetts for the month layoff. I remained on campus, loaded down with extra credit so that I could stay in school. You've never quite experienced loneliness until you've spent a Christmas by yourself. My Christmas dinner consisted of warmed over McDonalds, which I had purchased the night before just for this occasion. I received calls from pretty much everyone I knew. The month went by fairly fast, I spent the majority of it in the library getting my scholarly noggin screwed back on. Paul came up a few days earlier than expected which was greatly appreciated, especially since I had finished all my projects three days hence and was going absolutely stir crazy.

"Man is it good to see you!" I had been sitting in the dorm lobby watching the tube when Paul strolled in.

Paul came up and gave me a hug. "It's good to see you too man. What have you been up to?"

"Going friggen nuts," was my reply.

"Come on, let's go have a beer."

"I can't tell you how much I've been waiting for those words."

We went to a local bar, drank, played darts and shot some pool all night. It definitely felt like old times. It was then that I realized how little we had been doing this kind of thing. Just hanging out and rapping with each other.

"Hey Paul, I'm sorry that I've pulled away so much this last semester."

"You noticed that too?"

"Okay, so I guess I got a little wrapped up in the whole Beth thing."

"I totally understand, she's definitely the type of

chick that you can get totally wrapped up in."

"Tell me about it. But I promise I won't spend nearly as much time with her this semester as the last. And when we hang out it'll just be a guys' night out."

"Sounds good to me. When does she get back?"

I looked at my watch. "Two days, twelve hours and forty six minutes." Paul was looking at me incredulously, shaking his head. "Dude, I'm just kidding."

"Ass," he said as he nailed my arm with a punch.

*   *   *

Beth came back a couple of days later. There was a little awkwardness there. But we quickly got over it with a marathon love making session.

"Did you miss me?" I asked after our session.

"I saw Mark." If I hadn't been in bed I would have doubled over. I tried to regain control of my emotions before I spoke. I was unsure how to proceed, so I waited for her to continue. It didn't take long, I learned at least one thing about women, if you leave enough open-air time in front of them they feel compelled to fill it. "He told me that he missed me, and that he wanted to get back together with me."

"What was your response? Did you tell him about us?"

"I told him that I missed him too."

'What!!!' I screamed in my head. "I'm not sure I understand?" I was attempting to quash the mounting horror I was feeling. I wasn't doing too well with that.

"I'm not sure what to do, I have strong feelings for both of you. I've been going out with Mark for two and half years, it's hard to just let go."

"Did you spend time with him?" That was the best way I felt that I could broach the subject of whether or not she slept with him. It was vague but we both know what I meant. She never answered that question directly, that was all the answer I needed.

CHAPTER 12 - Seventy miles South of the Boulder Municipal Playground – Cheyenne Mountain

"Lieutenant, I asked you a direct question. What the hell is that?" Captain Moirane said. He was a man used to having his questions answered in a most timely manner. A little over 6' tall and built like a flying fortress, he struck a very imposing figure. Captain Moraine had worked his way up in the Marines Corps, he was what the troops called a Mustang. He was an enlisted man who had crossed over to the officer ranks. These types of officers have had arguably the most loyal following among their troops because they knew what it was like to be a grunt in the field. So it was with great hesitation that Lieutenant Blankenship, a boot lieutenant out of Georgia University, answered the Captain with a pure look of amazement.

"Sir, I just don't know, we've been tracking it for three hours since that civilian observer called it in to NASA. At first we thought it was a huge meteor but then twenty minutes ago it changed direction. It's on a direct collision course for Earth."

"I've got two questions for you Lieutenant. And I'm going to be very specific, and I want very specific answers. If you do not know the answers at this time, I want you to do everything in your power to obtain these answers. Because my next call is going to be to the President, and I had better damn well know what I am talking about. Do you understand me son?"

The lieutenant understood well enough to know that the term "son" was not used for endearment. "Sir, yes sir!"

"Lieutenant, I want to know EXACTLY how big that thing is and I want to know EXACTLY how long we have until it makes contact with my beloved planet!"

"Sir, yes sir, the science officer is en route now."

"What's his ETA?"

"I would say about now, sir," the lieutenant snapped.

"Captain, why was I awoken at this godforsaken hour? This had better be the emergency that the lieutenant made it out to be. I've had just about enough of your emergency response drills," Dr. Schoville said with just a hint of venom behind it. The professor a short balding man in his middle sixties who looked more like Larry the janitor than one of the world's leading astrophysicists. That point was further pointed out by his disheveled appearance. It was almost comical, blue jeans with pajama tops, and one slipper paired with one loafer.

"Why Professor, it's good to see you too," the captain said sarcastically. "I see that you've pulled yourself together well tonight."

"Oh do zip it Captain, as much as I like you, I have no desire to banter this evening," the professor said as he plopped down into his control seat.

"Professor, I would not have called you out of bed at this late hour unless it was absolutely imperative."

"What happened?" the professor grunted "Did the cow jump over the moon?"

"Object J-2378 has changed direction, Phil."

The professor looked up with a jerk. For the captain to forget protocol and use his first name obviously meant that he was serious. "But that's impossible, meteors don't just change course, did it collide with another object and veer off?" the professor asked incredulously.

"No," the lieutenant spoke. "One minute it was heading off into delta quadrant and then it seemed to hesitate for about ten minutes and then it turned to a heading exactly in this direction." The lieutenant appeared nervous and a little bit relieved; the man he was talking to was infinitely more capable of answering the captain's questions.

"That, my dear professor, is why we awoke you at this God forsaken hour," the captain added. The professor looked nearly as nervous as the lieutenant.

"Lieutenant, could you be a champ and get me a cup, a very big cup of coffee, I think I'm going to be here awhile," the professor said resignedly.

* * *

"Captain, for the two hours I've been studying this object, it is by no means a natural celestial body," the professor said later. Had his scientific side not been so curious he felt that he actually might have been afraid.

"Professor, for the record, what exactly are you saying?" the captain fairly demanded. "Do you really expect me to call the President of the United States and tell him a space ship with little green men is on a collision course with Earth?

"First off, Captain, I'm fairly certain that this ship will stop before it impacts with our planet, and from what I can tell there is nothing small about this vessel," the professor half-stammered out. "The ship appears to be roughly half the size of our moon and will be in a tidal influencing position in less than two weeks at its present speed. But I'll be honest with you, Captain, this ship hasn't been traveling the stars at its present speed unless it's somewhere in the neighborhood of a couple of thousand years old. I'm sure that these "beings" have some sort of hyper drive or "warp" drive if you will, that could have them in our neighborhood more in the vicinity of a day or two or quite possibly even an hour or two. If I were you Captain, I would get on the phone with the President *now*."

The captain could not even begin to fathom how he was going to start this conversation off. He had been through two wars and dozens of skirmishes, but at this moment, on this night, he felt that he was the most out of his depth he had ever been in his entire life.

"Lieutenant, call the President and get the Joint Chiefs of Staff out of their beds, I also want General Burkhalter up here as well."

"Sir, yes sir!" the lieutenant shouted, sweat now

pouring off of his face in rivulets. The captain noted that fact and was mildly amazed considering the 'mountain,' as it was affectionately called, was air conditioned to near freezing temperatures to keep the machinery running at peak performance.

Less than an hour later the captain found himself, via satellite hook-up, staring face to face with the most powerful people on the planet, the President, his military leaders and some of the most prominent cabinet members along with the senate and house chairmen.

"Good morning Captain Moiraine," the President said almost jauntily for this time of day. The captain was surprised that the President knew his name, much less that he was in an affable mood.

"Good morning to you Mr. President," the captain added as politely as possible. Just because the man was his boss didn't mean he had to like him, and that was definitely the case here. But then again the captain had never liked any Democratic leader in the Oval Office; the military was always the first to suffer.

"Captain, I have this fairly thorough briefing in front of me but I would like your opinion on this matter. I have some very conflicting theories and proposals being thrown around here, I would most welcome an outside opinion in this grave matter. What are your thoughts?"

"Sir, at this time it is near impossible to theorize on what these "beings" want. At this time we can't even be sure that there is life on this ship, it could possibly be some sort of probe. We can hope that if there are sentient beings on this ship that they are merely out on an exploratory mission as opposed to a military operation. However, it is my belief that we should prepare for a full scale planetary invasion, but I believe Sir that a pre-emptive strike, as some of your advisers are advocating, would be futile and more than likely fatal."

"Why is that Captain? My generals here feel that we should launch our shuttles armed with all the nuclear payload they carry, and strike well before this ship ever enters our orbit."

"Mr. President, with all due respect, these *aliens* ..." that even sounded funny to himself, the captain could hardly believe that he was saying the words aliens and wasn't making up a story for his sons. "Well, these aliens traveled from a distance that we can not even fathom at this time in our evolution, it would be a safe call to say that they are at least two hundred years ahead of us in technology. It is my opinion and my opinion only, Mr. President, that to attack them with nuclear weapons would only prove to these aliens that we are a hostile species and that we would need to be dealt with accordingly. Quite possibly they are merely curious about another intelligent species in space."

"Captain, what makes you think that they believe we are an intelligent species?" the President said, stress was beginning to strain his voice.

"Sir, it is mine and Dr Schoville's opinion that the only way they even noticed us was by radio and television transmissions. We had the computers running simulations for the last hour and as near as we can tell from the distance that that ship is from our planet, they are watching and hearing transmissions from roughly 1980ish. Sir, another assumption that we have made is that these beings most likely have already formed a not so flattering portrait of our species. The vast majority of our television matter is laced with violence."

"So my point again, Captain, what makes you think that those aliens think we're intelligent?" That earned a few laughs and helped to lighten the mood for a least a short while.

"All the more reason to strike as soon as possible!" the commander of the Army, General Forbes yelled. Always the tactful one.

"I understand your concern General," the President stated flatly. "But I agree whole-heartedly with the Captain's view, we would merely be proving to the aliens that what they are watching on our television transmissions is true, and most likely a full strike would do little more than be an irritation to this ship. No, we must seek a diplomatic solution, although it would be a lot easier for negotiations if we knew what the hell they were up to. Having the upper hand is the key to negotiations and I can assure you, gentlemen, that is not something we possess at this time. Mr. Secretary, could you please get me the Chinese Premier and the Russian President on the line. Thank you Captain Moiraine, I'll be in touch." With that, the huge monitor inside the "mountain" winked out. Captain Moiraine merely looked into the screen for a few more minutes, letting the full weight of these events hit him like a tidal wave.

The Captain turned from the screen and approached the lieutenant.

"Lieutenant, go home, enjoy the weekend. And remember, everything that you have seen and heard today is top-secret."

"I understand sir, I'll see you on Monday. Sir?" the lieutenant asked.

"Yes Lieutenant," the Captain answered, already half submerged in other thoughts.

"Are we going to be all right, sir?"

The captain turned back to fully face the lieutenant. "Son," and now it was clearly meant to be a term of endearment, "I just don't know."

CHAPTER 13 – Journal Entry 12

"Bud, what's up with you, you look like a whipped dog," Paul quipped.

"Paulie, Beth has got me in such a funk I don't know if I should fart or cry," I lamented.

"What's up?" he asked seriously.

"She didn't come right out and say it, but I think she got back together with Mark."

"Mike, I'm sorry, but I told you not to get too involved with her. She's a heartbreak looking for a place to happen."

"I know you're right, it's almost as if I can't help myself. I know I'm in over my head, but when I see her…"

"Yeah yeah, your other head takes over," he chided.

"No, it's not like that. Okay well it's a little like that. But there's more, it's almost like I'm falling…"

"Talbot, don't say it!" Paul looked mock horrified. "Don't spend your entire collegiate career on one girl, although she is one hell of a girl. Man, you'll miss out on so much, and you'd better remember she still has Joe Jock out at Penn State unless she told you that she has other plans for that particular problem. Face it buddy, you're her plaything, not the other way around. Women have needs too, you just happen to have what she needs now. Although I bet it's not really all that impressive." He chortled at his own wit.

"Blow me," I said, but he really did have me thinking that I was merely a pawn in a much larger game.

"Just ride it and her out, dude, I'm not saying to not enjoy your time with her, but don't get any more emotionally involved than you already are. I can guarantee that you will get irreparably burned. You are my best friend and I don't want to see you waste away our greatest party years."

"Thanks bud I appreciate that, and I know you're

right, but right now I have no idea how to stop this train. When I'm with her I just know she's the right one."

"Dude, she's just Miss Right Now, don't do this to yourself."

"I know, well no I don't know, let's go get a beer and shoot some pool, I haven't kicked your ass in something all day, I'm starting to get the DT's."

"Dude, just make sure you get some of your balls out of the way so that I'll have clear shooting lanes!"

The afternoon blurred to late in the night, whether distracted drunk or both, Paul beat Mike, fifteen games to nine.

CHAPTER 14

Wednesday February 3rd

"Captain, the ship disappeared!" the lieutenant fairly yelled.

"Lieutenant, I know that you've been pulling double shifts and you must be tired but you had better check your screens again."

"Sir, it was right there by the nebu... oh shit!"

"Lieutenant, please try to regain your military bearing, and tell me where that ship is!"

"Sir," the lieutenant whispered, his face an almost ashen gray. If the Captain hadn't known any better he would have thought that the lieutenant was dead.

"Speak up boy, what's the problem?"

"Sir, the ship has shown up in orbit around Venus!" the lieutenant almost cried.

*   *   *

"Yes Mr. President, the ship simply winked out of the Crab Nebula and approximately eight seconds later was in orbit around Venus."

(Pause)

"No Sir, we have not had any contact with the ship."

(Pause)

"Yes Sir, we *have* tried to hail them on every known frequency."

(Pause)

"No Sir, the ship has not changed its course in the last ten minutes. It is staying in a stationary orbit around the planet. My guess, Sir, is that they are aware that their ship will cause gravitational effects on our planet and are being somewhat courteous."

(Pause)

"You're right Sir, hanging around two planets away

and not signaling your intentions is not very courteous."
(Pause)
"No Sir, the press does not know about this yet, but any one with a telescope from Sears will be able to see this, it will be in the morning papers."
(Pause)
"Yes Sir I am fully aware of the repercussions that this will entail."
(Pause)
"Yes Sir, Defcon 5 has been initiated, I have alerted the other governments around the globe. We have done all that we can at this time. Sir, I believe that the next move is theirs."

"Captain, Sir," the lieutenant broke in "you might want to see this."

"Lieutenant, do you know that I am on the phone with the leader of the free world?" the captain muttered with a little more anger then he felt that the lieutenant deserved.

"Sir, the fact remains you should still see this." He motioned desperately toward the screen that had the live feed from the Hubble telescope, which was now pointed directly at Venus.

"Mr. President, could you please hold for a moment, we have some developing issues here."

"Captain," the President intoned, "I have three heads of state on a conference call. Could you please hurry."

"Yes sir, I'll be right back."

"Lieutenant what is it, and make it quick."

"Sir, the ship vanished."

"Any idea where it has gone, Lt?"

"Sir, it hasn't gone anywhere, it's just invisible to every sensor array that we possess. The only reason we know it's still there is the gravitational effect it's having on the planet."

"This just gets better and better," the captain muttered. "Mr. President, I'm sorry to have kept you on hold. Our public release problem has been solved,"

"How so Captain?"

"The ship has some sort of cloaking device Sir, it is no longer visible to the human eye, or any instrument known to mankind at this time."

"Captain, you have an optimistic way of looking at things"

"Sir, if I could speak freely."

"By all means, Captain, speak."

"Sir, this new event brings up some significant questions. We have to assume that they have been studying us by our transmissions and have decided that we are not yet ready for a visit from them and don't want to panic our populace or that we pose no serious threat to them technology wise. My belief, Sir, is that they are going to sit there for a while and contemplate our fate. If the public discovers their existence there could be panic in the streets, and if they attack, well Sir, if they attack there won't be much that we can do."

"Captain I appreciate your candor, but those are your views and unless you have some more concrete evidence I will as your Commander in Chief order that those opinions of yours go no further than this call. I will not tolerate rioting on top of this... visit."

"I understand completely Sir."

"Captain."

"Yes, Sir."

"Go be with your family, I'll talk to you first thing in the morning."

"Yes Sir, thank you Sir."

CHAPTER 15 – Journal Entry 13

And so begins April; the second half of freshman year was proving to be much more difficult than the first half. Beth had cooled things considerably as she wrestled with the demons that plagued her. Namely me, Penn Boy and her guilt. My heart would alternately leap and drop at the sight of her, even if it was only for a fraction of a second halfway across campus. I made sure to drop the one class we had in common that semester. I knew I'd never get anything done in there anyway. I tried to avoid her like the plague, which was sort of difficult considering that we lived in the same dorm and on the same floor. One good thing did come of all this mess, my grades soared. I went from an average 2.1 GPA to a semi-respectable 2.95. Not all-star material but great for a partier. I had actually gotten to a place within myself that I could accept the fact that Beth and I were pretty much over. Do women have a sixth sense in this manner? As soon as they feel that you are over them they come back and make sure to light the friggen fire up again.

"My head hurts. Dude, what's that smell," I snarled as I attempted to wipe the crusties away from my eyes.

"Oh man, I *so* ralphed last night," Paul half gurgled. "But I did get the majority of it in the trash can."

"What are the odds that we had a trash bag in that thing?"

"What do you think?" Paul semi chuckled.

"Bud, are you gonna get that thing outta here?"

"Mike, if I even look at it, I'll heave again."

"Aw this sucks," I said as I pulled myself out of the bed. With the puke bucket as far outstretched as possible I headed for the door and opened it. To my surprise, Beth was standing there about to knock.

"Oh man, what is that!" she cried as she shied away.

"Ginner had a technicolor yawn in this thing and I'm trying to get it the hell out of our room."

"How you feeling?" she asked.

Man, I don't care what Paul says, she *looks* like she cares for me. "I've been better and I'll be a whole lot better once I drop this damn thing in the dumpster."

"I won't keep you, I just wanted to know if you wanted to go to a concert Saturday night. I got tickets for Widespread Panic at Red Rocks."

"Who?"

"Don't worry about who, silly, do you want to go or not?"

"With you, I'd go to the ends of the earth." Maybe it was the aftereffects of the alcohol, hell, maybe I was still buzzed, but Beth gave me a strange look after that comment. Was she wondering why I would say such a thing or was she flattered? Women, they should come with some sort of instruction manual, although with my luck I'd get the book and it'd be in Braille.

"So I take it that that is your version of a yes?"

"Just let me know what time and I'll be ready."

"Just be ready by 5 on Saturday and we'll head out to Red Rocks."

"Gotcha, now if I could just go take care of some business, standing here with a bucket of puke is not my idea of a good time."

"Tell Paulie I hope he's feeling better. And I'll see you later," she said nonchalantly.

I guess I really wasn't expecting a kiss under these circumstances, but I'd take a squeeze on the shoulder as opposed to the casual way she left. I'd really better get rid of this bucket or it was going to get a little heavier.

"Hey Paul who the hell is Widespread Panic?"

"I don't know bro, sounds like some sort of heavy metal band."

"Oh." I winced. Listening to heavy metal didn't

sound like much fun with the headache I was nursing. Oh well, I'm sure I'd be back in fine shape by Saturday.

"Why what's up?" Paul half lifted his head from his pillow.

"Beth invited me to a concert at Red Rocks."

"Bud, the chick doesn't so much as say 'hi' to you in the past month and a half and you say yes right from the get go. You've still got a lot to learn, grasshopper."

I basically just stood there looking for all intents and purposes fairly stupid.

"Don't sweat it man, I'll ask around when I get up and see if I can find out what kind of music they play. Dumb ass."

"Paul."

"Yeah," he said grumpily.

"Don't you have a test today?"

"Already taken care of, my friend," and with that he rolled over and was again enjoying the company of his eyelids.

*   *   *

"Beth, Beth!" Paul yelled. "Hold up!"

They were just outside the entrance to the Student Union; people flooded around them on all sides. "You got a minute?" Paul said breathlessly.

"Yeah, I was just going to get a cup of coffee before my Sociology class."

"Excellent, I'll buy."

"What can I do for you Paulie?" as they sat at the small café set up to the left of the student union.

"Beth, well it's more of what you can't do."

"I don't get your meaning."

"Beth, I have no idea of what your intentions are with Mike, but I'll take it as a personal affront if you purposely hurt him in any way."

"I'm just having fun Paul, what business is it of yours?"

"First off he's my friend, and secondly I don't think

he's just having a good time as you put it." That caught her a little off balance, she really hadn't thought about their relationship being anything more than having some comfort from a person that was within arm's distance.

"I think he's starting to …"

"Don't finish that, Paul, I'm not ready for that and I don't want any of it."

"That's my point exactly Beth, if that's not where you want to go I think you should give him the heave ho and leave him be before his feelings grow any deeper."

"Paul, tell me this isn't some elaborate plan for me to get rid of Mike so that you can give it a go."

Paul laughed, "At one time, Beth, that probably would have been the case. I love you but more as a great friend than a potential lover, I'm honestly just looking out for my friend. Obviously do as you wish, but I hope you'll at least rethink your feelings and act accordingly."

"Thanks Paul, I've got to get going."

"See ya."

She was so deep in thought she did not even hear his goodbye.

* * *

"Hey Paul can you get the phone, I'm just about to win this level."

"Yeah I wasn't studying too hard," Paul said sarcastically

"You study? Are you feeling ill? Come on man, I've been trying to beat Bald Bull all day." Geez even to me that sounded like whining.

"Shut up already, I've gotta answer the phone. Hello? Hey Beth, yeah hold, on Mike's here."

So I tore myself away from the Nintendo and answered the phone. "Hey Beth, are you getting psyched to go to the concert?"

"Mike, I just wanted to call and tell you that I don't think that we should go to the concert."

"Why, is it supposed to rain?" I knew this was a futile

attempt at humor, I could tell from the tone of her voice that this conversation was not going to go well for me. A large knot began to form in my stomach.

"Mike, I'm thinking that we should actually not do anything together, I'm just not ready for the kind of feelings that come with this kind of relationship." I could tell by the quiver in her voice that she was near tears. "You know that I still have my boyfriend out in Pennsylvania."

I had thought about telling her I was willing to share but that was by no means the truth; I wanted her all to myself. Like a large cold Coke on a hot summer day, I wanted to drink her in, alone.

"I understand," I said, barely audible. One more minute on the phone and I might have cried, that wouldn't have been good for my image and it would have given Paul fodder to use against me for months. "Alright well, I'll see you sometime on campus, gotta go."

"Bye Mike, I'll miss…"

I hung up; I had no desire to hear those words.

"Fuck!!" I yelled

"What's up, man?" Paul said with more than a little concern.

"Beth dumped me."

"Oh man, I'm sorry, but were you ever really going out?"

"No not really, but you sort of get attached to the girl you're doing."

"Not me."

"Well you're different, you're a dog."

"Let's go get a beer and look at some chicks."

"The beer sounds good, the chicks can kiss my ass"

"That's the spirit."

*   *   *

"Dude get up, its Saturday morning, the birds are chirping, the bees are buzzing…"

"Dude, shut the shade," I moaned. "I still can't see straight."

"Too bad, Kelly across the way just got out of the shower and forgot to shut her shade."

Fifteen seconds ago I would have told you I couldn't have moved that fast if someone had set my bed on fire.

"Damn she has big tits."

"Yeah too bad her ass is as big a match," Paul quipped.

"What are you boys looking at?" Beth said from our open doorway.

"Ah, nothing," Paul said as he casually released his grip on our shade, plunging the room into near total darkness.

"No, please don't hit that switch," I begged. "Hit the one below it. If you turn the strobe light on I won't make it halfway down the hall."

"Hey Paul I know this is getting old, but could I please talk to Mike for a minute, I promise that it will only take a minute."

"Yeah that's about how long I've got to piss for anyway," Paul said as he brushed on by Beth.

"Eloquent as always," Beth said with half a smile.

Why did she have to come here, especially with the way I felt and how I looked. I learned you were always supposed to look your best when you ran into any ex so that way they could see that you bounced back fine. And here I was looking like last week's laundry. Smell included.

"I was wrong," she blurted out.

"About what?" Hope surged, adrenaline raced, I did my best to portray an even calmness.

"About everything, I think, I'm not sure exactly what is going on here, but I know I'd rather have you around than not."

"But what about Joe or John or Jock or whatever the hell his name is?"

"I don't know about him either. I know I love him."

Oh, *that* felt like a direct hit to my stomach.

"But I know that I also have very strong feelings for you too. I'm greedy, I want it all," she half-laughed.

"I'm sorry Beth, I also am greedy and I have no desire to share. I don't think that I could stand the thought of you in his arms when you go home for holidays or summer break or whatever, that would tear me apart much worse than this. If you want him, he's yours and you and me will stay with the status quo. If you somehow decide that you would rather be with me, I'll give you the time and space to make that decision. But I'll tell you now that I broke up with my girlfriend back home because I didn't feel that what I was doing was right, with her or with you or potentially with anyone else." That seemed to sting her; I guess she didn't think that I could already be thinking of another girl already, what can I say, I'm a guy. We're always thinking of another girl. Although in all fairness and truth the only thing that was going to cure my thoughts about her was time, lots and lots of time and maybe some beer. Lots of beer.

"Mike, I understand all of your concerns, but I was hoping we could push all of these issues to the side just for tonight. Can we at least go the concert tonight and be together?"

I really almost said no, but to look into her sea-blue eyes and say no was just something I don't think any man was strong enough to do. And with my hesitant answer of yes I had forever altered my life beyond any recognizable feature.

We arrived at Red Rocks around six o'clock that night. My watch told me that the year was 1988 but the people around me made me feel as if I had stepped into a time warp. It appeared to me to be somewhere around the 1968 or '69 era. The girls and even some of the guys had flowers in their hair, they were tossing Frisbees around, drinking beers, smoking bones and even the occasional trip was being taken. I thought to myself that I could really learn to like this time period. The girls for the most part had on old faded bell bottom jeans or long flowing sun dresses, most wore sandals, some just went bare-foot. The vast majority (much to my approval) had no idea what a bra was. I had been to my share of heavy metal concerts and I knew from experience that this was NOT a heavy metal crowd, the girls that usually attended those were the type that would beat the guy up if he did something wrong. I don't think that I had ever seen so many gorgeous women at one time, even on campus and I thought that that place was beyond belief. Whether I liked the band or not, the view was sure to be entertaining. Beth must have seen the grin that had unbeknownst to me spread across my face, because suddenly and viciously I was snapped back to reality with a sharp blow to the side of my head. A lesser man might have actually gone down on his knees. I rubbed my head while mumbling my apologies.

"We're here to see the band, not the women," Beth said a little indignantly.

"Just exercising my rights as a single man," I answered, hoping beyond hope that that was actually a falsehood. Her face fell ever so slightly.

"Come on girl, let's go check out this band," I said as I grabbed her by the waist. Her heavenly face looked up at me and something deep within my soul stirred. I had never been to Red Rocks but it was a sight to behold, it is or I should say was an outdoor amphitheater. The place was full of natural beauty. It was dominated by brilliantly colored giant sandstone formations. It was unbelievable to be nestled between two 400' high formations. The theater held roughly nine thousand people and was probably one of the most intimate settings for a concert that I have ever or will ever be at. Even when not watching the band the panoramic view of the plains was almost breathtaking, that and the fact that I was about six thousand feet above sea level. The band was awesome. I'd never had so much fun at a concert in my entire life. We got stoned off communal bowls and drank all the beer we could handle. It's the only concert I've ever been to where you never sat down, the music is just that good, you just stand and dance the whole show away. It was right after the first intermission that I began to get a buzzing in my head. I know what you're thinking. Yes, I was buzzed, but I was getting a buzzing sensation, almost as if a mosquito was around my ear, only this was bigger than a mosquito and it was a lot further seated back in my head than my ear. Others must have felt it too because on occasion I would notice some of my fellow concert-goers turning their heads over their shoulder to look up to the back of the amphitheater. At first glance I didn't notice anything out of the ordinary, but upon further review I noticed an object up in the sky roughly the size of a quarter, it glowed a translucent greenish color; I thought it was the moon. I figured that Beth should see this; I had never seen the moon with that color hue.

"Hey Beth, you should see the moon tonight it's unreal!" I shouted over the chorus of One Arm Steve.

"What's so special about it, it's not even full!" she shouted as she pointed to a spot directly over the stage.

"If that's the moon, what the hell is....?" I screamed. I'm sort of ashamed about that fact but I can guarantee you I wasn't the only one. Whatever it was it was huge and it was directly over Red Rocks. The whole amphitheater was covered up like a large Tupperware bowl, but this lid was far larger, it extended well over into the parking lots all around the theater. The last thing I cognitively remember was the green light that came out from the bottom of the ship. And I can tell you from the way people fled towards the exits they felt the same thing I did: terror, mind numbing terror.

CHAPTER 16

Sir, we have a situation," the lieutenant said with a start, he had almost begun to get used to the invisible ship orbiting around Venus. He wasn't necessarily comfortable with that fact but he had like everybody else in the "rock" sort of imbedded it into his everyday life.

"What is it Lieutenant, has the ship rematerialized?" The captain dreaded that occurrence above all, there would be rioting in the streets. Not only would they have to contend with the visitors but also a scared populace.

"No sir, three smaller ships have left the main ship and are heading this way."

"Lieutenant, get me the President," the captain said, visibly shaken. "Lieutenant, what's the ETA."

"Sir, at their present speed, less than two hours."

"Yes Mr. President, we have just confirmed that three alien vessels have departed the main ship."

(Pause)

"Sir, yes sir, we estimate their size to be roughly that of one of our aircraft carriers."

(Pause)

"No sir, we still have heard nothing from them."

(Pause)

"Yes sir, I will scramble all available fighters."

(Pause)

"Sir, I will notify all the governments around the world but they are watching the same Hubble feed that we are so I would imagine they are taking their own steps to avert this tragedy."

(Pause)

"Yes sir, I will notify you the moment anything changes."

CHAPTER 17 – Journal Entry 14

My cell, that sounds so weird. "My cell," I said aloud. I've never broken a big enough law in my life to warrant a cell. What the hell was I doing in a cell? Did I get caught with a big fattie at the concert? Naw, I would've remembered that. Wait a second, this doesn't look like a cell that a town like Morrison would possess. Then it hit with the full force of a cascading waterfall, this isn't Kansas anymore. I was on some sort of ship, and not only that, but I was being held prisoner on said ship. My cell was about ten feet by ten feet by, how original, ten feet. Although I have no idea what unit of measurement aliens use. Aliens, that sounds even more ridiculous than my being in a cell. I'm now convinced they are aliens because all of the conspiracy theorists in the world couldn't have thought that the government was capable of making that ship that hovered over Red Rocks. Oh my God, I thought to myself, Red Rocks, the concert, Beth!!! "Beth where are you?" I screamed vainly. The only articles that broke up the monotony in this cell were a chair and a hole in the floor, which I imagine was for refuse by the smell of it. The bus depot had nothing over this place. The front of the holding pen had no visible door but appeared to be made out of some clear sort of glass but I can attest to the fact that this "glass" was solid. I kicked it as hard as I could. I thought that I had shattered the lower part of my leg. The gate didn't even shudder, so much for getting some satisfaction out of breaking something.

"Do not do that again, hu-man."

I pissed myself, no I'm not just saying that I was so scared I could have peed, I literally let my bladder explode all over the front of my jeans. What stood before me was something straight out of a horror movie. If this were a movie

I would have changed the channel a long time ago. Whatever this thing was it had developed along the reptilian line of its species and to me it looked mostly like the crocodile side of that family. This beast looked to be at least two feet taller than myself. It had an elongated snout that ended in a bulbous fashion. It had no ears that I could see but what appeared to be ear holes. Its skin did not have the green, brownish tinge I would have expected from a reptile type of thing. It had more of a reddish glow to it, more on the shade of Red Rocks, but the skin texture looked to be more like our own native crocs. But I had never actually had any desire to touch a crocodile before, and I definitely had no desire to touch whatever the hell that thing was. Its bulk was impressive, in addition to its two feet of height advantage, it also outweighed me by two to three hundred pounds, and this thing reeked of power and menace and intelligence. Its eyes, by far, were the scariest part of this creature. They were cold and flat, with the pupil more in the crescent moon shape. But it was the way it stared at me. For all it was concerned, I could be its lunch. Oh please, don't let that be the case. Is this its refrigerator? Is this where it keeps its food fresh until it's ready to eat? Beth, where are you!

"Ssit down and Sshut-up hu-man!" it boomed.

Well, I thought to myself wryly, English must not be its first language. But I understood it enough to do as I was told. Thankfully it moved on. Well, so much for the Steven Spielberg ET type of alien. I think Ridley Scott got a lot closer to the truth. Once the creature passed the relief that flooded through me was near palpable. And then I started to hear voices. Oh great, not only was I stuck in a cell with alien creatures I'm also going insane. Wait, maybe I'm already insane and this is the outcome of that insanity. That would be far more agreeable than the truth.

"Pssst buddy."

"What and who the hell is that?" Boy, I'll tell you insanity isn't a fun thing.

"Hey number 1988!"

"What are you talking about!?" I half yelled

"Look above your head, that's your number, or should I say ranking."

"Who are you?" I asked

"I'm number 1987, I'm your next door neighbor," the mystery voice answered back.

"Oh thank God, I thought I was alone on this thing."

"Quiet down, if you yell too loud those things will come back."

"Do you know what's going on? Are we lunch?" I asked, almost hoping he didn't have an answer. Ignorance can be bliss.

"I've got an idea, but you might actually like your lunch theory a little better."

"What kind of information are you going to lay down on me."

"Word through the cell-vine is that us men folk are going to be used in a gladiator type spectacle. We are going to be the Progerians' entertainment and THEN lunch."

"We have to fight th-th-those things?" I asked incredulously.

"No, it's much worse than that."

"Worse than that?"

"We're battling each other."

"Who, me and you?"

"No, no, from what I can gather that number on the ceiling is sort of a preliminary ranking, think of the NHL playoffs where No. 1 plays the No. 8 seed, but in this case its No. 1988 versus 2212, to the death."

"Oh God," I moaned, the fear was crippling. "When does this happen."

"I think it already started," he replied.

"Who are you? I'd at least like to know your name before I die."

"My name is Bud Adams," he intoned. I had been hoping for some words of encouragement from him. Maybe something on the order of, 'you have a chance' or 'you're not dead yet.' Something that would give me some sense of hope no matter how false. Apparently he had resigned himself to his imminent fate, and had no desire to comfort another human being in distress. Misery loves company. I guess the aliens had good reason to put me this low in the rankings. At 5'9" and 165 pounds I really didn't cut an imposing figure. Well at least my first opponent, ranking wise, was more pathetic than me. More questions, worries and concerns ran through my head than was even remotely comprehensible, but it didn't take long until all of my questions were answered. One moment my cell front was there, the next moment it simply vanished, was it ever really there? I stepped out of my cell before it had the chance to reappear and I got my first real look at the vessel I was on. It was enormous, I was able to see hundreds of cells in each direction before the curve in the ship hindered my view. I turned to look at Bud Adams to see if he had possibly been freed. He was, but he was nowhere in sight. Do I make a run for it, where the hell would I go, do I take my chance with the guard, who am I kidding? So I did nothing, I just stood there like a knot in a piece of wood. An opaque doorway from the other side of the corridor opened up to reveal where my guard or one that looked very similar to him had gone. So now I knew that the holding cells were on an outer ring of the ship and the crews' quarters or duty stations were on the inside. But a lot of good that did me, knowledge didn't feel very powerful at the moment. The guard stepped out from the doorway and motioned for me to follow the indicator lights around the ship. He kept a safe distance from me, if I didn't know better I would think that he was more disgusted by my appearance than I was of his/hers, no clue? I had a fleeting thought to turn and charge it, but I didn't know if he was armed. By the look of him my charge would be no more effectual than hitting a bear with a fly swatter. So I did what was expected of me, I followed the lights for what seemed like a mile. All of the cells I passed were empty. Apparently these poor souls had met their fate already; I felt like a lamb being led to the slaughter. After passing the cell marked with the No. 1, the corridor opened up into a huge amphitheater. It was filled to standing room only with these creatures, although from where I stood there appeared to be two types of animal/things. There were the reddish ones that I had already met, and there were smaller ones with a slightly brownish tinge to them and a shorter snout. And from the looks of things they were the real ones in control here, because they had all the seats closest to the coliseum floor. The guard forcibly pushed me into a booth on my right that I had not even seen when I approached the theater.

"Ssit down and Sshut up hu-man," it snarled.

"You need to learn some more words asshole!!" I spat, I figured if I was going to die I might as well get a last jab in. I don't think that he had any clue what I said, he shut the door to the booth and left.

"Sit down hu-man," a voice boomed from the top of the booth in what appeared to be an alien version of a speaker. "Your briefing will begin now."

This did very little to calm my nerves, if anything it only made me more nervous, to hear the alien voice through a speaker made it sound that much more inhuman. I felt like a rat in a cage, a very small cage.

"You are here, hu-man," that snapped me back to reality, "in a competition like no other. Should you become the champion of these games you will win the prize which your kind cherishes the most." The first thought that came to my mind was 'pussy.' I'm sorry, I was an 18-year-old college student. "Freedom!" the voice boomed. Well, that was my second choice. "You will compete to the death, whether it is yours or your opponents." The voice might as well have been talking about last night's soccer score for all the inflection and feeling it put into those words. I yelled at the speaker to demand what had happened to my girlfriend, but my fears were not quelled, apparently this was a one way speaker and more than likely it was 'canned.' I don't think these aliens wanted to do anything more with us than to watch us die.

"The winner will be rewarded handsomely, the losers will be dead." Oh shit, I thought to myself, the voice didn't use plurals. There is only going to be one winner, out of what my mind figured were a possible 4000 or so contestants. I resigned myself to my fate, how could I possibly come out on the top of this? I was a self-proclaimed lover, not a fighter. And I wasn't even sure how good a lover I was and I had some practice in that field; the last fight I was in, I was 8 and I got my ass kicked by a girl. I know that's pretty humiliating, I got my ass kicked by an 8-year-old girl that had a crush on me. All I wanted to do was play baseball with my friends, so she threw me down on the ground and punched me in the eye. I of course told my friends that I was jumped by Jimmy Johnson's gang of friends and that's how I got my shiner. Nobody ever tells anybody that they got beat up by a girl. "Each battle..." whoa, back to reality or at least this skewed version of it. "...will be a one on one competition to the death. The only other rule is that you are permitted to use only one weapon at a time. And do not be fooled, hu-man, if you or your competitor do not abide by these rules at all times you will both be dead. If both of you do not fight, you both will be dead. Look to your right and my point will be proven." So I did just that, off to the right I spotted what appeared to be the variety of species that my guard was, there were four of them holding what appeared to be rifles, but I was under the impression that it wouldn't be lead that came out of that long barrel. How would it feel to be shot by plasma or whatever it was, well I guess it would be the same as being shot by lead, dead. And that thought sent chills right up my spine. I knew in the back of my head that everybody dies, but to know that I was mere moments from it made me think of what wrongly convicted death row inmates must feel. Terror. Pure, unadulterated terror. "Your first test will begin momentarily. You will be given one minute to prepare yourself in whatever way you wish."

"Wait!" I wailed. "A minute's not enough, I don't want to die, Mom!!!"

The door opened and the festivities began. The terrain was moving, well not quite moving it was shifting, changing, that's it, it was changing from the grated ship floor into what appeared to be small scrub, no they were definitely getting bigger, it was becoming a forest. Not a particularly dense forest, it actually reminded me a lot of the woods surrounding the Boulder area, oh to be back at school cracking a kegger. Could this all be a bad trip! Please? How could this not be a trip gone bad, I'm being held on an alien ship preparing to fight for my life on a platform that is terraforming in front of me? My legs were like wood. They were so stiff. I felt like I was in one of those dreams where a monster is chasing you and you can't run, although there was nothing 'dream like' about this. My very existence depended on my being able to move and defend myself. In contrast my arms felt like jelly, I couldn't possibly think to wield a weapon with them feeling like this. Weapons, that was what I was focusing on, there appeared to be weapons of varying sorts lined against the bottom wall of the coliseum, bows and arrows, swords, spears, knives, maces, unfortunately no plasma discharging weapons, because I'd really like to take out a couple of these crocodile looking thing's. But there was no weapon quite advanced enough to make an escape a plausible possibility. Who was I kidding, where was I going to go, I didn't even like to ride amusement park rides, did I really think I'd get far enough to grab a shuttle ship and pilot my way back home? No, my only chance was victory. The crowd had finally become silent as they waited in anticipation for the ensuing battle. While all of these thoughts were running through my head I watched as my opponent was forcibly removed from his holding pen and thrust into the arena on the opposite side. The guy looked more scared than I was. He was more than a hundred yards away and I could see him shaking from here. I'm not an intimidating fellow, and like I said I've always prided myself as being a lover, not a fighter. This guy was pathetic though, he looked to be about 55 years old, 5'5" or 5'6", maybe 130 pounds soaking wet. I think that he was one of the security guards at the gate at Red Rocks. If it was the same man, he also had a nervous tick on the right side of his face. Man, this place was almost a replica of Mile High Stadium, they even had a huge screen on either end of the arena. It was how I was able to tell that my opponent was more petrified than I was. Terror emanated from him, his eyes were all pupil, in the fight or flight scheme of things this guy was a jack rabbit looking for a place to run. I could see him begging the guards not to leave him there, and then I could hear him yelling in my direction to please not kill him. I wanted to tell him that I had not so much as killed an insect on purpose. But my gestures scared him even more because he shrank back against the wall; it was then that he grabbed a spear. So apparently this jackrabbit could bite. What was I doing, get moving, I thought to myself, or this pathetic old man is going to kill you, and if he does I would never be able to make the ones responsible for this injustice pay. He was still crying for alien mercy or possibly mine, but he was advancing and he had a weapon. My heart felt like it was in my throat. I had the distinct impression that I was going to choke to death long before he was able to get to my side of the battlefield. As he stepped forward I backed up, and in all my glory I fell over. I had tripped on a tree root and banged my head against a tree, I tripped on a tree root on a space ship. This was going to be real difficult to grasp the reality of. "Go to your death or go to your victory hu-mans!" a voice thundered from overhead. The crowd went nuts, the huge screens went blank, apparently they didn't want us watching what our opponent was doing. The aliens began a sort of hissing, it sounded like a battalion of tires having their air let out; the noise was deafening. I got up, my head still spinning from the impact, and I wiped the blood away. Just maybe the fall was the best thing that happened to me, I finally got moving and ran to the wall behind me and grabbed the closest weapon, a sword. I didn't know what I was going to do with it, I had no intention of actually using it on that man, and maybe if I waited long enough he would die of natural causes. But the need to have that weapon in my hands was somehow primordial, instinctual, it felt good. Blood pulsed through my veins. My senses were heightened to their max. I thought I could smell the fear of my prey, but more than likely I smelled my own fear. My eyes honed in on the slightest movement. My feet began to move with stealth that modern man had long since forgotten. I began to wonder if my forehead was beginning to protrude a little more. No time for intellectual thought, I began to surrender myself to the most basic of thoughts, survival. I had crossed what I took to be roughly half of the arena without a single cognitive thought beyond kill or be killed. I didn't even hear the crowd anymore. And then it hit me, my modern mind raced to catch up; fear suddenly and eagerly gripped me with a force equal to dread. I dropped my sword. It made a loud clanging noise as it slid down a small embankment. The crowd quieted, it almost sounded like they were holding their breaths. At the same time I heard him coming. Apparently he wanted to live too.

"I almost forgot that there was somebody in here with me." To this day I'm not sure if I said that out loud or not. I turned to look and there he was, about thirty yards away and closing fast, at least as fast as a 50ish-year-old could move. It was kind of comical. Here was a wafer thin man hefting a spear almost double his height, huffing and puffing his way toward me. It would have been even funnier if he wasn't huffing and puffing his way to *kill* me. 'Dude,' I thought to myself, 'have a heart attack and save us both the trouble.' I don't think he heard me. His face still contained that look of utter terror but now there was something else, what was it? It was determination. He *wants* to kill me. I unlocked my feet and luckily this time they weren't nailed to the floor like in so many childhood dreams. In fact they were quite the opposite, they felt like feathers. It's amazing what pure adrenaline can do for you, hell, look what it was doing for him. I moved with not a second to spare, the man went tumbling past me. He cart wheeled down the embankment more times than I could count. I've got to get my sword before he recovers. I ran down the embankment about ten yards to retrieve it; the man was another ten yards beyond that at the bottom of the rise. He was still on his back. His eyes were closed but I could tell he was still conscious, he was sobbing. He kept pitching his spear in different directions almost with the hope that I would impale myself on it. The crowd went crazy as I approached the downed man, sword in hand. When I was just out of reach of his outstretched spear I stopped. The man was begging and pleading with me not to kill him; if I had eaten any lunch I would have left it there on the forest floor. I let my upraised sword hand drop down and half-turned to leave, it was then that I noticed what that outcome would entail. The guards raised their weapons level with my head. So this was how it was going to end, either I went against everything that I was and killed this man, or the croc-things were going to melt my head. Survival is by far the most demanding of instincts, I turned to do that which most repulsed me in life. I was going to take another human's life, I had to kill. The man had stopped flailing his spear, his arms were around his head now; his breathing came in ragged sobs. I think that he had finally resigned himself to death.

"Sir," I said, my breath coming out in thin wisps, "Sir, I'm sorry. I'll make it as quick and painless as possible." Tears flowed from my eyes almost to the point of blindness.

"Sir, what is your name?" I asked.

"Tom Greenborough." His breath hitched in his throat.

"Mr. Greenborough, I promise on my soul that I will avenge your death."

"Thank you, son," he replied more calmly. He placed his arms by his side and said the Lord's Prayer. I waited for him to finish before I brought the sword crashing down through his upper chest. The shock of his breastplate collapsing almost jolted my arms out of their sockets, but once through his chest I felt the sword go all the way through his internal organs and stick into his spine. The sound was horrible, it sounded like a cockroach being crushed only a hundred times louder; the blood, however, that was far worse. I had pierced his heart and the blood flew up in an arc looking like some sort of macabre fountain. It stung my eyes and assaulted my mouth, it tasted like steel. The sword rose and fell once with the final beat of Mister Greenborough's heart. I fell to both knees sobbing and I cradled him in my arms. It was there and then through my apologies to his still warm body that I promised I would do all in my power to not make his death in vain. The crowd was in near hysterics. I had not noticed before but the guards had encircled me and motioned for me to get up. I half thought to grab the sword and do what damage I could, but no, I wouldn't make it two steps, and then my promise would have been futile. So I got up and let the guards do with me as they would. I was led back to a cell, not necessarily my cell though, the corridor I was led down appeared to be different, although it was in the same direction I had come. My adrenaline surge was waning, I could not think clearly and I was visibly shaking from head to toe. It was all I could do to walk straight. And then it dawned on me the cells that I was passing on my left were bigger, yeah, that was it, they were bigger, almost double the size. Then I came to the horrified realization that they were double the size because half of us were dead. I collapsed, whether from the shock of the truth or just because my body could no longer withstand the rush of stimulants I had been producing, I guess I'll never know. I awoke minutes? hours? days? later, I just didn't know, there was no way to tell the passage of time here. I awoke with a start. Whoa, I thought to myself, this room is a lot different from my last abode. There was a table in the middle of the room with a bowl containing what appeared to be fruit and a door that actually led to a bathroom, but what really caught my attention was what was on the far wall from my bunk. It appeared to be a large video screen. I walked over and hit the only button available; I hoped it was the power button. I was right, I stepped back as the screen lit up into life. At first I wasn't sure what I was looking at, it was just a bunch of names with a number next to them. Then it dawned on me that this was their rating system. The first round was over. 2,048 men were alive, and tragically 2,102 had died. I knew that my event wasn't a very artful and/or cunning one, so I figured that I would be somewhere in the middle of the pack in terms of ranking, but obviously there were a lot better warriors out there than me. I was ranked No. 1,738, almost the bottom of the barrel. I was paired against No. 310, one Hank Sterns. Things were not looking good. I barely survived against a 55-year-old man, how was I possibly going to take down my next competitor? I leaned against the wall pondering my mixed emotions but mostly to keep from falling over. The screen changed but it took me a moment to register this fact; what I saw on the screen both frightened and thrilled me at the same time.

Round Two had begun, and like a pay-per view event I sat on my bunk and watched. I never even looked at the food I was eating as the games started. No. 1, Thomas Durgan, was squaring off against No. 2048, one Albert Timmins. Timmins looked as if he had eaten his last competitor. He weighed in excess of 350 pounds, all of it fat, he must have fallen on his last victim. Sweat dropped from his brow, in fact, his whole body was wet with sweat and he hadn't even moved from where the guards had deposited him so unceremoniously. He was too busy biting his nails in nervousness to obtain a weapon.

"Get up you fat fuck!" I yelled at the screen. "At least defend yourself!" How the hell did he make it to this round, I wondered. It was later that I found out that his competitor had died of a heart attack as I had wished mine had. But if he thought divine intervention was going to happen again he was sadly mistaken. It was clearly obvious he was not going to see Round Three. Durgan was closing fast, the axe that he had obtained was held high. There was no tact here; Durgan went straight up the middle of Main Street in what appeared to be Mayberry. I think it was, they even had mockup dummies of Floyd the Barber and Barney Fife; where was Andy when you needed him. He would have stopped this slaughter. Durgan's body was a rippling mass of muscle clearly outlined in his tank top and jeans; this man spent the majority of his days in the gym from the look of it. He was monstrous, 6'2" or 3" of pure muscle. He was the type that walked the beach and made girls melt and smaller men look on with envy. He even had the looks to match the muscle, although that face was now contorted into a grotesque sort of war mask. He appeared to have painted blood onto his face in the way of the ancient Incans. He looked like the Roman God of war, all ferocity and determination. He was not going to be denied. I turned my gaze just a fraction of a second too late, I had seen in horror Durgan's axe hit home, straight on the top of Timmins' skull, and from the force and sound of it, I'm fairly certain he split the fat man in half. I shook like a leaf in a gale; my body was wet with a sheen of sweat. I was glued to the screen for what seemed like hours. I watched hundreds of battles and subsequently hundreds of deaths. I was becoming numb. The one fact that stuck in my head was how well the aliens had done on their handicapping of these events. Very rarely did a lower seed pull out an upset, and that was usually only when the higher ranked competitor made a serious blunder. I was not feeling very confident about my chances when I turned to see the guards entering my room. It was my turn and ready or not I had to go. I said a prayer but I wasn't sure to which god I was praying to. How many gods would help those that kill? I was led to the arena almost courteously. I guess winning did have some advantages. This time I wasn't even shoved through the door, although I did not get the luxury of gathering my thoughts in the isolation booth. Apparently everyone was supposed to know the rules by now. I waited patiently for No. 310 to enter the arena.

CHAPTER 18

"Is there any new news from Colorado, Captain?" the President intoned. The captain was under the impression that the President was more concerned with his plummeting approval ratings than with the semi-invasion of Earth. Three ships had deployed from the mother ship and had removed thousands of people from three different venues around the globe. One in Russia, one in China and one here in the good ole United States. The lack of response by any of the governments was astounding but really, what could they do, nobody was prepared for this scenario; there were no computer mock-ups for this, no drills. Nine thousand people in Morrison, Colorado had simply vanished. One moment the amphitheater had been packed with concert-goers enjoying a show, the next it was empty. Even the surrounding fauna had been uprooted. Anything that was living had simply ceased to exist in that spot, for some unlucky few who were actually half in and half out of the ship's radius, they were neatly sliced in two as if by a laser. In one example, some eye-witnesses were still visibly shaken as their friend had been chasing a Frisbee when the mass exodus occurred. They had watched in horror as his right outstretched arm, his leg from his knee down and a quarter of his face just disappeared. He was able to half turn to his companions, his one eye pleading with them for answers; he had not even been able to vocalize a scream because that portion of his brain had been removed.

The captain had no desire to be in Washington. He had always despised politics, he was a soldier, he did as he was ordered and he expected the orders he issued to be attended to with the same attention to detail. Everything in Washington came at a price. Every word here had meanings on multiple levels. Ulterior motives were the norm in this town. Here he was trying to avert a National Disaster, and the President, a pot smoking draft dodger, was more concerned with recent poll numbers. The President couldn't believe that the aliens would come to Earth on an election year.

"Sir, we've got some eyewitness reports but they are not all that reliable."

"How so Captain?"

"Well sir, most of the eyewitnesses are still pretty shaken up, or else they were under the effects of various types of drugs."

"Drugs, Captain?"

"Yes sir, it *was* a concert, it's tough to get an accurate picture of what happened from a person tripping on mushrooms," the captain noted sarcastically.

"Captain, I'm not much in the mood for humor today. I know you don't like politics much, or more specifically me. I know you think that I'm more concerned with poll numbers than the crisis at hand."

The captain looked up with a start, not meaning to, but the President had hit his thoughts on the button.

"Ah, I see by your reaction that I was correct. Captain, I am concerned with the numbers only for the fact that I need to stay in office to deal with this threat. If the Republicans get into office we both know their stance on this new crisis, hit it with everything in our power. Well I'll let you in on a little secret, Captain, that wouldn't do a damn thing."

"Sir?" the captain said, now a little curious.

"Captain, what you are now about to hear is top secret information only a handful of the most brilliant minds in this country know about."

The captain was hooked.

"We had prior knowledge of these aliens coming."

The captain bolted upright out of his seat. "Sir, how could you not let us know, we could have prepared ourselves!"

"Sit down Captain, we didn't have forewarning of

their intentions, only on their possible arrival. Do you remember that outbreak of anthrax in Kansas last year?"

"Yes sir, the National Guard was mobilized and pretty much shut down the town of Missoula."

"Well it wasn't anthrax, it was an alien probe. It actually wasn't all that remarkable looking, at first we thought it might be some sort of Russian device. The first inkling we had that it was not a terrestrial device was the fact that it had no burn marks upon it. Any satellite that could possibly survive reentry would at the very least have some serious burn marks on its skin. This was perfect, it was spherical, roughly the size of a VW bug, smooth as a polished stone. We had our scientists study it for months; they couldn't even get a shaving off of it to study what type of material it was. They radiated it, exposed it to molten metal and absolute zero freezing temperatures, nothing. We actually had no idea that it was even a probe until one of the scientists by accident discovered that it was sending signals on a super low frequency. It's actually a frequency that we just discovered and as of yet have not figured out how to send a signal on. Once we discovered there was a message piggybacking on the signal we had 22 Cray super-computers working non-stop 24-7 to decipher the message. The problem was that these machines were programmed to crack any language or mathematical code on *this* planet; we had no previous basis for the computers to rely on. So the gears spun inside the computers but we couldn't crack the code.. The only things we learned from the probe was that their technology was far advanced of ours, that the probe was indestructible and where the general direction of the signal was being transmitted. We were not even able to learn the planet of its origin. Near as our scientists can figure the signal is being sent to a black hole out in the Beta-Centauri area, and that the aliens must be using the hole as some sort of worm device to transport the signal to God knows where."

"Sir, I thought that nothing could escape a black hole's gravitational field once it entered it?"

"That's what we thought also, Captain, but apparently that's not the case. This probe is indestructible and I fear that the mother ship uses the same technology, and any direct assault on these beings will most likely unleash hell on earth. For the first time in my life I am afraid, Captain. Not for me but for our country, for our planet, for mankind's very existence."

The captain saw beyond his prejudices and began to admire this man. He could finally begin to understand with his charisma and bravery how he had been elected to the office of President.

"We have actually had contact with the ship." The President turned to look at his monitor.

"Sir, how is that possible? We at NORAD have detected no signal from the mother ship."

"Well Captain, you didn't know where on the frequency spectrum to look. And unlike the probe's unknown signals, this message came through in perfect English. Would you like to see a transcript of the transmission?" Without waiting for the captain's response the President hit his intercom button and requested his secretary to get the 'Project Blue-Fire' dossier.

The captain read and re-read the transmission, not entirely sure what to make of it.

"Humans, make no attempt to contact us or confront us, any and all perceived threats to our ship will be met with unbridled fury. We have come to your planet and intend to stay until what we have come for is accomplished."

"Sir, that's it? Nothing else?" the captain said, bewildered.

"Nothing Captain, it's very direct on what they'll do about any perceived threats, but not very clear on their intentions. We can assume from their actions thus far that their visit isn't entirely one of peace. But I will sacrifice those thousands that were taken for the good of the planet. That haunts me; I do not sleep very well at all. I know that sacrificing the one for the many is the prudent thing to do, but their souls torment me. And the fact that we are powerless doesn't sit well either. Even if I did not feel that we should give those people up without a fight, there isn't a damn thing on this planet that we could do." The president sounded nearly desperate.

"Nukes sir, would nukes do anything?"

"Captain, when the probe could not be deciphered or studied and after we learned of the imminent arrival of the ship we attempted to nuke the probe to see the effects. We broke the Paris peace accords by detonating that bomb. Well, the Pacific Island of Guimina was completely leveled, the probe however did not so much as suffer a surface scratch."

The captain shuddered. If the most powerful weaponry known to mankind didn't phase a mere probe, what could they possibly do against the mother ship? They were up against a master race of aliens and had no idea what they were here for. Were they to become their slaves or worse, their food? No scenario the captain came up with sat well with the dinner he had eaten earlier.

CHAPTER 19 – Journal Entry 15

A light sheen of sweat covered my body. I felt confident I had made peace with myself, but was I ready for a person seeded No. 310? More to the point, was I ready to die? He would have to be fairly big and intelligent, that new thought broke a brand new sweat across my brow and a failing sense of confidence in my heart. When I saw my opponent step forth from his side of the stadium, my worst fears were realized. Dan was huge; he was almost the same size as Durgan. At one time Dan Sterns was probably considered a good-looking man, but those days were over. This man was now a walking wound. Whoever had faced this man previously had almost completed the job; a foot long gash across his shoulder glistened with pus. And by looking at the sweat on his forehead I could tell he was burning with fever. He was hours away from dying from infection, but that was too far away to do me any good. It did, however, give me a chance, and a chance was all I needed. He also had a disfiguring facial wound that literally went from ear to ear that made Dan look like a horribly mutilated clown out of a Stephen King book. It was hard not think of him as simply smiling widely – very widely. But the misery in his eyes made it clear that that was no natural smile. A dark stain over the left knee was the source of this man's limp and all I needed to know. The field was one of small rocks and stony clumps, clearly designed for the very mobile and sure of foot. One thing I was certain of was that my competitor was no longer either of those things.

The crowd cheered at our entrances and our fates were sealed. Well, as I had learned from my baseball coach, to be truly competitive one must think like his competition. His motives, his desires and even his fears. This wasn't baseball but the advice fit aptly. Although I was only a pawn in a much larger game, I had no intention of sacrificing myself for the common good. So I thought like a wounded man/animal. An animal - hurt, cornered, defensive. That's it, I shouted in my head, he'll definitely be on the defensive and what better weapon to use on the defensive but a bow and arrow. Although I'm not physically intimidating he is in no shape to battle anyone hand to hand. He had not received those wounds from long range and he would be severely gun-shy of another frontal assault. The odds were on my side that this man was right-handed, in fact my life depended upon this assumption. Yes, I thought to myself, I know all about assuming things. I was now going to feel my prey out. But first, I got the necessities out of the way: I threw up, nausea striking my stomach more effectively than a fist. Was I starting to like this? No, I answered myself, it was a question of survival. Pull it together, Durgan would have already buried the proverbial hatchet by now, GET IT TOGETHER!. With that sobering thought in mind I started out, totally oblivious to the taut grin that was stretched over my face. Halfway across the arena I went to the right side wall and grabbed my weapon of choice for the evening, a mace. It weighed more than it looked. I was going to have to be careful that I made contact on the first swing as it would be difficult to bring it back around with any true speed or precision. Even halfway across the arena floor I had yet to feel true fear regarding Sterns. I was fairly certain that he had holed up in a somewhat secure and sheltered area and was going to wait until I was in full view before unleashing his hopefully lethal volley of arrows. I traversed another twenty-five yards through some short scrub grass and stones. It was now time to begin employing tactics. I had to be closing in on his firing zone, unless I had made a horrible mistake and he had circled behind and was even now ready to cut my throat. I spun around, more than expecting him to bear down on me, and there he wasn't. My nerves were primed, I was on edge. I had to stick to my game plan; it was time to play cat and mouse. The first thing I had to do was find out where the very large and dangerous mouse was hiding. This cat was going to be very cautious. 'Curiosity killed the cat' crossed my mind more than once. I looked across the surface of the remaining twenty-five yards or so and could see nothing except rocky crags and grassy outcrops. This place reminded me of a miniature Maryland with its rolling hills and green grass. There were dozens of places he could be holing up. My first break came and the smile I wasn't even aware I was wearing got even bigger. The place where the bow and arrow had hung in my last round was bare. I was right and Hank Sterns, whether he knew it or not, was as good as dead. The best he could hope for at this distance was one shot and one shot only, or so I hoped. I got down into a kneeling position and picked up a grenade-sized stone and hurled it side arm ten or fifteen yards back into the middle of the arena. Sure enough his dark curly topped head jerked up and he peered about looking for me. His eyes no longer appeared to have agony in them; when he realized that he had exposed himself for a mere rock, his eyes took on the look of a trapped animal, and terror reigned supreme. My stomach convulsed again. Being raised as a Catholic I should be helping a man that looked that desperate, but instead I was planning ways for his untimely demise. God forgive me. Thankfully I had nothing left in my stomach to bring up. After a few seconds the feeling passed. It was him or me and I didn't know him. I grabbed another rock and hurtled it almost directly in front of his hidey-hole. In a panic he stood up and fired blindly, luckily blindly because it still came dangerously close to the left side of my head. I'll swear to this day that I heard that arrow whistle by over the roar/hiss of the crowd. I jumped up from my crouching position and halved the twenty-five yards in NFL record style, it was then that the world slowed down to a snail's pace. No! I screamed to myself. This can't be the time or place to have one of those crippling dreams. I took a step, he brought an arrow out of his sheath, I took another step bringing the mace up, he began to notch the arrow. I took another step and brought the mace back beyond my shoulder, he fully notched the arrow and pulled back on the bow. Damn, I thought to myself, how the hell did he load that thing that fast, was I running that slow or was he moving that fast? I took another step and brought the full splintering force of the mace down onto the top of his head. The mace shuddered in my hand as the steel made contact with his head; his skull snapped like a dry branch under my foot and brain matter flew everywhere. So this is what it feels like to be Gallagher I thought nonsensically. Sterns crumpled like a Coke can under a car; his knees seemed to have blown out at the sides as his head and neck both skewed at right angles to each other. The mace had buried itself a good five inches into his skull so that the ball was resting directly above his now empty eye sockets. My first impression was that sweat had stung my eyes and filled my mouth but upon closer examination the metallic taste in my mouth would not go away. I spat, I heaved and then I collapsed. The bastard had gotten the shot off and it had struck true. The question now was how good of a shot had it been? The pain in my side was searing. Damn, I thought, I'm going to die by the hands of a dead man. I guess that's what poetic justice is all about. Blood flowed from my wound, a deep crimson red; even I knew that this was no superficial wound. In those old John Wayne movies I always thought that when the cowboy gets shot with an arrow and they show him holding onto it, they just did that for dramatic effect, but that's not the case. The mind just can't grasp the concept that you have this foreign object inside of you. The first inclination you have is to just wrench it out of you, but the slightest movement of the shaft sends agony blistering through every nerve ending so you basically just put your hands around it to keep it from moving around. I stayed there for a few minutes not really having any thoughts other than would I be admitted into Heaven after today's festivities. I thought not, but how bad could Hell be after this little jaunt in the park. Then I died.

CHAPTER 20

"How go the games, Krulak?"

"They go well, my Supreme Commander, the hu-mans are even more cruel and savage than we had originally thought. But for a few rare cases they have no regard for other human lives."

"It is amazing that this species has survived to this juncture in their evolution. Apparently we will only be speeding up their demise by a decade or two."

"I agree, Commander, and the entertainment is just what the populace needed after the last buckle we completed."

"Yes that was a particularly difficult space traversal, are the Genogerians behaving themselves?"

"Yes oh Great One, but all the killing has made them a little more unstable than usual. A couple of fights have broken out among the crew but only two deaths and five serious injuries."

"Maybe, my dear Krulak, we should have done on our planet what these Earthlings did on theirs."

"Sir, by wiping out Cro-magnon these hu-mans rid themselves of a valuable asset. Now they have to do their own dirty work."

"You are right my dear Krulak. If we had destroyed the Genogerians we would have succumbed long ago to the Fregtew. I still have a hard time believing that we have any commonality to the beasts though."

"Sir, we have as much in common with them as a piece of steel does to a sword. We are of similar material but we have been worked and honed to be a thing of beauty and power."

"I agree. As always Krulak, your faith has never

wavered, old friend. Please let me know when Round Two has been completed. You may go."

"By your leave, sir."

CHAPTER 21 – Journal Entry 16

I thought I had died. Apparently I had just passed out. I knew this to be true because I had some sort of strange wrappings around my wounds. I'm pretty sure Heaven wouldn't need any type of gauze to keep me from bleeding out. Unless God of course had a strange sense of humor, which by the way he probably does. If you need proof of that just look at the predicament I'm in at this moment. But I'm alive. For good or bad, I'm alive to fight another day. Man, how hollow had those words sounded a lifetime ago, now they ring as true as the Liberty Bell. I stood up from my bed and flexed my bad side. I felt remarkably well, the aliens must have some super-Neosporin, either that or I've been out for a long, long time. Curiosity won over morbidity; I crossed the room to turn on the 'Kill-O-Vision' as I had affectionately begun to call it. No battles were being waged at this time so all that appeared was a static list of the remaining contestants and their respective rankings. At first I thought it was a misprint. I had beaten Sterns, ranked at 310, and my rating by comparison had *dropped*. I was listed at No. 812. That meant that either the competition was that difficult or Sterns' injuries had severely hampered my chance at a better rating and an easier challenger next round. I stared at the screen in horror and dismay. I had hoped that I would have a relatively easy opponent next round, but the aliens had seen it differently. I had faced a man who had been close to death and I had almost joined him. How in the hell was I going to beat this next person? I was shaken out of my stupor when a countdown clock appeared to announce that Round Three was about to get under way. I had five hours to prep myself for another battle, how long was I out for? Well, I had five hours to fully recuperate, and depression had settled in deeply. I was thinking it was time for a nap. Backing up towards my bed, I put an arm out to guide myself down and touched something warm. At first I thought I was still dreaming, so I moved my hand back and forth a little without turning around. I was afraid to see what was there; I slowly turned, half-expecting to be face to face with Mace Head. The thought of him coming at me, brain matter still oozing out of his gaping maw, almost made me double over in fear. It was then that a high shriek brought me back to reality or at least a semblance thereof. The woman in my bed, upon opening her eyes and seeing me, recoiled in terror. She pulled the blankets around her and got into one of the tightest fetal positions I had ever witnessed. After the initial shock and surprise of finding another warm-blooded creature sharing my abode, I wondered what caused *that* reaction. I may not be Tom Cruise but I'm not the Hunchback of Notre Dame either, what gives? The whole situation might already have been somewhat humorous if I hadn't been as startled as her and fell backwards, lightly brushing my head against the table, but more ridiculous than that was the sound of my pride making a solid thunking sound as my ass hit the floor. I could do nothing more than laugh. Her eyes shifted from terror to bewilderment. As my laughing increased her eyes became even softer. I think that for a moment through my tears of mirth I even witnessed the beginning of a smile. Still trying to wipe the tears from my eyes and holding my stomach from splitting I continued to laugh and to my amazement my new roommate joined in. After a few more moments the merriment of the situation came to a drawn out finale. The wariness began to creep back into her eyes. So I spoke to try and calm whatever her fears were.

"Please," I whispered, "don't be scared. I don't know who you are or why you're here but I've done nothing to you so far, and I don't plan on starting now."

She looked me over carefully and must have decided that I was telling the truth, as she loosened her death grip on the blanket and actually stretched out her legs a little bit to relax the fetal position.

"Who are you?" I queried. "And what exactly are you doing here?"

"You mean you really don't know?" she uttered skeptically.

"I don't know much of anything right now other than the fact that I'm being held captive in an alien ship and so far I've killed two other human beings, and more than likely my time left alive on this ship is measured in hours as opposed to days, plus that was the first good laugh I've had in what seems like decades." She winced when I mentioned the part about my death, but I didn't know her from Eve so I don't think that my passing would greatly affect her.

"I'm a spoil." She seemed to have almost gagged upon that word.

'A spoil?' I thought to myself, all I could think of was milk. Why the hell would she be comparing herself to old milk? Ohh, now I get it, I must have hit my head a little harder than I thought.

"You're my spoil, as in spoils of war?"

"That's it."

"But that's crazy!" I said.

"This whole thing is a little crazy, wouldn't you agree?"

We both almost started the whole laughing bit again, but the pain in my side abbreviated that.

She continued. "We, meaning the remaining women, are made to watch all the matches as they are waged. We are awarded to the winner and he may do with us as he sees fit."

"You mean you have to clean this place if I tell you to?" I said jokingly. But then it struck me, if this girl was somebody's girlfriend that meant that Beth could possibly be with another man right now. My heart almost derailed, it hammered inside my chest as if it were trying to get out. She must have seen the concern in my eyes.

"What's the matter?" she asked with true empathy.

"Someone that I care about is out there," as I swept

my arm across the expanse of the ship.

"I'm so sorry, I know how it feels."

"How could you possibly know how it feels?" I shot back angrily.

"I also went to the concert with a loved one, and then I got to watch him die a horrible death in the first round. At least your girlfriend may still be alive."

"I am so sorry, I'm such an idiot. I've been alone for so long in this room I don't even know how to act around people anymore. I am truly sorry for your loss. It wasn't me was it?"

"What? No, it wasn't you, but it doesn't matter now anyway."

"Sure it does, how could I possibly face you if I had killed your boyfriend?"

"Fiancé."

I shut up, she truly did have me bested. My girlfriend was at least on the ship, but her boyfriend/fiancé had departed for a better place, or at least I had to believe that.

After a few moments of a drawn out and awkward silence she extended the hand of friendship.

"What's her name, or better yet what does she look like? I might know her. They let us stay together in one huge communal room."

I began to give her a description of my Beth and the more descriptive I became the more I noticed the light of recognition on her face. Hope surged. I was almost afraid to get any news because my mom always used to say 'no news is good news' and thus far in my life I had no reason to dispute that. Well, I thought to myself, now is not the time for the faint of heart. I said her first name... and my new friend said her last.

"You know her?" I asked incredulously "You truly know her?" Here was a person that had been in contact with my love, most likely just yesterday.

"Not really, but I know *of* her."

I don't understand what you mean." I was now

grasping for straws, I just wanted to hear anything about Beth.

"She is the Goddess of the Arena."

"What the hell is that!?" All the goddesses I had ever read about were always sacrificed for some stupid reason or other. This twist couldn't be good.

She cringed at my outburst but continued anyway. "She was chosen to be the most desirable among all the women here." She huffed as if to say 'what am I, chopped liver?' Which, my dear reader, I can tell you right now she was not. "And it was decided by our glorious hosts that she will be given to the winner of the entire tournament."

The image of that animal Durgan with my girlfriend did nothing to ease my nerves. The questions I had for her came out in rapid fashion.

"Please, I will answer all your questions as best I can, but please give me some time."

"That's the problem," I noted as I pointed to the screen where the 3rd round had just begun. "I don't have much time."

"Okay," she said. "I'm sorry. By the way, my name is Debbie, Debbie Zimmerman."

"I'm pleased to meet you Debbie." And under any other circumstances I would have been truly happy to meet her. She was around 5'3" with long blond hair, green eyes and a complexion that belied her hair and eye color, she was actually a little darker than I was and considering I had some Italian mixed in with my English heritage that made her look all the more exotic. She looked a lot like Michelle Pfeifer with a great tan and she had the body to match the face.

"Do you know why I'm still alive? I'm not a doctor but the blood I saw pouring out of me was a deep crimson, it was an arterial strike and by the way I was bleeding out I should have only had a few moments left."

"Well, from what I gather the aliens were more than a little peeved when in the first round an additional fifty-two victorious combatants died from injuries sustained in their bouts. They decided to step in from Round Two on and save the victors with their advanced medical techniques." Oh, I thought to myself as I absently touched the alien pack on my side. That explains that.

"Deb... do you mind if I call you that?" I asked.

"No, most of my friends call me that anyway."

"Why were you so terrified when I woke you, I know that this whole situation is crazy but I'm one of the good guys, at least I think I am."

A sudden nervousness clouded her face for an instant, than passed when she realized that I was only asking the question out of concern and with no hidden malice behind my words. I guess she finally decided I was telling the truth. Damn, I thought to myself, this was one attractive woman but I decided in the best interests of all to let my primary head do the thinking. It's amazing to be a guy, on an alien ship God knows where, with potentially less than three hours to live, yet I still was having strong feelings of desire for this girl I didn't even know.

"And why," I asked, truly curious now, "was someone as gorgeous as *you* "assigned to such a lowly ranking as myself?"

She visibly flushed. "You weren't supposed to win," she said quietly, hoping to not upset me. Too late, I thought. "The ranking system is almost always right. These monsters take pride in that fact. You, Mr. Talbot..."

"Mike," I interjected.

"Mike, you are considered an anomaly, they were actually going to let you die so that their predictions would be true, but I guess now you are some sort of curiosity to them. So far you are only one of fifteen that has gone against the odds."

"Lucky for me I guess," I said with very little inflection.

"And lucky for me, I suppose too." But she definitely put more feelings in her words than I had.

For the first time in a week I felt something besides

hate and pity, and for a moment in time I wasn't afraid. She responded to my smile with a kiss that could have easily melted into a love scene.

"I'm sorry," I said as noncommittally pushed her away, which might have been the toughest thing that I had ever had to do. "Deb, I'm sorry. But the girl I want to be with is still alive and she is on this ship somewhere. I still have a chance albeit a slim one to see her again, and I have to hold on to that as long as I can. It wouldn't be right to her, to me and definitely not to you. Although this might just be the hardest thing I've ever done in my life, including the battles."

She laughed a little and that helped to ease the mounting tension considerably.

"I understand, and Mike," she said ever so softly, "thank you for not taking advantage of me."

"Deb, I might be caged but I am not an animal."

We talked for hours about everything until we came back to my original question, which she had tried to skirt around for the entire conversation. She told me she was so afraid because Durgan had started a gruesome trend among the victors. She explained that not everyone had followed his lead but enough did to make it a very macabre event. Upon winning his second battle, quite easily she added, Durgan was awarded his spoil right there on the field. He then proceeded in front of the whole alien audience and the rest of the women (the spoils to be) to rip the clothes off of his newest acquisition. When that was done he pushed her down to the ground on all fours and mounted her from behind.

"He raped her right there in front of God and everyone," she sobbed. "Those fucking alien things were going crazy. That poor girl was screaming in pain, she was so afraid, I just wanted to go down there and help her."

It was at this moment that I wanted to kill all of those alien bastards, and not only for what they had done to me, but for what they had put Deb and the other women through.

"He was brutalizing her until blood began to come out of her."

That sickened me, how could you possibly take such a beautiful act and turn it into such a gruesome event?

"This went on for almost half an hour, he just kept doing it and doing it, and the girl, she was now just sobbing a little bit, the bastards even put close-ups of the whole thing on the big screen, they were eating it up. Finally he finished what he had started and then it really got bad."

"How the hell could it get any worse?" I didn't think that I wanted to know, but I was too involved now to not find out.

"He… he killed her," she stammered. "He drove his sword through her back and pinned her to the ground like a butterfly, it was horrific. She was so battered and bruised that the girl could barely muster up a scream. Many of the contestants followed suit after him with their own spoils, it was a slaughterhouse. I just cried and cried for those poor souls, and I am ashamed to admit it now but I hoped beyond hope that you would die also."

"I understand if I died I wouldn't be able to do those awful things to you. I'm so sorry that you had to see that. I know it's horrible inside the arena floor but I at least somewhat control my own destiny." I paused to gather my thoughts. "Deb, I know you're upset but I have to know…"

"What is it?" she whimpered

"What happens to you if I die in this next round?"

"Don't even say that! Please don't even think it!" she yelled.

"Deb, look at me, I'm 165 pounds soaking wet, I'm far from the bruisers that are out there now. I've faced one old guy and a half dead guy who almost killed me, my odds of going too far aren't all that great."

"Please!" she cried.

"Deb, what happens?" I asked a little more urgently.

"I go to your victor," she sobbed. "Please don't let that happen!"

I hugged her with all the strength I could muster, she winced in pain but she didn't want me to let go either. We cried for what seemed like hours but in reality it was only minutes. Then the screen roared to life.

"Gladiator, prepare yourself, your bout is about to begin."

All of our conversation ceased as we watched the events unfold on the screen. It was obvious more pomp and ceremony was attributed to the higher rankings. Durgan didn't even have an armed escort leading him into the arena. He appeared to enter willingly, all too willingly actually. The camera honed right in on him and I was able to get a good look at him. He looked like a wrestler in his garb, he even had what appeared to be a silk robe on. This really did look like Saturday Morning Wrestling only I wasn't on my couch at college and I definitely wasn't smoking a big fattie with Paul. Durgan even bowed before the crocs, and they loved him, they hissed back their collective approval. It was when they announced his competition that I knew something was amiss. His competitor for this round had died from his injuries sustained in the prior round. So even the alien technology was only so good, they did have faults. That was a good piece of news, if only I could get out of here to tell somebody. Durgan was getting a bye for this round and he was pissed; he was angry that he was not going to get the chance to kill another human being. How far from the edge had this man been on Earth? It couldn't have been that far that he was pushed over the edge like this. And then as he turned to his spoil his eyes gleamed. No, I mean they really twinkled, if it wasn't for the evil grin that spread over his face I would have actually thought that he cared for this woman. I was riveted to the screen, I felt like I was watching a train wreck in action. The camera pulled back from the massive structure of him to the shrieking and shivering form of the woman in the center of the arena. She was tied to two posts, so that she was spread eagled and naked standing up. Tears flowed down her eyes in rivulets; she could not take her eyes off of him. She knew this monster and she knew that her fate was sealed, but that didn't make it any easier to swallow. He slowly sauntered his way to the center of the arena. The crowd was going crazy, they were actually throwing flowers onto the floor of the arena.

"They're as sick as he is!" I shouted to no one in particular.

The woman renewed her shrieking and screaming with a vengeance. He approached her and actually walked around her once, slowly. The woman desperately tried to follow him with her eyes all the way around; he finally came to a stop in front of her and just stood there, eyeing her up and down. It was the kind of once over that could get you in trouble for sexual harassment on our planet. He looked at her for another few seconds with her just quivering and crying and then bang, he punched her full force in the nose. Her nose cracked with an audible pop. What was once a beautiful aristocratic nose was now a shattered piece of flesh and cartilage on her face. Blood poured out and her eyes instantly blackened. The crocs looked like they were foaming at the muzzle. I had hoped that that punch would knock her out so that she would not have to endure the inevitable torture that he was about to rain down on her. But whether he had pulled the punch just enough, or she was just strong enough to withstand it I don't know, but she was still cognizant, the terror in her eyes revealed that her senses had not been dulled in the slightest. Durgan removed his robe and let it gracefully fall to the floor, he then undid his kilt and with one quick motion he fully violated this woman. She went slack. This once probably strong and vibrant woman just gave up the ghost, she had accepted her fate and was most likely now making peace with her God, but to me it didn't seem that he was listening at the moment. That animal was everything men had striven not to be, he was more the missing link than a human. He let out a triumphant yell as he came and even stepped back and beat his chest like King Kong. He pointed into the audience and yelled "This one's for you!" The camera zoomed onto the person he had been talking to. I fell against the screen, it was Beth. Her face was pure hatred and terror. The camera flashed back just in time to catch the sword as it made its way through Durgan's newest spoils' neck. I shut the screen off before the woman's head had a chance to hit the ground. Deb was crying and I was dry heaving into the toilet. It was a long time before I was able to regain my legs and stand up. When I finally exited the bathroom Deb was still whimpering a little bit, but she must have been dreaming of the atrocities because she was now fast asleep.

They came sometime after I had fallen asleep. At first I thought Deb was trying to awaken me. But the feeling was unmistakable, cold and clammy and immensely strong. They felt dead to the touch and their eyes did little to change that appearance. I jumped, Deb jumped too. Tears flowed from her eyes anew.

CHAPTER 22 – Journal Entry 17

"Wake up hu-man, it is time to die," the guard stated. If I had known any better I would have sworn he laughed, but through the mass of teeth they have it's nearly impossible to tell if they even possess any human-like emotion.

"Gladiator No. 812, follow the lit arrows to the stadium, do not stray or you will be shot."

"I guess that means me."

"Good luck Mike," and then she kissed me, not one of those auntie kisses, but a full-fledged passionate kiss. My knees literally knocked together, another couple of seconds and I would've wobbled to my knees.

I had to be strong. I was not only fighting for my own survival but also for Beth and now Deb, the burden that was being laid upon my shoulders was almost too much to bear. If it wasn't for the guards holding me up, I most likely would have collapsed on the floor.

"I'll be watching Mike, and I'll be praying for the both of us."

"Thank you," I said weakly. She wiped away a tear as I rounded the corner.

I stood in my familiar place awaiting my introduction and my competition. The crowd seemed to have worked themselves up into a frenzy, a shark feeding frenzy. Bloodlust was in the air. I tried my best to scan the arena stands where I thought Beth might be, but I couldn't see through the lighting that was flooding the arena floor. We wouldn't want those friggen aliens to miss any action in the shadows. No. 212 came in, he appeared to be about 5'10" or 11" and was extremely well built. And he did not have so much as a scratch on his entire body. A repeat of No. 310 would not happen this evening. The high, tight haircut he was sporting did little to calm my fears. He gave me the distinct impression that he was at some time or still was an active member of the armed services. 'Please God.' I thought to myself, let it be the Navy and not the Marines. He had that air of self-confidence about him that reeked of drill instructor. He didn't seem to be concerned with me in the least.

The unceremonious shove from behind clued me in to the fact that it truly was time to do or die. Great, the arena motif this time was tropical jungle, I get to fight what appears to be a Marine on Vietnam territory; the odds seemed stacked worse than I thought. This day was not getting off to a good start.

I pondered using a bow and arrow. A long range weapon was something that I needed over someone who definitely had better training and better conditioning, my idea of a good workout was going a couple of rounds with the Nintendo. But long distance had been denied to me tonight. From where I was standing I figured that the longest shot I could probably get off would be in the neighborhood of ten yards due to the tropical foliage. Definitely too close, the memory of Mace Head was still too vivid to risk that avenue. I would never be able to swing the mace fast enough and I was afraid of a sword fight, he would overpower me entirely too easily. But my only alternative was a knife and I had no desire to smell his breath with my last. So I grabbed a spear. It felt good in my hands, it was light and deadly, it was just what I hoped I needed. For the first time in three rounds I found myself on the defensive. I didn't think that there was any sense to sticking my proverbial neck out any further than it already was. I gathered just from one look at him on the Jumbotron that Mr. 212 was going to go on the offensive, and why shouldn't he? I didn't appear to pose much of a threat to him. So I did what any scared kid would do, I climbed a tree. Unless he was using a bow and arrow this sort of put us on even terms.

It seemed like I was up in the tree for hours. Sweat

poured off of me, I was concerned that he would see the moisture dripping out of the tree. I did not want to wipe the sweat away either though, I was more afraid of him seeing the movement. At last Mr. 212 found his way towards me. He was going through the jungle as one that was well versed in that area. He seemed a little perturbed that this was taking so long, but confidence still shone brightly through his gaze, always checking around himself and placing his feet where they would make the least audible sound. He even occasionally glanced up into the trees. If he wasn't out to kill me I would have really been impressed with him. I hoped that the trunk of the tree and the branches would shield me from all but the most diligent of searches. Patently and patiently he made his way in my general direction. I knew when the time came I could not hesitate, he would not give me a second chance and neither would I in his position. The time had come; he was directly below me, fifteen feet directly below me. My heart raced, my mouth went dry, time slowed down. It was now or never… my leg cramped as I was about to spring, my fricken leg cramped, so what was to be a graceful death dive turned into a perilous plunge. The Marine must have felt something amiss for he looked up in time to notice my hurtling body and my poised spear ready to puncture his breast. He turned incredibly fast to avoid the majority of the thrust, but I still felt the unmistakable scraping of metal on bone as the spear plunged deep down the length of his left arm. He reacted with the speed of a cat; it appeared to me that he was oblivious to the pain. He swung his sword with full force and would most likely have cut me in half had I not been rolling away from him, the momentum of my ungraceful dive saving my life. How long could this kind of luck last? As it was I had shattered my left arm again, but I was definitely more in tune with the pain in my shattered arm than old Mr. 212. I finally stopped rolling to notice he had recovered and was coming full tilt for me, sword raised and ready to strike. He had no fear. Groping with my right hand, I was trying to scamper away, back pedaling at a much slower rate than the jarhead was racing forward. Reaching back my hand fell upon a palm sized object, it was a rock and it was just what I needed. I stood up, trying desperately to block the pain of my arm out, and hurled the rock as hard as I could. I can't say that I was truly aiming, I just threw it in the general direction of the death mass coming my way.

Pay dirt: a puckering sound erupted as the rock blew out his right eye. Blood flew everywhere and his eye dangled uselessly down by his chin. His forward progress had been stopped and this Goliath was on his knees. His one good eye burned at me. This man was by no stretch of the imagination out of the race yet. His left arm and right eye were useless but he still attempted to finish his mission. He carefully put his sword down, never taking his good eye off of me, and proceeded to rip strips of cloth off his shirt. He was making a patch. I ran. This guy was the Terminator, no matter what you did to him he just kept coming. I needed to patch myself up a bit and more importantly I needed to get rearmed. The pain in my arm ebbed somewhat but it was quite clear that I was now a one-armed warrior.

"Hey you little motherfucker, come out and playyyy!" He was taunting me. Could this be happening? I had inflicted wounds that would have killed 95% of the population and this guy was taunting me. I was scared shitless, what if this really was a Terminator, maybe the aliens were messing with me. No, get it together man, you saw him bleeding, get a weapon and get moving. I grabbed a sword and I ran as far from that voice as was possible in this jungle arena. I then proceeded to dig a hole in the ground, hoping that I wasn't digging my own grave. The ground was soft, more like potting soil than a true forest floor, but I guess I couldn't blame the aliens for their ignorance; maybe I'd thank them for the softness of the soil in some special way if I ever got off of this heap. I made the pit around a bend in the trail, trusting in the fact that he would not have enough time to notice my trap as he rounded the corner. When it was complete I backtracked about twenty yards and unwrapped my damaged arm; I wanted to make sure that he had a blood trail to follow. With any luck he would be so focused on finishing this job that he wouldn't be able to tell that I had covered the same ground twice. I returned to the pit and crawled into what I hoped wasn't my final resting place. I grabbed a thin reed and snapped it off so I could use it as a breathing tube, then covered myself as best I could with twigs, dirt and leaves. I could only hope that he hadn't been watching any of this, because if that was the case I was a dead man. I was positive that the pounding of my heart would give me away, by either the noise or the unsettling of the dirt on top of me. But I could do nothing to calm myself, the thought of him plunging his sword into me at any moment was all I could think of. My breathing was getting ragged; I felt that I was suffocating. I didn't think that I was getting enough air through my plant stalk. I was just about to exit my hole when I felt him, yes, *felt* him coming in my direction. His steps were slower and they did not have the same subtleness as before. The small sliver of plant that I was using as a breathing hole was suddenly gone; he had trampled it with his foot. Dirt poured in. He had to be able to tell from the difference in his footing that I was under him. The advantage was his or mine for the taking. I panicked. I used every bit of strength I could muster and in a defensive gesture I thrust my spear straight up and luckily into my now suspecting victim. The spear entered him almost too easily. I had caught him in a manner that will haunt me and all mankind forever, directly in his scrotum. Even in what had to be total shock he still had the awareness to try and kill me. He tried desperately to drive his sword into my now exposed neck. I'm sure the only thing that saved me was his lack of dimensionality. With one eye completely useless his depth perception was off by a mere fraction, but it was still close enough to leave a substantial gash across the left side of my neck. Another quarter inch and he would have cut my carotid artery. His crumbling body shook, my spear twitched from his death spasms. But through it all, his one good eye never left mine. He was still pissed and if he hadn't died just then he would have killed me.

Once again I was wounded to the point of unconsciousness. I awoke to the careful ministrations of Deb. Oh how my head ached, didn't the damn aliens have pain medication? While Deb was tending to my mending arm a stunningly beautiful brunette was placing a new bandage on my neck. At first I looked at her in bewilderment and then it dawned on me she was my newest spoil. Unfortunately No. 212 must have killed his first spoil so I would not able to liberate another, at least for the time being. But was all this false hope, how many times could I dance with death and not have to take a bow?

"I think he's waking up," the brunette said.

"Mike, Mike, can you hear me?" Deb said, her voice laced with concern.

"Yeah I'm here, any chance of some water, my throat tastes like dirt," I managed to croak out.

"I was so scared, you fought so bravely but I still thought that you were going to be ki..." she cried, tears welling up in her eyes before she could finish.

"Me too, but the fact remains I'm still alive and I've got the thirst to prove it."

"Oh I'm sorry, I'll get it right now."

"And what's your name," I managed to say to the brunette.

"I'm Stephanie," she said somewhat nervously.

"You've no doubt talked to Deb?"

"Yes."

"So you know that you have nothing to fear here?"

"After talking to Deb it's not you I fear, it's what happens if you..."

"Yeah, die, I know."

"That's not what I meant!"

"Sure it is. Don't get me wrong, I understand your concern. Your fate is directly tied into my own and you have no control over it whatsoever."

"Before this," she stammered, "I was just a groupie that toured with Widespread Panic. I've never hurt anybody, all I wanted to do was have a good time."

"Listen, Steph," I said. "We're all in the same boat, mere weeks ago I was attending college, not going to classes, partying my brains out and in the process, falling in love. But now we have to do all that we can to help each other out through this mess. I have no desire to die for those croc-aliens."

"Me neither," she sniffed.

"Good, now if you could please hurry Deb up with that water, otherwise I'm going to die of thirst."

When Deb returned with the water I grabbed her with my good arm and planted a kiss on her that the gods would be envious of.

"Oh, Mike I think I love you!" and then she began to cry in earnest. "I think the stress of this place has intensified my feelings. I mean, I just lost my fiancée and here I am talking about loving you. What the hell is wrong with me?"

I don't know if I would have wanted to reply or not, but either way the point was moot, I succumbed to my exhaustion and fell fast asleep. I awoke hours, possibly days later. I was so disorientated that I was unsure of which. Deb was next to me spooning my body; Stephanie had taken a blanket and was fast asleep on my couch. My couch!? I really was moving up in the world. I got up as carefully as possible so as to not disturb either of my guests. I needed to know how my last outing had placed me. I wanted, no, I *needed* to know my ranking. I knew at most there could only be in the vicinity of 600 men left and any ranking over 300 in my present condition would in all likelihood be the end of me. But I was in no way prepared for what the screen showed me, I was ranked No. 33. I had to pull a chair out from the table to keep myself from toppling over. The scrappy kid from downtown Boston was now considered a contender. I was lost in my own world when I felt the hand on my shoulder.

Surely it can't be time for another fight. But it wasn't time for fighting. It was Deb's hand and it was time for love. She gently guided me back to the bed. Kissing me softly on my mouth and down my chest, she half pushed me down onto the bed and proceeded to kiss me from the top of my head to the bottom of my belly. I started to protest as she began to pull my boxers off, but she was having none of it and shushed me with her finger over my mouth. She slowly removed her blouse and panties and I was lost in her. I tried my best to not wake Stephanie, but unless she slept like the dead there was no way she wasn't awakened by our lovemaking.

It must have been embarrassing for her. And I'm sure it was even more embarrassing the next morning when she attempted to wake us up in the most unobtrusive way possible, because we had fallen asleep in a heap of tangled arms and legs and we were both as naked as jaybirds. Deb upon awaking visibly flushed.

"Steph, I'm sorry. I didn't mean for you to see this," she said as she pulled her blanket up over her breasts, leaving me all that much more exposed. Unfortunately for me I couldn't move quite as fast with the damaged arm and various aches and pains; it took me a good thirty seconds to get my boxers on, and I felt the flush in my face as I had two sets of eyes on me the entire time.

"Come on you guys, give me a break," as I almost fell over when I got my leg caught in the shorts. After I had finally got myself into somewhat of a presentable manner, Stephanie replied to Deb.

"There's no need to explain, you both obviously care for each other. And it's great that you can share that love."

"Thank you," Deb said, sighing. "Do you have anybody special on this ship?" Obviously that hit a sour note with Stephanie, she recoiled as if she had been slapped, and not wanting to push any further Deb let it go.

After a few moments of awkwardness, Stephanie went to the kitchenette area and made some lunch. Dinner? Hell, breakfast, I don't know. We sat and ate and idly chatted for a while when out of nowhere Stephanie blurted out that she had gone to the concert with Durgan. Deb dropped her cup, juice sprayed everywhere. I could have caught bugs with my mouth, my jaw had dropped that far.

"We've been going out for three years and he's always been somewhat of a bully," and she added hastily "but he's never acted anything like this, not even anything close. He's always been extra protective of me and treated me like royalty. I don't know who that person out there is. I can't even imagine that we were once intimate, he disgusts me beyond words, I feel as if he has violated me every time he rapes and kills those other girls." The anger mounted in her voice, she was nearly shouting. Deb went to comfort Stephanie as the shouting suddenly turned into sobbing.

"You know Stephanie, if by some small miracle I ever reach him. I will have to do everything in my power to kill him. It'll be the only chance any of us has."

"I know," she said with a clear tremor in her voice "The man I loved is no longer here, he is already dead to me. What happened to him?" she implored.

That was a question none of us knew the answer to, nor in all actuality wanted to find out. With the field of competitors getting smaller I guess the aliens felt the need to draw things out so as to add to the suspense and tension. We were given more time off each subsequent round. I was not complaining, because even with the advanced medical attention I was getting I still ached from head to toe. I was lucky I didn't break my neck when I fell out of that tree. It was going to take all the careful ministrations of Deb and Steph to get me back to full health, and who was I to complain.

Most of my waking time, which was beginning to increase, was spent either on the weight bench which the aliens had supplied or watching "reruns" of the past gladiator battles. I wanted to learn all that I could about my opponents. The tendency of more violence among the victors was an alarmingly increasing occurrence. A woman's chance at survival stood at a mere 40%. Six out of every ten women were killed right there on the arena floor, and who knows what happened to the ones that lived when they got back to their champion's room. I'd be surprised if more than half of those lived to see the next day. The disease of violence had hit hard. It was unimaginable that these hippy wannabe concert goers could turn into such violent creatures. I guess given the circumstances and the stresses we were under that it wasn't that far-fetched of a notion. We were all turning back to our baser instincts, but if our predecessors on Earth had killed off the fairer sex in the fashion and rate that was going on now, we would all be extinct. That I had the tenacity or will to kill another human being still left me weak-kneed if I thought about it too much.

My next battle was against No. 579, Andrew Jenkins. By watching his tapes it seemed to me that this man won more by luck than by skill, he sort of reminded me of myself. He was smaller than I was, but definitely more agile. It seemed that lightning quick hand speed was another of his virtues. This man had an uncanny ability to detect where his competitor was coming from and would thus lie in wait. One thing I noted with interest was that his preferred weapon was a knife. And every victim he faced, well, faced wasn't a good word. Stabbed in the back would be a better description. He never saw any of his competitors' faces as he killed them. And for some reason or other the killing blow was always delivered in the small of the back. He looked well practiced at this routine; I could picture him in a dark alley at night lying in wait for some unsuspecting victim. Man, I thought to myself, Widespread Panic drew out all sorts. The little Rat Man, as I affectionately began to coin him, seemed to like the shrieks and throes of pain that ensued from this type of blow, it was not a quick mortal blow, but it was a mortal blow nonetheless. The camera zoomed in towards Rat Man's face and caught a smile of sheer delight; he looked like a kid that was about to get an ice cream cone. He took great pleasure in watching his victims flail about and try futilely to reach behind their backs and take out his weapon, which was slowly draining their life away. As his foe dropped to the ground to conserve what little life force he still contained, the Rat Man would finally make his frontal assault. That was, of course, if they had dropped their weapon first. He would step in front of the person and just start mad kicking them in the face. Truly a little shit if I ever did see one.

I prepared for my fight against Rat Man mentally, physically, and spiritually. I was ready and it was time. When we finally made it to the arena Rat Man did little to convince me that he wasn't part rat. He was always looking around and twitching; he made my skin crawl. His shifting eyes were disquieting, they were always darting around looking for a place to run and hide. He constantly raised his head and sniffed at the air. I wondered, maybe he *was* a rat and could smell his victims coming? And his 5'4" frame made me look like a giant. The terrain this time looked like something from an Isaac Asimov book. It appeared to be a city after a nuclear holocaust. Rubble was everywhere. Pieces of buildings stood but much more of them lay in pieces on the ground. This looked to be Rat Man's home territory, I was wondering if he had put in this request. From what I could tell on the big screen there appeared to be many hiding spots and only one or two possible pathways through the litter covered streets. Was the little turd licking his lips? No it had to be a trick of the light, it looked like he was even rubbing his hands together. We've got to get this over with before I lose it completely.

The battle was going pretty much to plan, I wasn't dead and that was a great plan thus far. I had prepared for one form of attack, if Rat Man changed his routine in any way I could be in for a serious run. I started down the narrow litter strewn path that at one time could have been Main Street in any city. These aliens were really good at reproductions. From the looks of it they must have been watching us for a good long time. My heart was pounding in my chest, even more than normal in these situations. Fear gripped me like a vise; I had a premonition of a lamb being led to the slaughter. Then it happened, I felt a thud in the small of my back. I fell to my knees more out of relief than anything else. It was finally over.

* * *

Debbie screamed in horror. "Oh dear God no, please don't let him die!" She stared at the screen in utter disbelief, unable to comprehend that her new found love was about to die and so was she. Tears flowed heavily from her eyes. Her vision was so blurred it was all she could do to tell in which direction the screen was, focusing on anything was beyond reason. But she wiped as hard as she could with her shirt sleeve when Stephanie yelled in a jubilant tone.

"He's still alive, he's still moving!! Get up!" she shouted.

Could it be? Deb thought to herself, could he actually take a stab to the back and still be alive? If Rat Man would just get closer so that Mike could kill him the aliens would actually come in and fix him up. It was too much to hope for, and now she was hoping for the aliens to intercede.

Rat Man finally felt good. He felt as if he had come into his true calling. He had always been the brunt of his so-called friends' jokes, but these aliens, well, they were ugly but they loved him and all he had to do was keep killing people. He got the jubilation from the throngs and all the free women to do with as he pleased. Life was actually good. He didn't even care that he had not been ranked so high, it made killing his opponent all that more satisfying. His 5'4" skin and bones frame made it incredibly easy for him to hide in some of the most unusual places. And he felt as if he could move more silently than should be normal. He was truly coming into his own. These ugly alligator things had given him more in the last month than all of society in the last twenty-four years. In fact, up until two weeks ago he had been a virgin, not something he was particularly proud of, but it was now no longer something he had to be concerned with. He loved this place. Maybe the adrenaline surging through his veins or the self-induced high he was on made him unaware that the knife had not struck home, because he took his time reveling in his glory. The smile on his face convinced Mike that he had absolutely no idea what was going on, except for the cheering of the crowd. True to form Jenkins aka Rat Man came in front of Mike to finish off this battle with his signature move. The crowd became silent, holding their collective breath to let out the roar upon the conclusion. Debbie and Stephanie watched in horror, embracing each other in their perceived final moments. Beth, higher up in the stands, shed a tear.

*   *   *

Time stood still. My heart beat once, Rat Man reared back and let loose a bone crunching kick. My second heart beat brought my left arm to block the brunt of the kick, although I felt that he possibly may have shattered my arm again. On my next heartbeat my right hand came up and thrust the sword which had been trailing on the ground in and through the frail frame that once belonged to Jenkins and was now a soulless shell. His eyes grew wide in disbelief.

"You're dead," he whispered. "I killed you, you're supposed to be dead now, they love me, can't you hear it?"

He must have been listening to the voices in his head; the crowd was as silent as a hockey stadium after a playoff game in which the home team loses in overtime. I pulled my sword out of him and mustered my strength to stand. I didn't think my heart would ever calm down. Even in death, his eyes had a gaze of disbelief forever frozen in them. I pulled my shirt up and to everyone's amazement unstrapped the cushion from my weight bench. The aliens did nothing. Deb and Steph cried and laughed in relief. Rat Man's corpse still stared in disbelief.

I yelled up to the stands. "Isn't this what you wanted? You ugly fucks! Isn't this what you wanted?"

More than likely there were only one or two in the stands who knew what I was saying; the rest probably thought that I was doing some sort of war chant. And that they did love, they went crazy. Hissing and cheering and clapping, it was sickening. I walked to the center of the arena and claimed my spoil. She was another blonde; my favorite flavor, I thought to myself. Don't let this place take you down with it. Keep it together.

"Please," she said. "Don't hurt me." Her voice was pathetically weak, to me it seemed that she had already resigned herself to a gruesome fate, no matter what the outcome on the battlefield today.

"Don't worry," I said, trying to be as reassuring as possible. But a picture is worth a thousand words, and here I was approaching her with a sword, my chest heaving from the surge of victory and the blood and gore of Rat Man all over me. What a sight I must have been. "I'm here to save you my dear," I said in my best Clark Gable impersonation. It wasn't that good. I'm not sure that she was going to believe anything I said up to that point, but the tone I used and the true smile did more to calm her down than any of my actual words.

"Come on, let's go home," as I cut her bonds. "You can meet the other women."

"There's more women at your place?" she said in disbelief.

"No matter what you've witnessed out there, I leave it on the arena floor. The women who are at my cell are free to do as they wish, at least within the confines of the cell."

That actually seemed to cheer her up a little bit.

"Now if you could do a little something for me." She eyed me warily. "I could use your shoulder to lean on, my back and my arm are throbbing. I'm afraid I might fall over and I don't want those things getting anywhere near me." So she leaned in close and supported enough of my weight to get me back to my cell, with my dignity intact. And that was how I met Leanna. I'm pretty sure I slept for twenty-four hours straight and no matter how long it truly was it was definitely a deep sleep, because when I awoke I found myself in a totally new room. It was almost as big as my old house.

There were three bedrooms and two bathrooms, a full kitchen and a den. I was wondering what real estate went for out in space these days. You'd probably have to pay a pretty penny for a place like this. I could almost get to like this, especially since I found myself wrapped up in Debbie's arms.

"I didn't think that you were going to get up at all today, sleepy head," she said playfully. "You know you scared the crap out of me out there. See, you got me so upset I actually cussed. I never cuss."

I was preparing my comeback when she put one finger over my mouth and made a shushing sound. I had begun to like her shushing techniques. With her tongue she outlined my now hardening nipple and traced a line of saliva all the way down my flat belly. For two days we stayed in that bedroom, never venturing far except to grab the occasional drink or a sandwich.

To look at my 'prison' one would have thought I was a multi-millionaire caught embezzling funds. Donald Trump in his heyday would have been envious of this place. But the most prized possession in the entire room was the window. It was no larger than a foot across and a foot tall, but it let us see that there truly was an outside to this ship. Even if it was cold, vast, distant space, it was still infinitely better than the confines of this alien vessel. It allowed us to see our planet, our real home, even though it seemed light years away. How far is Venus from Earth anyway?

"Do you think anyone down there can see us?" I said to no one in particular, but wanting everyone to hear. It was then that the newest addition to my entourage spoke.

"I've been thinking that same question over and over, why don't they send help? And then I realize where we are and that more than likely this ship has some unbelievable defensive capabilities."

"I'm sorry," I said, "but what is your name?"

"Leanna. Leanna Cantrell. And I wanted to thank you for saving me."

"And Leanna, I wanted to thank you for carrying me

back."

"It was the least I could do," she smiled. She blushed ever so slightly but quickly controlled herself when she saw Debbie's eyes on her. Obviously Stephanie had informed our new guest about the house rules. The budding tension was broken with Stephanie's shout from the den.

"Look, the new ratings are coming up!"

I found myself being drawn to the screen, the competitive spirit in me was coming out in full force. I was sort of horrified at my morbid fascination for this tournament. But I had to know. It wasn't a long wait either. There it was, and as if one we all let out a collective sigh. Luckily as advanced human beings we were above mere superstition, or at least I hoped so, because there I was, lucky No. 13. The field had trimmed down to a svelte 306 men. (Out of 4,000 plus, this place was unbelievable.) Even with all their advanced technology two more men had died needlessly. Well they would have died anyway, I thought to myself, sooner or later, it was just a matter of time. I spent the remainder of the day? Night? How do you tell that kind of thing in space, do the aliens even care? In any case, I spent the next few hours watching reruns of the events and I had to be honest my next opponent scared me the most. He wasn't big and he wasn't small. He was actually just about my size. He was the type that had made it thus far on wits, more so than power. So it was safe to assume that he was at this exact time watching *my* re-runs. This looked to be my toughest event yet.

"What's wrong Mike?" Deb said as she curled up tight next to me on the couch. Apparently the scowl on my face was very noticeable.

"It's my next opponent."

"What about him? He doesn't look very remarkable."

"My point exactly."

"What do you mean?" She sounded perplexed.

"Well, he's not huge, he's not terribly fast, yet there he is. Still alive and kicking. He's smart. He didn't overpower any of his competitors. He outsmarted them. His road thus far looked twice as tough as mine."

"Oh, I see what you mean," as she sat up and took real notice of the man that could potentially end her very existence. "But you're smart too," she said, but her voice had lost some of its conviction. Not another word was spoken for quite some time. The significance of the conversation hit Deb deeply, she line for line inherited my scowl. The similarities between my mirrored opponent and myself, however, ended at the conclusion of each match. My competitor quite literally looked insane. After killing his latest victim he began to dismember him. That was about all I could handle, I had eaten a good lunch and had no desire to see it again. I shut the screen off. I had found his weakness anyway.

"Leanna," I said, removing my hand from its resting position on Deb's stomach. Deb seemed a little perturbed that I disturbed her, but she did her best to hide that she felt that way.

"Yes Mike," Leanna answered warily, trying not to let her voice waver in any way. She wished to have that hand on *her* stomach but she had no desire to cross swords with Deb, at least not yet.

"Do they let the women watch these reruns?"

"Yes, and we make sure to watch every one."

"Why?" Stephanie said as she turned away from the book she was reading. "Don't they make you sick?"

"They do, they're horrible," Leanna trembled. "But we have to know our fate. Don't we? We have to silently cheer for one or the other in the ring to win; our very survival depends on it. And sometimes when the two men in the ring are both insane we can merely hope that death is swift," she sobbed. The room fell silent. The women waiting to become spoils were living in a hell no less worse than mine, just in a slightly different location.

Leanna finally broke the silence with a smile in her voice. "You're one of the favorites."

"Excuse me?" I asked in disbelief.'=

"Well, you are *so* cute," she said, quickly glancing at Deb continuing on anyway. "And smart, and plus the obvious fact that none of your women suffer the fate that so many do now."

"I understand completely," I said "And yeah, I am kind of cute aren't I?"

"And big-headed," Deb said as she threw a pillow at my enlarged ego. Obviously I wasn't too fast because the pillow caught me right on the side of my noggin. We all laughed, it was the first time in a long time that we were all finally at ease with each other.

"So you believe that any of these women will recognize me?" I asked hopefully.

"Most certainly, but if you don't mind my asking, why are you asking?"

"I just think that I'm going to need a little help in this next round. That's all."

Nobody knew my plan and at the moment I wasn't in the mood to explain any further.

Deb later admitted to me in bed that she did not at all like Leanna's revelation.

"What do you mean Deb?" I knew the answer but egging her on was fun, what can I say. Sometimes I'm a shit.

"I don't like the fact that you are now a desired commodity."

"Would you rather I looked like the hunch-back?"

"You know what I mean, why are you mocking me?"

"I'm just playing, cool your jets woman."

"I'll tell you what. If anyone tries to make any moves on you I'll make the tournament look like a sandlot football game."

I laughed, but she didn't see the humor.

"And I just bet that you would Deb, I just bet that you would."

The next few days were tense ones. Up to this point in my life I had never felt so much accumulated tension. I was having a hard time with the women. No, they got along fine, it was the responsibility that I now shouldered for them. Back on Earth I could barely take care of myself, now I was responsible for the very lives of these three women. That weighed heavily on me. I avoided all three like the plague. I just couldn't bear the thought of anything bad happening to them. I would have gladly given my life if I had any opportunity to spare theirs. But the only way I could keep them safe was to do the very opposite. I could not spare the lives of my opponents, I had to be ruthless and that's just not who I was. It was a lot to wrestle with in those proceeding days. Deb tried her best to offer support and comfort but she also had to wrestle with her own demons. The potential of losing her lover and possibly losing her own life kept bleeding through into the membranes of her very existence like poison. She even had to wrestle with the alternative: what if I kept winning? I'd eventually get Beth back and then what would happen to her? She was torn. Neither scenario offered much comfort. It was two weeks until the next awaited match came. The tension never loosened its grip the entire time. The girls spoke to each other less and less over the following days and then it was usually only in passing that any comments were made. Deb seemed to pull back more and more every day. But nobody could be blamed for any strangeness of feelings that surfaced. When the day of the fight finally arrived it was more of a relief, at least now I could get out of this cell and try once again to shape my own destiny as opposed to just obsessing about it. Deb wept openly as once more my door vanished and I made my way to the arena. Leanna's eyes seemed to be watering a bit, but the biggest surprise was the total lack of emotion on Stephanie's face. I'm pretty sure that the weight of the previous weeks had finally found a way to settle down on her shoulders. She appeared to have physically aged years just in the past few days. So there it was, I left my semi-castle with some mixed feelings. At this point I seriously doubted that I was ever coming back. Oh, the sweet relief to just let go, to not have to shoulder this burden anymore. I trudged onwards towards my fate.

*   *   *

As soon as the door once again materialized, Stephanie turned to Deb.

"Deb, I had a dream last night," and with that sentence the floodgates opened. Steph's chest rose and fell with each gasping breath as her hot tears burned tiny rivulets into her cheeks. Terror began to surmount in Debbie.

"What is it?" she cried out as if in extreme pain or possibly fear or more than likely both.

"I dreamed that Mike was killed," Stephanie choked out. "It was so real, I kept yelling to him to turn around, but, but, he wouldn't listen."

"Steph, it was just a dream," Deb said as she tried to calm Stephanie and herself down.

But Stephanie just kept crying and wailing, so Deb did the only thing she could think of, she smacked her hard, right across the face. Both women stopped crying and could only stare at each other in surprised shock. And for the first time since they met, they shared more than negative feelings about one another and their situation. Almost as if on cue they both took a step forward and embraced each other. The crying intensified. Leanna joined in more for the comfort than any true liking for either woman. But it still felt good anyway. They finally let go of each other after what seemed hours and turned to the screen to watch their own fates unfold.

"Oh GOD NO!" Stephanie shouted out.

"What, what's the matter!" both girls turned to look at the color rapidly draining out of Stephanie's face.

"That's the terrain I saw in my dream!" Stephanie shouted with pain in her voice.

CHAPTER 23 – Journal Entry 18

The crowd, its usual reserved self, looked like something out of a Saturday afternoon baseball game in the Bronx. The Yankees versus the Red Sox, no less. They were going crazy. I again lost my lunch; it was the best I'd felt in the last two weeks. I was also hungry, but not in the food sense. I hungered, no I yearned for victory. These aliens liked me; true, it was mainly for the sport of it, but they still liked to watch me fight and I hoped preferably win. I wonder if they gambled on these things. Do they handicap? They must, I reasoned, why would they go through the trouble of having a ranking system in place? I reaffirmed my vow that if I survived these insane games I would do everything possible to kill all those responsible for this travesty. But it was time for NOW, not later. There would be no later if I did not get through the now. I felt very zen at that moment.

The arena floor had been laid out in a desert motif, how quaint. They even had small cactuses and Joshua trees covering small sand dunes. Actually some of the dunes weren't quite so small, some appeared to be in the neighborhood of fifteen to twenty feet high, plenty of places to hide and lie in wait. It would be virtually impossible to hear somebody coming at you, but neither could they come upon you with any speed; the sand was soft and made all movement difficult. I could see my potential spoil from the spot where I stood; she was exactly mid-way between the two gladiator entrances but pushed back against the far wall. I knew that Beth had been watching me through all these battles. What did she think of me? Could she possibly still love me? If she ever even had. If anything, we had always been quasi-peace activists in school, not actively involved but we always supported their efforts. Thankfully, I was not given the time to pursue these debilitating thoughts any further. The battle was about to commence. My competitor was introduced first; they even had the custom of introducing the challenger first. How long had they been watching us? The door behind me closed as my introduction was being announced. I hope whatever they were saying about me was flattering but I didn't speak alien so I really had no idea why the crowd was going ape shit. I tried to block the noise out with images of tranquility and peace but the only views that kept popping up into my head were those of my own dismemberment and darkness closing in on me. I banished those thoughts as quickly as they came, and tried my best to focus on the task at hand. I grabbed the weapon that was closest to me; it was a small lightweight-throwing axe. I was actually happy; I figured it would do nicely. Axe in hand I started to run as fast as I could. The sand crust always breaking away at the last push making my progress seem frustratingly slow. The crowd began to whoop and clap or at least their own damn version of it.

Deb turned to Stephanie. "What the hell is he doing, he's running to his death?"

"That's what I saw," Steph replied flatly.

My biggest fear of running flat out and paying no attention to my surroundings was finding my opponent lying in wait, just waiting for me to crest a dune and chop my legs out from under me. But I felt that the potential reward was well worth the risk that I was taking. It might be my only chance. Besides, I reasoned, he would have to be running just as fast to catch up to me and then get into an advantageous place. I figured the threat to be relatively low. Although this was my life and the lives of four women that I was gambling with, I'm not sure the stakes could get any higher. The girl looked up in sheer terror as I approached her at full tilt. She had to think that I was mad. Here's this friggen guy coming straight at me, running as fast as he can with an axe held high. I just kept thinking to myself, please whatever your name is, don't pass out or everything that I am trying to do

will be for naught. But I figured that I would have wet myself
by now if the roles had been reversed. I couldn't spare the
breath to forewarn her and I didn't want my competition to
know what I was up to. That could spell instant disaster for
both of us. And then she began to scream, a full-throated
scream. Oh no, I thought to myself, I chose wrong. He had to
have heard that even over the mob; my time was limited. I
approached her, axe high in the air. She had added
uncontrollable shaking to her repertoire. I swung, the girl
slumped, no, don't pass out!! I think I heard Beth scream.
The crowd was silent, for once. The girl's hands came down
as I severed the rope that bound them over her head. Luckily
she didn't pass out. She picked up her head after realizing she
wasn't quite dead yet and looked me straight in the eyes.
Hers were still wide with terror. The best I could do was to
try to calm her down with a shushing sound and hold the axe
down in a non-threatening manner. It seemed to me to take
hours before it dawned on her that I wasn't there to kill her.
Her sobs wracked her body, it looked more to me like she
had a killer set of hiccups than anything else. At any other
time that thought might have seemed humorous. After a few
tense moments of this I felt she was ready and motioned for
her to follow me. I grabbed a short sword for her which hung
on the wall near her station. She seemed surprised that I
would arm her but she accepted it eagerly. Hopefully she
wouldn't have to use it, but if I got myself killed today at
least she would have the opportunity to defend herself
against Psycho Man. She was beginning to come more into
her own and understand just what was going on here. She
knew that I meant her no harm and that the odds of us getting
out of this alive were greatly increased when it became two
against one. My confidence increased. I was fairly certain she
wasn't a trained killer but her athletic body would do in a
pinch even if for only diversionary tactics. For the first time
during the games I was at an absolute loss as to what plan of
action I should take now. I sincerely hoped my confusion
wasn't showing, I didn't want my new ally to become

unnerved by my indecision. At the moment anyway she appeared to be relatively calm, possibly because for the first time since she got on this strange trip she now carried her own destiny in her right hand. I hoped that her strange calmness would not leave her during the heat of battle. Utterly clueless as to my next move, I warily went forward, always on the alert for an attack. The girl followed closely, she also was on full alert.

We progressed forward for what seemed hours. I was beginning to think that he had somehow circled around us. But I reasoned that that was impossible, there wasn't really anything to completely cover him while circling past, we would have spotted him at some time. No, he's laying low, we just need to be careful when we come up over the dunes, unless of course he's buried himself... Too late!!! I screamed as the blade entered my leg just above my ankle. I felt it scrape against my bone; I could hear my muscle being cut as the blade exited right below my knee. He pulled the blade back and as he did so I could feel it scraping against my shin. I fell like a stone. Blinding white spots shot across my eyes, I could see nothing except pain, and it was savage. He had used my own tactic against me. I barely made out his shape as he jumped out of the sand to complete his handiwork. I couldn't even raise my sword, because number one I had dropped it, and number two both of my hands were clamped against the wound on my leg. I knew that this was the end; I just wished that I could have kissed Beth one last time.

"You're a fuck!" I yelled, mere moments before I passed out.

The next thing I consciously remember was waking up with Deb looking down at me. But how could that be, did that maggot kill her too? Am I dead? Do they have pain in Heaven? Oh no, I'm in Hell? I did my best to try to get up but the searing pain in my leg prevented that. My teeth were chattering uncontrollably. From across the room I could hear Stephanie's voice. I couldn't even begin to concentrate on the words, the pain had put me into another whiteout. It was many moments more before I was able to regain some semblance of consciousness. I was able to focus on objects even if the edges were blurry.

"Am I dead?" I managed to stammer, not really sure which answer I wanted to hear.

"No, but it was close," Deb said gravely, tears now forming in her eyes. "Tanya saved your life, you clumsy thing you." Her attempt at humor did little to stem the tide which was now flowing freely. She grabbed me and hugged me, luckily she didn't shake me or I know that I would have passed out again from the pain.

"What happened to him?" I asked incredulously.

"Tanya stabbed him in the back as he was moving in to finish you off, he was so intent on killing you he never even noticed her." A noticeable shudder ran through her body as she explained the details. I drew her close to try and drive away the demons that were bothering her.

"And I'd kill that bastard again if I had the chance!" Tanya yelled from across the room.

"He killed her best friend in the last round, talk about your poetic justice," Deb said. "She still has nightmares."

"Still? How long have I been out this time?" I moaned. At this rate I'd sleep the rest of my time on the ship. I felt bad for Tanya and her nightmares, but the fears of what might have been far outweighed the action she took.

"A week."

"A week! When's the next round start?"

"Another week."

"Deb, I can barely move after a week of recovery, how am I possibly going to be in any type of fighting shape in another week?"

"That's not your biggest worry," she said softly, obviously seeing the strain on my face.

"What could possibly be worse?"

"There was a huge power struggle over you. The gladiator overseers, I guess that's what you'd call them, some of them wanted to have you executed. They said that you violated the rules and received outside help. But a slim majority felt that you used extreme cleverness and improvisation and heralded your actions as very advanced tactics. The minority had to acquiesce on two points so as to not have any further arguments regarding you," she said with a sigh.

"And just exactly what are those two points?" I felt that I already knew the answer to one of them; the pain in my leg was testament to that fact.

"One, they did the bare minimum to fix your wound, basically to just make sure that you didn't die."

"And the second?"

"They dropped your ranking down to 152nd, last place."

"Death sentence," I mumbled.

"What? Don't say that!" Deb cried.

"Come on Debbie, they left me injured and dropped my ranking. I have only come out of one fight unscathed and I was healthy for all of them. I'm going in there now with one good leg against my toughest competition. What do you think is going to happen!?"

"Stop yelling at me. I don't know the answers. I only know what I want, and that's you. I don't want to be on this god-forsaken ship playing the aliens' god-forsaken game. I just want to go home." She broke down in heart wrenching sobs.

"I'm sorry, I'm sorry, I didn't mean to upset you any more than you are. I... I'm just not feeling too well at the moment. Could you please close the door on your way out, I would really like to get some shut eye."

"Of course," she said as she wiped the few remaining tears away from her face.

But sleep was the last thing that happened that night. I thought about all the wondrous and glorious ways that I was going to die next week. It's amazing how humans think, I mean I've always known I was going to die but when you put a date on it, it becomes almost insufferable. Death seemed to be all around me. The smell of it seeped through my bandages. If I tried hard enough I felt that I could catch a glimpse of him gleefully wisping around my room waiting for his opportunity to come. "Not yet you bastard!" I yelled. The women huddled together in the adjacent room looking at each other in bewilderment. They did their best to comfort each other, but they knew the score as well as anybody. If I died they died, plain and simple just like algebra, a=b.

The next day, or what I perceived to be the next day, I awoke and jumped out of bed. Oh crap! I thought to myself, I am going to pay dearly for that move. I waited for the blinding pain to sear the front of my brain, and then I waited a little more and then I waited just a little bit more. Ah there it was, but it certainly wasn't the stampeding of wild stallions that I expected, it was more like a lone small donkey. The blinding pain had been replaced by a slow steady throb. I finally opened my eyes and unclenched my teeth; I must have been somewhat of a sight.

"What the hell is going on?" I yelled

"What do you mean?" Deb said as she entered the room with a huge smile.

"You know damn well what I mean, woman. Yesterday…"

"Three days ago," she interjected.

"Okay three days ago you were all depressed and I was in a great deal of pain."

"Well from what I can gather," she started, "is that large amounts of drakka…"

"Huh?" I asked

"Money," she continued. "Drakka is money on this ship." I nodded in understanding, barely. "It is wagered on these events and apparently there is a fairly significant amount of drakka or money riding on you. So an alien doctor was paid off."

"They have corruption too? It's good to know that that's not just a human condition."

"So you feel better?" she asked hopefully.

"I'm almost perfect," I said as I grabbed her in my arms and twirled her around, and was regretfully rewarded with a doubling of the pain. I tried my best not to let her see me wince.

I felt curious enough or possibly morbid enough to sneak a peek at my wound. I unwound the bandage that had this incredibly sticky feeling to it, but stuck to nothing but itself. Man, would the doctors on Earth love to get a hold of this stuff. When I was done I could only stare in disbelief. What had been a life threatening gash and at best a handicap making wound now appeared to be no more than a briar scratch. My skin didn't even look as if it was going to scar in any way. As I reapplied the bandage, I was convinced that within another day the throb and scratch would cease to exist. My mood healed almost as quickly as my wound. As long as I was mobile I still had the proverbial fighting chance, and I was oh so close to seeing Beth again.

I knew it had to be done but I was having the hardest time convincing myself to do it. I walked into the adjoining room where the women were. Stephanie appeared to be about to speak. I shot her a glance that could have frozen a glass of mercury from twenty-five yards away. Needless to say she got the hint and let whatever she was about to say drop off her lips. I made a beeline for the huge screen. I soon discovered that in these advanced rounds the competitors could do more than just watch reruns; we were also given short snippets of information on each contestant. Lord knew I could use all the help I could get. But to be honest, all I was concerned with was Durgan's last competition. The terrain had been similar to my last bout. I couldn't believe what I was seeing. Even though they say seeing is believing it was still difficult for me to grasp. Durgan was even bigger than when I last saw him. Schwarzenegger at his prime was never this big. I had hoped that possibly the added bulk would make him slower and less agile. But almost as if he heard my thoughts he did a standing back somersault for the benefit of the crowd. Obviously this was his new signature move before every fight. The aliens had to be feeding him straight steroids, there could be no other explanation for his massive increase in size, strength and speed. What was even more surprising was his nonchalant attitude. He looked like he was going out to get some lunch, not kill another fellow human being. He couldn't even be bothered with getting a weapon. No. 254, one Derek Sanderson (a formidable looking character himself), opted for the two handed sword.

I was not under the impression that something as unwieldy as a two-handed sword was a good idea against an opponent so fast. But I think that he was also under the false impression that all that bulk was going to make Durgan a lot slower and more vulnerable. Big mistake, one that I personally wasn't going to make. Durgan had no fear, he just strolled up the middle of the arena like he owned the place. Sanderson, upon seeing that Durgan had no weapons, decided to take advantage of the fact. He came running at Durgan as fast as the sand would let him, sword raised and poised to strike. Mistake number two, upon approaching closing distance Sanderson lowered his weapon. With lightning quick speed Durgan stepped to the side and avoided the strike, leaving one foot behind and with his right hand pushing the flailing Sanderson to the ground with a resounding thud. His sword unfortunately went flying through the air and landed some fifteen feet away. Durgan deftly placed himself between Sanderson and the sword. With what seemed like considerable effort, Sanderson raised his body from the sand. Blood oozed down both of his knees and dripped from his hands. Warily approaching Durgan, he never saw what hit him. If I hadn't had the luxury of rewind I wouldn't have caught it either. With blinding speed Durgan did a roundhouse kick that would have easily broken the neck of a less statuesque man. As it was, Sanderson's jaw was clearly broken and some of the bone had even protruded from the right side of his face. I thought that if he were to live he was going to have a hell of a time eating, but I don't think that was his biggest concern at the moment. He went down faster than a hooker at a convention.

Even as dazed and confused as he was, I'm pretty sure he knew what was going on. Durgan picked Sanderson's slack body up and proceeded to raise him up over his head with no more effort than a basketball player puts into lifting a basketball. He then found the nearest Joshua tree and threw Sanderson on it. The spiny plant pierced Sanderson's body in multiple places. The scream that came from him was one that will haunt me till the end of my days. Durgan had no desire to make this a merciful and quick killing. He proceeded to put his foot on Sanderson's midsection and push until some of the spiny leaves began to make their way through to the other side of his body. Thankfully his screaming began to lose some of its velocity, blood began to fill his lungs and served to further stifle the noise. Shock mercifully was settling in; Sanderson's eyes got the thousand-yard stare. To rouse the crowd even further Durgan pulled off one of the spiny leaves and jabbed it directly into Sanderson's left eye; apparently he was not far enough in shock. He managed one more scream that rivaled all the previous ones combined, then gave one final convulsion and stayed there. I tried to imagine that he was just a scarecrow stuck to Velcro, that was far more palatable to swallow than the truth. I was about to turn the set off but my lack of better judgment prevailed. I wanted to see what Durgan did with his newest spoil.

He strode with all the pride of a peacock to the woman who was helplessly tied up. What he did next surprised and disgusted me. He knelt down on one knee before the woman and yelled up into the stands, "I will have no woman but the Goddess of the games" With that he stood up and put his hands on either side of his captive victim's head almost as if to caress her and with a sudden twisting motion he broke her neck. That was probably the most humane thing that monster had done on this ship since he arrived. She was dead and that was that. I was not as appalled at the death as I should have been; I guess that I was getting desensitized. What horrified me more was the thought of that Cro-Magnon with my Beth, *that* was ripping my soul apart. Well, I thought to myself, he vowed to have no other woman, so I must also do the same. I had to focus on one thing and one thing only, survival. But now the focus wasn't so much on myself anymore, I had to do it for Beth. The guilt I felt for having been with Debbie was already beginning to consume me. I had needed her then, I still needed her. When I felt that I wasn't going to survive I needed her comfort but now that I had a chance, even as slim as it was, I had to focus all my attention on that possibility. Beth was my reason for living and fighting. I no longer needed or wanted Deb's comfort, I told myself. I know that sounds selfish but I had to be true to myself in order to be true to Beth. I decided to check the rankings to see who my possible opponents would be, if I made it through the next round. That's when my biggest break thus far showed itself. I kept telling myself it had to be divine intervention. If so I would forever be in debt to the one I called God. The competitor's names, vital statistics and rankings came up and by some twist of fate only 151 names showed up. Sometime between the decision of the alien board and now, one of the victors had died. It was only later that I learned it was not by wounds suffered in battle but by a jealous woman in one of the competitor's growing harem. These women were proving more and more to be my allies. Confidence was beginning to build; now it was time to see what No. 2 was made of. I went out into the other room and approached Tanya. She stood there proudly, hands on hips. Apparently the other women had filled her in and she had no fear of me. That was a good thing, I thought to myself. Even if I didn't make it through to the end, I had given these women something invaluable: hope. I grinned at her and she grinned back. No words were needed; we both knew we had saved each other's lives out there. Most likely her actions weren't as altruistic as I would have hoped, but either way the outcome was the same. I was alive and I could continue on my quest. And yes that's what I felt it was, a quest. I was now on a mission I did not yet fully understand the magnitude of.

I turned on the Jumbotron to check out No. 2, Adam Kirkland. My confidence waned ever so slightly when I saw him. He was nowhere near the size of Durgan but every part of him was pure muscle. The best way I could describe him would be to take a picture of Patrick Swayze and shave his head. Obviously this guy had studied martial arts before he ever stepped into this three-ring circus. He, like Durgan, didn't believe in using weapons, he had no need for them. Kirkland disposed of his latest victim quicker and with more finesse than Durgan had. It was almost an art form the way he killed him. I'm relatively sure his competitor never felt a thing. His foe had thrust his spear at Kirkland's torso, but he quickly evaded the attack. He put one foot behind the man's leg and literally tripped him over his shin, a mere fraction of a second later the heel of Kirkland's boot was smashing through the bridge of that poor man's nose. Pieces of cartilage into the brain cavity did the rest of the work. Unfortunately Kirkland saw no reason to be quite so merciful to his spoils. The woman shrieked in terror as he approached. Obviously she knew something I didn't. What I watched so sickened me that I vowed I would kill him just for that single act. With the woman still tied up, hands over her head, he delivered a hard karate blow to her arm. The elbow gave way and bent the opposite way from which God had intended it to. With a sudden fury Kirkland kicked in both of her knees. Her legs bent backwards like an ostrich's. The audible crunching of the bones could even be heard over her shrieks. The woman just kept screaming and Kirkland just stood there, hands on his hips looking at her as if he was admiring his work. And then he just walked away. I was yelling at the screen at the top of my lungs.

"Damn you, finish her you fucken bastard!" I spat. This man was far crueler than Durgan, if that was even possible. He just left her hanging there with a broken elbow and two broken knees. I think it was shock that finally killed her, the sobbing stopped after twenty minutes but her tears went the distance. Forty-five minutes later when her final death throes were over I was shaking uncontrollably. I had cried so much the front of my shirt was damp. What was even worse was that the aliens with all their advanced medical technology just left her there to die. I once again vowed revenge for all the souls that had lost their lives here, but especially for Kate Hellsboro, the girl they left to die. They would pay with blood or whatever flowed through their crocodile-like veins. The first plan of action was to figure out a way to eliminate Adam Kirkland. But with God on my side, how could I lose?

Deb asked a question, breaking me out of my contemplation. "Mike, can I talk to you?" Her voice sounded distant, almost as if spoken through an intercom system. I don't know how many hours I had been sitting there in the dark but I still felt no relief from the internal pain I had experienced earlier. Debbie repeated herself before I was really even sure somebody was talking to me. Her voice groped in the dark, looking for my ear like a blind man in unfamiliar territory.

"What is it Deb?" I replied slowly and with a hint of an edge.

"Are you alright?" she asked tentatively.

"What do you mean Deb?" I snapped, "Do you mean in the physical sense? Because yeah, I'm in the best shape I've ever been in. I've got muscles in places I didn't even know existed. Or do you mean my mental state? Yeah, I'm as sharp as a razor. I can think of more ways to kill a man than you can imagine. Or do you mean spiritually? Because I'm sure God just loves the work that I'm doing down here. And you know what Deb? I'm starting to *like* it. I feel more alive when I kill somebody than at any other time. Even more so than when we're making love!" That seemed to sting her like a bee, she outwardly winced. "I'd rather snap someone's neck! Don't you see what I've become? I'm losing my ability to empathize. I've seen more death and torture and destruction of the human soul in the past couple of months than most people see in a whole war. And we're doing this for the enjoyment of a civilization that couldn't give two shits about us. Sometimes I think it would be easier if I just went into the arena and fell on a sword." If Debbie's facial expressions could have been capable of making noise I would have been able to hear her face drop even in the gloom of the bedroom.

"Stop that, don't talk like that!" she implored. "We have got to survive, we just have to!" She seemed to be saying that more to herself than to me.

"Please leave," I motioned. "I just want to be alone for a while."

A while turned into two weeks. I didn't so much as say hi to any of the women the entire time. The aliens came and I went with them without uttering a word, and not surprisingly no words were offered in return.

Well, one thing I couldn't count on anymore was the help of a woman. Since my last fiasco all women captives were kept up in the stands until completion of the battle at hand. For the first time since I got on this ship, I saw Beth. I guess I was early because she was just being led to her 'Guest of Honor' seat. I know that she saw me too because she paused for a moment and almost made to wave but then thought better of that idea. My heart had somehow made its way into my throat. Sweat leaked out of every pore and I hadn't even moved yet. I had almost forgotten the deep feelings I felt for her. No time for reflection though, Kirkland was already being led into his side of the pit. When I entered my side of the pit the crowd hushed into complete and utter silence. While I had my chance I yelled at the top of my lungs so that all could hear, even though the message was for one only. "I love you!" And barely audibly, so that no one heard but I *knew,* Beth repeated those same words. And so the saga continued. I picked up a spear. I hoped that Kirkland hadn't developed any new moves in the last two weeks. The terrain this time out was only a small grassy hill in the middle of the arena that flattened out on the top. But it effectively hid my competitor from my view and vice versa. I knew from watching him that he would be approaching at a steady pace up the slope and he would be unarmed. I checked my homemade knife which was hidden in the belt loop of my trousers. I hoped it wasn't noticeable. The laws of the games strictly prohibited the use of two weapons. I hoped that this rule didn't apply to homemade ones. I'm not sure how favorable the alien board would look upon another infraction from me. It had taken me nearly a week to sharpen the strip of metal I had taken off of the fridge. And still I wasn't sure if I would be able to deliver a killing blow with it. I was fairly confident it would cause injury but it had to be enough to slow this monster down. I walked toward the hill with a pace that would make a turtle happy; I was in no rush for this showdown. Obviously Kirkland was, though, the crowd began its incessant buzzing. I was certain that these croc-aliens were capable of smelling death. Well let them, for one of these days it would be their own deaths they smelled.

But enough reflecting. Kirkland was coming and he was coming fast. And the bastard was smiling. I think it was the sight of the spear. I'm pretty sure he thought I was going to be as easy as his last prey. That was fine with me, the more confident he was, the better I felt. He would be less wary in his over-confidence and eagerness to finish the job.

"That's right," I mumbled to myself. "Stick with your normal routine, and you'll be dead in another twenty seconds."

And so we squared off. I felt as if I was performing an instant replay for the NFL but this time the ending would have a different outcome. I slowly jogged towards him, spear in hand. I jabbed at him with the spear; he feinted right and dodged left. My heart jumped; he was doing exactly the same routine. With his left foot out his left hand grabbed the spear, with his right hand in the small of my back he used my momentum against me to force me to the ground. As he pushed and gravity took over, I began to twist my body.

When I hit the ground I was already in motion; my hand
found the hidden knife. I pulled it out from behind me as I
began turning my body away from his kick. His right foot
missed my face by no more than a shoe's width. He seemed
to hesitate with the change in the game plan. But that was
something I would think about later, I was acting purely on
instinct at the moment. With one deft motion I drew the
sharpness of the blade across his Achilles heel. The tendon
snapped like a broken rubber band and he fell fast. His face
was twisted in agony. I still had no follies about going in for
the kill just yet. He may have been down but he was far from
out. The lethality of his hands hadn't been diminished in the
least with the crippling of his leg. Extreme caution was now
the order of the day. I wasn't going to give up the advantage I
had fought so hard for. The crocs were silent, must have been
a bunch of them that lost a crap load of drakka on that last
move. They looked stunned. They didn't like the unexpected,
by all their accounts I should be dead by now, but much to
their future chagrin I still had a few more battles left in me. I
don't know what I was thinking but it definitely wasn't about
the task at hand. I began to drift off; I started to think about
my first encounter with Beth and how I knew that there was
something special there just from the way her skin felt on
mine. I hoped beyond hope that we would once again be able
to unite but I wasn't sure if she would or even could love me
after witnessing my destruction of human life. She had
always been an advocate for peace and a vegetarian to boot.
Could she handle a soul mate that violated her most
fundamental principles? I hoped so, the thought of going on
without her hurt more than the broken rib I had just
sustained.

"What the…?!" I yelled as I snapped back to my
predicament. Kirkland had sensed my thoughts were
elsewhere and was kind enough to help me back by
projecting his left foot into my rib cage. One, possibly two
ribs snapped with the dryness of a twig under a hot desert
sun. But the pain made it feel as if my entire side had

collapsed. I was in trouble, he had punctured a lung, my breathing was becoming shallower and the blood that rose up my throat was also a good indicator. I figured I had about a minute to finish him off before I was the dead one. Wouldn't that just screw up my plan? Kirkland was also aware of the damage he had inflicted; he started to pull himself away from me as fast as a one legged man can, which believe it or not was amazingly fast. I stumbled after him but my breathing was becoming more difficult, I was drowning in my own blood. My heart raced in fear, my thoughts drifted to my mother. I missed her toasted cheeses for dinner, Eddie Peak, my best friend in the first grade, Betsy Hoegler, the first girl I ever had a crush on. Mandy, the first girl I was ever intimate with. Breaking a million on Missile Command. Kate Hellsboro. A blood splattering cough racked my body, I fell face forward; I barely had enough strength to turn myself over. Kirkland, seeing my potential demise, was coming back for the kill. His eyes gleamed with the prospect of another victory. He appeared to me to look more like a serpent than a man. If I could only concentrate on something besides the pain, but everything began to become unfocused. Images kept fading in and out. Kate Hellsboro. 'Who is Kate Hellsboro?' Recognition through the pain. Kirkland also noticed the change in my face, the clearing of my eyes, he hesitated and my opening arrived. With Kirkland literally in my face I stuck my crude but effective knife straight into his throat. If I had been a surgeon it would have been a perfect tracheotomy. Blood criss-crossed my face, air bellowed out of the hole. He still had the presence of mind to try and finish me off; he attempted to break my neck, but I was never going to give him that opportunity. I just kept sticking the knife into the side of his neck until he had to accept the inevitable, life as he knew it was now over. He rolled off of me and tried to cover his multiple wounds with his hands but the blood poured through every crevice. I felt the need to let him go into the afterworld with one final parting shot.

"Hey dumb ass!"

He actually acknowledged my words and turned to look at me.

"If you had just left me alone I would have died all by myself in another minute or two." With that final shot his days were over, but even though my eyes were closing I had the distinct feeling it wouldn't be forever. For some strange reason I thought I smelled a cheeseburger.

"I think he's coming to!" I heard from a galaxy far, far away.

"Someone get a wet cloth." That galaxy didn't sound so far away I thought.

"He's opening his eyes," a familiar voice said, but for the life of me I couldn't figure out where it was coming from. I thought to myself, I hope my eyes aren't open because I can't see a thing. The world looked as if I was viewing it through an ace bandage. I could see shapes but no distinction whatsoever.

"I can't see," I mumbled weakly.

"And by the sound of it you can't talk either." A small laugh broke out among the women in the room but it felt more like relief than humor.

"We all thought that we were going to lose you," a tender voice said. I could hear the strain in it.

The name Deb popped into my head long before I was able to associate it with the voice.

"How long?" was all I was able to mutter.

"You've been out for close to a month," a voice unfamiliar to me said.

My face must have gone slack, but she still continued with the explanations even after seeing my disdain.

"Well dear sir, you got your lung punctured, and an artery to your heart was also nicked. The aliens are still in disbelief that you are alive. They are more than a little upset, by all of their scientific data you should have died the moment that your rib was broken."

Well, that was all the information that I could handle for this month, I fell back asleep but not as deeply as before.

"Mike, can you hear me?" What a soothingly comforting and familiar voice I thought to myself. "I know it's over between us." I was about to reply but from her tone I was under the impression that she was talking more to herself than me; the fact that she thought I was sleeping did not deter her from her speech. "I know the comfort we brought each other was temporary. It was just our way of coping with this insanity and the stress. Only I didn't know that I was going to fall in love with you. To be honest I didn't even think that you were going to live past the first round I saw you in. And I think maybe that you had the same thoughts and maybe you felt it would be better to at least go out with a smile. But now I think you're going to survive and I think that you also believe that you are going to make it through this nightmare. Nobody could've done what you've done so far. Granted your strategy has been superb, your stamina incredible, but ah my love, your luck has been..."

"Has been guided by the hand of God," I rasped.

Deb gasped in amazement that I was awake. "You bastard, you let me go on and you were awake this whole time!" she yelled.

"Well, even us heroes need ego boosting every once in a while," I murmured.

"You ... you..." her face reddened with the prospect of using the appropriate terminology. Before she was able to find and use the sailor's vernacular, I spoke.

"Deb, I love you."

"But?" Wow, she did know me well.

"But Beth is and always will be my first love, and I think my soul mate. You were there at a time when I so desperately needed someone. You made me happy and kept me going especially when I didn't think that I had anything left in me. But I truly feel that the end is drawing near, whether it is for my victory or my ultimate demise. I can feel it in my bones; in my very soul I can feel it. And because of that I have to be true to Beth and myself. Being with you now would only be selfish."

"I know," she said softly. "But I'd rather have a small piece of you than no part at all." She left the room before her watering eyes began to tear.

After a brief reprieve Tanya came in, more breathtakingly beautiful than I had remembered, but alas I had no time for such frivolous thoughts anymore.

"They have a fight slated for you two weeks from today," she said bluntly.

"That's just dandy, I can't even leave this bed right now to take a whiz, but in two weeks I'll be back in the arena fighting."

Her entire demeanor reeked of concern. Although I know she cared for me I was under the impression that she was more concerned with her own well being than with mine. And that was completely understandable; I didn't fault her for that at all.

"Don't worry," I said. "I'm sure that I'll be able to piss by myself in two weeks."

She laughed and I laughed and damn it, it felt good. Up until the time my ribs said otherwise.

The aliens had held off on the ratings until they were sure that I was going to pull through. My survival was probably going to set off a shit storm, because a lot of contestants were more than likely studying the opponent they would next meet with me out of the picture. So they had in most cases wasted a month of studying time on an opponent they would not be facing. Thoughts of Beth filled my head constantly, life without her seemed incomplete. Debbie had become solemn and withdrawn over the last few days; unfortunately I couldn't afford to be good company to her. I didn't feel that I had the capacity for it.

No. 2, I thought to myself. Not bad, not bad at all. But with 74 other competitors left that meant that Durgan was going to get another bye, which meant the rest of us were going to do our best to kill each other while sustaining grievous injuries and he just kept getting stronger. Apparently God, or at least the aliens, didn't like that scenario either. The aliens wanted to see the gruesome Durgan at work so they revoked his bye and were going to randomly assign it. I was under the suspicion that 'random' was too strong a word. These aliens probably had ties to the mob. I was convinced that my number wasn't even included in the randomization process. And there it is, No. 13 got the bye. Well, on to the task at hand.

CHAPTER 24 – Journal Entry 19

My next opponent, No. 74, Shawn Timmins, was one of those rare individuals that prove that you can't judge a book by its cover. Especially when the cover weighed in excess of 360 pounds. He was about 5'10" or 5'11" and fat, not big and bulky, just plain fat like his brother. If I ever got off of this ship would I be able to go to the Timmins' household and look their mother in the face? And tell her what, that her boys had died valiantly, at a stupid alien contrived event? Shawn was huge like his brother, but all similarities stopped there. He moved effortlessly and with a precision that a figure skater would be proud of. I had no clue how this incredible bulk of a man had made it this far. I watched all of his previous clashes and discovered that I was going to be truly saddened by killing him. He was one of the few contestants left that was worthy of living. By all accounts, he never let one of his competitors suffer needlessly, and it appeared that the women were relieved when he won. They obviously knew their fate with him would not end up with torture and death. However I might feel about him, I still had to look out for number one, or in this case No. 2. I deserved to live just as much as the next guy and I was not going to let those feelings disrupt my ultimate goal, which was to get off of this ship and give these aliens some payback. This man was blessed with a grace that belied his enormous size; he must have lulled all of his competition into a false sense of security. He had to have a lot of muscle mass to move that much weight around that fast. He, unlike me, did not make it to this level on luck alone. He was skilled, but I found a chink in his enormous mass. And I planned to exploit it for all it was worth, and in this case that meant his life. My competition was in two days and I did aerobic exercises almost that whole time, I had to regain some of my former strength. I said nothing more than the precursory niceties to the girls. Deb had withdrawn from our makeshift family, she did little more than eat and sleep. I felt concern but it was buried deep, it was more like a back burner type of concern; if I wasn't actually looking at her I didn't think about it at all. By the time my front door dematerialized I was able to, as promised, take a piss on my own. Also, due to the expert care of our hosts, I felt almost 70 to 75 percent back to my normal self.. Not as high as I would have liked it to be, but a lot better than dead, I reckon. For once I actual entered the arena with no fear, whether it was pure folly or total confidence, I'm not sure. It finally felt good to not want to heave at the beginning of a bout, but the flip side of that was I was about to kill a man and I was not concerned about that little tidbit at all. I was saddened at the prospect of never again being that boy who had come onto this ship. Would my own mom even recognize me? I seriously doubted it.

The battlefield this time was a mockup of a department store. It looked just like Wal-Mart, there was a produce section off to the right, sporting goods straight ahead, a row of registers to the left. Sporting goods, huh! What are the odds they'd have rifles there? I didn't think that would happen but it might be worth a jaunt down that aisle to check it out. First I grabbed a spear and then I strode up one of the aisles. Much to my chagrin everything was merely a mirage, unlike previous scenarios all of the goods in this store were nothing more than smoke and mirrors. The floor and the shelving felt real enough but if you tried to pick up a bottle of Wisk your hand would pass right through it. So even their computers had limitations. It was good to know that this opponent was not omnipotent. Well, so much for a rifle, I might as well go to the task at hand. And there he was, entering the same aisle that I was in. We had about twenty-five yards of distance to close on each other before we clashed. Alright, time to put Plan A into effect. This had

better work because there was no Plan B. Mr. Timmins
seemed pleased that I was headed straight for him, apparently
looking at him gave people the misinformed notion that he
could in no way move his bulk quickly enough to strike or
even repel an attack. I picked up my pace a little and brought
the spear up over my head and threw it for all it was worth.
Well, I'm not Swahili and he was fast. He dodged it with
little to no effort whatsoever. I stood for a second as if
dumbfounded. I let him go on the offensive, something I
knew that he was not used to but would do if the cards
favored it. He ran at me, sword upraised. I stayed as long as I
dared, he moved fast, faster than he even looked on the tapes.
I heard, hell, I *felt* the tip of the sword as it cut a six inch
swath through the back of my shirt as I hauled ass away.
Smelling fear and blood he chased me. I made sure to stay
close enough so that he wouldn't give up the chase but far
enough so that I didn't become his next victim. Man my legs
burned, it had been a long time since I had sprinted; my lungs
ached for air. But I could hear Timmins laboring, he sounded
like a bulldog on a 95-degree day. He was panting and
snorting and I bet if I had big enough balls to turn around he
would have been drooling like one also. I could sense he was
falling further and further behind. I sped up and then slowed
when I felt the distance was right. Timmins was hunched
over with his hands on his knees breathing for all he was
worth; catching his breath was becoming an exercise in
futility. Well, time to up the ante. I sprinted to the end of the
aisle and cut up the next one running for all I was worth and
circled back to the far end where I had first spotted him. Poor
bastard, he was still hunched over gasping for air. I halved
the fifty yards in eight or nine seconds, scooping up my spear
as I ran. He was possumming! He stood, twirled and ran right
at me at full sprint. I again chucked the spear at him but this
time he was more like a charging bull than a dancing pony. I
scored a partial hit; blood welled up from the wound in his
side but he never slowed. This time I had no time to feign
surprise, my forward momentum had brought me to within

inches of his sword. I did not have enough time to turn tail, I ducked down and dove to the right. Timmins' bulk brought him another twenty feet before he was able to get his mass moving in another direction. I scrambled for a few feet on all fours, I wasn't trying to look pretty I was just trying to escape. Every moment counted, he was again right on my ass. If he had a spear I would have been impaled a long time ago. My legs were throbbing, I had a stitch in my left side, but I was not going to slow down to resolve that problem. After another twenty-five to thirty yards of him pursuing me I could tell he was dropping off again. I felt confident enough to take a glance over my shoulder and yes, he had stopped and was once again hunched over hands on knees, but this time his shirt was soaked through. Sweat was dropping into his brow and off his chin. I would remember to be careful of the puddle he was making lest I slipped on that. I figured I had more time but I had no desire to prolong this, I once again grabbed my spear. Timmins lifted his head just enough to eyeball what I was doing. He knew, he eyed me and smiled.

"Touché Mr. Talbot!" he yelled between ragged breaths.

"What are you talking about?" I asked. I was not about to give him any more breathing room.

"I see what you're doing," he rasped, "I may be fat but I'm not stupid. I'm glad I'll be losing to you instead of one of those other animals. Maybe in a different place we could have actually been friends."

"Maybe," I said warily "But you know what I have to do."

"I do," he answered. "But do me two favors?" he asked.

"What?"

"Take care of my women, and then please take care of these insects," and he gestured with his hand to the crowd.

"I promise on my very soul that I will do both of those things for you and for every other decent person that has died here." With that promise made he dropped his sword. Was this another trick, was he just trying to lure me in? I couldn't take that chance.

"Defend yourself!" I yelled

"My time here is done Mike, just do it fast."

"Shawn, pick up your weapon, don't make me do it this way."

"Come on man, you know as well as I do I don't stand a chance against Durgan or anybody else for that matter. I've been watching you since this began, you have a way about you. You could actually pull this off. No, it's better this way. The women have a better chance of survival with you than they do with me. I care more for them than for myself. Just do it!" he yelled.

His voice startled me, I think I jumped. I was wishing that it could be me letting the weight off of MY shoulders. He was about to die and he seemed immensely relieved. Is that how I'd feel? I wondered.

"Mike, this isn't a trick. Finish me off or they'll do the both of us in. Just look over there," he said as he pointed to the right hand side of the stadium. The guards were already zeroing in on us, and up until now I had not noticed the hissing and booing from the seats. The crowd wanted death and they wanted it now, they didn't care whether it came from my spear or the guards' weapons.

"Do it," and he dropped to his knees. "Do it now," and then he clasped his hands over his head. "Do it or all of our women are dead."

I approached him slowly, tears welling up in my eyes. Then I had full on tears coming down my face, I was crying like I was in the 1st grade and somebody had stolen my favorite lunchbox. I picked up the sword he had discarded and walked completely around Timmins so that his back was facing me. The crowd hushed, the guards put down their weapons. I raised the sword with both hands but I had to take one hand to wipe my eyes. I wanted to make sure that this was a clean killing blow and I could barely make out his bulk at the moment. I could tell that he was also crying; his back rose and fell in the spastic way it does when people are sobbing.

"I'm sorry Shawn."

"Me too." he cried.

I cut his head off; it was amazingly easy, like the proverbial hot knife through butter. Blood spurted out of his severed neck and the body fell over. His head rolled another five or six feet before coming to a rest. Of course it was face up and he still had a tear in his eye. Oh God, I thought, please don't let him be cognizant right now. This is already going to haunt me. Just then his mouth moved wordlessly, and I hurled everything I had ever eaten in my entire life. My guts screamed as I evacuated my innards. When there was nothing left my body looked for more, dry heaves threatened to rip loose every muscle in my rib cage, and still his mouth moved. God please forgive me! The crowd was going nuts; they apparently liked good old-fashioned beheadings.

I couldn't sleep for a week, every time I closed my eyes Shawn's head would haunt my dreams and every so often in my five minute dozes before I awoke screaming and sweating, words would actually come out of his mouth. Words of blame, of acrimony. Tension in the Talbot household was at an all time high. I wasn't sleeping and we had doubled our population. Needless to say I wasn't the most popular guy to half of these women. Some of the girls that had been with me for a while were actually concerned that I might be in some danger from one or more of Shawn's women. And then bless her heart, Debbie snapped out of her self-induced fog to bring some sanity to the household.

"Quit your bitching!" she yelled to the newcomers semi-huddled in the corner of the room. "Your champion…"

"Shawn!" one of the girls yelled.

"Shawn, he wanted Mike to win, he gave himself up to protect all of you! He knew he wasn't going to win and he didn't want to lose to any one of those other animals still out there. What do you think would have happened to all of you if he lost to Durgan?" Most of the girls shuddered; some were still not letting go of their anger. "Did you not all watch the battle? He gave himself up willingly. He wanted Mike to protect all of you, all of us."

"He didn't have to kill him!" one of the first girls to be in Timmins' harem called out, she was a pretty little thing with short blonde hair; her name was Karina.

"And what then?" Deb yelled. "You saw the guards, they would have killed them both, without blinking. And do you know what they do to spoils with no champion? They kill them! They just bring them out to the center of the arena and mow them down. End of story. So we will quit all of this in-house bickering and we will move forward. I'm sorry Shawn died, from what I could tell he looked like a decent person."

"He was!" the same little blond cried out.

"But these aren't decent times, but Shawn did the most decent and selfless thing he could for you and us. He sacrificed himself so that all of us stood a better chance of staying alive. And right now girls, that's what it's all about." I don't think there was a dry eye in the house, I retired to my room as both sets of women got into the middle of the room and had a huge group hug and cry fest. I had nothing left, I was tapped. I think I had heaved every possible emotion left in me. I slept for three straight days and not once did Shawn Timmins intrude on my thoughts.

Unfortunately for me, Timmins' selflessness ended up hurting me. In his willingness to let me kill him, the aliens felt that I had not lived up to my ranking and demoted me to 25th, not that it truly mattered. Out of the 38 of us that were still alive none of my remaining battles were going to be easy. But I had another month or so to prepare.

CHAPTER 25

Washington DC – Pentagon
"Do you think this is a viable plan?" the President asked his Chiefs of Staff.

"Sir we don't know if it is, but it is the only plan that we have," answered one of the President's more liked advisors. He was Dr. David Witherdrot, the Chief of Homeland Security. "Sir, we have heard nothing further from the ship since they took those hostages almost six months ago. To do nothing makes us look weak. Especially to an increasingly hostile and paranoid population. For good or bad, we need to do something."

"Yes, I understand the need to do something," the President uttered. "I've got pressure from groups that didn't even exist half a year ago. I just don't feel confident that this is the course I wish to take."

"Mr. President, we understand your concerns, but we feel that this shuttle is our best offensive weapon."

"And what of the hostages?" the President asked.

"Sir?" asked the Chief of the Military.

"The hostages, General, are they just fodder?" the President snapped back.

"Sir, we've been through this. We have to protect the many, even at the cost of the few."

"That doesn't make it any easier General."

"Sir, whether you like me or not. The fact remains as a military man I would rather avoid conflict at all times. It's always been politicians who scream WAR; whereas we military men have always advocated peace. But in these times sir, I believe that our hand has been forced. The aliens sit there parked on our doorstep, and say and do nothing. They could be waiting for reinforcements, they could be just deciding which way would be the best way to attack. Hell sir, not to get morbid, they might just think of our planet as a drive thru restaurant and they're just finishing up. What do we do the next time they come to visit? I don't think that we offer them a dove."

"General, what if they are trying to ascertain whether or not to contact us?" the President asked.

"Sir, with all due respect. The best scientific minds on this planet have been working on that very question for almost the entire six months. They came to the basic conclusion that the aliens have enough information at their disposal to have come up with a decision in their first week of orbit around Venus. No sir, their expert opinion is that the aliens are deciding on how to take us down in the most efficient way without doing untold damage to the planet. For all we know sir, those people they grabbed are test subjects for some type of viral agent that will reduce our population to thousands or maybe even hundreds. Sir as a species, our days may be numbered in the single digits. We owe it to all humanity to take this one final shot. If nothing else, we need to show those bastards that we won't go down without a fight."

"General, I understand your vigor. But what makes you think these nuclear weapons will have any effect whatsoever on the mother ship? We didn't even scratch the probe the last time we tried something like this."

"Sir, there is no guarantee, but the explosives that are on that shuttle are on the magnitude of 75 times the power of the one detonated off of the atoll. It's our best chance."

"I hope this doesn't just piss them off," the Chief Science Officer intoned.

"Well speak out now, Dr. Nisorini. You've made your opinions known, no sense in keeping them bottled up now," the President motioned. He did not like Nisorini in the least; he was a member of a growing segment of the populace that had become increasingly fatalistic. Depression and suicide were running rampant throughout the country, and the world for that matter. The President had always been a die-hard optimist, if you were still alive, you still had a chance.

"Sir," Dr. Nisorini said with a nasal twang. "The aliens thus far have done nothing to us."

"Except take twenty-five thousand or so people off our planet against their will."

"Except that sir, but at this point we really don't know if they have harmed them in any way. It just might be a way to introduce themselves. It has been my stance that we should not anger these aliens in any way. To do so could bring untold horrors down on the rest of us."

"So we should just chalk those people up as losses?" asked the President.

"That is my view," Nisorini droned. For being such a brilliant man he had not the least amount of common sense. The President had merely been baiting him, but Nisorini bit hard. Well at least, The President thought he knew where the good doctor stood. Not that he valued that opinion very highly.

"Well, thank you Dr. Nisorini. You have made up my mind," the President said.

"You are welcome, Mr. President." Nisorini beamed like a child that had received a gold star in his notebook for a good day at school.

"General," the President said.

"Sir?"

"Launch the shuttles."

"Yes sir!" The general hopped on the phone to tell NASA to get their asses in gear. It was now time for operation Blue Dragon.

The President wished he had a camera. Nisorini's face was worth the proverbial thousand words. The President couldn't decide whether Nisorini was going to cry or start stomping his feet.

CHAPTER 26 – Journal Entry 20

No. 13 was a guy from Jersey. He was an Italian man, but not your regular Italian, this was more your Guido variety. Come on, you know the type. He drives a Camaro, wears huge gold chains, most likely with the Italian horn on it. Has wife-beater t-shirts (tank tops), if he does wear sleeved shirts he has one side rolled up with a pack of smokes in it. And more than likely he uses more hair gel than your sister. Yeah, you know the one. Generally they are on the bullying side of things and this one looked to be no different. I didn't want to stereotype him but he looked like he did side work for the mafia. He stood about 6'1" to 6'2", jet black, greased back hair, and huge arms that hung low. He just optimized the tough guy look. He looked like a thug, and he appeared to be very used to a variety of weapons, although he tended to shy away from the bow and arrow and spear. Probably with his arms so large he wasn't able to get a proper throwing motion going. I had a month to study this guy, and I felt that I was going to need the entire time. I'd been watching his events for a solid week and as of yet I had not discovered a single weakness. He was smarter than his looks belied. He was cautious; he knew how to fight with or without weapons. And most importantly he wasn't insane, probably because he had already seen his fair share of violence in his time and this was just a new wrinkle in a standard way of living for him. He went about his business as if it were a business, very methodically and precise. He didn't extend himself to any great degree and as of yet he had made no mistakes. This man had not so much as suffered a scratch during the entire games. His competition, on the other hand, had not been so lucky. Was that a weakness? Lack of passion. If it was I saw no way to exploit it. I could see why the aliens had ranked him subsequently so low; he didn't do his job with any particular flair, he just went out there and did what he had to do. And now it was my job to figure out how not to let him do his job, on me.

While I watched and trained, Deb and I grew further apart, but she did not withdraw as she had previously. If anything she took over control of the household with a new and determined vigor. We had 12 women plus myself living here in our 'household.' It was increasingly difficult to find time to myself. This place was always bustling with activity. I tried my best to be pleasant but I didn't know half their names and in all actuality I had no desire to learn them. I already felt overwhelmed with the thought of protecting them all; I had no desire to get to know them any better. But sometimes when I just sat back and looked I wondered if this was the same type of view Hugh Hefner had enjoyed for so many years. Luckily or not Deb had made it crystal clear that my bedroom was completely off limits to everyone for any reason. I had my refuge, but I guess she figured if she couldn't have me, nobody could. And that was fine, I longed for one, and one only. With about a week left before my next bout, my biggest surprise to date on the ship happened. I and the rest of the gladiators were given a tour of the ship. To this day I don't know the reasoning behind it. I'm sure they felt we were no threat to them. But I had the distinct impression that to them we were beneath them on the evolutionary ladder. I can't imagine taking my pet hamster on a tour of my house. Did some of these aliens know what it was like to be cooped up with a harem of women? Was that it, did they feel bad for us? Or was it gratitude at the display we had been putting on for them? Don't get me wrong, we were heavily guarded by the larger of the two species, the ones known as the Genogerians, but we were being taken on tour by the smaller species that definitely seemed in command of things. It would have actually been a great diversion from the normal routine if it hadn't been with the very people that wanted to, or at least had to, kill me. No. 13, Tony Rizino, eyed me up and down once, and then apparently he made up his mind, because he never once looked at me again for the entire day. I, however, studied him for the full two hours of our tour, and did not discover a chink in his armor. If anything he looked more imposing in person than on the screen. His arms looked a full foot longer than mine, so much for hand-to-hand combat.

"This, hu-mans, is where we eat." Our host spoke as he led us through a cafeteria that wasn't very far removed from the ones on Earth. The greatest difference would be the troughs that were on the far sides of the cafeteria lining both sides. I wouldn't have been too sure what those were if not for the fact that a couple of the Genogerian guards were at the troughs sloughing away. Well so much for manners, they had scraps of food all over the floor and pieces of flesh hung greedily to their snout. "You will have to excuse them, hu-mans, they have yet to learn the importance of manners." Our host seemed to sneer at his last comment. I understood that there were two very distinct races here, but it was unclear to me whether this was due to some twist in their evolution, or this master race had simply taken over the planet that the Genos owned and had made them slaves. Was that our fate? I might have assumed that except that some of the scraps on the floor appeared more than likely to be of human origin. One did not generally eat their slaves.

And so we traveled through the cafeteria and beyond to what could only be labeled as the shuttle bay. Hundreds upon hundreds of spaceships of varying sizes and shapes were lined up along the hull for as far as the eye could see. They didn't look much like the ships from Star Trek or even Star Wars, but I was still fairly able to tell which ones were mere transports and which ones were used for battle. Some of the gun ships even had what appeared to be other alien vessels painted on the outside. I guess in a lot of ways we were a very similar species, they also liked to know how many kills they had, much like our aces in the great wars. What are the odds I could fly one of those things? Slim to none. Could I make a run for it now? The guards looked slack but I still didn't think I'd make it ten feet before I had a plasma burst in my back. And even if I made it, then what. I couldn't fly the thing and I sure as hell didn't have any clearance to get the shuttle doors opened. Someone had to let our planet know. These guys weren't here to say hi. The only reason this ET was phoning home was to let them know how the impending invasion was going. Our demonstration was merely a means for them to study our warfare tactics up close and personal. Hell, what better way to do it? They were learning all about our cunning and our brutality, while we were entertaining them. Talk about killing two birds with one stone. And we were all too wrapped up in our own existence to see the true bigger picture: that they were merely using us as test subjects to further their cause. By surviving and killing each other we were in effect giving them the weapons with which to kill our entire planet. It was then and there that I began to formulate my plan to get off of this ship and let Earth, my planet, know the true intention of these things. If they came here because of the message Carl Sagan sent out so many years ago, I was going to kick his ass too. The tour guide of our little group was droning on about the vast array of ships they had. And how many civilizations had fallen under their rule. And that soon Earth would become part of the Strolactic Empire. Ah, so I finally had a name, but the ugly bastard never disclosed any vital information. Like how does one fly one of these things. Oh well, there has got to be more than one way to skin a cat. Or gut a crocodile as the case may be. I got the impression that this tour was more of a 'Look how awesome we are, puny hu-man' tour. That could be just my slant on things, but being from New England you tend to take the rose-colored glasses off before you look at things. Our next stop was the training area for the warriors; another interesting note there was not a Progerian, besides our guide, in sight. The stop after that was the sub-helm according to our guide. On a starship of this magnitude apparently there were seven such sub-helms that were all under control of the main helm, which we were informed we would not being seeing. No alien race had ever seen the main helm and according to Brystrar, our guide, none ever would. Another point that seemed to interest no one but myself was that there were no Genos on the helm either. So along with being two distinct species they had very clear lines of delineation on their tasks. Is that a weakness? And if so how could I exploit it? I was having as much difficulty with this task as I was with finding and exploiting the weakness of my next opponent.

I was startled out of my thoughts by the hissing/talking of our guide.

"So, hu-mans, you have seen part of our ship, I will allow a small amount of time for questions."

Holy shit, this would be the first time we had actually been allowed to speak to them, what questions would we ask, what questions would they answer? We were each allowed one question and it went in order of ranking. I tried desperately to think of a question that would not be asked before it became my turn. I had little to fear in that department. Here we are in front of a vastly superior technological society, and we can ask them virtually anything regarding the cosmos, and the questions that were laid out were more along the lines of what you would ask your neighbor. "What do you eat?" although that could have been more out of concern than anything else. "How long do you live?" There were a couple of questions that piqued my interest. One of the more fascinating was, 'Do you believe in God?" That was actually Jersey Man's question. Brystrar's answer had been somewhat hesitant and blatantly evasive, but the general gist I got was that no, the Progerians had no need for a God but the Genos wholeheartedly believed in a higher being. I was wondering to myself if the Genogerians believed the Progerians to be this higher being; that could be used against them somehow, but not while I was on this giant can. When my turn came around I figured I would get some clarification on Jersey Man's question and also on my own thoughts.

"And what is your question hu-man, and please hurry it is getting past my noon meal time." The reptile licked his lips as he pondered his next meal. I hoped it wasn't leg of human.

"What exactly is your relationship to the Genogerians?" I asked as off-handedly as possible.

"That is a very good question for a hu-man, no wonder I have been winning so much drakka with you."

I knew it! There's the proof that they have been gambling on us the entire time. We're just a football game to them. Well that answered that question.

"Our worlds mirror each other in very similar ways." I personally highly doubted that. "On our planet we did not have a planet shattering event like the comet that destroyed almost all life on your planet. Our 'dinosaurs' as you call them merely became smaller in stature while their brain cavity increased. Along that evolutionary line we had a split from early Genogerian to modern Progerian much like your own between Cro-Magnon and Homo-Sapien. We, however, had enough sense not to destroy what would become our greatest allies in our quest for galactic domination. In essence we are the brains behind their brawn."

Wow, they weren't technically slaves but they were definitely doing the brunt of the dirty work. But to me it didn't look like they minded all that much. Being closer to their baser instincts must have made them perfect warriors, but would they be able to act without the head? Could that be their weakness? But I still had the problem of being able to relay this newfound information to Earth. I had so many questions but Brystrar had made it abundantly clear that he would answer one and only one question from each of us. And it looked as if we were getting to the point where his patience was beginning to wear thin. He looked at us much the same way we looked at him, in disgust and revulsion. All in all it was a very informative day and it hands down beat the hell out of being in that female-dominated beehive that was my house. There's a guy for you though, I'd rather be out with a bunch of guys that would rather see me dead and a bunch of aliens that didn't care if I was dead or alive, than having to spend the entire day in a house full of women. What is this spaceship coming to? I laughed out loud; the guard didn't see the humor and pushed me just a little harder into my abode than need be.

"You're alright?" Stephanie yelled from the top of the banister.

"I'm fine," I answered, "We just went on a little tour."

"Oh thank God, we thought they might have taken you to execute you or something unimaginably horrible like that," Stephanie half-cried. "Deb's beside herself in anguish."

"Well could you please just let her know that I'm good to go. I'm dog-tired. I just want to get some sleep." I guessed that I was being a little selfish but the sooner that Deb could get along without me the better off she'd be.

"I really think that you should be the one to tell her that," Steph threw in.

"Steph, listen, I know that I'm not the king of this or any other domain, but could you please just do this for me. Staying away from her is hard enough, if I see her crying I don't know that I can take it."

"Then why not just be with her, if it hurts both of you this much to be apart why should you?" she asked.

"You know the answer to that," I raised my voice just a little too much.

"Mike, you know as well as I do there are no guarantees in life, and all bets are definitely off in this place."

"So is that your way of saying I'm a dead man walking?" I said my voice now getting a little louder.

"Now hold on, you know I don't think like that. If I was that fatalistic I wouldn't have bothered getting out of bed in the morning, what would be the point."

"I know, I know." I now was trying to calm her down as her voice was beginning to peak.

"I honestly think that somehow, someway you're going to get us out of this hell hole."

"I'm glad you feel that confident, because honestly Steph I don't feel the same way."

"I don't want to hear that shit!" she yelled. My head snapped back from the sheer voracity of it. "All of our lives also hang in the balance." It was then that I noticed the growing crowd of females that had gathered to watch our tirade. "If you keep thinking like that then we are all doomed, and I personally will have none of it!" She was nearly shouting now, at this rate I figured the guards would be in here at any moment to quell the disturbance.

"Steph!!" I shouted at the top of my lungs to finally quell her. "I love you but if you don't shut the fuck up I'm going to come up there and smack you with a big stick." She actually finally shut up, the gears in her head must have been turning a mile a minute; her face was beginning to blossom in patches of crimson, and I could tell she was about to let loose a volley of insults. The girls watching could do nothing more than stare in disbelief with the turn of events. This had to be better than afternoon soaps. And then it happened, first it was a snort, then it was a chuckle, and then I full out lost control, I started laughing. It's amazing what stress can do to a person. When Stephanie realized that I was merely egging her on she began to laugh, she actually had to hold onto the banister to keep from falling over. And that will be the moment that I use to always remember Stephanie, long blond hair flowing over a beautiful laughing face, tears of joy streaming down her eyes. It would be the last time I ever saw her laugh.

"What is all this noise?" Deb said, emerging from her room as she wiped the sleep and old tears from her eyes.

"Mike was just telling me," Steph snorted, "how he was going to beat me with a big stick!" and then she started laughing anew.

"How is being beaten with a big stick funny?" Deb asked seriously.

And then I lost it, again. Deb stared at us for another minute or two before throwing her hands up in disgust and retiring back to her room. Steph and I both pointed and started laughing again. The range of emotions that this ship put me through were vast and extreme in both directions. Even if I could get off of this ship, would I ever be able to fit back into normal society? Who knew, but the fact remained, I had to try.

After I grubbed down some food I forestalled sleep in favor of watching some more of Jersey Man's battles. There had to be a weakness somewhere, it would mean my demise if I could not discover one in time. As I began to watch his matches for the third time that day, a theory came to mind. Granted it was only a theory, but it was the first formulation of a plan that I had yet to develop and I was going to roll with it. So with that in mind and figuring that I was not going to get any new information today I decided to catch up on some sleep. And for the first time in a couple of weeks I actually slept well. So well in fact that I never even stirred when Debbie joined me in the bed. I awoke the next morning feeling refreshed and light hearted, but that possibly could have been due to the fact that my nose was in Debbie's hair and it smelled just like a strawberry field on a hot summer day. A couple of more whiffs and I would have been there. Debbie turned, and noticing me in my rapture just shoved me away.

"Don't be getting any funny ideas just because I'm in your bed," she snapped.

"You're the one who came here," I retorted. "Why are you giving me a hard time?"

"I was just cold."

"There are extra blankets in the closet," I answered matter-of-factly. She huffed and puffed and blew through the doorway. Geez, I thought to myself, I think I pissed her off.

Jersey Man's time had come and he was going to find himself in some trouble. I entered the arena first this time, once again being the underdog. The crowd's response wasn't nearly the same. Apparently my contingent of fans was growing smaller, but there were still a few die-hards who must have made some serious drakka on me. The terrain this time was fairly plain, but it was gorgeous. Under any other circumstances I would have felt great peace with the world. It was a grassy meadow, with foot long golden green grass that actually swayed in the breeze. How the hell was a breeze possible, but I guess on this ship pretty much anything was possible. The aliens even piped in cricket and bird noises, this place could have made a fortune on Earth. Instant vacation, you could go anywhere on the planet and more than likely anywhere off of the planet. How cool would that be to take a leisurely stroll on the Martian shores? Or possibly check out a meteor hit on the moon? The possibilities were endless. But alas, back to the here and now; the announcer was just finishing up his introduction of Mr. Rizino and I didn't think he would waste his time letting me indulge in my reverie. Well, it was time to put my plan into action and now that I was standing here it didn't seem quite as good. It looked better on paper than in the real world. But it was way too late in the game to be changing now. The meadow motif greatly worked out to my favor, it gave me plenty of time to start haranguing Jersey Man. I ran to the far side of the arena across from me and grabbed a bow and arrow, and then ran to the back edge of my wall to stand by where the spear stood. A guard raised a weapon level with my head. If I so much as brushed up against that spear while the bow was in my hand he would surely strike me dead. The crowd looked on in amazement, they thought I was committing suicide. I, however, had no intention of giving them that satisfaction. Rizino had seen me running across the arena like a madman, yet he didn't seem perturbed about it in the least. I don't think he gave a rat's ass.

"Hey you fucken guinea!" I shouted. He looked at me and then looked around and pointed a finger to his chest as if to say 'You talken to me?'

"Yeah you mook, I'm talking to you!" I yelled again.

I couldn't really tell from this distance but I would swear to this day that I saw the first real facial expression from Rizino since this whole thing started.

"It's wops like you that make us look bad," I yelled as I pointed to myself.

"Shut up you fuck!" he yelled as he quickened his pace.

"Good, come on you fucken dago!" I yelled.

Well I went and did it now. I pissed him off. "I'll kill you, you little fuck. Nice and slow too," he promised as he increased his pace to a full on charge.

Well, it's do or die, I thought to myself. I have to wait until he's close enough that he's committed but not too far that he is able to realize his folly. With fifteen yards between us Rizino was charging like a mad bull with sword upraised, he definitely wanted to cut me in half. I raised my bow and arrow and drew back. Recognition dawned in his eyes, he knew the score; I had set him up and he had fallen for the trap. He also knew it was do or die, he was going way too fast to do anything with his momentum except come straight forward. Either I hit and killed him or I missed and he killed me. Well as fate would have it, we were both wrong. I shot and I struck but it was far from a mortal wound. The arrow hit on his left side and actually passed right through the fleshy part underneath the rib cage. But curiously the arrow had another strange effect, which I had not been prepared for at all. With about five yards between us, Rizino pulled up and just stared down at the blood pouring out of the wound in his side.

"I can't fucken believe you shot me!" he yelled over and over again. He was truly insulted that I would have the nerve to actually wound him. What was I thinking? This had to have been the first time he had ever suffered a wound by the hands of another. He was so used to doling out punishment he didn't have a clue how to receive it.

"You ffffuck!" he spit as he yelled. "I'll kkkill you for this!"

"Yeah, I've heard that before." But I wasn't playing with him; if he actually got his wits back about him he was still incredibly lethal. I did not think that stopping was going to be part of the plan. I hesitated, not knowing whether to finish him off with the bow and allowing my not so good aim to become a factor or grab the spear and give him a chance to come around. I had no desire to get close. I notched another arrow and let fly. At fifteen feet even a child would have had a tough time missing. The arrow hit with a solid thunk square in his chest. You could have literally heard a cricket chirp in the arena; the aliens had ceased all noise.

Rizino blinked once in utter amazement looked down at the arrow in his chest, and then spoke his final words.

"You can't kill me." I don't know if he was asking or not but the job was done, he fell face forward onto the arrow, driving it straight through his back. It let out a large popping sound as it broke through the skin. I didn't so much as look twice at the body as I headed out of the arena. My thoughts had turned elsewhere. I was really hoping for chicken tonight when I got back to the house. The guards brought down my latest spoil, a pretty brunette although a little too tall for me. She looked to be about 5'10". At 5'8" I had never liked going out with girls taller than myself, hopefully she could cook. For some damn reason I was famished. I left the arena and only a handful of aliens were making any noise. It seemed to me that my guard may have been giving me a wider berth today, I didn't think he was all that frightened but even he was amazed at the unconcerned attitude I had adopted upon killing my latest foe. If he had the ability to mind read he would have seen that I was shaking like a leaf on the inside but he didn't need to know that.

"What's your name?" I tried valiantly not to stammer. But it was hard with my heart beating inside my chest like a jackhammer.

"Carla," the girl answered nervously. She was also a little thrown off by my attitude.

"Well Carla, can you cook?"

"Um, some." She looked at me sideways, still trying to get a bead on me.

"Well then we'll get along fabulously." And that was the last thing I said to anybody for the entire night. I'm sure she didn't mind in the least.

"Are you alright?" more than one girl chimed out. Deb however knew better, she didn't say a word. I headed straight for the kitchen and luckily food had been prepared. Regretfully not chicken, but meat loaf would have do to. Nothing caps off a good day of killing quite like a nice slice of meatloaf. Although it can be a little disconcerting to eat a meal while thirteen women are watching your every move. I guess I'd better eat with my mouth closed tonight. I was going to sleep the sleep of the dead. Not quite the Rizino dead but dead none the less. I ate, I wiped my mouth with my shirt and I headed up the stairs into my loft bedroom. Apparently Deb wasn't the only one that could read my mood that night. Nobody asked another question or spoke a word in my direction that evening. I slept and I dreamed, I was hoping to sleep dreamlessly but that was not in the cards. I dreamed of every person that I had killed thus far. All of them looked at me with the quizzical Rizino look and asked how I could have possibly done that to them. I was wondering if there was a Heaven and had any of these people made it there. And if I made it to Heaven and met these people would they still be mad? Do you ever really get over being killed? How could you? It did not make for great sleep. I was actually happy when Deb came in and interrupted my nightmares.

"Mike, you up?" as she shook me a little harder than I thought was needed.

She had startled me and I instinctually reached up and grabbed her by the throat. She had begun to gasp and scratch my arms before I became aware enough of my surroundings and let her go.

"I'm so sorry Deb, you scared the crap out of me," I replied.

"Well just think I how I feel," she said as she began to rub her neck

"You know I didn't mean it, right?" I pleaded.

"Yeah I'm pretty sure you didn't mean to kill me. I shouldn't have startled you out of your sleep, especially since you were tossing and turning so much."

"No, I'm thankful to be out of that world," I said with true conviction.

"I know we've been down this road before."

"But," I said.

"Are you alright? You looked sort of possessed out there. You're starting to get that look about you like some of those others," she said with disdain.

"I'm not sure." I replied. And I wasn't. How can you go around killing people and hold on to your sense of who you are? "I'm having a hard time finding the person that first came onto this ship. I mean yeah, I was nervous about last night's bout, but it was a lot further buried than it should have been. I know that every time I go into the arena it's either him or me, and I know that it has to be him. It's as black and white as that. All the moral issues seem to go right out the window the minute we start. I'm sorry that they have to die, but I'm not sorry that I'm the one doing it. Does that make sense? Or am I just going insane?"

"No it sounds sane enough," she replied "I'm sorry that you have to go through this, and I know that the burden you carry when you think of all of us makes your job even tougher."

"Deb, if it wasn't for you and the rest of the girls, I would have given up a long time ago," I replied.

"Why do you say that?" she pleaded.

"If it wasn't for all of you, the guilt that compiles upon me with each killing would have been too much. I think I would have let Timmins do me in. I'm truly afraid for my Judgment Day, how could St. Peter possibly let *me* through the gates?" I was almost crying.

"He'll open the gates wide when you get there. You

are our savior, Mike; you put everything on the line to make sure that all of us here stay safe. Your sacrifice alone would have him open the gate. But I know the true you also, you are a very caring and compassionate person, I can see how this is eating you up inside. I'm not sure that I could do what you do even with all these other people's lives on the line. God won't have a choice but to leave the door wide open when you finally kick the can in sixty or seventy more years."

And I laughed, I was counting my life minute by minute and Deb was figuring for the next fifty or sixty years. "I love you Deb, you're just the dose of what I need tonight. And I hope that no matter what happens in our lives that you'll always be there."

Her face fell a little, but in true form she tried to hide it before I noticed. She understood that I still meant to get back with Beth at all costs, and that she was not included in that equation.

The next few weeks went by pretty much uneventfully. I was studying for midterms and my roommates were busy doing household chores. Although I can guarantee you there isn't a freshman male alive that has the quality and quantity of women as I did. Although on that same line of reasoning, there isn't a freshman whose life depends on passing his next test, although maybe in the abstract. Definitely not in the harsh cruel way that I was talking about. My ranking had improved some but not anywhere near the top tier I was looking for. I felt like Rodney Dangerfield, I couldn't get any respect. I was ranked 10th which still made me an underdog. But it was still better than being grouped in the final three, instead of offering any byes this round the aliens opted instead to have a three way among Nos. 17, 18 and 19. I hoped that this wasn't a trend that they planned to continue. They were having that tri-event a full week before the main course began. I hate to admit it but I was as excited about that fight as I was with opening season of Monday night football. The only thing missing was the beer. But I planned on being fully prepared for my bout before I sat to watch that one. My next opponent appeared to be from the island of Jamaica, he was a very dark skinned man named Jacob Farley. He wasn't particularly big but he was well built, more on the wiry side. He could dole out punishment as well as receive it. In his last bout he had been speared straight through the leg and still had the presence of mind to sever the arm holding the spear. Unfortunately for Joe Parkerson, the shock and finally the blood loss did him in. Farley didn't move, maybe the pain was too great or more than likely he just wanted the front row seat for the impending death. He was a scary looking fellow. I can't say that I was particularly thrilled about fighting him, but of the nineteen of us left I felt that I was the weakest link in this chain. Farley varied almost all of his styles to adapt to the competitor he was fighting. If the opponent was bigger and/or faster he would grab the bow. If Farley was bigger he opted for the sword. If the terrain did not allow for a clean shot with the bow he headed straight for the spear. And he was proficient at every piece of gear that he handled. He was going to be a tough nut to crack, but I had to believe he would opt for the sword against me. Great, I knew by what means he wanted to kill me but as of yet I had not figured out an adequate defense. Or offense. Maybe if I could get a hold of some killer alien weed and roll him a fat bone he'd stop and smoke it and I could club him over the head while he was eating a Twinkie. No, that probably wouldn't work, where would I get a hold of a Twinkie? I had the inklings that a major headache was coming on, I began to rub my neck as best I could. And then I felt it, the touch. The touch of one who knew how to give a great massage. Tanya had come over, noticing my discomfort and had begun to rub my neck. Had I not been so delighted in the feeling I would have noticed the daggers being thrown my way by Deb. If looks could kill I don't know which of us would have been dead first, Tanya or me. Tanya, however, had noticed the stare and simply chose to ignore it. Under any other circumstances this would have been phenomenal, two gorgeous girls fighting for my affections, why doesn't this stuff happen in the real world? No it only happens on alien spaceships hundreds of thousands of miles away from anybody who would actually believe that this was happening. When I finally did look up Deb had retreated from her spot at the top of the stairs, but I found out later that they had one doozy of a spat after I had unfortunately gone to sleep. I could have used a little enjoyment. Especially from two women vying for my attention, and it would have also been nice to witness a confrontation that did not end in bloodshed. But from what I heard from the other girls it could have gone that far had some others not stepped in. Man this just never happens to me, where the hell is the Kodak when you need it? The month went by a lot faster than anticipated, things in the house stayed somewhat tense. I guess when your life is on the line you'll always be sort of tense. Tanya and Deb didn't actually work out a truce, but when I shunned Tanya's next advances it kept Deb at bay. At least she finally realized that I meant everyone except for Beth.

I never did crack the secret behind Farley. I saw no obvious or not so obvious flaws in his fighting style. The man made very few mistakes. Tonight's bout was going to come down to who made the least amount of errors. I had been lifting and doing cardio the entire month, in fact it's the first time in a long time I didn't have to spend the majority of my downtown recuperating. So I figured I would match him in weapon selection and go sword to sword. Neither of us were sword-wielding swashbucklers. He might have the advantage in strength but I was confident that I had him in speed. So like I said before, it was all going to come down to who made the biggest mistake first.

Once again I was led into the arena first and listened to the crowd hissing and booing. Apparently I cost a lot of money to the ugly bastards. Well too bad because unless they bet on me tonight they were going to lose a bunch again. Farley came in after a few moments and received the lion's share of adulation from the throng and he didn't seem to mind. He bowed in the general direction of Beth and then proceeded to bow to every corner of the arena. They ate it up. I stood there hoping he pulled a muscle or something with all that bowing. But he didn't.

Here was a twist; the aliens did not terraform the arena, they left it flat gray and lifeless. It looked much like a warehouse, maybe that was the effect they were shooting for. It didn't really bother me as I had no intention of hiding anyway. Farley went to the far wall and grabbed a sword; I did the same. And then we just started walking to meet in the middle. There was no particular rush or sense of urgency. Both of us knew what had to be done, but hey, where's the fire. When we got roughly ten to fifteen feet away from each other, Farley actually bowed to me and saluted me with his sword. I thought that was a really classy thing to do, so I returned the bow, but I kept my head up just in case it was a ploy to catch me unawares. It wasn't. He waited till I stood completely back up and then advanced, but much more warily than he had the first forty-five yards. So the dance of swords began.

CHAPTER 27

"Ground Control to Major Tom, Ground Control to Major Tom."

"Butch, you know I hate it when you do that, my last name is Thomas and I'm a Colonel now, Major!"

"I know Ray, sometimes I just can't help myself."

Ray Thomas was the commander of the shuttle USS Liberation and had been dealing with his best friend Major Pat (Butch) Hatfield's long running joke for years. He knew that Butch had been happier when he made Major then he himself had been. Butch had been calling him Major Tom since they were boot lieutenants out of Annapolis.

"How are things going up there, Ray?" Butch asked, adopting a more serious tone.

"Major, when are you going to start using military protocol?" the colonel asked half seriously.

"Come on Ray, I've never used it before, why would I start now. Besides I'm your kid's godfather, that transcends all military ranking."

"Somehow I don't think you'd be saying that if the ranks were switched," Ray replied.

"Yeah, but then *I'd* be in charge and you'd have to do what I said," Butch laughed.

"That'd be the day." Colonel Thomas snorted, he wasn't too thrilled with his lack of military bearing at the moment but Butch always seemed to have that effect on him. If he had never met Butch Hatfield he was sure he'd be a full colonel by now instead of a light one. But if he had never met Butch Hatfield he would never have met Butch's sister Gina, and then he would never have had the light of his life, little Devlin. Some things were definitely worth the tradeoff.

"No, but seriously, Ray. How are things going up

there?" Butch sounded a little stressed out.

"They're going as well as can be expected, Butch. We're traveling as fast as this bucket will go and we're still a couple of months out. If the aliens decide to move at all, we'll never be able to catch them."

"Why'd you do it Ray?"

"Why'd I do what, Butch?" although he knew full well what the major was talking about.

"Why did you volunteer for this mission, there are a hundred captains out there who would have gladly given their right arm to fly this mission."

"And what? Should I have sent them to their deaths?"

"I'm not saying that, but they have less to lose. You've got a beautiful wife and my godson. Ray, my sister is shattered."

"I'm not quite dead yet Butch."

"Come on Ray, who are you fooling, this is *me* you're talking to. I've known you longer than anyone. You flew this mission because you knew the outcome and you couldn't bear the thought of someone taking your place. But you have more to lose."

"Would that make any of their deaths any less significant, Butch? How could I possibly send someone else when I know the odds of success are almost zero? I don't even think they'll let this ship get close enough to receive our transmission."

"Abort the damn thing, Ray. Pull a fuse, I can create a computer glitch here that'll make your ship look like it's dead in the water."

"Butch, you know this has to be done. If for no other reason than to let those bastards know we aren't going out without a fight."

"Ray, you read the reports, if by some grace of God you do get close enough you know the chances of you doing anything more than scratching their hull are one in a million," Butch said with urgency in his voice.

"You don't know that Butch, the scientists said that

they believed that the original probe and the ships that took those people are more than likely made from similar materials but different ratios."

"So you're basing your whole mission on the results of a radar screen?"

"What else do we have? I didn't sign up for a suicide mission. I know the odds are horrible but if there is still a chance, I'm taking it. Even if our 'transmission' does nothing more than shake their dishes around I'll be happy. They'll know that we'll go to any length. Maybe they'll even second guess their reasons for coming here."

"And maybe we're just stirring up the hornet's nest."

"Listen Butch, we've been round and round on this. What kind of husband would I be to your sister or father to your godson if I didn't do everything in my power to keep them safe from this threat? I'd never be able to live with myself."

"I know Ray, we just all miss you down here. I have no one's ass to kick in darts on Thursdays."

"If I remember correctly pal o' mine, I was winning three games to two before I left."

"Just don't forget you promised me that you were going to finish the series."

"I'll be back Butch, one way or the other I'll be back."

Butch did not like the tone his longtime friend had used. He guessed a couple of months out in space could cool anybody's jets. That would definitely give you enough time to really think out the probabilities of success for this mission. The odds had to rank up there somewhere with the USA hockey team defeating the Russians in the 1980 Olympics. Possible but definitely not probable.

CHAPTER 28

"Sub Commander Krulak, we have intercepted a message from the Earth vessel Liberation," the crewman noted to his superior.

"What did it say, crewman?" the sub commander asked.

"Sir, they are using some sort of arcane 512-bit encryption. It's been a long time since we've had to decipher something so crude, it should only be another minute or two."

"Crewman, until you have that message decoded do not bother me."

"Yes, Sub Commander." If reptiles could sweat he would have been, the sub commander was not someone to be trifled with. He hated being bothered for trivial events. The crewman had even debated whether to inform him of this latest development. They had been monitoring this space shuttle since it had departed Earth, but it had been more of a curiosity factor than out of any actual concern.

"Sir, the translation has come through," the crewman said, visibly shaken. More important crewmen than himself had been sent to the 'games' for less, such as bothering the sub-commander with immaterial matters.

"Well what is it crewman, I can hardly wait to see what these puny hu-mans are up to."

"Sir, there was some discussion about a transmission."

"A transmission? Crewman," the sub commander said sourly, "what kind of transmission? What do the scans of their little ship show?"

"Sir, there are four life forms on the ship and some minor radiation leakage, but so insignificant that it has to be from their computer equipment as opposed to any type of explosive device."

"Is there any sign of plasma ionic dispersion or anti-matter fluxuations?" the commander sighed heavily.

"No sir, we have been studying their technology for months now and they are at least one hundred to possibly two hundred years away from that type of technology."

"No, crewman, you have it wrong, these puny humans will be under our boot heel in less than a year; they will never attain that goal."

"Yes sir," the crewman grunted obsequiously in agreement.

"Well then crewman, if they have no plasma discharge weapons and no anti-matter weaponry and barely enough radiation to power a computer monitor, then why are you bothering me. The largest conventional Earthling weaponry discharged directly on the hull will not even disturb my drink. So unless you wish to become the next challenger in the games I suggest you go back to something worthwhile and go check the status of the invasion launch."

"Sir, yes sir," the crewman stammered.

"Sub Commander Krulak?"

"What?" the sub commander said irritably, and then turned to note his superior officer standing behind him. "Sir, what can I do for you." The obsequiousness in his tone matched that of the lowly crewman from a moment before.

"Well, if you are not too busy I would like to talk to you regarding this Earth vessel."

"Sir, anything," the sub commander said as he nervously licked his chops.

"Calm down Sub Commander, I have no intention of sending you to the barrens of Sverlock. I just wish to know what you feel about this ship."

"Sir, what do you wish to know?" the sub commander said, visibly calming down.

"What is its purpose?"

"Sir, we have been monitoring their transmissions but

as of yet have come up with no viable explanations as to their purpose. My guess, sir, is that they are coming here on some sort of diplomatic mission."

"Does this ship pose any type of threat?"

"No sir, none whatsoever, what could these puny humans possibly do to us?"

"Krulak, I have seen the smallest germ take down the largest warrior. What if they are the germ?"

"Sir, we have scanned their ship for every type of known weaponry and we can find nothing. That ship couldn't even hold enough explosives to take down our smallest cargo transport."

"What about their nuclear weaponry? It's a small threat but a threat nonetheless."

"Sir, our scans show nothing more than minor radiation leakage, probably from their onboard equipment. A bomb the size they would need to harm us in any way would have pegged our scans."

"Then what do you propose we do about our 'guests,' Sub Commander?"

"Sir, I say let them come. I see no reason to waste any of our resources and our time by getting rid of them. By monitoring the planetary media we know they are still waffling in regards to us. They don't know whether we have come in peace or to take total control. The longer we let them debate the issue, the easier our task at hand becomes. If we shoot this ship down, they will galvanize and make our job just a notch more difficult. I say let them come and then maybe we can even throw them into the games."

"I like your reasoning Sub Commander, carry on."

"Sir, yes sir," the sub commander said as he opened his mouth wide in an attempt to diffuse the heat that had been building up inside of him.

CHAPTER 29 – Journal Entry 21

Damn that hurt, the vibrations up and down my arm almost made me drop my sword when it first came into contact with Farley's. I was beginning to regret my choice of weapons, Farley was stronger than I and he was a step or two higher on the ladder of usage with said sword. He had me backpedaling every time he swung, it was all I could do avoid acquiring a gaping wound on my chest. As it was I had suffered a semi-serious gash on my left arm and an annoyingly painful cut along my right side. I wouldn't bleed out from either of them but if he kept adding to them I might be in some trouble. We kept parrying, ah, finally I got him to break out in a sweat. It wasn't much, but I didn't want to go out without at least having him work for it. If he didn't fall over soon and land on my sword I was going to be in some trouble, at this pace fatigue would be a problem and soon. Farley looked like he could do this for days. The crowd's buzzing was beginning to get louder, maybe they were getting the blood scent. I was certainly giving them enough to enjoy.

"Mr. Talbot just give yourself up, you know that I have you beat," Farley said almost matter-of-factly in his Jamaican accent.

I would have replied but it was all I could do to breathe and dodge, I had no time for useless words at the moment.

"I begin to tire of this Mr. Talbot, the crowd wants a kill and I aim to please." With that he renewed and doubled his efforts. My future was beginning to look bleak.

"Bite me," was all I was able to muster. I was tempted to turn tail and run so that I could catch my breath but with Farley this close I wouldn't make it half a step before I felt the cold steel of his sword cut me in half. It was time for desperation. I would either make it or I wouldn't, I knew by playing his game my moments of being alive and well were numbered.

"Farley, how bout we call this a draw," I said as I gasped for air.

"I would man, but the guards be havin' none of it," he answered. And I think he really would have gone for the draw, but he wanted to die about as much as I did. So it was either kill me or be killed by me, but he sure wasn't going to let the guards do it. Damn, he hit my thigh, that was the deepest one so far. I was slowing down and he was beginning to take me apart piece by piece. I had backed up as far as I could go, he had pushed me back to my starting point, and I literally had my back up against the wall. There was nowhere to go except sideways so there I went. Farley had renewed his attack probably thinking the end was near. And it was, just not the one he had envisioned. I knew hand speed wise I was quicker than him, and now was the time to implement that. I slid across the wall to where the mace was stationed. I had to time this right or not only would Farley kill me, the guards would finish the job. Hey, I thought, was there such a thing as double jeopardy on this ship? I guess that only applies on Earth. Farley swung at my head for all he was worth. I ducked and dropped my sword. Before the sword had a chance to hit the ground I grabbed the mace and brought it up just in time to catch Farley's back swing, and like a good little mace the chain wrapped around the blade two or three times. I let go of the mace while Farley desperately tried to untangle his weapon. I retrieved the sword and drove it straight through his mid-section. I would have thought that those rippling muscles he had in his belly would have prevented the sword from entering or at least slowed it down. But it slid in as if he had been swimming in tenderizer for a week.

"Well that's it, man." And those were the last words Farley ever uttered. He was another one I was going to have to chalk up for the nightmare list. He didn't deserve to die here, and I had no right to mete out this justice. One day I was going to have a good old talking to these bastards but for now I was going to claim my spoil, get cleaned up and go to sleep for a week. It appeared that I had won a few of my fans back, the crowd was going nuts. When in doubt take the points and bet on the underdog. I was tired, who am I kidding, I was bone weary. But at least most of the wounds I sustained were far from life threatening. For one of the few times I was actually able to meet my spoil and not have to be carried back to my living quarters. She was a black girl, gorgeous, maybe 5'7", jet black hair that stopped just shy of her shoulders and dark brown liquid eyes. She was a knockout. I know it sounds prejudiced but I hoped to all hell that I hadn't just killed her boyfriend, or somebody that she knew. But she seemed relieved enough when she was led to me. I'm thinking that she would not have been nearly so pleased had I just skewered her beau. We didn't say much on the way back; I was still too hopped up on adrenaline. My entourage at the house was immensely pleased that I had suffered very few wounds, I thought to myself, they're getting as desensitized to all of this as much as I am. I just killed another human being and they wanted to know what I wanted for dinner. Maybe that was just the way they coped. Did they not yet fully realize what would happen if I lost?

"Hey Steph!" I yelled across the room.

"Yeah Mike. What do you need?" she yelled through the din.

"Could you check the vitals on Farley and see how many guests we should be expecting later. And thanks."

"Sure thing, I'll check now," she yelled even louder, apparently the women were finally letting their collective breath go and it wasn't quiet. It appeared to me that all of them were talking at the same time, how do they do that? But women are funny that way; they can talk at the same time and still understand each other perfectly. Men on the other hand step on one word of their friend's speech and they have to start over. It was harder trying to follow one of their conversations than the battle I just had.

"Deb, could you please tell me when the grub's done, I'm gonna lie down."

"Don't you think that we should get you cleaned up before that?" she asked with genuine concern.

"I'm just going to hop in the shower and into bed. I'm pretty drained. Adrenaline crash can be tough," I responded.

She nodded but I could tell that she still didn't think that this was a prudent course of action. If I waited an extra second I'm sure I would have gotten the whole spiel on infection and bacteria and bogeymen under the bed. But in truth I just needed to get out of that room and that seemed the most graceful way to go about it. Do you think if I ask the aliens they would give me guest quarters? It's got to be worth a shot.

"Deb, please make sure that you guys prepare enough food for the newcomers, make sure that we have some cake too, they're going to be upset and maybe you guys could bond over some chocolate or something."

"You really don't understand women, do you?" she responded.

"Please tell me that's rhetorical, cause I don't have enough in me to go a round or two with you."

Apparently she didn't see the humor, she turned her head so fast to go in the other direction that her hair whipped up and slapped me across the face. Wait, she probably did mean that. No, I was way out of my league on this ship. The men I could handle, we each had a job to do, and we knew each other's roles. But women, well she was right, I had no clue. All I knew was that they were soft in all the right places and they smelled pretty. Sometimes it's good to be a man.

I had just meant to rest my eyes and actually join in for dinner, if for no other reason than to let the new women meet me so that they could put some of their fears to rest. But coming down from adrenaline can be as bad as any drug; it took my body a full sixteen hours to recuperate. I awoke in time for brunch the following day. I must have been out cold, because I hadn't even awoken when someone, probably Deb, had dressed my wounds. So she pretty much got her way anyway. Ah, natural order was restored in the world. The new women had arrived right after dinner the night before. Farley had been a decent host, he hadn't abused any of them, but they were summoned for his every beck and call. To him they were pretty much glorified servants. A couple of the original girls giggled a bit when they noticed my embarrassment when the new girls came up and bowed to me. I could have done without that.

"Please," I said "Get up."

"Yes master," they said as one, they obviously had had a lot of practice.

"And no more of that master crap either," I said as my cheeks reddened even more.

"I think he likes it," Tanya giggled as she nudged Stephanie.

Deb didn't see the humor. She threw a glance at Tanya, but she merely shrugged it off. However when Deb gave that same glance to the newcomers, they scurried like mice caught in the pantry.

"Deb, please make sure that doesn't happen again. I definitely don't need or want that kind of attention."

"What kind of attention do you want?" she asked

"Why are you starting with me, I just got out of bed, and all I want to do is go eat some blueberry pancakes. Did someone piss in your Cheerios?" I hadn't really meant to add that last bit, but the day had already gotten off on the wrong foot, there was no reason to stop now. But much to my surprise she acquiesced. I'll never understand women.

"I'm sorry, the stress of this place is really starting to wear my soul thin. Not only do I have to worry about your fights and what could potentially happen to the rest of us, but also I have to deal with this household. I must quash a dozen fights a night. Women just weren't meant to live communally. I'm sure for the most part guys would be fine.

But the jealousy runs rampant in this household. They practically kill each other just to decide who is going to bring you juice in the morning."

"I had no idea it was like that," I said, astonished.

"You see what I want you to see. Most of these girls won't even talk to me. Most of them downright hate me." She was beginning to cry.

"Why?"

"Because of you," she moaned.

I might be slow but I caught on pretty quick this time. They were jealous because she had been with me. So now she was caught between the rock and a hard place. She couldn't get solace from the women and she couldn't get comfort from me.

"Well we might as well make it worth your troubles," I said.

She looked up at my eyes and wiped a tear from hers eye. "Do you mean it?"

"You can sleep with me, but I mean sleep and nothing more."

Her face fell a little bit, but I'm sure the mechanics in her mind were working overtime. She had her foot in the door, and I'm sure she was under the belief system that she would be able to throw that door wide open given a little time. Lord knows I wanted the comfort, there was still no guarantee I was ever going to see Beth again. The way these women were acting I might be lucky just to make it to the next bout. I was feeling more anxious now than I ever had since being on this ship. I was so close. There were only nine of us left. But what was I getting close to? I knew that I would get to see Beth, but then what. I'm fairly certain they weren't going to give us a shuttle and let us live happily ever after on Pluto or something. Would they bring more people to fight? Would they just leave us in the houses until we died gracefully of old age? Or would they just kill us when our entertainment value was gone? These were aliens and so were their thoughts. There was no way to predict what they were going to do with us. I was trying not to think that far ahead but it was difficult. I wanted to see Beth so bad, but there were eight of the biggest baddest killing machines who had other thoughts. Yeah, I definitely wanted the comfort and companionship of Deb; would I be strong enough to resist? If I let her back in now and then won the tournament, then what? It was there and then that I made my decision to find a way off of this bucket. Whether it was on a shuttle or a body bag I was sick of being these aliens' entertainment. Now I just had to find a way out. It was long into the night when my door opened. Deb had not forgotten our agreement, and the night would get longer still.

CHAPTER 30 - Journal Entry 22

I had one of the most peaceful rests I had had since coming onto this ship. I didn't dream about fights or aliens or even women for that matter. I relived a slice of life, more specifically a small sliver of my childhood. It was a time long before any of this present nightmare materialized. It might just have been one of the best summers in my life, we were fifteen. It was the in-between time before we were truly adults and not quite kids, we hadn't started the heavy experimenting with booze, drugs and ultimately women. We were explorers, oh not your garden-variety ocean explorers or even space explorers. We explored a place called Indian Hill. It was the summer after the 'initial discovery.' It was a place probably no more than a mile from our houses but it might as well have been ten thousand miles from any place we called home. Just to get to the 'Hill' required no small amount of danger. First was the required pass through Rusty Grant's territory, he was the local bully and at 16 he was huge and we were afraid of him. But luckily he was slow. So unless one of us was dumb enough to trip, we could generally make that part without too much difficulty. The next major part was the train trestle we had to cross. Dennis had somehow garnished enough courage to make this crossing without too much bellyaching. Although we did our best every time to let him know only wimps were afraid of heights, every single one of us never said so much as a word while we were crossing the trestle. It was all business then. We'd go one at a time, head down, watching where our next footfall would land. The rest of us, whether already over or waiting our turn, kept a vigilant eye out for the train. Even at that tender age I knew what it meant to have your balls crawl up into your belly. The trestle was in the neighborhood of one hundred fifty feet across and fifty feet down into a raging river. That however was not the catch. The catch was that much like Stephen King's Stand By Me, there was a curve in the track less than a quarter of a mile away. It was a difficult maneuver to not constantly keep looking up at that bend. The biggest fear was being in the middle of the bridge and looking up to see the train bearing down on you. It had happened more than once but luckily none of us had ever gotten our foot stuck, but your heart would still pound for minutes after the event was over. I guess if we were a little brighter we might have gone down to the local train station and gotten a schedule but what kid thinks like that? Anyway we were explorers, danger was our middle name. Once past the train tracks we would have to traverse the embankment that led down to the river and then cross said river. Enough people had 'explored' Indian Hill as to put together a makeshift bridge across the river, but it usually included some pallets or small trees. It was generally not very stable and for some reason or other it was always slippery. More than once one of us had taken a plunge. But once over we felt like masters of our universe. Our parents could never find us here, we were free, at least until dinnertime. When you came up the embankment you would approach a beautiful huge oak tree that seemed so out of place, it was the only tree in the entire meadow. We always thought it looked lonely. Off to either side were the hills that we liked to explore, these unlike the meadow were covered with trees and hid all sorts of treasures. There were old cars that had been ghost ridden off of small cliffs. We once found an old boat. I have no idea how that got there. My mother was pissed when I came home with the ship's steering wheel. I didn't have a good explanation for that one. Indian Hill was off limits; I couldn't tell her that was where I got it. Once in our deepest search we stumbled across an actual log fort. We were amazed, but we were also leery. Whoever made this wasn't a kid so we threw some rocks at it from a distance to see if we roused anybody out of it. Nobody showed, so we picked our way through the brambles and scrub brush to gaze in. It was a kid's paradise. It had to be around fifteen by fifteen feet made with some pretty good-sized logs; it stood about five feet tall and was covered with a green tarp. Whoever had built it took great care to make sure it wouldn't be found by the casual observer. But we were explorers. It was about fifty feet off the normal path and through some of the thickest scrub we had thus far encountered. When we got in we found our biggest surprise. Rusty and his friends had built this masterpiece, and their names were carved into the woodwork. I wanted to leave; I had no desire to get pummeled today. But then Paul found the coup de grace, Playboys. That pretty much put an end to any of our thoughts on leaving.. They were three of the most beat up magazines any of us had ever seen. They looked like they had gone through the wash, twice. They were the best things any of us had ever seen. And then Dennis stumbled over a bottle of Jack Daniels, what the hell, we tried it. It burned worse than the Tabasco sauce I was forced to swallow when I swore in front of my mother. But the aftereffects were quite soothing. So there we were, dancing around this cabin singing and shouting like Indians. If Rusty and his friends had been anywhere within the vicinity we would have been dead meat. But the gods were shining down on us that day. It must have been the effects of the alcohol but Paul felt the need for some false bravado.

"Let's take this fort!" he shouted.

"Yeah, we'll just stay here and defend it with big sticks," I laughed, "Rusty and his friends won't mind."

"No I'm serious," he said, and by the look on his face I knew he was.

"What do you mean?" Dennis piped in. "Rusty and his friends will kill us."

"Not if they can't find us," Paul smiled evilly.

"What do you mean Paul? They built this place, of course they'll find it," I moaned. My mom would kill me if I got blood on my clothes, especially if it was mine.

"Not if it's not here." His smile grew even bigger.

"What are you talking about Paul?" Dennis answered. "You drank too much?"

"No, no, I mean if we take this thing apart and move it somewhere else," he said.

All of our eyes lit up then, we would have the coolest fort and at 15 years old that still meant a lot.

"But what if they find it, they'll know we did it," I pleaded.

"We'll just have to hide it even better than they did. I've got a plan."

So for the next few days we all raided our parents' garages for tools, pick axes, shovels and saws. We moved about a half mile further through the brush, we cleared a spot roughly the dimension of our soon to be palace, and we started digging. It was the hardest work any of us had ever done, but we loved it. We dug a huge hole, six feet deep and fifteen by fifteen feet across and wide. We couldn't believe the work we had completed, it was awesome, and it was just a hole. Now the real fun was to begin. We took turns having a scout, that person would have a walkie-talkie and keep an eye out on the only route available to enter Indian Hill. We fortunately only had one false alarm, we would learn later that Rusty and his pseudo gang had probably stopped visiting this place months earlier. They were out of their exploring stage, they were driving and girls where pretty much all they wanted to explore now. But we didn't know that then and we always felt that we were moments away from mortal danger. Log by log we moved that fort doing our best not to leave a telltale trail back to our new hide out. We borrowed another huge tarp from Dennis's dad and that became our makeshift floor. Then piece by piece we stacked our logs against the earthen walls. For ten hours straight we worked on that fort, we dared not leave that part for another day. If by chance Rusty came up here they would see their fort being ransacked and would just lie in wait for us. We capped it off with the original tarp and then cut down a few more logs and placed them on top. Than we covered that with pine needles and scrub brush and whatever else we could find. The only way anybody would ever see this place would be to literally step on it. It was awesome. We had even dug out our sloped entrance on the far side to make it that much more invisible. Paul stole a gas lantern from the local hardware store and I stole a couple of bottles of booze from my parents' never used liquor cabinet. I think it was a bottle of crème de menthe and some Bailey's Irish crème. But we didn't care; we had an awesome fort, Playboys and booze. What more could a fifteen year old want? We spent virtually that entire summer up there, bringing our treasures there to display on the walls like trophies. It was one of the last happy summer I ever had before the whole teen angst stage moved in. From time to time I would go up there by myself when I needed to get away from my mother. Unfortunately the spirit of the place had diminished, without all the mirth and friendship it just became a hole in the ground; the Playboy's had been replaced with newer Penthouse's but even that couldn't make the atmosphere any lighter.

And what a quandary my life had become, I had had one of the best night's sleep in months, remembering some of the best times in my life, but when I awoke I had a strange taste in my mouth. It was later that I realized it was the taste of bittersweet. Oh how I wished I could go back to those simpler days. But the fates had stepped in, and they were not to be denied.

"Mike, get up!" A disembodied voice yelled. All I could think was that I didn't feel like going to school today.

"Mike get up!" Geez she was adamant today.

CHAPTER 31 – Journal Entry 23

"They're posting the new rankings and I really think that you should see this!"

"That definitely wasn't my mother, where the hell?" and then I woke up. I liked my dream world much better. Even if it was a time long forgotten. The worst I would suffer back then was a bloody nose, not a spear in the belly.

"I'm coming!" I shouted. "Just let me put on some pants." Damn, that didn't sound good. If I had been a little more awake I would have chosen a better selection of words, especially with the tension that was flowing through this abode.

"You're ranked sixth!" Tanya shouted with an almost gleeful tone. "That's awesome."

"Yeah," I replied sarcastically. "If there were more than nine of us left."

"Oh," she sighed as the wind flew out of her sails.

"It says that you're fighting the third and fourth ranked contestants. What does that mean?" Francesca, one of my new acquisitions said.

"No, you must be reading it wrong." Or so I sincerely hoped. "I should either be fighting the fourth seed or the sixth seed or by some grace of God I should have a bye."

"No, it says you're fighting Leonard Bernstein, No. 4 and Troy Trentner No. 5, what does that mean?" She was almost pleading.

And so I paid a little more attention to what I was actually reading. The aliens had decided to do one on one on one-ers. Basically it was going to be every man for himself in a three-way. This was a very twisted and unwanted surprise. The odds of dying in this mess had increased geometrically. Not only would I have to study two men's fighting techniques, I would also need to try to figure out how they would interact with each other *and* with me. If they decided to team up against me and get me out of the way first I was a goner. But I had to believe that each of the other men would consider me the weakest link and would rather have my help in eliminating the other and then try to finish me off. Or else they would just play renegade and kill the first thing that got in their way regardless of who it was. This was not a pretty turn of events, and of the three men going into the ring I was picked as a 50 to 1 long shot of being the one coming out alive. Troy, the No. 5 guy, was in the neighborhood of 6' tall, he didn't look overly impressive but according to his bio he had been a fitness trainer another lifetime ago. He was agile and fast, his preferred weapon was the mace, and he wielded it like it was a child's toy. Even with a miss he was able to bring it back around before his competition was able to parry a thrust. Leonard, No. 4, was even less impressive but there he was. He looked like a lost accountant but the man had an uncanny ability with the bow. He had killed everyone he faced with that bow and arrow. I don't know how many of you folks saw Lord of the Rings but he was as impressive with that bow as was Legolas the elf. I watched in fascination as he placed two perfectly aimed arrows into the chest of a running man from fifty yards away before that man took his second step. I don't think the poor bastard had even registered the fact that he had been shot by the first arrow when the second one slammed home. A deal with Leonard was out of the question, he wouldn't give two shits who was coming. I can't imagine that he was afraid of either one of us. But Troy, well, he had to be a little concerned with the speed and accuracy which Leonard possessed. But I wasn't even sure if the both of us together had a shot in hell. And could we possibly build enough mutual trust in that short of a time knowing full well that we would have to kill each other before the night was through? What a fucking mess. I was scared, and I didn't want any of the women to know. I'm sure that they were suspicious but the drama in this place was already to a boiling point, I didn't wish to be the flashpoint. I had not a clue what my next plan of action was. Luckily the aliens opened the door for me and I took full advantage.

Word came down the following day that the Supreme Commander wished to visit with the final nine warriors. Maybe he wanted to express his undying gratitude for our showmanship. I would have loved to have made it his dying gratitude but such pleasantries had to wait. If the Supreme Commander wanted to see us then that's what we would do. I just had to take full advantage of that fact.

We met the Supreme Commander the following day with his entourage. Apparently we were either too far beneath him or he didn't speak English, because he never once addressed us personally. It was all through one of his men or women (I still had no clue if this species reproduced sexually or asexually). He basically just wanted to thank us for a job well done, and as gesture of goodwill he laid out a spread worthy of a king. There were lobsters and steaks and every imaginable food along with, bless his heart, beer. It was a bitter beer but it was beer nonetheless. The only thing that would have made it a good night would have been if I wasn't with eight guys that wanted me dead, but I was truly unconcerned with all of them save one, Troy. I tried desperately to make contact with him without appearing to make contact with him. Leonard didn't give a care about anyone else there, he paid no attention to anything except the food and the beer. Durgan was too busy attempting to intimidate everyone. The rest I felt were much more on my wavelength, yeah they had confidence and some swagger but they were also leery. They were aware of everything going on around them, they like me were attempting to size up their competition, and it was then that I noted Troy looking directly at me. My heart leaped into my throat; this might be the only chance I had, and if he misconstrued my message we both would be sunk. I pointed at my chest and then at his and mouthed the words 'me and you.' At first he had a quizzical look upon his face and then my hopes sunk as anger began to cross his face. I think he thought I was directly challenging him. And then thankfully recognition dawned; he nodded once in agreement. So the plan was set. I could only hope that he would hold up his end of the bargain. And to be honest it wasn't much of a plan, we had merely bargained to forestall our own demise in favor of killing the far more dangerous of us three. What a twisted world we had stumbled upon, in all the imaginable tangents I could have foreseen my life going into, this one wasn't even on the scope. After I had made my intentions clear to Troy I actually partook of the abundance in front of me. In some respects this could be my last meal, who knew. The beer was bitter but it was beer nonetheless. And it was not as bitter as my thoughts as I dwelled on the upcoming battle.

CHAPTER 32

Outside Vail, Colorado

"That's it Dewey you've got it. Now stay steady and squeeze the trigger, don't pull it," Paul said as he moved down the firing line to check on the rest of the recruits. It wasn't much of an army, twenty-two people to be exact, but he knew the government was covering up the whole alien conspiracy. Dewey had been in the parking lot when the ship came and took his friends away. No matter who he pleaded his case to they always turned a deaf ear. And he was sick of it. Paul, after his latest visit with Senator Allard, had decided to take matters into his own hands. Not many people took him seriously but he had a small decently armed and growing militia. And he had left enough fliers on campus so that when the shit did hit the fan the rest of the non-believers would have a semi-safe haven. Paul had never been one to embrace military affairs, that was always best left to those who were trained for such things. But by sheer luck or divine will he ran into a character named Frank Salazar, a former Marine, who had been taking a few classes on the campus to further his education. Paul and Frank didn't necessarily see eye to eye but they both believed in the cover-up and the impending invasion. Nobody comes down to earth and scoops up ten thousand people or so without some kind of ulterior motive. Frank still had some connections at the reserve station in Colorado Springs. The sergeant of the armory was sympathetic to this new cause and was also a ranking officer in the newly founded Colorado State Militia. M16A2's and the corresponding ammunition had somehow fallen off of a truck bound for Twenty-Nine Palms and landed in the militia's arms. The makeshift army had found an old hiker's cabin, the kind that are built way out in the wilderness so that if someone is caught out in severe weather, they might be lucky enough to stumble across one of these shelters. The cabin itself was used mainly for meetings; the men had started building bivouac huts. They figured two would be enough to house them all comfortably. Paul had them build twelve. It was difficult to train against an enemy when you didn't even know what they looked like. The majority of their days were spent on honing their survival skills such as chopping wood for the coming winter, storing food, keeping the generators in peak operating condition and building and reinforcing the original structures. And when the basic chores were completed, the men all practiced their shooting under the watchful eye of Frank. He was by far the most qualified having attained three expert badges while in the Corps. And he had been thoroughly pleased with the progress of his men. Eight of them were without a doubt experts, ten were good enough that you didn't want to be in their line of fire, and three, well those three needed a little more tender loving care, and a lot more ammunition. Well at least Frank knew which three to put on the perimeter defense. If you can't shoot you have to be closer to the action. Frank saw to the training and the discipline of the men. He felt that they were truly beginning to gel into a fighting force. He wouldn't want to take them up against Marine regulars but these guys could give the army a run for their money. Paul saw to the day-to-day affairs, recruitment, and if he couldn't get a warm body he was always looking for cold hard cash. And there were a lot of people out there who wouldn't publicly admit to what was happening, but when it went down they also wanted that safe haven. The U.S. government hadn't even mobilized the National Guard yet. By this stage of the game U.S. Marines should have been stationed at every major city. Frank was under the impression that the National Guard couldn't fight their way out of a wet paper bag in a rainstorm, and at best they would take three to four full days to mobilize. The way these ships moved they'd be lucky to have a three or four hour warning. No, these small bands of brothers had made the decision to not go out like lambs, helpless to the slaughter.

"Frank, how is Generator Four doing? Paul asked

"So far so good but it's going to need a new valve before the winter sets in. We don't want to get caught up here without enough juice when the snow sets in."

"Alright I'm running down to Boulder today, I heard there are three more recruits and a couple of thousand dollars in donations coming our way. Ask the men if there is anything special they want while I'm in town. Oh, and Frank..."

"Yeah," Frank said as he turned back around.

"Tell the men that two out of the three new recruits are women, and if they are anything but perfect gentlemen, I will let you use them for targets."

"Yes sir," Frank said with a grin. He knew Paul wasn't kidding. "Dude, you really should have been in the Marines."

"Dude huh? Is that a military term?" Paul smiled. "Naw, I could have never been in the Marines especially with those god-awful haircuts."

"You mean high and tights?"

"Yeah those friggen things, besides women love this long hair."

"Well I guess we all have our faults," Frank snorted. "I'll get Bivouac Eight set up for the women."

"Frank."

"Yeah boss."

"Make sure there are no extra holes in the sides."

"I'll check on it myself, Paul. Drive safe, see you tonight. Hey, why don't you snag some Mickey D's on the way back. Stop at the one in Georgetown and tell the manager, a pencil necked little geek named Richard, that you know me. He'll hook you up."

"Excellent, and get on Dewey will you, his shooting is terrible. I don't even want to be in the same room with him when he shoots darts."

Frank smiled. "Hey Paul, someone has to be on the front line of defense."

"Alright, alright I'll be back in a few hours." Paul turned and hopped into his brand new Jeep Wrangler courtesy of the dealership owner who had a son training here at this very moment. What a strange twist of events his freshman year had turned out to be. His dad had told him these would be the most memorable times of his life. Somehow he figured this wasn't what his dad had meant. 'Mike, I swear to you and Beth that I will avenge your deaths.' He felt with utter conviction that all those people had been slaughtered and he meant to do all that was in his growing power to do something about it.

CHAPTER 33

Washington D.C.

"Dr. Schoville, what are the chances that the aliens can see that bomb?" the President asked with just a little more conveyed tension than he wished the cabinet members to see.

"Well Mr. President, I think the proof is in the pudding," the professor answered in all seriousness.

"Dr. Schoville, pardon me," the President said as he rubbed the bridge of his nose. "I'm tired and I'm more than a little worried, what exactly do you mean?"

"Well sir," the professor said without missing a beat. "Our shuttle is still there. If they suspected the magnitude of the device on board I have no doubt that they would have eliminated it a long time ago. And to be honest with you sir, they still have a long way to go and we know the aliens could strike at their leisure."

"And that is my concern," the President noted.

"Mr. President, if I may." Captain Moiraine stood up.

"By all means Captain, your opinion is always welcome here."

"Well sir, like the good professor noted, if they knew of the device on board they would have eliminated the threat as soon as the shuttle left the planet. With that new platinum wrap around the warhead I don't think even the most advanced scanning equipment in the galaxy would detect anything more than some random naturally occurring radiation."

"Captain, what is the prognosis for the crew of the shuttle?" the President said , once again rubbing the bridge of his nose.

"Sir, they were all volunteers and they knew exactly

what they were getting into," the Captain answered as neutrally as possible.

"I know they were volunteers. I am asking you as a military person, what do you believe their odds of coming back from this are?"

"Sir, knowing that they have to get close enough to loose that missile without giving the aliens a chance to blow it up or move their ship... well sir, they'd never be able to get their ship far enough away in time, they would be killed by the initial blast."

"So in your expert opinion you think..."

"I think we should be preparing drafts for the parents, wives and children of those men."

"Thank you Captain, that is all." The President sat back down in his chair, bracing himself for the whopper of a migraine that was mere moments away. But he knew he had one more task to complete before this night was through.

"Alright, everybody is dismissed for the evening but please wake me should any new events arise." Although he was fairly certain sleep would once again not visit the White House. "Captain."

"Yes sir."

"Send in Mrs. Cavanaugh on your way out."

"Yes sir, right away sir."

Mrs. Cavanaugh was the President's personal secretary and had been at his side since he was a lowly district man back in Massachusetts. She entered the room and assessed the situation at a moment's glance. "Joseph, why don't you go upstairs and get some sleep," Mrs. Cavanaugh suggested with concern written all over her face.

"I would love to Mrs. C, but the fate of the world I fear is resting squarely on my shoulders."

"It's going to be tough to hold the weight of the world up when you yourself are barely standing."

"Point well taken, but I have to do this one final thing before I call it a night. Could you please take some dictation for me?"

"Certainly Joseph."

"Mrs. C, when are you going to start calling me by my title?"

"Joseph, I've known you since you were a wet eared kid out of Harvard, you've never called me Betty and I've never called you by whatever title you had at the time. That's just who we are. I see no reason to change that now."

"I guess you're right Mrs. C. Now is not the time to change anything more than what already has been. That's the first time I've felt like smiling in the last month," the President said with a twinkle in his eye.

"Ah, there is the Joseph I know and love."

"And now back to the reason why I wanted you here."

"Do you want me to start on the letters to the families of the shuttle crew?"

"Mrs. C, you really need to stop listening at the door."

"How else am I going to make sure that you're doing the right thing? Go to bed Joseph, I've written enough of these letters to know how it's done."

"And that's the problem Mrs. Cavanaugh, I keep sending brave young men to their deaths and here we are safe and warm in our home."

"It's the lot you drew in life and don't go feeling all sorry for yourself, you are a true leader of men. You've averted at least two great wars since your time in office and the one war you had to fight you made decisive decisions that saved the lives of countless thousands. And you are now sending some of this country's bravest men on a suicide mission to save potentially the lives of billions. You've known all along that the few always have to be sacrificed for the many."

"Once again Mrs. C you've gone where none of my top advisors will ever go. You tell it to me straight. Not necessarily what I want to hear, but always what I need to hear. But no, I will not leave you here alone to write these

letters." Mrs. Cavanaugh began to protest but the President just motioned her to sit back down.
"Dear Mr. and Mrs…"

CHAPTER 34 – Journal Entry 24

With one week to go I did not have a lot of confidence in my alliance with Troy, was a nod enough to trust my life to this man? I watched his bouts, but I saw no overt signs of him being any less sane than myself. As far as I could tell he also didn't hurt his women. Maybe this made him honorable or maybe it didn't but my best chance still lay with him. Deb had become more reclusive than I ever had and Stephanie had practically vanished from sight. Tanya slowly but surely took over the daily household affairs. The house had seemed a lot more subdued these past few weeks, possibly due to the fact that the end was so near, and nobody knew their fates, not with any certainty anyway. I conditioned my body for six hours a day, whether it was on the treadmill or practicing martial arts movements. I was quite literally impressed with the machine I had become. Too bad it took death matches to get me into shape, but for good or bad I was a bona fide lean mean killing machine. The women folk seemed especially nervous this time around or maybe my senses were just a little bit more heightened, either way I was walking on the edge of a razor. It hurt to walk up there but it beat falling off into the abyss. I said my prayers and had a sort of group hug with the women more so for them than me. I was attempting distance, but women are like that, all touchy feely, what are you gonna do.

I headed off to the games. I walked into the arena first because I was the lowest ranking which this time didn't bother me that much, it gave me a chance to survey the area that much longer. The aliens had scaled down the football size arena into something more along the size of arena football. And this arena was round unlike its rectangular predecessors. I guess it gave them the chance to squeeze more fans into this place. And it also gave none of the competitors any advantage. We would all be let in at equidistant points around the circle. Leonard entered next and was not given a rousing applause, apparently his lack of variety in the kill didn't sit well with the masses. And there it was, my extra time paid off. His weapon of choice was about thirty yards to his left and forty yards to my right. My mind was racing, could I get there before him? He was scrawny but he was fast and he had a ten yard head start. And the footing could be treacherous. It was a jungle motif, but not a necessarily dense one. They must have had complaints about obstructed views of kills. There were trees and vines but they were spread out, mostly there were twisted roots on the ground. Running could prove perilous. Troy was finally led in on the far end of the circle, he was a good sixty or seventy yards away from the action, and I still had no way to tell which side if any he was playing for. The buzzer lit and I hauled ass. Leonard saw my move and also started to sprint. Shit, I thought to myself, he's friggen fast. I had made up about five yards before he fully realized what I was attempting to do. But that was it, he was closing in fast, would he have enough time to grab the bow, turn and fire? I almost faltered, my feet slid, and the aliens went nuts. They were expecting an early kill, well they were right. He was less than ten feet away and I was twenty to twenty-five feet away. I almost sheared off, had there been anywhere around to take cover I would have. But I was out in the open and I was committed. I didn't even want to turn to see what Troy was up to, for all I knew he was sitting back at his entrance just waiting to see which one of us bought it first. Not a bad idea, I wish I had thought of that earlier. I was still running full tilt when I noticed Leonard had a small problem with the bow, the string got hung up on the hook it was suspended from. I just might make it, and then it came free. Damn he brought it up fast. I had so fully committed myself to the charge I didn't even bring a knife to a bow and arrow fight. So I did the only thing that I could, I ran straight into him.

Not as if I was tackling him, but I just kept running as if he was never there. There was a loud snap as we collided, I was pretty sure I had dislocated my left shoulder. I guess the protrusion from my shoulder gave it away, that and the flaring pain, but I had taken the little bastard's rib out, he was screaming like a little girl. But it didn't stop him, he knew the drill, it was do or die time. My momentum had driven him against the wall and that had lent him some support, to my regret he had never let go of the bow. I was carried directly into the wall, and unfortunately these weren't padded like in major league baseball, no, these had more of the consistency of National Hockey League walls. I crumpled like a tin can, I hope he made a clean hit. I rolled over to face my exodus, Leonard had finally regained enough of his poise to stop his screaming. I think I punctured one of his lungs because he was sucking a lot of air, but his five minutes of life were ten times the amount that I was looking at. He raised his bow and pulled the string back and then his face just disappeared. The cavalry had come! Troy had planted his mace square in Leonard's face. The arrow still came dangerously close to my head, but to this day I will never forget the vision of Leonard's face turning into pulp right before my eyes. Fragments of bone and tissue flew everywhere, and an eyeball went into the stands where one of the Progerians made a handy snack out of it. It was if I was watching life one frame at a time, I could watch as each individual pieces of his face went flying into different directions. Then time stood still and then it raced ahead; Troy was coming my way and he had a mace, I was still partially dazed from my wall contact and I'm pretty sure I had a concussion. Well, I thought to myself, at least I made it easy for him. And then he surprised the hell out of me, he offered his hand. The aliens were pissed, they were throwing things on the arena's floor. Some of the debris looked like femurs; they probably had a fried leg stand somewhere in this hell hole. Well it couldn't get any worse, I figured he could either kill me on the ground or standing up. At this point it made little difference to me.

"Come on man, grab my hand."

"What are you doing?" I said as I desperately tried to shake off the effects of the concussion.

"We had a deal, I didn't know if I could trust you or not, but you more than held up your end of the bargain, and I am a man of my word. Or in this case, nod. Get up, collect your thoughts, grab a weapon and let's finish this." So I reached out with my good arm to his proffered hand and stumbled wearily to the wall, furthest from where Leonard's body lay. I wanted as much time to regroup as possible. I was still half expecting a shot to the back of the head, but true to his word he never left the spot where he had helped me up, not until I gave him the thumbs up anyway. The aliens did not like this turn of events, here was another of their inherent weaknesses, they had no honor. I don't believe that they had any clue as to the motives that were taking place in front of them on the arena floor. I walked as slowly as I dared so as not to anger the guards. They hadn't raised their weapons but they also weren't at parade rest either. My head rang like a bell, my left shoulder was on fire. I had one arm to defeat a heavy weapon user, maybe it would have been more humane if he had just finished me off when he originally had the chance. My only chance against Troy was to reset my shoulder. They always made it look so easy in movies and on TV, but I'm telling you right now, if anything more than a fly had even breathed on my shoulder I would have been crying like Leonard. The thought of actually ramming it into the wall terrified me. If I didn't do it hard enough and it didn't pop back in I risked the chance of passing out from the pain, and honor or not Troy would have no choice but to finish me off and go home. I risked the chance of passing out even if it did go back in. So I went for broke, I got a five foot start and dove straight at the wall, twisting my shoulder as it made contact. It ground in like glass encrusted fingernails on a dirty chalkboard, my vision began to tunnel and I was on the verge of passing out. And then it passed. The best way I can explain it is if you are in a car and the urge to defecate hits you so violently you can think of nothing else as the sweat pours off your brow. You clench your ass cheeks together in a vain attempt to keep in what so desperately wants out. Your stomach twists in a knot. The back of your shirt becomes damp with sweat. You begin to scan the horizon for any viable alternative to get the liquid lava out of your hindquarters. When you finally do find some unsuspecting diner, it's all you can do to get your pants off without leaving a little surprise behind. Damn those button fly's. Then your ass doesn't even get to make contact with the toilet seat before the refuse begins to pour out. I felt sorry for the poor minimum wage worker that would have to clean that toilet. Even as you finally let go with the sweet release, your stomach is so churned up you have to fight back the urge to evacuate from both ends, no, that just won't do. And then as quickly as it started it's over, only now you feel like a million bucks, hell, ten million bucks. You could probably conquer the world now. If you can survive that you can survive anything. It's a euphoric sensation and it's not just a quick fleeting feeling, it lasts and lasts, just like that friggen bunny. Yeah, the bathroom smells and looks like hell, and the toilet's not going to flush right for a week, but you feel fucken great. And yeah that's what my shoulder felt like right now. I could move it again, yeah it was going to take some special alien juice to make it right but it worked for now, even if it sounded like I had rocks rolling around in there. Troy began his reluctant striding over to my spot. He took no pleasure in this, and I believe he was under the wrong assumption that I was still greatly handicapped. I felt bad, the man had quite literally saved my life and now I had to kill him, but that was the nature of this game. Three men in and hopefully at least one out. I grabbed a sword with my right hand and I played the part of a left sided cripple. Every time I attempted to grab the hilt with my left I would wince and drop my hand back down to the side of my body. He had to be figuring I had no chance to wield a two handed sword with one hand. And towards me he came, he had a scowl on his face and I did not think that he would give me another reprieve; we had fulfilled our bargain and now it was time to finish this affair. I feebly held up the sword, and onward he strode. He raised the mace knowing full well that I'd never be able to deflect it with one arm, more than likely he'd drive the mace and my sword into and through me. I don't know and never will know why he hesitated. Did he think that this was too easy? Was it a trap? Or was he distraught over having to kill the first ally he had in this place thus far? I begged him in my mind not to change his game plan now, the euphoria was beginning to seep out of me to be replaced by a giant red spot in the center of my skull. But his hesitation was momentary and he came forward. As he swung I moved right and grabbed the hilt of the sword with my left arm to bring it in a slicing motion across his abdomen. It was a deep cut, I almost lost the sword to the vacuum of his innards. As I sliced further through and his forward progress brought him to the other side of my attack, the sword released itself from him with an audible sucking sound. And then the sight of Leonard's destroyed face would have actually been a welcome one at this time. Troy's innards spilled out, he dropped his mace as he desperately tried to place them all back inside. Foot after foot of intestine just rolled out of him, the smell was horrendous. His eyes glazed over in shock and sorrow, and he was crying. It was the worst thing I had ever seen. He fell to his knees right on top of his intestines. He attempted to rise but became tangled up in himself. I didn't know what to do, I was so horrified by what I was seeing I couldn't move. I was frozen. He turned his face to me and it was framed with his innards; he begged me to kill him, he pleaded. But yet I still couldn't move, my legs felt as rubbery as the substance that oozed out of Troy.

"Kill me," he whispered. "Oh dear God, please just kill me."

"I... I... I can't," I stuttered out.

"I'd do it for you."

And that was all I needed to solidify my resolve. I drove the sword through his back and into his lungs and mercifully through his heart.

"Thank you," were his dying words.

He thanked me for killing him. I knew from that point on I'd never be the same person. My fate was sealed and I was petrified. I don't even remember the walk back to the house. I would have liked to blame it on the concussion but I'm thinking that was not the case. I had been altered, and for the life of me I couldn't imagine it being for the good. It's not like I had been enlightened, no it was the opposite, if there was such a word I had been endarkened, and I was afraid. I was afraid for my very soul.

CHAPTER 35

Somewhere outside of Georgetown

Paul stopped in the first good-sized town outside of Vail and pulled in to the Texaco station to use the payphone. He would have used his cell but he was fairly certain the good old U.S. Government had that tapped. He actually kind of liked that fact, that way he could feed them whatever information would benefit him. He knew that they knew about the location of his training facility outside of Vail, but his alternate would not be compromised.

"Wags buddy, what's up?"

"Paulie, how you doing my man?" Dennis was a longtime friend that Paul could trust, loyal almost to a fault, he was just the type of man Paul needed for the Defense Corp.

"Dennis, have you gotten in touch with Ron yet?"

"Yeah, I talked to him yesterday."

"How'd he sound?"

"He sounded a little weirded out. I'm not sure he's grasping the whole concept of his little brother being beamed aboard a spaceship. But he knows something is wrong, and that the government is trying to cover it up."

"Okay, more importantly my friend, is he willing to help?"

"He seemed hesitant at first, he started hemming and hawing about permits and stuff like that. I thought he was going to say no, but then he just looked me square in the eye and said fuck it. 'They fucked over my brother now it's payback time.' And that's pretty much how the conversation went."

"Excellent, when do you think you'll get that done?"

"Well my man," Dennis said exuberantly. "With

some help from Kev, Dino and a few select others and Ron's heavy machinery, I'd say no more than two to three weeks."

"We don't have that kind of time, I'm expecting either a raid from the Feds or an attack from our out of town friends. I need to be able to move in a week, ten days max."

"That's pushing it Paul, there's a few more guys that are sort of sitting on the fence about this. I guess I could push them a little harder."

"Wags."

"Yeah Paul."

"I appreciate everything you're doing out there."

"I'm doing it for Mike."

"You and me both my friend."

Paul hung up the phone and shook his head. He couldn't believe that a three minute phone call to Massachusetts just cost him $3.75.

CHAPTER 36

"Ground Control to Shuttle Liberation. Ground Control to Shuttle Liberation." The delay caused by the distance was a lot less than one would expect, but enough to make talking awkward, which was why as Ground Control was finishing up their second attempt to hail the shuttle Colonel Thomas had already started talking.

"This is the Space Shuttle Liberation, go ahead Ground Control."

"Say again, Shuttle Liberation, I was still talking when you began."

This was what it was like talking to mainland U.S.A. when he was stationed in Hawaii, the colonel thought to himself.

"I say again Ground Control, this is Colonel Thomas of the Space Shuttle Liberation. Ground Control, where is Major Hatfield?"

"Ah, Colonel, he, he's taken some time off to be with his family."

The colonel couldn't blame him. These could be the last few days of our civilization. And the colonel knew that Butch was taking this mission a lot harder than even he himself was. When Butch found out that Ray was going on this mission, he had volunteered himself also. Ray had turned him down. When Butch had confronted him on it, he merely answered that he wanted Butch here on Earth to take care of his kids. He had known from the get go that this was a one way ticket and he'd be damned if he made Butch's kids fatherless too.

"What can we do for you Ground Control, do you want a bowel movement or something for your bio-sensors?"

"Ah no sir, General Burkhalter wanted to say a few

words."

That got the colonel's attention, not that he really had any respect for the rank in principle, but he did for that man. Of all the generals he had ever met, he felt that only two or three had actually earned their rank through their battlefield expertise, and not their political know how. And General Burkhalter was definitely in the former category.

"Hello Colonel, how are things going up there? How is your crew's morale?"

The colonel found himself assuming the position of attention. He knew that he was hundreds of thousands of miles away and the general couldn't even see him, but there he was in zero g's at the position of attention.

"Sir, morale is as high as it can be, but the men do have a few requests."

"By all means, Colonel, but please be advised that we have been told by our senior science staff that these transmissions are being monitored and most likely decoded."

"But how is that possible sir, this is the most advanced technology known to man?" and then the Colonel realized that he had answered his own question. "Sir, the men would like a few words with their significant others." He made damn sure to omit the word 'last' in the previous sentence. No sense in letting their eavesdroppers know their intentions.

"We should be able to arrange that Colonel. But in the meantime, Colonel, please know that you have the utmost admiration and respect from your colleagues and myself."

"Coming from you sir, that truly is an honor."

"Over and out Liberation."

"Over and out Ground Control... and goodbye," the colonel added inaudibly.

CHAPTER 37 – Journal Entry 25

I sat in my enormous living room and stared at the Jumbotron. So there I was, ranked last, can you believe this crap? I couldn't buy respect in a whorehouse. Three people left and I'm ranked third. This was worse than betting with my brother Ronny, at least I knew where I stood with him. I just kept losing, it was never hard to know where you were. But here, I keep winning and I'm losing, how does that make any sense? But then again none of this really made any sense. I was fully expecting another round robin event but the aliens wanted to draw the suspense out. No. 2 Sam Pontiff and myself were to battle to the end to see who would have the privilege to meet Thomas Durgan, who by all accounts had gotten even bigger. He looked like he was growing taller and more muscular, what hell were they feeding him? I had actually hoped for a one on one on one event again, I'm fairly certain Sam would have sided with me until we possibly finished Durgan off, although I would have liked to have another two or at least three people in there with us for insurance. I'm not sure if a battle armored alien guard could have stood up to Durgan these days. Any semblance of sanity had left that man the first week he was on this ship, and he had done nothing but spiral even further into that insanity since then. Sam was a study in the opposite, he was methodical and thorough. Proficient I guess is the word I'm looking for. He had been somewhat of an underdog through the earlier rounds, but he had proved himself big in the last three or four rounds with some huge upsets. He had the appearance of a surfer dude gone bad. To glance at him quickly you would have seen a man with shoulder length bleached blonde hair, roguish good looks and a quick smile. I'm sure once upon a time he was a pot smoking laid back dude, much like my friend Paul whom I missed dearly. But on closer examination of his eyes, you would take notice that whatever light of goodness that had shone in them had dimmed and been replaced long ago with a cruel and bitter darkness. He took no joy in his kills but neither did he shy away from them. At 5'10" he wasn't necessarily huge but you could tell any surfer residue had been burned away. This man had been using the weight bench religiously, he was ripped. I was trembling, I hadn't even realized it until I looked down at my hands and they were shaking. I wasn't necessarily shaking because of Sam, although he definitely scared me. No, I was shaking because I was two rounds away from Beth, and I couldn't even begin to explain to her the things that I'd done since we'd been apart. How do you go about explaining the unexplainable? Oh God, I will have gone through all this for naught. No, I said to myself, stop thinking like that, you have kept these women around you alive too. But for what? I asked myself. For further slavery for more events? I'm pretty sure they weren't going to put me out to pasture after this was over, if I lived. Isn't the first sign of insanity when someone talks to themselves? My mind was racing in a thousand directions but it always steered back to one thing, Beth. The girl that I felt in my heart I was destined for. My soul mate. But how tarnished was my soul, how black and dirty was it now? Even if she accepted my on the physical plane, would she reject me on the spiritual, would her soul be so repulsed by mine that her heart would have to follow? I had to get out of here, I had to go for a walk. So I went up to the door that wasn't a door and just started shouting.

"Guards!!! Guards!!!" The women stopped everything that they were doing and froze, they just stared at me. I felt that I had entered into one of my early pubescent daydreams. Come on you know the one, where you are able to freeze women so that you can do whatever you want to them. Oh you never had that one? Maybe I am going insane.

"What is it hu-man?" The guard looked vaguely

pissed, almost like I had interrupted a card game or whatever they did in their free time around here.

"I need to get the fuck out of here!" I shouted, not realizing that the door only stopped me, not my voice.

"What is phruck?" the guard said, having some serious difficulty with the "f." It almost sounded like an Asian. Great, I have an Asian crocodile guard at my force field door. Did I truly just lose it that night I called my brother from a bad acid trip? Maybe I never came down. God please, maybe I'm really right now just locked up in an insane asylum and someday some brilliant man will invent some drug that will get me out of my drug induced insanity, how awesome would that be? But in the meantime I guess I'd better keep up with what's going on in this alternate universe.

"No I just want to get out of here."

"Stop talking hu-man!" he shouted, maybe he also didn't realize that the door didn't stop sound waves. And that was that, he turned and walked back through the invisible shield on his side of the deck. I had contemplated shouting again, but I didn't think he'd be nearly as congenial this time around. I was about to head back to my room when I saw a sliver of light down the corridor. I craned my neck to see, but the angle just wasn't right. I hoped I hadn't ticked off his card buddies and now it was time for payback. And then the smiling face of what could possibly be my initial guide from the previous tour was at my door. I didn't mean to be specieist but they all looked the same. He let the gate down without so much as a guard by his side.

"What can I do for you Mike?" I jumped back, I had never expected him to use my name. "Are you so surprised that I should know you by your Earth name?"

"Ah yeah, I'm a little shocked," I said as I was trying to regain my mental balance.

"Learning your name was the least I could do after all the dr… Money that you have earned me."

"I'm glad I could be of help," I said with my best Bostonian sarcasm attached to it. Unfortunately the wit was lost on him. Oh well, apparently there is no sarcasm in space.

"Why thank you, so what can I do for you?" he replied politely. He still looked like he could eat my head with one bite. It goes back to that whole trusting the smiling dog thing. It's a hard concept to get over.

"Well first thing's first, you know my name, what is your name?" Now it was his turn to be taken aback. I had no sense of why this was.

"We do not share our names with any one that is not of our race, even the Genogerians do not know their commanders' given names."

Whoa, so they don't even consider the Genos to be on the same plane as them? My guess was that they used the Genos in these games when they couldn't find an unsuspecting alien civilization. How long had they been doing this?

"But you can call me 'Frertek,' it means roughly 'one who guides' in your primitive language."

I had a snappy retort all set for that one, but then I might just anger him and if he didn't eat me outright he might not allow me to do what I so desperately wanted to do.

"Well Frertek, I would love to get out of here."

"I am sorry Mike, but no one is permitted to leave this ship, especially someone of your stature." And I know he didn't mean that in a good way. Man, I wish I had a baseball bat, cause I'd be slugging him upside his large noggin.

"No I mean out of this house, I just want to get away from all of them." I tried as casually as possible to motion to where all the women were. But he did not have a clue. How the hell could they be so far advanced from us? They had to have had outside help. "The women, Frertek, I have to get away for a while from all these women. I just want to go for a walk."

"Why would you wish to get away from your harem, Mike? Is this not the way that kings in your early years lived?"

"Yes Frertek, but when the king said jump his harem

would say how high. If I said it they would tell me to go take a flying leap." No recognition in his eyes, he didn't get it again. "Do you procreate, Frertek?"

"No, we have no need for such a thing; we are androgynous and asexual," he said very matter-of-factly.

"I guess that's sort of a blessing." Again with the blank stare. Okay, back to the direct approach. "Frertek, will you take me for a walk just so I can relax?"

"That is the least I can do, but be advised Mike that I am unarmed and at all times a guard will be no more than fifteen feet away. If you were by some means able to overpower me." It sure sounded like he used sarcasm there. "You would be shot immediately, and you have never experienced a pain more intense than that of a plasma discharge. It will burn you from the inside out. It is a most excruciating death, or so I am told."

"I have no illusions of escape Frertek, I simply wish to..." I was about to say stretch my legs but I was afraid he might take that too literally. "To go for a walk, to just leave this house for a while."

"Lead on Mike, you may go where you wish except for any door which has a red triangle on it. Those would be strictly forbidden to your kind." He really had no idea how pissed off he was making me. But I had been granted my wish so I wanted to make the most of it. I headed in the general direction of the arena, I had never been there except obviously on game day, this would be my chance to check out the place without any life or death pressure placed on me. And I wanted to see where Beth sat, maybe, hopefully, she had a seat with a very obstructed view, but I highly doubted it. The arena was deathly quiet; nobody was in there except myself and my guide. The place was enormous, on the scale of Mile High Stadium, maybe even bigger. How big was this ship? I walked onto the floor from my normal entranceway, the floor had not been altered in any way, no sense in wasting power with no event on. It was a very unremarkable looking surface for all the wondrous things that it could do. I pointed up into the stands.

"Frertek, could I go up into the stands?" I asked innocuously.

"Why certainly Mike, I see no red triangles around here." I couldn't tell if he was being sarcastic or straightforward. Thinking that I was a lesser being though, I had to opt for the latter.

"Frertek, where exactly does the Queen of the games sit?" My heart was pounding.

"It is not far from where you enter the arena. She sits about midway in the arena and five rows up. She sits in the seat marked with the flowers."

I all but ran to the seat, maybe some of her scent still lingered behind. If I concentrated hard enough maybe I would still be able to feel her presence. I inhaled deeply, I smelled something but whether it was just my overactive imagination I'll never know. But I would have sworn that I smelled the sweet vanilla scent that was Beth. I turned to the stadium floor, and then it hit me like a ton of bricks. She could see every disgusting thing I had done, perfectly. People on good old planet Earth paid huge bucks for these kinds of seats, just for the fact that you could see everything.

"Our Supreme Commander sits directly in front," Frertek broke through my horror. "He also has been watching your gamesmanship. He is very impressed with your skills on the arena floor. But he does not believe that you can beat either of the two opponents left," he said very matter-of-factly. What did he care, it wasn't his life he was talking about. I could have been an insect for all the emotion he showed about my expected demise. I noted with great interest where the guard stations where. There was one right next to each of the gladiators' entrances but curiously enough there were no guard stations that were noticeable anyway, anywhere around the Supreme Commander's chair. He obviously had no concern whatsoever in regards to assassination. Maybe that was only a human folly.

"Is this Supreme Commander a pretty popular guy?" I

asked casually

"What exactly do you mean by popular, Mike?" Frertek asked almost if he was trying to grasp a question out of a non-developed infant's mind. And I guess for all I knew about their culture I was just that.

"Do you vote in your leaders?"

"Oh no, hu-man." I must have really been looking ignorant, this was the first time Frertek had slid down into the Genogerian method of addressing me. "He is the Supreme Commander by birthright. He can be challenged only by those of high blood and only during the Marquetith."

"The mar what?" I asked, puzzled.

"It is something much like these games, it is much more ritualistic though. Very seldom do injuries occur during their bouts. But the winner is crowned the Supreme Commander."

"How often do these ritualistic fights take place?"

"Roughly two and half of your earth years."

"And once the bout has been decided it cannot be challenged?"

"No hu-man, we do not have impeachments like on your planet, he is our Supreme Commander and all on this ship would die a thousand deaths before we would see any harm befall him. Come Mike, we will go to the eating hall, all this question and answering has made me hungry. And do not worry, it is not the Genogerians' eating time, you will not be subjected to see any of your peers eaten."

"How comforting," I answered.

"Yes, I agree." They really don't have a sense of humor. How do you go this far into your evolution without laughing? Maybe that's how the Germans were always kicking ass on our planet.

It actually ended up being a relatively enjoyable lunch. Frertek was quite chatty and gave me a lot of insights into his civilization. I think he was what we on Earth would call bragging. He was always comparing it to the foibles of my planet.

"You know Mike. if we had been around here when your Earth smashing meteorite had hit we would have stopped it. Our planets are very similar except for the obvious fact of who won out in the evolutionary tract. My kind by right should be ruling your planet; it took an interstellar mistake of vast proportions to change that outcome. So basically we are only taking what was rightfully ours from the beginning." I dropped my juice. It spilled all over my shirt, but I didn't even notice.

"So, so, you're here to stay?" I stuttered.

"Well not me personally, but once the invasion is complete we by all means plan to make this one of our colonies."

"You're just going to take our planet?" I cried.

"It is only yours by mistake hu-man, and at the pace you are going we are only speeding the process up by a few years at most."

"What gives you the right to come from God knows where and take what is ours?"

"We take whatever we wish to. We are not hampered with the overabundance of emotions that you hu-mans have. This planet will be an excellent colony for us, and with a minimum amount of work to restore it."

"So you are just going to come in and wipe us out as if the meteorite never hit?"

"Oh no Mike, we plan on using your kind for our physical labor, and like the Genogerians we will most likely use you in our conflicts throughout the galaxies. Your kind has proved over and over again your skills at killing, treachery and trickery. You will fit in most well with our scheme of things. And the way that you procreate so quickly will make a wonderful food source."

"You're going to eat us?"

"Well, not all of you." It seemed by his tone that he couldn't believe that I was outraged with the fact that we were now a step lower on the food chain. "Do not be alarmed Mike, while we do plan to greatly reduce your numbers we have no desire to extinguish your species like you do to so many of the other species on your planet. To kill you off would not be beneficial to our species. You work hard and kill gloriously, and when prepared properly you taste wonderful."

"How comforting," I said for the second time today.

"Quite," he answered. I really think he thought that I was appeased.

That little bit of conversation put a huge damper on the rest of my meal. I tried my best to show Frertek that I was thoroughly pleased that they weren't going to wipe us out, only enslave and eat us. I think I would have much preferred option one. Mankind would be more inclined to fight to the finish if they knew it was a matter of extinction or not. Just take this small group of concert-goers for instance. We had butchered each other for survival, would we have been so inclined had we been told we would merely be enslaved and a certain portion of us rooted out? I don't think so, we would have settled for the more peaceable solution because the survival rate would be significantly higher. What of the quality of life? Was a mere increase in quantity worth the degradation in quality? I'd rather go down guns a blazing to these things than to die an old decrepit slave having done their bidding my entire life. That one flash of existence would have infinitely far outweighed the dragged out dredge my life and my future generations' lives would become. And so I kept with my plans to get off of this ship. Although I must admit it was much more smoke and mirrors than anything of true substance. But I rationalized, smoke and mirrors pretty much summed up my entire time here thus far. I would first need to get through my next competitor and that in itself was going to be no easy matter. I don't think he would care if I told him that I needed to get off of this ship to tell our home planet of the imminent danger that they were in. My guess is that he just wanted to finish me and Durgan off and he would be quite content to spend the rest of his days aboard this ship doing their bidding. Who knows, I could be wrong but that was my impression and at the time I had no one else's to go with. I prodded Frertek for as much information as I could about the ship, pretending as best I could to be completely awe struck about everything he said, which actually wasn't that far from the truth. When someone tells you that the ship you are in is roughly the size of Texas, you have to be a little dumb-founded. I guess Frertek was in a good mood or maybe he thought I had no chance of surviving the next round, or maybe it just didn't matter to him what I knew. What could I do with any information he told me anyway? It's not like there was a Radio Shack on this place. Although maybe there was. He told me that the entire outer hull that wrapped around the ship was the hangar which contained somewhere on the order of ten thousand ships. The next inner layer housed humans, I learned that my 'window' was merely a projected image on a plasma screen, I felt cheated, other non-friendly aliens or their version of livestock. The next inner layer contained close to ten million Genogerians, their warrior class. The inner layer contained the more advanced race of Progerians, or so he said, they roughly numbered in the two to three million range and then the inner sanctum where only those of the high blood were quartered, and there was where the Supreme Commander reigned supreme.

"So you don't intend on destroying Earth." I stated.

"Oh by no means, if we had wished to do that we would have done so long ago and been done with it. But your planet so closely matches our own in terms of gravity and atmosphere and it comes neatly stocked with an endless food supply. It would be detrimental for us to destroy your planet."

"How do you plan on taking our planet? You have watched us fight, you know that we are not merely going to lie down and let you waltz on in."

"Waltz on in?"

"I mean just come to our planet and hand it over."

"No, the plan is a simple one that we have used

throughout the galaxy. We will demoralize your planet. We will start with an overwhelming display of force and then offer what your people call an olive branch. Once your people have realized that they cannot resist our awesome might we will have won. Your kind will roll over like all those before you have."

"And how exactly do you go about displaying this awesome show of force?" I knew it was a long shot but I had to push, what could it hurt? He seemed to like to brag and I was a captive audience.

"It's quite brilliant in its simplicity. First we level two or three of your largest population centers around the planet. The sheer magnitude of the destruction is usually enough to quash any resistance, but occasionally a small faction or two will rise up and that is when we loose the Genogerians on them. To have terror reigned on from above is one thing, but to fight these creatures up close and personal has made stronger species than your own quake and shiver. The longest we have ever had to battle for possession of a planet was I believe eighteen of your Earth months. The Drenodiuns were an incredibly resilient fighting force."

"Were." I interjected.

"Yes, they proved entirely too difficult to bend to our will so we did away with them."

"What do you mean you 'did away' with them? You wiped out a whole species because they wouldn't just surrender to a hostile alien force and give up their home planet, their freedom and ultimately their lives to you?!" I was fuming. My planet's very existence was hanging on a thread. A thread which the Progerians held.

"It really wasn't that big of a deal, they tasted horrible no matter how much seasoning you put on them."

"What happened that you destroyed them all?"

"They were a lot lower in their development than your species is right now. They were somewhere more along the lines of the late 1700's in their technology. Their weapons were very crude. We obliterated a few of their larger settlements but they did not have the mass media like so many planets do. They actually had no reliable means for the news to carry. It was weeks, sometimes even months before news of these atrocities spread, so the seed of doubt had not been planted into them like it will be on your planet when images of Brazil razed and burning are flashed across the globe in live time. When the Genogerians landed the Drenodiuns fought for everything they were worth. They fought, they died, they inflicted a lot more casualties than we had anticipated, and they just wouldn't give up. Even when we could come to a tentative agreement with one country, none of the others would follow suit. And after we fought from country to country and finally had them succumb to our rule, still they fought. The governments called them rogues or rebels, but we knew better, we knew the governments were funding their operations. The Supreme Commander decided, especially since they tasted so bad, that ridding the land of them would do us no undue harm or misfortune. We removed all of our troops and dropped huge pods of poison onto their planet. Within three weeks all the Drenodiuns that lived on that planet were either dead or dying."

"How could you?"

"Oh do not worry, the poison is very fast in the breakdown process. We were able to inhabit the planet less than six months after the pods had done their work. Clean up after these attacks can be tedious but colonists seldom mind difficult work. The poison was specifically designed to kill only the Drenodiuns so food was still in abundance, even more so because obviously the top predator of the food chain had been eliminated."

"So you didn't destroy the whole planet?"

Frertek snorted. "What would be the sense in that? Contrary to your popular beliefs on Earth there are not hundreds of thousands of habitable planets out there. They are very rare and precious. To destroy a perfectly good planet makes no sense, it makes no sense whatsoever." And he seemed a little peeved that I would even think that his species was capable of such a thing. Geez, what was I thinking.

"Frertek, what happens to me if I win this competition?" Would he answer?

"Well as you know Mike, I statistically doubt that you will win, but because you asked I will answer. As we travel from galaxy to galaxy you would be paraded around as the champion of the Earth games. More than likely you will face champions from other species. You will keep fighting to live or you will die."

"So there is no happy ending to this fairy tale?"

"Being among a superior race should be enough reward in its own." And there wasn't a hint of sarcasm in his voice. Well, I guess if you kick ass all across the galaxies you have a right to be cocky. If I ever got a hold of a plasma weapon he was going to be the first to taste it. But as I had been for a long time about a lot of things, I was wrong again. Frertek babbled a little more and I nodded at the appropriate times like a good little lap dog and he eventually led me back to my house. Now I was actually relieved to be coming back. The women didn't say anything but they also appeared relieved that I hadn't offended anybody and ended up on tonight's menu. I was exhausted; Frertek's ramblings had worn me out. Now I felt like I had the weight of my life, all the women's lives, and the lives of everyone on my planet squarely weighted on my shoulders. Even if I won what would I be going back to? Certainly not the planet I had left. Well, I reasoned, at least our internal Earthly disputes would cease to exist. But the alternative wasn't any better, not by a long shot. One thing I took from Frertek was that Earth still had time. This ship, as vast as it was, was not a true invasion/occupation force, it was a scout. The real battle cruisers were a good three to four years off even with their buckle drives, whatever that meant. The scout ships were just that, scouts. They were there to put the fear of God, or whatever deity the Progerians worshipped, into the doomed species and to occasionally chase off any other species that might be trying to move in on their intended territory. The universe was vast but not so vast that on occasion two competing species wouldn't fight over a planet or a system. The battle cruisers were the true invaders, but a scout ship could still deliver considerable damage.

CHAPTER 38

Outside Vail

"Hey sir, ah Paul, I was wondering something?" Frank asked tentatively.

"What is it Frank, you look a little perplexed, do you need to go move a bowel or something?"

"No, no, that's not it, but with the recruitment of so many personnel..."

"Speaking of which, oh I'm sorry to interrupt, but how many people are we up to now? I've been so busy with appropriating supplies I haven't got a chance lately to go out there and see what's going on."

"We just topped one hundred."

"Damn, no wonder we need so much stuff."

"They need more."

"I've got just about everything that I can think of on this list, what more do we need."

"It's not a physical thing sir, I mean Paul, it's not something you can hold but it is something you can hold onto."

"Frank, you're talking in circles, come out with it."

"Sir, I mean Paul, we need leadership."

"Well then, make yourself a general and let's be done with it."

"Paul, that's not how it works. These people here, they came because of you and your ideas, they merely see me as an instrument of yours."

"So you're saying I should just stop with all this requisitioning stuff and go play soldier."

"Basically in a nut shell that's exactly what I'm telling you to do. These people came here to learn how to defend their homeland and if necessary die for it. Go get

Dewey to do all this appropriating and paperwork, he's very adept at it and it will give you a chance to get out there and be with your personnel."

"You make this sound like an army."

"What do you think this is? And speaking of which, any time you get a mob this big together under stressful situations you're going to have problems. We need to instill some discipline, definitely into the newbies."

"Frank, this is the kind of crap I avoided like the plague in college. I didn't even fill out the form at the post office when I turned eighteen."

"Well like it or not Paul, you are now in command of the first planetary defense army and as such I think that you need to start acting the part whether you want to or not."

"Well Frank, you were in the Marines, what's a good rank for me?"

"Well to be honest I always thought full bird colonels were the baddest asses in the Corps, they weren't so high and mighty that they couldn't come out and do physical training with the troops. They mostly seemed like regular Joes with a little more responsibility. I knew colonels in the corps that every one of his troops would willingly follow to the death. And that's the feeling I get with our troops when they look at you. They'd follow you to hell, and to be completely honest I think they might just do that before this whole thing is over."

"Well then Frank, Colonel Ginson it is, and just exactly what rank would you like to garner?"

"I've always fancied myself a captain."

"Congratulations Captain Salazar. Now I just need to get us insignia and some uniforms and we'll be all set."

"Already done sir." Frank pulled out a set of camouflage fatigues with colonel wings on the lapels.

"Pretty sure of how this conversation was going to turn out Frank?"

"Just a little bit, sir."

"Captain." Frank snapped to the position of attention. Paul thought to himself that this was going to take a little getting used to. "Captain, please send in Private Dewey Johnson." Frank smiled with the corner of his mouth, said "Aye sir," did an about face and left the command tent.

CHAPTER 39

NORAD

"Captain Moiraine."

"Yes General." The Captain had been awakened by his lieutenant when the call from the general came in over the scrambled line. He had been in a deep sleep and found it relatively comforting that he could awaken so fast when the need arose. His mother would be so proud. As a youngster it had taken nothing short of soaking him with cold water to get him out of bed and on his way to school.

"Captain Moraine, are you there?" Apparently he hadn't woken up nearly as well as he first believed.

"Sorry sir, the line faded out."

"Captain, have you been keeping an eye on those zealots up by Vail?"

"Yes sir, we have a satellite that primarily monitors their doings. Sir, may I speak freely?"

"Go ahead Captain, I have never been one to stifle your opinions even if you would let me."

"Sir, why are we wasting so much time and resources on this small band of militia?"

"Well Captain, there are a couple of reasons. Number one, we don't want them alarming the general population. So far they have kept their theories pretty close to the vest. Their recruitment is very limited and selective. We just want to make sure that they don't get the country's panties in a bunch and secondly... well, secondly we're funding them."

Now the captain was fairly certain that he had not fully awoken from his sleep. "Sir, say again?"

"We're funding them, this is known only to myself, their leader, Paul, a supply sergeant in the Springs and now you."

"But sir, why would you help out a fanatic militia?"

"Because they are at least preparing for the inevitable. The President is so busy trying to negotiate a peace with a species that won't even acknowledge our existence except to scoop some of us up for God knows what purpose. He won't bring any of our troops back from the Middle East or Europe, this is the time when we should be monitoring our own, and he hasn't even mobilized the National Guard. Not that I think that those buffoons could win a war even if they were fully activated and on alert."

"Sir, what could you possibly think this rag tag bunch could do?"

"Captain I just don't know, but that Paul's got moxie and I like him. He actually approached me and convinced me of his intentions. He knew full well I could have thrown him in jail just for mentioning it, but yet he went full steam ahead anyway. And you know Captain, sometimes the smallest cog in the machinery has the biggest role. And something deep down in my gut tells me that this is the case here. So basically Captain, I want you more to keep an eye on the activity around the mountainside as opposed to the activity in the camp. I don't want any of the local police messing this up. You, my fine Captain, are going to run interference for, I believe he is now called Colonel. Yeah, Colonel Ginson."

"Sir, how am I possibly going to do that?'

"Easy Captain, you are going to join the Earth Defense Militia. Over and out Captain. Any questions, you know where to reach me."

All thoughts of sleep had completely left the captain. So there he was watching an infomercial for a juicer at three in the morning with an ice cold Budweiser. He didn't know if it was the late hour or the cold beer, but that juicer really looked like a good buy.

CHAPTER 40 – Journal Entry 26

Orbiting Venus

I had less than a week and I had yet to find any viable strategy regarding my next opponent. He was as smart if not smarter, he was as big if not bigger and he was fast and yes, faster than myself. He displayed a wide range of excellence with almost every weapon. He had stood toe to toe and won, he had tricked opponents and won. He had even fallen into a trap and was deft enough to get out, get the upper hand and still kill his opponent. This fight was going to take everything that I had. And even that prospect didn't seem very fruitful. I had no clue which weapon I even wanted to attempt with him. Luckily the Progerians took care of that small detail. The remainder of the week flew by, I don't know how because I sure wasn't having any fun. But there it was on the screen, game time; only I didn't get to sit back and watch the Giants with Wags and a cold beer. Everything that I had planned hinged on one man. The fate of the entire planet Earth itself seemed to hinge on this battle. If I lost, we as a species would pretty much have sealed our fates. But if step one in my at least ten step plan went as planned, I would be the victor here and one step closer to warning my home. The problem however with plans is that they rarely go as planned. Joe Pontiff had no desire to be my latest victim and the Progerians had made this round of the battles the toughest thus far. I was introduced first as seems to be customary for me. I surveyed the arena to get the lay of the land and that was when I noticed the first thing that was amiss. There were no weapons on the walls at all. One would reason that the aliens quite possibly hid them within the arena tapestry. But that would also be a falsehood, because the arena was merely a level dirt surface, there was nowhere to hide anything.

Anxiety rose within me. Fighting was hard enough but hand-to-hand combat to the death was almost a little more than I could bear. My legs literally began to wobble. I looked up at the big screen as soon as Joe was receiving his introduction. He also surveyed the arena, and he knew what was happening also. He did not seem in the least concerned, and why should he. I had thus far not proven to anybody that I was very adept at this style of fighting. Perhaps the powers that be realized this and were finally finding a way to get rid of me. The horn sounded and the bout began. I did not move for fear of falling over, I didn't want to give Joe any more confidence than was absolutely necessary. He started heading towards me but he was cautious, he was making sure that I had not set up some sort of elaborate plan. I don't know what he was thinking, but I had nowhere to hide and nothing to use. But I guess when it's your life on the line it's better to err on the side of caution. I felt like a deer caught in the headlamps, I couldn't move backwards and I didn't dare move forward. I felt naked without a weapon. I felt small, I felt puny. I wanted to run, but there was nowhere to go. And yet he kept approaching. I knew he was coming but I felt like I was stuck in a Twilight Zone show. Every time I looked at him he never appeared to be getting any closer. But I'm pretty sure it was wishful thinking on my part. If he never looked like he was getting here than just maybe he wouldn't really get here. But my body knew what my mind failed to grasp, a little thing called reality. He was coming and if I didn't get a groove on I'd be dead before the next minute ticked off.

Was he saying something? Why was he wasting his breath, unless he was telling me he surrendered I really didn't want to hear it.

"...thing personal."

What? Did he just say nothing personal, he was coming over to crack my neck in two. Not somebody else's neck, *my* fricken neck. How the hell was that not personal? I instantly flashed back to good old Tom Greenborough, only in this scenario I was Tom and I was begging for mercy. But there was no mercy here, only death. The place reeked off it. I swooned, "shit," I thought as I collapsed to my knees, "I'm going to pass out." And apparently Joe could tell by how my face had drained of all color that I wasn't faking. This was no elaborate plot, my flight or fight mechanism had pretty much fried itself. I was the proverbial fish out of water. Joe wasn't taking any chances, he moved in fast as my eyes began to roll up into my head. He was a no nonsense type of guy, no sense in dragging out the inevitable. I couldn't stop thinking of all those women back at the house. They must be flipping out. It wouldn't take a rocket scientist to see that my numbers had finally come up and they were all snake eyes. So this is how it ends, so close to the finish line and I fell, what a fucking bummer. And then Joe's hands were on either side of my head, he was going to twist my neck like a bottle cap. "I hope it doesn't hurt." I thought to myself. But his hands on my head and neck electrified me, the only way I could describe it was like he was the jumper cable and I was the dead battery. My fried flight or fight mechanism coughed, sputtered and sprang to life. And there it was, Joe's crotch was directly in front of my face. I wanted to relate this story and say that I threw my closed fist up and punched him as hard as I could in the jewels but that wouldn't be the truth. I don't know why I did it but I did it. I bit him, I bit him so hard I literally crushed his right nut in my mouth. Don't get me wrong, I'm not very proud of that fact, as I write this line I'm still debating about whether or not to delete it. It was horrible, it had the same consistency as that of biting into an unpeeled avocado, and then it burst. Joe immediately went rigid and attempted to scream, that part may have been the worst. The pain for him was so intense he couldn't even vocalize it. I don't know which of us was more in shock, him just stuttering in pain or me with his burst sack in my mouth. Thank God for cotton shorts. I let go and Joe fell over. He didn't even attempt to break his fall, he fell straight backwards still wordlessly mouthing his agony. The sensation of the whole event had turned my stomach, I had ruined this man with my mouth, it was by far the most vulgar thing I had done to date. "Oh please," I thought to myself, "don't let there be another event to compare to this." I turned and retched up everything that I had eaten for the last two days, and still I couldn't get the sensation of his scrotum bursting in my mouth out of my head. When I finally turned back to look at him he was still rigid as a board staring straight up at the ceiling. He hadn't even moved his hands to cover his damaged goods. And for the second time in this whole hellish nightmare someone begged me to kill him. And I had to, you can't do what I did to another man and not finish the job, I still had that much humanity in me. I didn't know if I had enough strength to snap his neck. I was afraid of botching that, and I wasn't sure if I could take any more of this inhumanity. So I brought the heel of my boot directly down on the bridge of his nose. I heard the splinter of bone, and the splash of blood, but I didn't stop to check if my first blow had done the trick. I wasn't brave enough for that. I wouldn't be able to look at him if I hadn't finished this. I brought the heel of my boot down on his face again and again, to the point where there was no face left. I had crushed virtually every bone in his face and driven his eyes down into his brain cavity. Not only was there a massive amount of blood but also brain tissue began to splatter all around. And yet I stomped on. I know that at that point I had finally lost it. Even the aliens had had enough. Two guards had to pull me off of him, they literally had to raise me off of the ground and still I kicked, strings of brain hung off my treads. I had crushed Joe's head down to half of its former self. But it really wasn't so bad. His face was so mangled it didn't even look human, and that was almost something I'd be able to live with, almost. To this very day it doesn't take much effort for me to relive every moment of that. After so many years it's still that close to the surface. The guards had to carry me back to my quarters, I was so dysfunctional at the moment that if they hadn't carried me they would have had to drag me. When they got to my apartment they deposited me on the foyer and left. I was vaguely aware of my surroundings; the women were just staring, mouths hanging open, dumbfounded. Just think how I was doing ladies. And then the cavalry came to the rescue. Stephanie.

"What the hell are you all looking at? Your champion is back and he needs our help." That seemed to galvanize them. "Tanya, get his boots off." I don't know what she did with those shoes, but I never saw them again, and I'm a much happier person for it. "Gabriella, get some water! Rebecca, help me with his pants and shirt!" And all of a sudden the house was a blaze of activity, I was stripped, scrubbed, redressed and put to bed, all without me doing much more than moving the appropriate body part when asked to. I slept remarkably well that night. Maybe that's how madmen do it. Without a conscience, I mean. How else after the horrors I inflicted that night could I be otherwise. That was the last waking thought I had that evening. I awoke the following morning feeling absolutely refreshed; I couldn't begin to explain the lightness in my heart. Had I lost that much humanity? The women folk for the most part were very wary around me. How far over the line had I traveled and would I or could I even come back over it? Did I want to? It was so much easier on this side. No conscience, no worries, no pain. I felt great but yet I knew that was a horrible thought process. I must have had some horrible facial expression on my face because the women avoided me like the plague. You would have thought that I had leprosy. It was later I learned that it was the lifeless grin on my face that had scared the shit out of all of them, even Deb and Steph. Nobody dared disturb me today. What was going on, I felt great and no one was even congratulating me on my win, the ingrates.

"Huh, I wonder what ranking I am today?" I yelled and laughed. The women all but tried to blend in with the surrounding furniture

"I'm going back to my room, I strongly suggest nobody make any noise." I don't even think they were breathing at the moment. Hours later a little brunette named Bridgitte dropped a bowl on the floor and all the women froze, so sure they were of me busting out of that room and killing her. Bridgitte wept uncontrollably for an hour. I didn't even know the whole thing happened, I had been dead asleep almost from the moment I entered my room.

CHAPTER 41

Vail

"Hey Colonel, you got a minute?" One of the newest enlisted men to the militia poked his head into the command tent.

"What can I do for you Private...?" Paul hesitated for a moment. "Anderson." Paul took great pride in learning the names of every man and woman in his new army, from the highest to the lowest.

"Sir." Paul still had not gotten used to that yet, but he was learning. "Sir, I was in town this morning picking up some supplies and I ran into this gentleman outside of town. He said he had heard rumors about what was going on up here and that he may or may not be interested in rendering his services."

"Did he give you a name, Private?"

"I think he said More Rain or something to that effect."

"Was he talking code, soldier?"

"Sir?" the private looked at Paul with a comical expression.

"Don't worry about it Anderson, just send him in on your way out please."

"Yes sir, right away sir."

"Ah, so you're the infamous Colonel Ginson that I've heard so much about." Captain Moiraine said as he sauntered into the room. He was not happy with his new assignment and it showed. Paul had known sooner or later Burkhalter or the FBI or CIA or one of those alphabet organizations was going to send a mole. He had no idea that it was going to be such a lightly veiled placement.

"What can I do for you Mr. ..."

"Moiraine, Sam Moiraine."

"Mr. Moiraine."

"I came up here to see what exactly was going on up here and if it was to my liking whether or not I would stay."

"Aren't you a little old to be playing army, Mr. Moiraine?" Paul asked with a slight smile on his face. This could actually work to his advantage. Having a known spy, he could be used as he saw fit. He could make it look like these guys were just a bunch of goof balls with some extra ammunition. That would greatly ease the prying eyes if they thought they were a bunch of buffoons.

"I'll have you know Colonel Ginson that I still can run three miles in under twenty minutes," Moiraine said, heat starting to flare under his collar. He was a decorated Captain in the Marines and here he was taking heat from a self-appointed Colonel of a rag tag bunch of near fugitives.

"Have much need for that out in the civilian world, do you Mr. Moiraine?"

Moiraine eased back a bit, he had almost blown his cover in the first three minutes, and he had no desire to tell the General he couldn't even get enlisted into this quasi-military endeavor.

"Well if you can't tell by looking at me, I'm prior military."

"Prior, Mr. Moiraine?" And now it was Paul's turn to ease up. If he led on that he knew what this man was up to they'd just send another who might be much more difficult to root out. Who knows, maybe this guy is here to take the pressure off of the real spy. Oh what a wicked web we weave. You gotta love the Internet though, he had background checks on every one of his troops, and he had no desire to bring down any more heat on this fledgling organization than absolutely necessary. He really only had two or three people in his unit that he had some unanswered questions about, and they were not so much as able to pee on their own without being shadowed. At least until they showed their true colors or proved themselves loyal.

"Prior, Colonel. I know a lot of things about how to organize a successful fighting machine. But I am only here if the cause is justifiable. If you're here to overthrow the U.S. government or to hire your services out to foreign campaigns, I'm out of here. I have no desire to be with traitors, or for that matter, mercenaries." Moiraine said with a sneer.

"Hold on Mr. Moiraine. Simmer down a bit. We are not here to take down the U.S. government, in fact that would be the direct opposite of our intentions. We are not here as mercenaries. We are not up here playing glorified games of paintball. We have one reason and one reason only to be up here."

"And what is that?"

"Defense."

"Defense from what, Colonel? Radical Muslim fundamentalists?"

"Moiraine, I don't know how much you're trying to hide from me but I've got a fair idea you know what's going on in the real world. Call me crazy if you want, you wouldn't be the first, but I started this fighting unit for defense of our planet. My best friend on this woe begotten world was dematerialized in front of hundreds of amazed and horrified witnesses. Now granted, the vast majority of these people were on mind-altering substances of one sort or another. But when the government pulled out the old mass hallucination card I knew something was fishy right from the git go. I've got ten or twelve of them I could round up for you in three minutes that will swear on their lives that they witnessed a huge ship literally take nine thousand or so people right out of Red Rocks. We have heard rumors of the same thing happening in Russia and China but those governments clammed up even more so than our own. We also have visual confirmation of a huge ship staged or poised if you will in orbit around Venus." Moiraine's face fell, outside of the military he had no idea anybody else knew about that ship.

"Ah, I can tell from your face you know something about this ship."

"I've heard rumors," Moiraine lied.

"We have an amateur astronomer in Maine, a good friend of mine that just happened to be checking out weather patterns on the planet of Venus when right before his eyes a huge ship, roughly the size of Texas or so I'm told, materialized and then just as suddenly dematerialized. Now my friend also likes to partake of the funny left handed cigarettes on occasion so I was prone to believe that he had witnessed one mother of a hallucination. But lucky for him and for us I guess, he always videotapes his sky watches, as he calls them. So there he was cleaning up that videotape for two days before he had the gumption to call me with it. He sent me a copy before he called the U.S. government, who by the way summarily confiscated that tape and all of his sky watching apparatus."

"You still have that copy?"

"Oh that copy and a hundred just like it scattered across the country for safe keeping."

"What's to say that this 'ship' isn't some sort of anomaly on the master tape?"

"Well you see my friend began to have those same doubts. It's kind of hard to swallow the fact that a huge alien ship has literally parked at your doorstep. So before he made the fateful call to the powers that be, he studied the planet's atmosphere with a little more scrutiny. You see apparently when something that big orbits around a planet it tends to have minute gravitational effects."

"Which he recorded."

"Right you are."

"And you have a hundred or so of those tapes scattered across the country."

"Again correct."

"But that still doesn't explain your whole military campaign here."

"Well you see Mr. Moiraine, I do not believe that these aliens have come to our fine planet on the up and up. If they had come in peace as we so often see on the creature double feature movies, I don't believe that they would have come and scooped up literally thousands of our people. My theory, and trust me I have doubted myself far too often, my theory is that they are studying those people. I am fairly certain those unlucky souls, my best friend included, are being subjected to the cruelest form of inhumanity. And therein lies the bulk of our problem, how could an alien civilization be deemed inhuman? They are by their very nature inhuman. They are alien. I am not one hundred percent sure they have come to annihilate us, just yet. But Mr. Moiraine, I fully intend to go down kicking and screamin', not crying and whimpering."

And beyond his better judgment Moiraine began to like this renegade. "Then why not tell the whole world what you know, show those tapes."

"Moiraine, I've watched those tapes over two hundred times each and I still don't believe what I saw. And you know as well as I do, John Q. Public is not ready for this type of information. The average Joe is concerned with the monthly mortgage bill and who the Bears are playing on Sunday. I have no desire to start riots in the street. The government knows what's going on, they have their hands full. I do not intend to throw any fire on that flame. But I also am not waiting idly by to wait for them to get their act together. It's not like they know what to do either. This isn't standard operating procedure these days. I had fully hoped that they would have called back all of our troops, but I guess they don't want to destabilize world power at this crucial time either. So there it is my friend. We are a new style military force for these times. We do an unbelievable amount of conditioning and combat training, we're getting prepared. So we put the word out there very subtly, people know something's going on, they're just not too sure what it is. If they come up here and they want to stick around then we let them. But it's not a free ride; everyone up here becomes part of the fighting force. If and when the shit hits the fan Mr. Moiraine, this just might be the safest place to be in North

America. If those aliens come down to start something they are going to hit military targets first. This place won't even be on their map. And once we get a glimpse of them, then we can go into action ourselves."

"I'm impressed, Colonel. I really thought I was going to come up here and run into a little Hitler wannabe. But you really seem to have your gear stowed away up here. If you don't mind, I think I'd like to stay awhile."

"How does the rank of Captain sound, Mr. Moiraine?"

"That'll do just fine, thank you."

"Great, then if you can just give me a few minutes Captain, I need to get a few things out of the way and I'll introduce you to the rest of the officers."

"Yes sir, Colonel, very well."

"Dismissed, Captain." And with that Captain Moiraine did an about face and left the command tent.

CHAPTER 42 – Journal Entry 27

Orbiting Venus

Durgan was next, there was no possible way to avoid that fact. His time, or more likely my time had come. He was an animal, no not quite. The aliens, *they* were animals. Come to think of it I'd rather take on one of the guards than Durgan. Sure they were bigger. But pound for pound Durgan was meaner. He was hopped up on some sort of go-go juice from the Progerians. Apparently he had big drakka backing his move for champion. If the aliens pulled another stunt like last time, having no weapons in the arena, even I personally would bet on Durgan winning. The women tried their best to be uplifting and consoling. They even tried an intervention. It was a couple of weeks before the match and they tried to coax me out of my room. Which by the way I hadn't left in the previous two weeks. I saw no reason to leave now, I knew my ranking and I knew Durgan's ranking. I knew his style, raving mad psychotic lunatic. What more was there? All of my exercise equipment was in my room, and food came whether I ate it or not. I had no desire to be amongst the living when I felt so dead. Deb tried her best but I wasn't having any of it. I'm certain she was the one who arranged the 'intervention.' What a pile of you know what that was. All the women came into my room with candles, I had no desire to get all touchy feely and find my inner femininity. If anything I was attempting to go even farther down the other path, and I let them know in no uncertain terms who the boss was around here. Now I know that this wouldn't have flown at home, but alas this wasn't Earth and therefore I wasn't bound to those rules. I kicked each and every one of them out including Deb and I told them that if they weren't bringing food or water into my room then they had absolutely no place there. I had really expected some sort of rebel uprising, but not a one of them even so much as whispered some disparaging remark. I'm sure they waited till I was well out of earshot before they attempted anything along those lines. No sense in pissing off the unchained lion. Even Frertek had come, I suppose in some alien way to say his goodbyes. The odds of my winning the next bout were at best one hundred to one. If this were pro football I would have been spotted twenty-eight points. Frertek had become more than a little peeved when I had not taken up his invitation to lunch. He had even gone so far as to strike Stephanie when she had blocked his path to my room. For me to interfere would have been fatal for us all, I didn't think that a purplish bruise on the cheek was worthy of all of our lives. So when he had slammed open my bedroom door, I was in the semi-catatonic state that I had adopted since the end of my last bout. He stared at me for what seemed like minutes, ranting away, and it was at this time I wished that I had known some Progerian speech because I would have sworn that he was swearing. Maybe he bet his next paycheck on me and now saw no way to recoup his losses. Because I truly looked insane, and the funny part was that not even I was sure whether or not I had crossed that line. It's a scary time in one's life to look inward and find a completely different person looking back. Frertek stopped by one more time about three days before the big dance. Stephanie did not, however, place herself in harm's way this time. He sauntered into my bedroom like he owned the place, which I guess he did in some fashion, and it was clear to him that I had not stirred an inch. Even the spittle on my chin was meticulously placed to look as if I hadn't even the desire to clean myself off. And there it was, it definitely sounded like the last long string of alien profanities, if he had stood there any longer I might have started laughing. The true problem would have been that I most likely wouldn't have been able to stop. Would Durgan get the same enjoyment out of killing me if I was laughing like a raving madman? Probably. I don't think he'd care if I was cradling kittens in my hands, a kill was a kill. I called Deb and Steph into my room the night before the bout, and I pretty much laid everything on the line. They were all ears. Although I believe some small dark well hidden place deep inside Deb hoped for my demise. For if I lived, she would lose. But the good part of her, which included the vast majority, outwardly rooted for me and my victory. Stephanie was more the pragmatist, she saw the inherent dangers and risks of my plan, but the rewards far outweighed the negatives. This was the proverbial rock and a hard place, it was our turn now. We would take hold of that rock and throw it at the hard place and see what happened. Ninety nine times, no make that nine hundred and ninety-nine times out of one thousand that rock would merely bounce off, but maybe, just maybe in this instance we would be able to crack either the rock, or the hard place, or more unlikely but much more desirable, both of them.

CHAPTER 43

Closing in on Venus.

"USS Liberation, this is Ground Control. USS Liberation, this is Ground Control, do you copy?"

"We copy loud and clear Ground Control. Nice to have you back Major Hatfield," the colonel said with true delight in his heart.

"Oh you know me Colonel, I just can't stay away too long," the major said, and the funny part was that he couldn't stand to be away from his post for too long. He had over six months of leave time built up and had been promising his wife for ten years they would go on vacation, but every time he got close to it he would get cold feet and back out. The military was his life and these men and women around him were also his family. He would lay down his life for any of them, as he knew that they would do for him. He was so concerned that the one time he left would be the one time they needed him the most. So for ten years he had placated his wife with three-day weekends and the occasional 96er. That's four days to you non-military types. A Friday and a Monday wrapped around a weekend.

"How are the wife and kids, Butch, do they still like piggyback rides?" Butch knew the code well enough, piggyback meant was any one listening in on the transmission.

"Well you know, Colonel the entire country likes piggybacks and especially our new friends, it seems that they've always liked piggybacks. Emphasis on always, Colonel."

"Hey Butch, any chance that once they got off of the piggyback ride that they'd kick our ass?"

"That's doubtful Colonel, if someone was going to

get off of your back and then kick you in the keester they would have done it a long time ago."

"That's good to know I think. Any luck with our last request?" the colonel asked hopefully.

"Yeah we've got some people here that would love to share a word or two with you, but good buddy, please have you and your crew be very selective in your choice of words, with the distance between us we're afraid that we'll lose transmission."

So basically the colonel was just told that he couldn't say goodbye to the people that meant the most to him in the world. How does one be matter-of-fact with the ones he loves at a time like this? But he knew if any of his crew or himself for that matter fouled up and started down the wrong path, the powers that be would yank the cord on this long distance call in a heartbeat. And that was another thing, he wanted to say goodbye to his wife in private, not with the whole damn military world listening in. But he had chosen this ride too long ago to now buck against the rules. And so he carefully briefed his crew on the do's and don'ts of their conversations. They were as pleased as the colonel but they were soldiers and they knew their place. He let his crew say their non-goodbyes before his wife of fifteen years took the mike.

"Hey Lauren, how are you doing?" Oh God, she was already sobbing, he knew there was some peon sergeant with his hand on the kill switch.

"Lauren honey, it's me Ray, are you crying because the Giants lost another close one?" Lauren knew enough about the situation that if she didn't pull it together soon she wasn't even going to get her pseudo-goodbye to the only man she had and would ever love.

"Those damn Giants," she said with a quiver in her voice.

"That's a girl, they'll pull it together next season. Don't you worry, just when you think they're down and out, there they are always by your side. I need you to be strong for them, Lauren. For our little Giants. Can you do that Lauren?"

She more nodded her head in agreement but the Colonel heard the mini whispered 'yes' come through the speaker as if she had shouted it.

"That's my girl. Because the little Giants are going to need a strong coach in the times to come. I've already talked to the assistant coach on this Lauren, and he wants you and the team to move in for these difficult rebuilding years. Do you understand Lauren?"

"I get it now Ray," as she choked back the tears. "Sometimes you just have to take one for the team. Even if it is a huge one."

"I love you Lauren."

"I love you too Ray." And it was the colonel that pulled the plug on this transmission, another second more and he would have started crying. Or worse, he might just have pulled on the yoke and turned the damn ship around. For just one more minute in her arms he would've done just that.

CHAPTER 44

Inside the Mother ship

"Sir, these humans just might be the most idiotic race that we have encountered thus far."

"Why crewman, what is going on in their communications?"

"Sir, they are hundreds of thousands of miles away from their home planet, about to encounter a civilization that they are not sure whether is friendly or not, and all they are talking about is an arcane game that they call football."

"This will be our easiest conquest so far, crewman. Our shore leaves will be doubled for making it such an easy effort." The crewman and his chief both laughed, they were already considering where they would go on their respective journeys.

CHAPTER 45 – Journal Entry 28

Orbiting Venus – But not nearly as nice
The day of reckoning had arrived. I wasn't too particularly thrilled about it. The women even less so. The majority of them believed that I wouldn't even rouse out of my catatonic state to make even a last gesture of defiance. Oh come on, you've all seen the t-shirts from back in the late seventies that had a mouse giving the eagle the finger right before the eagle was about to have his lunch. Well my growing legion of followers didn't even think that I was going to make that effort. And to be honest I wasn't sure if I was or wasn't. The guard came, Stephanie told him that I hadn't moved in weeks and that I was still in bed. The guard was less than amused, he crashed open my doors, this seemed to be a reoccurring theme among them. This time the doors were going to need some attention before they were serviceable again. But it really didn't matter, one way or the other I was going to be gone. The guard picked me up by the back of my pants. I felt like a little kid getting a 'superman' ride. I didn't appear to be fatiguing him in the least, but apparently he didn't like the way I just dangled there, so with a low grunt he hefted me over his shoulder like a sack of potatoes. And there it was, his rifle. It was no more than a foot away from my hand. But even that close, if I grabbed it how would I dislodge it from his shoulder? And then what, would it have some sort of safety device I'd never be able to figure out? All these thoughts and ten times that were running through my head. The arena approached a lot faster under his strides, we were just coming up on my entrance. I could hear the electricity buzzing in the crowd. Yeah, this was going to be a big draw night for them. But I figured it was going to be a lot like our Super Bowl, a lot of hype and

not much more. Normally the games leading up to the big event were much more noteworthy than the actual championship event. And I didn't figure that that was going to change today. For whatever reason, my guard had slung his rifle sling across his chest with the rifle resting on his back with the muzzle pointing down. I moved as slowly as possible so as not to bring attention to myself, I just reached out and placed a finger on what I was ninety-five percent sure was the trigger. I was on his right shoulder and the rifle pointed away from me down toward his left leg when he stepped. I was even less sure that his leg was in the line of fire but it wasn't like I could take a gander across his back. If I missed or just grazed him I wouldn't have to worry about Durgan, because of all the things I wasn't sure of this evening, I was sure this guard would kill me in an instant regardless of the consequences. I waited till his left leg was at its apex behind him and then pulled the trigger. Nothing happened; oh shit, there is a safety. And then I watched in horror or glee as my abductor's leg literally dissolved right before me. I guess it's hard to see stuff when you have your eyes closed. He fell over immediately; I think that he was in too much shock to even register the fact that he had just lost his leg. Falling eight feet wasn't any fun either, I slammed against the far wall thinking that I had once again dislocated my shoulder, but now was not the time to worry about that. He was in the process of attempting to flip himself over, if he did, it would take me and three other people a half hour to get that rifle up from under him. I kicked him where every animal is the most sensitive, square in the eye. That pain did register and he was beginning to howl. My time alone was growing short, luckily he was entirely too busy with his ruined eye and missing leg to give a shit about his rifle. But I still had the sling to contend with and that thing looked like it could tow a car. I had to finish him off; even an errant lashing out from him would break me in two. I just kept kicking him in the head till my leg ached. I was afraid I was going to cramp up, there I'd be, massaging a charley horse with a dead guard, I didn't think that would go over so well. After seven or eight kicks he stilled. I don't think he was dead but I wasn't going to check his pulse either. I unslung the rifle from him and not a moment too soon. I don't know what the guard said as he emerged from the arena floor, but I'm sure it was something along the lines of "What the hell is going on here? What is the delay? Get your ass in here!" But whatever it was I wasn't waiting for an interpreter. Shoot now and let God sort them out later. The second guard flew back into the arena with a fist-sized hole blown right through the middle of him. And much to my chagrin the whole scene had made its way on to the big screen, because they had been waiting for my grand entrance. Well I gave them a grand entrance, probably not what they were expecting though. I ran in and took a sharp left into the packed stands. Every single one of them had their eyes on me or on my image in the screen. The Progerians were surprisingly subdued; I guess they really didn't like to get their hands dirty. Whereas none of them were moving, the guards were running at full tilt to converge on my location. But they weren't shooting. They didn't want to risk taking out any one of their leaders. I luckily had no such compunction about it. If anyone stepped in my way, whether trying to get out of my way or merely to block my path, the outcome was the same. I shot them, they died. I had no clue how many rounds this thing held, sooner or later I was going to find out. The thirty to forty yards I had to traverse to get to my destination were the most blood littered I had yet ever encountered, and the guards had yet to let a shot fly. I arrived where the Supreme Commander would be sitting, and to my astonishment he was still there. He never moved, even with all the bedlam going on around me. All I could think was that he was so confident in his position he didn't think anything could touch him. I don't know if Crocodiles or Progerians sweat but when I placed the rifle against his head two things happened. First the Supreme Commander actually gave me a look of surprise and secondly and more importantly the entire arena came to a standstill.

The guards stopped all pursuit, which was a good thing because three or four of them were less than twenty feet from where I stood. Nobody moved a muscle.

"Stand!" I yelled at the Commander. "Fucking stand you ugly bitch or I'll blow your head off."

"No need to shout hu-man," he said as he stood. "I understand you perfectly, but what gives you the right to put a weapon to MY head, you puny little hu-man."

"You know what gives me the right? I'll tell you," and I rattled off all of the names of the victims that I had killed for their entertainment. He didn't get the connection.

"You know you'll never make it out of here hu-man."

"If I don't, neither do you, your Excellency." And I knew he didn't get it but the Excellency part was laced with dripping sarcasm.

"Beth, get down here!" I yelled. I didn't dare take my eyes off of the guard that was closest. I couldn't tell but he seemed to be inching closer.

"Beth, hurry up!" I yelled again.

"That could be a small problem," she yelled back. I risked a glance over my shoulder; a guard had her by the scruff of the neck and did not appear to be willing to negotiate.

"Listen Mr. Supreme, you tell your henchman to let Beth, I mean the Queen of the Games go or I'm going to put their boss's brains all over the arena floor." I was spitting by this time. One of the guards was inching closer; it was a no-brainer, I didn't consider him worthy of living anyway. I perched the rifle over the commander's shoulder and blew a hole right through the guard. I even felt a little special, as I had taken out an extra paying patron behind him too.

"Now back to you Mr. Supreme, I hate you and your kind and I have no problem with killing as many of you as I can before I run out of ammo. But I guarantee you'll be one of the deceased."

"You just killed the Prime Minister of Arabak. Mr. Talbot, I will personally see to your death."

"Well, now that we're over the niceties let's get back to business. He lets her go now or you and a bunch of your friends are going to die." He spoke to his guard in that halting choppy croc-speak, but the gist off it was pretty much let the girl go and back away. I hoped he hadn't added any extra instructions but that problem would have to be dealt with at a later time. Durgan strode into the arena just at that moment. He seemed very befuddled to be entering without the cheers of his admirers. It was then that he saw on the big screen the carnage and who I was holding prisoner.

"You let him go now Talbot! Or I'll fucken kill you." He was shaking with rage as he spat this out.

"Uh, I'm a little busy right now Durgan, you're just going to have to wait your turn," I answered back. I didn't even have to yell. The acoustics in this place were great and it was very, very quiet.

"You have no right to take this away from me Talbot. I'm moments away from my biggest glory and you're fucking ruining it for me."

"I'm sorry Tom. I know that I should have just laid down and died for you today but I wasn't feeling very giving. Sometimes it's just not in my nature. My mother always accused me of being a taker and not a giver." Durgan was enraged, he started to enter into the stands but the guards weren't letting another rogue human in. The guard closest to him stepped in his way. Durgan didn't care, he punched the guard square in the solar plexus and the guard doubled over in pain. With some effort but not all, not by a long shot, Durgan grabbed him around the neck and pulled upwards, severing the guard's spinal cord from his neck. He walked through a second guard like he was tissue paper. Thank God for Durgan, he actually took some of the heat off of me. Two of the guards now had their rifles trained right on Durgan's head. He didn't have a weapon or a hostage and he was in the wide open. He stopped his advance, but the rage inside him was boiling over. His face was beet red, veins were sticking out all over the place. He was quaking like a volcano about to erupt, somehow I didn't figure that to be the flight part of the fight or flight scenario.

"I'm going to kill you Talbot!" And I knew he meant it. But I had bigger fish to fry at the moment.

"Like I said Durgan, you're going to have to wait in line just like everyone else." He literally howled in rage and frustration. Beth in the meantime had made her unobstructed way down to me. I gave her a small hug and I could feel the ever so slight stiffness when I touched her. Well that answered my question. She wasn't going to mind if my savagery saved her but after that I didn't think she'd want any part of me. Well, like I said before, I had bigger fish to fry at the moment, love or lack of wasn't on the list quite yet.

I needed to act and I needed to act fast. But in what direction? I hadn't really believed that I would get this far. If I made the Progerians clear a path that could possibly give the guards a clear shot at Beth or me. If I left them where they were, would one of them make a move? I knew that the Progerians preferred the hands off approach but if pushed to the edge would they attack? I really didn't know them well enough to make an informed decision. I was fairly certain though that the guards would take full advantage of any opportunity. I had sort of made up my mind. Rifle pressed firmly to the Supreme Commander's head we moved, Beth pushed ahead with the Supreme Commander following her and me bringing up the rear. Durgan was still screaming at the top of his lungs.

"Hey Durgan!" I yelled over my shoulder. "Stephanie doesn't say hi." Holy cow, that shut him up. I think I could feel him boiling with rage. Apparently he never knew that she was my roommate, and I just let him ponder on what may or may not have happened between us. I don't know why I felt the need to antagonize him, but that got him moving again. Only this time he was running across the arena floor to meet me at the other entrance. Oh shit, he was going to foul everything up.

"Stop him now Commander, or the guards are going

to have some Supreme brain to clean up later." He may not
have understood sarcasm but he understood the threat just
fine. He said something in his native tongue, a blue flash
passed by us no further than three feet away and that was the
end of Durgan's right leg. It just sort of disappeared; I saw
white bone protruding from below his kneecap and nothing
else. He fell in a heap screaming and writhing in agony. I
almost felt pity for him, no actually I didn't but I didn't want
to sound too inhumane. Well I now knew that the guards
were excellent shots; I almost crawled up onto the Supreme
Commander's back. As it was there was no more than three
inches from any part of my body to any part of his. I might as
well have been a human fur, the way that I was draped over
him. To shoot at me the guards ran the risk of the exit
discharge going into their leader and as bad as they wanted to
kill me that was in direct proportion to how much they didn't
want to harm their leader. For the most part the crowd parted
as my small troupe made its way through. But once, whether
on purpose or by accident one, of the Progos shot a foot out.
I nearly stumbled, as it was I had to grab on to the
Commander's belt to keep from toppling over. When I had
regained my full balance I quickly turned the rifle and blew
off that foot. Nobody else's feet even came close after that.

"There was no reason to blow off my Computer
Engineer's foot," the Supreme Commander said calmly. He
was a cool cookie under pressure, I'd give him that much.

"Well you see Mr. Supreme Commander, sir. I
basically did it for my entertainment and enjoyment." He
stiffened much like Beth had when I first touched her. We
finally reached the entrance, the two dead guards were still
there but they now had fifteen or so live companions waiting
right around the bend.

"Call them off, Supe. You know the drill. Hole in the
head and all. Tell them to put down their weapons." The
commander hesitated. I jammed the rifle even further into his
skull.

"Now!" I screamed.

He complied; they hesitantly put down their weapons. "Now tell them to back away from the weapons and to open my cell door."

"Oh come on hu-man, where do you really think this is going to end up, tonight I will be eating dinner in my quarters and I guarantee you will be the main course. Let me go now, we'll fix up Durgan and you can die like a man in the arena."

"Um let me think about that. Uh, um, gee no, you *fuck*, now tell them to do what I asked."

He resisted so I shot a guard square in the chest, it smelled a lot like chicken. If I ever got the chance I was going to eat one of these things, just to see if the smell resembled the taste. The guards almost advanced on me. The commander raised his hand and spoke their native tongue, they backed away from their weapons and one ran back down the corridor. Whether to get help or to open my cell I wasn't sure.

"Beth, grab a rifle!"

"Mike, you know I hate those things."

"Now is not the time to be a liberal, grab a fucken weapon, now!" She reluctantly picked one up.

"Now keep that thing aimed squarely at the Commander's chest, anything happens to me just drill a hole in him."

"I... I don't think that I can do that."

"Beth, do you know that it's this animal that is responsible for all the carnage that has gone on here."

"I know, but more killing is not the answer."

"Alright Beth, then I'll put this weapon down and we'll negotiate. I'm sure Mr. Supreme Commander will be willing to hear me out. Right before he serves me up with a nice brandy." After a moment's hesitation she pointed the muzzle directly at his mid-section. Whether or not she would pull the trigger I didn't yet know. I grabbed as many rifles as I could possibly handle and still be able to fire if the need arose.

"What's all the commotion?" Deb and Steph rounded the corner to see our little Mexican standoff. Beth had the gun pointed at the commander, I had a handful of rifles in my hands. At least twenty guards were against the far wall, probably debating a quick rush on me and I had another ten or twelve guards behind me deciding on their own course of action. Steph saw the jam we were in and immediately grabbed a weapon for herself and Deb. A couple of the bolder girls also came and grabbed a weapon.

"Now listen ladies," I said, trying not to sound condescending. "These things have no safety and a hair trigger, do not point it at anything unless you are going to shoot."

Stephanie yelled, "Like this?" and proceeded to blow holes in five of the guards, all their thoughts of making a charge died with the five on the floor.

"Uh yeah, something like that," I said in shock and no little admiration. I nudged the commander in the back. "Tell the guards to lie on the ground before she takes out some more frustration." The commander now realized that he had more to worry about than just me, and lost some of his original swagger. He spoke, they knelt. The commander, having witnessed the savagery of the 'lesser' sex, obviously now wished that he had also pitted them in the games, they would have made for some entertaining viewing.

"Does anyone else smell fried chicken?" Steph asked quizzically. She looked up from her still smoking barrel.

"Yeah it does smell a little like KFC," I answered with a sick grin.

"Oh that's so gross." Beth was turning a little green. Apparently her jaunt on this ship hadn't been nearly as brutal as the rest of ours. She still seemed to have some of the refinements of civilization hanging about her. The rest of us, well, the rest of us didn't have that problem.

"You tell the guards if they so much as peek a snout around that corner we're going to blow the rest of their friends away."

"Friends?" the commander said. Wow, they didn't understand friends; I guess I couldn't play that card.

"I'll blow the rest of their fellow soldiers away." *That* he understood.

I wasn't sure if they weren't showing themselves for fear of getting their leader hurt or their compatriots, but either way, they never rounded that corner. We slowly made our way around the curvature of the ship, continually running into armed guards waiting for the chance to pounce. But we weren't exactly defenseless and more importantly we had the king of all hostages. At least half of the women were armed and I do believe they were more likely to use them than myself.

CHAPTER 46

Outside of Venus Airspace

"Colonel, I believe the main ship is attempting to hail us!" Captain Emerick shouted from his seat. He wished that he had not lost his military bearing but it was too late now. And besides, who else except the people on his ship would ever know.

"Well, what are they saying Captain?" The colonel was a little impatient, it had been a long journey and the end was in sight, literally. The mother ship could be seen from a thousand miles away.

"I'm not sure sir, it seems to be a repeating message and it was on one of our lesser used frequencies. I'm just waiting for it to restart."

"Let me..."

"Wait, here it is...." the captain piped in the message over the intercom system.

"American Hu-mans of the Space Shuttle USS Liberation." Well, the Colonel thought to himself, apparently they had been listening to their comms with Earth.

"We are the Progerians from the planet Aradinia. We regret that we have not yet made ourselves known to your general population. We feared that your primitive species might riot if we came unannounced. We took random crowds from across your globe to let them see us for who we are, so that these new emissaries could spread the word about us on your planet. We thought it might be easier for your primitive minds to accept an alien species if you heard it from your own kind."

"Well at least they're not arrogant," the colonel snorted. He received a few laughs from his crew but the unsettling alien voice over the tinny speaker did not match the words being heard.

"We welcome you and your crew aboard our ship. We will prepare a feast in your honor. Please reply once you have received this message, and follow the grid coordinates to the proper docking location."

"Colonel, what are we going to do, they could be leading us into a trap."

"Captain, if they wanted us dead they could have done it the moment we left Earth. Let's play their game for now; if we don't like it we'll change the dealer. Hail them back, tell them we gladly accept their invitation. And then dial up Houston for me."

"Yes sir!" the captain said. Hope had surged a little in the captain. Perhaps they were a friendly, albeit arrogant species. Maybe they weren't bent on global destruction like so many of his fellow countryman believed. He sincerely hoped so.

"Sir, I've got Houston on the line."

"Hello Houston."

"Hey Colonel, how are things going up there?"

"Well, we just received a message from our new friends."

"Oh yeah?"

"That would be affirmative. Seems that they have invited us for dinner."

"Did you say dinner?"

"Roger that."

"Any idea what's on the menu?"

"As long as it isn't us I don't care."

"You know the risks of docking?"

"Yes, I know the risks."

"We don't want them to see our present until the right time."

"Sir, I don't think this is a refusable invitation."

"I'm not saying that Colonel, but you may want to take great care."

"General, I know this is an unexpected turn of events,

but maybe they are who they say they are. If not, well then our present might be better delivered inside than out. They may acquiesce once our package is delivered."

"Colonel, you are aware of the consequences?"

"General, we've been through this a thousand times. We are all volunteers in this endeavor."

"Roger that Colonel, give me a call from the inside. I'd love to know what kind of hosts we are dealing with."

"You and me both General, you and me both. USS Liberation out."

CHAPTER 47 – Journal Entry 29

Inside Mother ship

We huddled as close to the outer bulk as possible. It was impossible to tell where exactly the next guard station would open up. We had already fried three guards that had absolutely no idea what was going on. They were probably coming from an all-night card game. They stepped out from one of the opaque doorways and seemed as stunned to see us as we were to see them. Stephanie blew two of them away before I even saw them. Tanya took out the third one. It happened so fast they hadn't even begun to reach for their weapons.

"Wow, these weapons really are incredible," I said, as the third of the guards fell. "Hey Supremie, how long do these things last?" I wasn't sure if he'd answer a direct question so I thought if I irked him in any way he would answer me out of arrogance.

"Why should I give you any more information than you already have, dumb hu-man?"

"Because Mr. Supremie, you can answer me now or you can answer me after Stephanie here takes off one of your hands. I bet that wouldn't go over so well with your council, would it. That whole thing about showing no weakness and all. I'd hate to see you removed from your lofty post because of an injury you could have avoided." I wished they sweated because I just knew he would be. He may have been in battles before, but they were in his youth and I can almost guarantee he had never felt so powerless in all his years.

"They'll last roughly three of your Earth years with regular use. The more or less they are used will affect that time line."

"These don't need to be reloaded?"

"No, they are a completely self-sufficient unit. They are disposable, to use an Earth term. When the energy cell within them dies the weapon is recycled."

I was truly amazed. If this was the small arms weapons they gave to their guards what else must they have in their arsenal? I'd love to get my hands on some of the 'big guns,' so to speak.

"Is there any sort of indicator light?"

"Indicator light?"

"Something to tell you when the cells are getting low."

"The last hundred or so shots will turn from the cobalt blue color to a brilliant red. But we do not have weapons over two years old in our fleet, just to avoid such a problem."

"I guess that's lucky for us."

"Quite," said the Commander coldly.

*　　*　　*

"Captain Emerick, could you come over here please."

"Sir, we are just about to land in their bay, I'm not sure if I should just leave Bootie over here by himself. I'd hate to start an intergalactic incident because the lieutenant bounced our ship off their helm."

"Captain, I think the lieutenant will be alright for a minute. There are a couple of procedures I would like to go over with you."

"Aye aye sir."

"Besides, I watched the lieutenant in the simulator, he only bounced the ship off three or four asteroids. Isn't that right Lieutenant?"

"Sir, it was five." And everyone got a laugh out of that.

"Captain Fitzy, I want you and Captain Emerick to hide in the cargo area with our gift. I will leave my comm. button on," as he duct taped over the talk button. "If it sounds like we are in distress or they try to take this ship while we're out of range, you know what to do."

"I know sir. I'll say a prayer for all of us."

"Well we should be a lot closer to Heaven from here, hopefully God will respond fast."
"Good luck Colonel."
"It's not luck we need Captain, it's faith."

Inside the ship

We inched our way along the corridor until we finally came across the bulkhead that led to the bay doors. Unbeknownst to us at this time the Space Shuttle USS Liberation was entering the 'Julipion' as she was known on board. Prayers were being answered, I just don't believe it was those of the crew of the Liberation. I did not like the exposure that walking into the docking area left us with. And the Genogerians had no intention of letting us off of this ship. There had to have been at least a hundred of them, probably more but I couldn't see over them to tell. It was more than a little disconcerting to have that many guns pointed at us.

"Girls, I need three or four of you to point your weapons directly at the commander." I was trying to take control of the situation as quickly as possible. Some of the women looked mere moments away from full-fledged panic. The last thing I needed was some of them shooting indiscriminately or running away at full tilt, or possibly just falling over in terror. As it was my nuts wanted to crawl up inside my belly, and I would've joined them given the chance.

"Ladies now! We have got to stay cohesive; I need three or four weapons trained directly on the commander. If they open fire I want him to be the second person to fall." Tanya and a couple of others pulled their gaze away from the guards and leveled them on the commander.

"Now it's your turn, Mr. Commander, tell your men to back away slowly, and if they kill me or anyone else in this little party of ours, you will die next. Now tell them!" I spat into his face. He complied but it was clear that he did so reluctantly. It seemed to me it was taking way too many words to convey this message. I wanted to cuff the commander upside the head but I think that definitely would have started an all-out fire fight.

"That's quite enough Commander!" I said softly into his ear.

"But I'm not done," he said indignantly.

"If they haven't got the general idea by now then your guards are a little thicker than I thought." He was not thrilled that I made him stop, but these handy dandy pulse weapons when leveled at your head make for very strong persuasion.

The commander may have lacked the ability to recognize sarcasm but he was by no means an idiot. He had risen to his position of power with wits and strength and I had no doubt that he had some sort of elaborate plan set, but for the life of me I could not figure it out. Everything was happening so fast, it was difficult to comprehend what was going to happen five seconds from now much less five minutes.

"Mr. Supreme, it is time for us to select a ship," as I rudely shoved him towards the vast array ahead.

"I cannot pilot a ship that is big enough for all of us by myself," he said routinely. And so here it was. One way or the other he was going to get one of his men on board.

"No your Supremeness, you're just going to have to give me a crash course on how to fly one of these things."

"I can do no such thing, my men train for years before they are allowed to pilot one of these ships. If you are my co-pilot we shall surely crash and burn. And that would be such a pity after how far you have made it." Was that sarcasm? "I am going to need one of these guards to co-pilot the ship."

"Ah, see your Lordship, there is your first mistake."

"What?"

"I know for a fact that these guards are no more than guns for hire for you and your kind. There is no way any of these Genos would be allowed to train for one of these ships. The only thing they would be allowed to do would be to ride in one. And I have a feeling that it would be in the far back."

"Very good Mr. Talbot, you are very crafty for a human." The disdain almost poured out of his mouth with those words, but I accepted the compliment anyway. I in no way expected that to be his last ploy but it at least gave me a few more moments of breathing room. We shuffled our way in a very tight knit cluster. One grenade would have taken out the lot of us. We were at this instant completely surrounded, as we shuffled along so did the guards, whose numbers seemed to be rapidly growing as news of the event passed through the ship. We were in a circle about fifteen feet across and the aliens gave us another fifteen feet on all sides. It was a strange sight and had I not been dead smack in the middle I would have thought it very humorous looking. As we moved forward one step the guards in front of us moved back one step and the guards in the rear moved up one step. I had no idea what kind of ship we were heading for, for all I knew it could be the equivalent of an alien tractor-trailer, but it looked plenty big enough for us all. It was roughly the size and shape of three standard sized school buses melded together. It wasn't pretty, but as long as it flew I didn't really give a shit.

"Commander, tell your men to make a clear path to that ship straight ahead. I don't want anyone in front of us or we start blasting a path." The commander spoke and like the parting of the Red Sea we had a clear path straight to the ship.

"Steph, get a couple of the girls and go ahead and check to make sure that the ship is clear."

"Gee thanks, would you like me to get you a cup of coffee too?"

"Steph, I love you, but could you please not bust my balls right now, I'm a little busy." She smiled; I think that she was enjoying the hell out of this. I guess being somewhat in control of your destiny was a lot better than having no clue what was going to happen to you and having no control over it whatsoever. So Steph and a couple of the women went up to the ship, and after a few tense moments they came out and gave the all clear sign. I had a couple of ladies stay at the bottom of the gang plank and guard the entrance while the rest of us made a hasty retreat into what I supposed was some sort of troop transport. I had turned to tell the women at the bottom to come on up before we closed the hatch when all hell broke loose. I heard it way before I saw it, a trap door in the floor of the transport had flipped open and a guard sprang out. It was too late for me to do anything in my defense; his weapon was trained right on me and I was looking over my shoulder at him with my weapon still pointing out of the ship. So close, I thought to myself, so fucking close, at least the women would still have a chance. He fired; my mind was racing so fast I was literally able to watch the blue spark of death heading straight for me. Unfortunately my body wasn't nearly as fast as my brain or I would have been able to dodge the sucker. I hoped the pain wouldn't be too bad. And then when I for sure thought the charge would strike me, it didn't. I had been in motion the entire time and was able to bring my weapon to bear on this new assailant and I fired true. His head just melted away; there was a spinal column jutting up from his shoulders and not much more. A few of the women began to scream and ran towards the hatch. I was yelling at them to stay in the ship, when I realized with great sadness who they were running towards. Stephanie had seen the trap long before I had and had raced to place herself in front of the shot. She had been hit and I could tell before I even got close she wasn't going to make it. The women at the bottom of the hatch were yelling up to us, near hysteria in their voices. The guards were shouting, they were looking as if to make a rush. I wanted to cradle Stephanie in my arms, but we had other pressing matters at the moment.

"Liliana, Francesca, start firing!" I yelled.

"What?" They both seemed on the verge of tears. I ran down the plank, gun a blazing. A few of the bolder guards had been within a few feet of the landing when I cut them down. The girls finally began to open fire and within seconds dozens of the guards had fallen. They were beginning to make a Genogerian death wall in front of us, so much so that the other rushing guards were having a tough time getting around their fallen comrades. We just kept the guns blazing.

"Deb, get the commander to shut the hatch!" I screamed. She didn't move, she was still holding Stephanie in her arms. "Deb, now or you're going to be holding a lot more than just her." I think that finally sunk in, she moved quickly, grabbing Steph's gun as she went. My guess is she wasn't going to take no for an answer. The guards got sick of making a mad death rush to the hatch, so they began to open fire. Francesca died fast; she had a mere moment to lament her stomach wound before she was struck for the second time square in the chest.

"Liliana, get into the ship!"

"I'll go when you do!" she yelled back.

After what seemed decades the hatch began its incessantly slow climb upwards.

"Alright now Liliana, I have no desire to be called Hop Along. Run for it." And run we did, with an entire army of Genogerians behind us. A few actually grabbed on to the hatch as it finally closed, and all they were rewarded with was the right to be called Lefty or Righty as the case may be. Or in one poor bastard's case, Stumpy. It was still disconcerting to have so many of them surrounding us. We could hear them below us and we knew it was just a matter of time before they launched some sort of assault.

"Oh Stephanie," I moaned, "why did you have to do that?" I cradled her in my arms, tears streaming down my face. She had been gut shot and was still alive. But the pain was taking her and death was all too prevalent.

"I did it for you," she said gently. "You have sacrificed so much for our safety, it was time for a little payback."

"Stephanie, thank you," I sobbed. "I will always love you, and I promise I will never forget you." And that was it, her eyes closed and she still had one of her slightly crooked smiles on her face. She went out the way she wanted to, fighting. And that's the way I'll always remember her.

"That's your problem, hu-man. You are too sentimental," the commander said with a sneer in his voice.

"Fuck you!" I shouted, wanting nothing more than to gut shoot him so he'd know what it felt like to die a slow, agonizing death.

"And too easily unsettled."

"And fuck you again, why aren't we flying yet?" as I stood up and headed towards the commander. My weapon was raised, I had so much wanted to bury him right there on that ship. But that would have done the planet Earth such a great disservice, and I had more than myself and Stephanie to think about.

"I cannot start the ship until my men leave the area."

"Listen closely because I'm not going to say it again." I planted the weapon square on his snout. "As soon as you start this ship, I'll guarantee they'll move away. And to be honest with you I really don't give a fuck if a few of your men turn into fried crocodile nuggets." He hissed, but he saw my rage and had no doubt of my intentions. The ship started and more than a few dozen Genos did become crispy critters, which made it all the more satisfying.

"Let's go. Open the doors and let's get this bucket moving."

"I can't open the door, they are automatically sealed when life is detected in the launch area."

"Well then, order your men out of here so we can leave."

"No matter what I say, they won't leave. They will not let me be taken off of this ship."

"Order them or die."

"I'll order them, but then you're going to have to kill me. Because they will not move. But we can negotiate, if you like." And he opened up his snout in what appeared to be his award-winning smile, but the only picture that stuck in my head was of the Big Bad Wolf in the Little Red Riding Hood story.

"What's the deal Commander, you'll fry me instead of slow roast me before you eat me?"

"No, I'll keep you alive, a few of your women will have to be sacrificed, but your safety will be guaranteed."

"So you're saying that all I have to do is sacrifice a few of my companions and you'll let me live out the rest of my years in relative comfort and safety, completely enslaved on your ship."

"Exactly."

A few of the women who didn't know me so well were actually a little flustered and I would assume worried.

"Go fuck yourself." His toothy grin disappeared as quickly as it had appeared. "Get this ship moving now, I won't warn you again. If you don't or if you try some new stunt I'll kill you and take my chances with all these controls." He started the ship in the general direction of the hatch and with great satisfaction I watched through the rear view monitor as a dozen or so more guards instantly vaporized. I would have been a lot happier had Stephanie not just been killed, but it was still a very satisfying moment. The guards backed up enough to be away from the deadly exhaust but they would not leave the hangar. I was at a complete and utter loss.

CHAPTER 48

"Which one of you is Colonel Thomas?" Well, that ended any doubt on whether or not they were listening in on our comms, the colonel thought to himself.

"I am." The colonel walked forward, sweat pouring off of his face. All of the science fiction movies he had ever watched had not prepared him for the sight in front of him. They were bipedal alligators or crocodiles, he could never figure out the difference. They were the most savage and vicious looking creatures he had ever seen. And the toothy smiles did little to allay his fears.

"Welcome Colonel to the Star Scout Julipion. We have been expecting your arrival for months. My name is Brystrar and I will show you to your holding cells."

"Holding cells?" The Colonel wanted to turn tail and make a run for the shuttle now.

"Oh I am sorry, the translation does not work well. To your um… quarters. Is that a more appropriate word?"

"Yes, that is infinitely more appropriate."

"Is there anybody else on board? We were under the impression you had two other crew members besides yourself."

"No, just me and Lieutenant Johnson here."

"Hmm strange, yes strange indeed."

The colonel knew they knew he was lying; the question was what would they do with that information.

"Colonel, I am going to have to ask for you and your lieutenant's firearms. We are very leery about hull breeches and such."

"And what of the dozen armed guards you've got here?"

"Come come, Colonel, you came to our ship, first

uninvited, and now armed, surrendering your firearms would be the much more diplomatic solution. Besides you are outnumbered four to one, no no, I mean six to one."

The colonel had been unholstering his sidearm when way down the bay he noticed a huge commotion going on.

"Brystrar, what exactly is going on down at the other end of the bay?"

"That is of no concern to you. We are running drills."

"I think I see blue flames, are they firing at each other?"

"Colonel, I will not ask again, hand over your firearm or we will take it by force." The guards who had seemed almost bored with the entire proceedings now took up arms and had them upraised at the colonel and the lieutenant. Not exactly pointing at them, not yet anyway.

"I'd feel a whole lot better about giving up my pistol if I knew exactly what was going on down there," the colonel said as he pointed down to where the ruckus was.

"Colonel, do not tell me that you flew all the way out here to get yourself killed over matters which do not concern you?" The firing at the other end of the bay got increasingly more intense, the guards here seemed to be itching to get into the fray. The colonel thought they just might shoot him and the lieutenant so they could be done with their detail up here.

"Brystrar, all I am asking is what all the commotion at the other end of the bay is all about?" The colonel watched as huge plumes of energy seemed to fry a score or more of these creatures. "We both know that is no drill down there, I can tell from here that your men are dying."

"Very well Colonel, we are in the midst of quelling an escape attempt."

"Humans, Brystrar?"

"Colonel, your sidearm."

"Is it humans, Brystrar?"

"Colonel, look out!" the lieutenant shouted, but it was not soon enough. The colonel took a hit to the thigh, he watched in disbelief as his leg just seemed to disappear.

"Captain, I've been hit, several unfriendlies here."
The colonel started shooting rounds, the first one hit dead
center in Brystrar's head. His head snapped back from the
force of the bullet. If the bullet had not killed him the broken
neck would have. But the colonel did not get another shot
off. Three shots from the guards hit true and vaporized the
colonel.

The lieutenant just started shouting, "The colonel's
down, the col...." and that was it, the lieutenant died without
ever getting a shot off. The captain knew from the sounds of
it that the colonel and the lieutenant were dead. He more than
half wanted to give himself up. That had to be better than the
alternative didn't it? But he had sworn to the colonel he
would carry out the final aspect of their mission..

"Dear God, please forgive me for what I am about to
do. And dear Lord, please tell my family that I will always
love them." And with that said he pressed the detonator. He
did not feel a thing, so quick was his passing that he believed
that the bomb had failed to detonate. But there was the tunnel
of light, so apparently God had approved or at least forgiven
his actions. The explosion was much more catastrophic in the
launch bay. The explosion killed every living thing in that
launch bay not protected in a thousandth of a second. The
shuttlecraft was lifted up and hurled against the far side of
the bay. But the bay door problem had been solved, the
explosion had ripped a huge chunk of the outer hull away, it
had to have been at least a mile long by half that same height.
The damage was mesmerizing. With the instant
depressurization breach in the hull all of the ships in this
launch bay that had not been completely destroyed were now
being sucked out into the vacuum of space.

"What the hell was that?" I pulled myself up off of
the Commander, luckily I had fallen into him and smashed
his head into the bulkhead, because if he had not been
knocked semi-unconscious he would have easily
overpowered me and taken my rifle. But as luck would have
it my full hundred and seventy pounds crashed into his head

as opposed to his four hundred and fifty plus pounds the other way.

The commander shook his snout, and blood flew in rivulets. I was not thrilled to be sprayed by Progerian blood.

"It appears that your visiting dignitaries blew up a bomb."

"The who and the what?" I asked dazedly.

"Your planet sent a shuttle to our ship, and apparently we grossly underestimated its strength. We were planning on taking the crew and the ship captive to show your planet that you have no offense or defense against us."

"Looks by the size of that hole in your hull, you definitely screwed that up."

"Yes," he said with a sneer. "It seems that you humans are full of a great many surprises," as he looked directly at me. "I strongly suggest that you sit down and strap yourself in."

"Why Commander, I didn't know that you cared."

"I don't, but we're about to be sucked through that hole, and I don't want you to mistakenly take my head off."

"Ladies, everyone alright back there?"

"Yes," came some wobbly voices. "For the most part we were already strapped in," Deb piped up.

"Why didn't that bomb destroy this ship like it did the majority of the others?" I asked.

"When we powered up, the ship's shield defense system was automatically engaged. Had we not been powered up we would have been vaporized like everybody else that was in the launch bay."

"Damn shame, damn shame," I said again. The commander looked at me funny, he was debating in his mind whether I was being honest or not. I wasn't. I felt for the crew of the space shuttle, but they knew their mission, and their mission had succeeded beyond their wildest wishes. It would be months or possibly years before this launch bay was operational, and that was going to put a huge crimp in the Progerians' plans.

CHAPTER 49 – Journal Entry 30

"Ground control to USS Liberation. Ground Control to USS Liberation. Sir, I've been trying to reach the shuttle for over half an hour. Their comm. must be down."

"Major, you saw the spike on the charts, their comm. isn't down. It's non-existent," the general said with deep regret in his voice.

"That can't be it. That can't be the end of them. Can it?" The major could not believe he had just lost his best friend. How could he go to the colonel's wife and tell her she was a widow and that her sons were now going to grow up without a father? He didn't believe that he could do it. He began to cry right at the console. "Ground control to USS Liberation," he sobbed in desperation.

"Major, pull yourself together!" the general said, but with concern interlaced through the stern words. "I've got to believe that we did little more than stir them up and we are going to need all the experience we can right here, right now. I know its difficult son, but there will be plenty of time to mourn after all this is over."

"Yes sir, I understand sir, it's just that we went through the academy together and I'm his kids' godfather. I don't know how I'll ever be able to face his wife, my sister, again."

"Son, we are going to lose a lot more fine men before this campaign is over. We have to focus on the task at hand. If we lose our grip now, we'll never be able to regain it."

"Sir, yes sir. Would you mind if I took a break to go compose myself?"

"Not at all Major. As a matter of fact, why don't you

take the rest of the day off? But be back here first thing in the morning. We are going to have to go over all the data we are receiving to see if we put a dent in that ship."

"First thing tomorrow. Aye sir." The major turned to head out of the control room when static began to pour through the overhead speakers. Hope surged through his chest like a tidal wave.

"Hello Earth. Hello Earth." It came through tinny and was not couched at all in proper military jargon. But the major reasoned that in a stressful situation military procedure can and usually is ignored.

"Colonel, Colonel, is that you?"

"Earth, please respond. Can you hear us?" The tinny voice came through again, the signal was starting to pick up some strength.

"Colonel, this is Ground Control, do you copy?" The major actually had his fingers crossed; it had to be them, who else could be broadcasting from near Venus.

""I'm sorry, this is not the colonel, my name is Mike Talbot, I am aboard the alien shuttle vessel 'Star Hopper.' I have with us one highly ranked hostage and a bunch of very happy civilians slash jail breakers."

The general motioned for the microphone. "I'm sorry son, my name is General Burkhalter, could you please repeat your name again."

"Sure thing General, my name is Mike Talbot."

"Were you at Red Rocks son?"

"That would be affirmative sir."

"How did you come to be flying back home with a hostage on an alien ship?"

"Sir that's going to be a long story, and I'm not one hundred percent sure we won't be hunted down and killed." The general couldn't believe the calmness in this youth's voice for the words he had just presented. "So I want to make sure that I get out a few things before that possibility happens. I can also guarantee, General, that this call home is being monitored."

The major covered up the mike and spoke softly to the general. "Sir, how can we be sure this isn't some sort of elaborate trap."

"Major, it just might be, but since we're not talking to anyone else at the moment we might as well hear out what he has to say."

"Sir, General, you still there?"

"Yes son, I'm still here."

"Our systems took a pretty good jolt from the explosion. And occasionally things will flare out for a while." Holy cow, the general thought to himself. This ship had witnessed the explosion first hand.

"Sir, first off. These aliens are not friendly. I repeat not friendly. They are extremely hostile."

"Well Major, if this is a trap it is sure is a darned crazy way to start one," the general said softly out of range of the mike pick-up.

"Go on son."

"Well sir, from what I've gathered in my extensive stay aboard the ship, they are highly evolved species resembling crocodiles or possibly alligators or both. Their evolutionary path closely mimicked our own with one glaringly different fact."

"What is it?" The general was on the edge of his seat.

"They didn't have a planet crippling meteor hit. They had all those extra years to evolve and become the assholes that they are. They didn't have to start from scratch like our planet did. Sir, they are coming to Earth with the full intention of taking it over and enslaving us. Sir, we are to become their new food source. They like the way we taste. Sir, I hope the months that that ship has been parked out there have given you enough time to get it together down there."

The general was upset, he had let the President talk him down on the defense buildup and now it was going to bite him in the ass big time. He made a mental note to himself to throw what was ever necessary to Paul's growing troops.

"Sir, the explosion is going to throw a huge wrench in their plans but this species is very industrious and clever, it won't hamper them forever."

"Son, what can you tell me about the explosion?"

"Sir, to be honest with you, we felt it more than saw it. But I witnessed firsthand the damage it did, and it was incredible. It had to have vaporized at least three hundred to three hundred and fifty of the Genogerian guards."

"Genogerians?"

"Yes sir, that is a sort of sub-species. There are the Progerians who are the ruling class, and the lesser-evolved Genogerians who do their dirty work. The Genogerians would be roughly equal to Cro-Magnon man on Earth had they survived. The Progerians realized early on that they could use this species for their own benefit, so you see the notion of enslavement runs deep in them. The Progerians are big on war as long as they don't have to physically be involved. I have some theories about this sir, but I don't wish to express them over the party line. With the way this ship flies we should be in your air space tomorrow. Could you please send up landing coordinates? I will make sure that my distinguished guest follows them to a tee. Sir, I am pretty exhausted and I plan to get some shut-eye here soon. But before I do that, I just wanted to express my deepest gratitude for that man or men that sacrificed their lives so that we could have this chance at freedom."

"You said us son. How many of you are on board there?"

"Roughly thirty sir, I can't get a straight count because I can't even see straight. It's been a long and difficult day."

"For us too son, for us too. You get some rest. We'll send the coordinates up to your 'pilot.'"

"Thank you sir, I'll see you tomorrow. Over and out."

"Over and out."

"Sir, you can't let them land here."

"Don't worry Major, I have no intention of leading a potential enemy straight to our command center. I want you to get every National Guard on the Eastern seaboard awake and ready. I'm going to have that ship land at that old landing strip in upstate Maine. Go pack a bag Major, we're going to Vacationland."

* * *

"Deb, could you please get two girls to keep their rifles trained on him at all times. Have them rotate out every hour. I have got to go get some sleep or I am going to fall over." I headed down the aisle and my breathing almost stopped, Beth was in the middle of the aisle waiting for me. And to be honest it didn't look like concern and love on her face. I wasn't in the mood.

"We need to talk," she said in an urgent voice.

"It's going to have to wait."

"I don't want it to wait." Man, I don't remember her having a spoiled streak in her. Maybe all that 'Queen of the Games' crap went to her head.

"Beth, I've killed over a dozen other living beings today, I'm a little bushed. So unless this ship is on fire it's going to have to wait." She shut up but she didn't look pleased about it. Screw her, I thought. I risked my very being for her, and she was itching to tell me to get lost. Well another eight hours wouldn't change anything.

Either this ship was a lot faster than I had anticipated or I had slept a lot longer than eight hours. I wiped crusties away from my eyes and tried my best to orient myself. The women on the other hand looked downright giddy, I can't say that I blame them. Earth was huge in the window.

"How much longer Commander?"

"Five, possibly six of your Earth hours." His face wore the complete opposite expression than that of his passengers. He seemed almost sullen. Wow, the High and Mighty Supreme Commander beaten that easily. I didn't think so. I would double the guards until the military took him off of my hands.

"Have you slept at all, Commander?"

"Progerians, unlike most of the lower species, only require three to four hours of sleep per night and can go for up to five days without sleeping at all. With no visible signs of fatigue. Unlike you lesser species."

"Ah there's the Supreme Commander I've come to know and love." He didn't find it in the least amusing. As far as I knew, the Progerians didn't even have an equivalent word for love. Why would they, they were asexual. Well, maybe you'd have to love yourself to have offspring. I snorted through my hand. The absurdity of that thought caught me off guard. Once again the commander was not amused.

"Commander, how old are you?" The struck me as a question that I wanted answered. If he would comply or not, I wasn't sure, and I wasn't going to threaten him for that little nugget of knowledge. I'd let the military decide upon that. I wanted to be as far away from this little bit of insanity as was humanly possible. The commander just sat and stared out the window, I guess staring at the ever-growing inevitability looming in front of him. Just when I thought that he wasn't going to answer, or quite possibly hadn't heard me, he spoke.

"One hundred and twelve of your human years."

"Holy shit!" I said as I spit out the water I had been drinking. That was not a number I had been expecting. "Is that old for your species?"

"It is old, I would be considered in the autumn of my years. But a reasonably healthy Progerian lives to an average of one hundred forty-five to one hundred fifty years. Unless, of course, an unnatural event occurs," as he once again returned his gaze to my looming planet.

I thought to myself, in another lifetime I might have been able to muster up some pity for him. But I searched deep within my soul and there was none. He was a monster worse than any ever dredged up in the nursery rhymes of my youth. I hoped that the military pried every possible piece of information out of him by whatever means necessary and then threw his dried up husk on the nearest trash heap. He had been responsible for at least nine thousand or so human deaths that I knew of. And needless to say all the other poor civilizations they had bumped into. No, the world, scratch that, the universe would be a much better place without him in it.

"Deb, have you gotten any sleep?"

"I got a few hours but I wanted to make sure that all the girls were rested and that he was covered by at least two people at all times."

"Why don't you go get some shut eye? I'll take care of the guard duty from here on out."

"Thank you," she said wearily. "We need to talk later."

"I know, I know. I've been getting a lot of that lately."

She raised one eyebrow, then turned to head towards the back of the ship.

"Tanya, could you please make sure there is always one lady up here with a weapon trained straight on his back? But I want the shifts rotated on the half hour. I don't want any one getting itchy fingers, and I don't want anyone getting lax. I'm getting worried that the closer we get to home the more desperate he's going to become."

"Why don't we just tie him up?"

"Do you know how to drive this thing?" I asked. She got the point.

"But if he gets desperate enough won't he just crash this thing into the first mountain he sees?" she asked with an edge of fear in it.

"I don't think so. He might be desperate but he's not suicidal."

"Are you willing to stake all off our lives on it?" That question hit deep. Was I? Did I know him well enough? Could I ever know him well enough? I was wrong about human intentions all the time. He was a friggen alien. I had no idea what was going through his mind.

"Commander." I turned back around. "How difficult is it to drive one of these things?" He either had super sensitive hearing or his thought process was similar to ours.

"Why, are you afraid I might crash this ship?"

"No let's just say something were to happen to you, like a heart attack. Would I be able to land this craft?"

"Not a chance hu-man. First off the controls are so advanced to your puny little brains that it would take you three solid years of intensive training to even begin to be able to understand and use them. And they are also DNA coded so that only Progerians can fly them."

"DNA coded," I said. "You have a lot of people stealing these, do you?"

"We've had problems in the past."

"What, I'm the not the first person to ever make an escape?"

"Oh no, hu-man you are the first," he sneered. "We had a Genogerian uprising over a millennia ago. They stole a bunch of our ships and attacked the Capital. Since then we have DNA coded all of our ships to ever prevent that from happening again."

"Oh ho, trouble in the home land!" I laughed.

"I do not see the humor, hu-man. At least our war was a species rebellion. Your own kind fight all the time. You fight over imaginary lines in the sand or for a metal that is more common than you can imagine."

That hit deep too. Damn, they knew all of our deepest darkest secrets. I bet if they had the Progerian version of Jerry Springer on their home planet, Earth would be a hit mini-series.

"Gold is common?"

"There are whole meteorites made of gold. Almost all the species we have encountered except for yours view gold as nothing more than a nuisance metal which is in the way of more precious minerals."

I changed the subject; he knew too much dirt about our planet anyway. "So basically you're saying that I can't fly this thing."

"Hu-man, the only thing you could manage would be to crash. Do not worry; though I feel some anxiety about this landing I have no intention of endangering my life. For I know that a full scale rescue attempt will be launched, and the plan that we have laid out will go into effect just a little bit sooner than expected."

"You sure seem very confident about that."

"I know my species well, hu-man. Your kind will pay dearly for your assault on my ship and for taking me hostage." He started to rise as his voice did.

"Slow down Commander, take it down a notch. I more than likely won't kill you, because I want to get home. But that girl behind me, well, she lost two of her best friends and her boyfriend on your ship. She would like nothing better than a reason to take you out. Now I strongly suggest you be seated and we'll go on with this flight."

"Of course," the commander said as he composed himself and sat back down.

CHAPTER 50

Outside Township 573 – Northern Maine – Hudson Army Air Base

"Major, what's the status on the ship?" the general asked as he wrung his hands. The general wasn't sure who was more interested in this encounter, the military or the legion of scientists that had been called up here.

"Sir, I'd have to say no more than an hour from their present position." The major was tense. The anger he had for this unseen enemy was vast. If he had been a civilian he thought that he would take a shot at this hostage. But military protocol, bearing and discipline forbade him from seeking his revenge. That would have to wait, but he figured payback was only a matter of time.

"Did you call the radar stations along the Eastern seaboard to let them know to disregard any and all unidentified blips on their screens?"

"Sir, I had the lieutenant's team take care of that yesterday."

"Very good Major, and did..."

"Yes sir, Project Bluebird will go into effect in approximately forty-five minutes." Project Bluebird referred to the project that the U.S. government had been working on since the Soviet Union first launched a satellite. It was basically a way to jam any and all signals to and from any satellite. From time to time the government had used this to disrupt communications in other countries. And then there was the miscue in the winter of 1985, when they had blacked out all television signals during the Olympics for over an hour. The government had feverishly denied any and all acknowledgement of that little pearl. Project Bluebird was for the most part a success, but it had never been tried on every satellite in orbit around the planet. The signal they would need to produce would be enormous, and most likely very easily traced. But the government felt that they would rather take blame for that disruption than for actually acknowledging the landing of an alien vessel on U.S. soil. The pros far outweighed the cons.

"Very good Major. Are there any other questions that I need answered before I ask them?"

"No sir, sorry sir," the major flushed a little bit. Probably better not to piss the general off at this exact moment. "Sir, is the President coming here?"

"No, he felt it would be better to have plausible deniability should this all blow up in our faces."

"Probably not a bad idea." It was going to be tough to deny this though. They had a full squadron of F-16's and Stealth fighters here, plus a battalion of Marines and twelve M-1 Abrams army tanks, and of course the local National Guard who had to be called so as to not hurt their feelings. Pretty tough to move that much machinery without an executive order. Especially to a little Hoboken place like this one.

"I know what you're thinking, Major. But if something does happen you are looking at the fall guy. According to any paperwork I ordered all this for military maneuvers. Basically an elaborate practice.

"Sir, why are you jeopardizing your career?"

"This wouldn't be the first time I've jeopardized my career and for far less. I know the bio we pulled on this Mike fellow makes him only 19, but he seems to have the situation well in order. Unless of course this is a trap and they want to do some testing of their weaponry on us."

"Do you think that's possible sir?"

"Not really, but I didn't bring all this machinery because I'm one hundred percent convinced either. Not that I think we'd stand a chance even with all this stuff. But it's still somehow comforting. Don't you think?"

The major thought that perhaps the general had been

in the military a bit too long. But he'd be damned if he let him know that.

"Sir, you really think that all this weaponry, the most advanced equipment on this planet wouldn't be enough?"

"And there it is Major."

"There what is sir?"

"The most advanced weaponry on this planet. That shuttle craft that's coming in most likely can fly circles around our F-16's and probably packs a bigger punch than the bomb we just hand delivered them."

The major really hadn't stopped to think about just how advanced these beings were. And now he wished he hadn't. It sent shivers right through him.

"Major, I want you to scramble all of the planes as soon as we get to T minus thirty minutes. Understood?"

"Yes sir. T minus thirty minutes."

"Good, I'm going to go finish my crossword puzzle."

The old man might be crazy, the major thought, but he sure did have balls of steel. The major was about ready to pee on himself and the general was going to do crossword puzzles. The major figured in the next forty-five minutes or so he was actually going to see it all.

CHAPTER 51

"Dennis? Hey buddy, how's everything going?"

"Right on schedule, Paul."

"Therein lies the problem."

"Problem? Did you say problem? What's up?"

"I need you to get ahead of schedule."

"Paulie, if I do anything more than what I'm doing I'm going to arouse a lot of suspicion."

"What are you using for a cover story right now?"

"Contaminated soil."

"Nobody's said anything about the cement trucks?"

"No, we actually made a small road coming in here that is well off the beaten path, and we divert traffic on the main road so that nobody sees a thing."

"Can they be trusted?"

"They've been bought my friend, and nothing speaks better than the almighty buck. By the way, where are you getting this kind of bread?"

"I'll explain when I get out there, you wouldn't believe the connections I've got. There's another thing I want you to do for me bud."

"What's that?"

"I want the addresses of every person on this project that is not in on the know."

"Gotcha, but why?"

"My friend, that is definitely something you don't want to know."

"Your word is my command."

"Alright bud, and remember I'm going to need this done in four months instead of six."

"You realize that means more people."

"Do what you have to, but I want addresses for them

all. Later."
    "Later Paul."

CHAPTER 52

Township 423 - Maine

The commander landed the ship at the appropriate coordinates without any tricks or attempted deception. He must have been very confident in his rescue squad. And from just a cursory comparison of technologies, I could see why he would be. We had a difficult time making it to the moon, and they were traveling across star systems. What did he have to fear from us?

"Just remember Afghanistan," I said into the smug commander's face.

"What does the reference of your Earth country called Afghanistan have to do with anything hu-man?" the commander said in his most contemptuous way. I guess he was what we on Earth would call putting on his game face. He had to realize that he was about to become a prisoner of war and more than likely believed that he would be beaten and tortured. Or maybe he even thought we had our own version of the gladiator games.

"Afghanistan was invaded by a far superior technological civilization that was bent on the absolute destruction of that country. But for years the Afghans fought, tooth and nail, grudgingly giving land measured in inches instead of the proposed miles the Soviets wanted. For years they defeated the vastly superior Russian army, but not with technology."

"Than with what, hu-man, you are beginning to bore me."

"With something I believe that your kind does not have," as I poked him in the chest. He flashed his pearly whites at me, but quickly regained control of his anger as three rifles pointed directly at him.

"What is it?!" he asked exasperatedly.

"Heart," I answered.

"Silly hu-man." And he laughed that horrible grating metallic laugh that only evolutionary evolved crocodiles had. "Yes we have hearts."

"Not the heart in your chest."

"Then what hu-man? You make no sense."

"We have the kind of heart that makes you go on when all seems lost. We have will and determination and spirit, your invasion will not be the roll over you and your kind believe it to be."

"We have encountered many worlds hu-man, and they all talk big and boastful, but when the guns start blazing your kind will fall in line as quickly as all the rest."

"I think that you're going to be in for a big surprise, Commander," I answered softly; my anger was very near the boiling point. But now it was time to give him some back. "But either way Commander, you're going to be sitting on the sidelines watching how this unfolds." He didn't answer but it was clear from his body language that he didn't much like that.

The ship no sooner came to rest when we were surrounded by what seemed like the entire East Coast National Guard. There had to be at least two to three hundred men with rifles pointed directly at us, that wasn't even counting the eight or nine tanks that had their turrets aimed at us. It was very disturbing to say the least. I didn't make it all this way to get killed in my own backyard by friendly fire. I was about to open the hatch to make them ease their fingers off their triggers, when a hummer came to a screeching halt alongside the ship.

"Mike Talbot, can you hear me. My name is General Burkhalter. Please do not open your entryway," he said over his bullhorn. "Our scientists are afraid of any alien contamination and want to quarantine the lot of you before we debrief you and your fellow travelers. Is that understood?" I gave him the thumbs up through the front window.

"Great, we travel all the way back from Venus and we're going to be stuck in a quarantined lab for who knows how long." I was hot, I was sick of being confined first by aliens and now I was going to be confined by my own kind.

"We are going to seal the hatchway and then you will be allowed to exit into the rear of a transport van. Please make sure that our 'guest' disembarks first."

I understood the concern they had. And I sure didn't want to be the person responsible for unleashing a new and improved version of the Black Plague. But I wanted to be far away from this whole party, hopefully holed up in some little dive with a couple or three cases of nice cold beer. But it was beginning to look like it wasn't going to happen any time soon. Those tanks might look impressive but I was pretty sure they wouldn't stand up to more than two or three blasts from the small arms I was carrying, much less what their fighter ships were capable of unleashing. And I knew without a reasonable doubt that the mother ship knew exactly where we were. They could probably track the commander from his vital signs. Just like in all those Star Trek movies.

The commander left the ship on his own accord much to the gasps and horrified stares of the detail that was ordered to watch him. Even in full de-con suits I could tell from their body language that they were shocked and scared of their new captive. Just think how I felt, boys, when I had to look at him when I was his captive. That was infinitely worse. One of the guards had to be replaced after he began to hyperventilate in his suit. Whether it was the heat in the suit or the sight of the commander I'm not sure. But even through the suit I thought I could smell that he had soiled himself.

"Oh fuck, get him out of there!" the general yelled over the bullhorn. "National Guard can't even guard a prisoner right." Although this was no ordinary prisoner the general had still hit the nail on the head. This was the true national guardsman slash weekend warrior, twenty-five pounds overweight and the janitor at the local school on his off time. His idea of warfare was when they all got together once a month to play paintball. But he usually just found it as an excuse to go drink beer up in the paintball headquarters. Most of them were only here for the health benefits. Usually they didn't even know which way to point the rifles they were carrying. The mess that was Staff Sergeant Bruce Gardner was unceremoniously hauled away into another waiting van. We would have to wait our turn. Our getaway ship was sealed back up and the commander was taken to parts unknown.

"What's going on?" one of the girls cried from the rear. "Why aren't they letting us off of the ship?"

"Don't worry Suzy."

"Susan," she said indignantly.

"Whatever."

She crossed her arms.

"We need to be quarantined before they will let us out, and then I'm sure that they will want to debrief us to no end."

"But I'm not contaminated. And I don't know anything!" she whined in a high pitched voice that suddenly made the commander's grating laugh seem enjoyable.

"Of that I have no doubt Suzy." And luckily she shut up. It took them a couple of hours to get another van rolling, they had not been prepared for a National Guard flip-out, and so had to start from scratch with a hermetically sealed van. We were all uncomfortable, tired and irritated when the replacement ride finally arrived. The negativity seemed to flow out the second the hatch was opened, but staring at those inhumane decon suits was still unsettling even though we knew they were inhabited by humans.

One suit stepped towards me.

"Welcome home Mike," the suit said as it extended a rubber clad hand.

Check out these titles in the Zombie Fallout Series

Zombie Fallout

It was a flu season like no other. With fears of contracting the H1N1 virus running rampant through the country, people lined up in droves to try and obtain one of the coveted vaccines. What was not known, was the effect this largely untested, rushed to market, inoculation was to have on the unsuspecting throngs.

Within days, feverish folk throughout the country, convulsed, collapsed and died, only to be re-born. With a taste for brains, blood and bodies, these modern day zombies scoured the lands for their next meal. Overnight the country became a killing ground for the hordes of zombies that ravaged the land.

This is the story of Michael Talbot, his family and his friends. When disaster strikes, Mike a self-proclaimed survivalist, does his best to ensure the safety and security of those he cares for. Can brains beat brain eaters? It's a battle for survival, winner take all!

Zombie Fallout 2: A Plague Upon Your Family

This story picks up exactly where book one left off. The Talbot family is evacuating their home amidst a zombie apocalypse. Mankind is on the edge of extinction as a new dominant, mindless opponent scours the landscape in search of food, which just so happens to be non-infected humans. In these pages, are the journal entries of Michael Talbot, his wife Tracy, their three kids Nicole, Justin and Travis. With them are Brendon, Nicole's fiancée and Tommy previously a Wal-Mart door greeter who may be more than he seems. Together they struggle against a ruthless, relentless enemy that has singled them out above all others. The Talbots have escaped Little Turtle but to what end, on the run they find themselves encountering a far vaster evil than the one that has already beset them. As they travel across the war-torn country side they soon learn that there are more than just zombies to be fearful of, with law and order a long distant memory some humans have decided to take any and all matters into their own hands. Can the Talbots come through unscathed or will they suffer the fate of so many countless millions before them. It's not just brains versus brain-eaters anymore. And the stakes may be higher than merely life and death with eternal souls on the line.

Zombie Fallout 3: The End…

Continues Michael Talbot's quest to be rid of the evil named Eliza that hunts him and his family across the country. As the world spirals even further down into the abyss of apocalypse one man struggles to keep those around him safe. Side by side Michael stands with his wife, their children, his friends and the wonder Bulldog Henry along with the Wal-Mart greeter Tommy who is infinitely more than he appears and whether he is leading them to salvation or death is only a measure of degrees.

As Justin continues to slip further into the abyss he receives help from an unexpected ally all of which leads up to the biggest battle thus far.

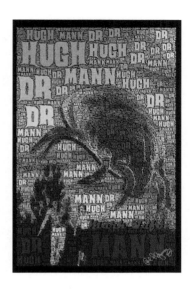

Dr. Hugh Mann – A Zombie Fallout Prequel 3.5

Dr Hugh Mann delves deeper into what caused the zombie invasion. Early in the 1900's Dr. Mann discovers a parasite that brings man to the brink of an early extinction. Come along on the journey with Jonathan Talbot is bride to be Marissa and the occasional visitations from the boy with the incredible baklava. Could there be a cure somewhere here and what part does the blood locket play?

Zombie Fallout IV: The End...Has Come and Gone

The End...has come and gone. This is the new beginning, the new world order and it sucks. The end for humanity came the moment the U.S. government sent out the infected flu shots. My name is Michael Talbot and this is my journal. I'm writing this because no one's tomorrow is guaranteed, and I have to leave something behind to those who may follow.

So continues Mike's journey, will he give up all that he is in a desperate bid to save his family and friends? Eliza is coming, can anyone be prepared?

Watch also for:

Mark Tufo is hooking up with Severed Press for a zombie novella entitled '**Timothy**'
http://severedpress.lefora.com/2011/04/12/mark-tufo/

and for the story '**My Name is Riley**' published in the Undead Anthology by Rymfire books!

Printed in Great Britain
by Amazon.co.uk, Ltd.,
Marston Gate.